IMPULSE &
INITIATIVE

WHAT IF MR. DARCY DIDN'T TAKE NO FOR AN ANSWER?

ABIGAIL REYNOLDS

SOURCEBOOKS LANDMARK™
AN IMPRINT OF SOURCEBOOKS, INC.®
NAPERVILLE, ILLINOIS

Copyright © 2008 by Abigail Reynolds
Cover and internal design © 2008 by Sourcebooks, Inc.
Cover photo © Getty, David De Lossy

Published by Sourcebooks Landmark, an imprint of Sourcebooks, Inc.
P.O. Box 4410, Naperville, Illinois 60567-4410
(630) 961-3900
FAX: (630) 961-2168
www.sourcebooks.com

Library of Congress Cataloging-in-Publication Data

Reynolds, Abigail.
  Impulse & initiative : what if Mr. Darcy didn't take no for an answer? / Abigail Reynolds.
    p. cm.
  ISBN-13: 978-1-4022-1357-1
  ISBN-10: 1-4022-1357-3
  1. Bennet, Elizabeth (Fictitious character)—Fiction. 2. Darcy, Fitzwilliam (Fictitious character)—Fiction. 3. Social classes—Fiction. 4. Young women—Fiction. 5. Courtship—Fiction. 6. Sisters—Fiction. 7. England—Fiction. I. Title. II. Title: Impulse and initiative.
  PS3618.E967I47 2008
  813'.6—dc22

                        2008011834

Printed and bound in the United States of America
          BG 10 9 8 7 6 5 4 3 2 1

Dedication

To
David
with love

Chapter 1

IT WAS NEARING NOON on a hot June day when Colonel Fitzwilliam stepped out of the stuffy coach into the raucous noise of London. Since it was only a short distance to Darcy's house, he decided to take the opportunity to stretch his legs after the long ride rather than hire a carriage. Paying a boy to cart his luggage for him, he set off at a quick pace.

He sincerely hoped that his cousin would prove to be in town. He could not be certain, since Darcy had been such a poor—in fact non-existent—correspondent since their trip to Rosings. Georgiana's last letter had not indicated any planned travels, so presumably she would be there. He would prefer to see Darcy, though, so that he could at least attempt to resolve whatever it was he had said or done that had offended his cousin.

Darcy had clearly been angry and upset when they left Rosings, but had been unwilling to discuss his concerns. At the time, knowing that Lady Catherine had called Darcy in for a private conference just before their departure, Colonel Fitzwilliam had assumed that his mood was related to that event, and that she must have finally overstepped the boundaries regarding Darcy's supposed engagement to her daughter. But now, after nearly two months of uncharacteristic silence from Darcy, and despite several letters sent to him, he could only conclude that Darcy's anger must have been directed towards him. Try as he might, he could not recollect anything more offensive in his behaviour than the usual teasing he engaged in with his cousin. Well, he would just have to jolly Darcy out of his sulk and find out what was on his mind.

He rapped sharply on the front door and was admitted by a servant who knew him well enough not to comment on his unexpected arrival. He was informed that Darcy was out, but Miss Georgiana was at home and would receive him in her sitting room. Disregarding the offer to show him in, Colonel Fitzwilliam strode down the hall and walked in.

"Cousin Richard!" Georgiana said delightedly. "What a lovely surprise! I thought you were still in Newcastle!"

He kissed her cheek in greeting. "Sorry to disappoint you, sweetheart. His Lordship decided that Major General Bradford needs to discuss certain matters with me immediately, so there I was, sent off post-haste to London with nary a chance even to tell you I was coming. Can you put up your poor wandering cousin for a few nights while I suffer the slings and arrows of the Major General?"

Georgiana smiled. "Oh, Richard, of course. Why else would we keep your room available?"

He bowed slightly. "Let me excuse myself then to make myself presentable for the company of a lady, which, after roasting for two days in the most uncomfortable coach in England, I assure you that I am not."

"Of course. I will be here when you are ready. And, Richard," she added, her voice becoming serious, "I am glad you are here. I need to talk to you about William."

"So something is up in that quarter. I suspected as much. I shall be interested to hear all about it."

In his room he was grateful to shrug out of his sweaty uniform while one of the menservants vainly tried to unwrinkle the garments he had packed hurriedly in Newcastle. "Well, they will just have to do for today," Colonel Fitzwilliam told him. "Perhaps you could spruce up the rest for tomorrow."

A knock came at the door as he was buttoning his waistcoat. Philips, Darcy's long-time butler, was on the other side. Colonel Fitzwilliam waved him in.

"Welcome to London, Colonel." Philips looked unwontedly nervous. "I know you have just arrived, but I wondered if I might be so bold as to beg a moment of your time."

"Of course," he said amiably. "What can I do for you?"

"Well, sir, I hope you will not think this excessively forward of me, but when I heard you were here, I thought perhaps . . . I should take the opportunity to speak with you about a concern that I have, that is to say that the staff in general have, but we have been at a loss as to whom to approach about it."

"Well, I'll be happy to hear you out, but surely if this is a staff concern, would Darcy not be the one to address?"

"Yes, sir, of course, but you see, the concern is, well, *about* Mr. Darcy, sir. He just hasn't been himself of late."

The colonel held his chin up as the valet began tying his cravat. He was quite surprised that the loyal and reticent Philips would approach him about Darcy at all, much less with a concern. "Not himself? What do you mean?"

"He seems very, well, withdrawn, I would say, for lack of a better word. He spends most of his time alone in his study, and we, the staff that is, have noticed that he often seems to be, well, in some distress. He goes out most evenings, although he doesn't seem to look forward to it, but then when his friends come calling, he isn't at home to them, not even Mr. Bingley. Mr. Darcy has never been what I would call a man of many words, sir, but now we don't hear much of anything out of him beyond requests and thank yous, even his valet. And, well, there are other things, but I'm sure you see the problem."

"What other things, Philips?" Now he was truly concerned.

"Well, sir, he's been short with Miss Georgiana a few times. And he has taken to staying up half the night, sometimes reading, but sometimes pacing or just staring off into space. And, begging your pardon, sir but as you know Mr. Darcy has never been one for excessive imbibing, as it were, but there have been several occasions when he has gone through more than a bottle on his own, though Cook says it is a challenge to tempt him to eat much of anything. I don't mean to complain, sir, he has been no trouble to us, but, well, we are worried. I don't know what he would say if he knew I was talking to you about him like this, sir."

"You were quite right to bring this to me, Philips, and you may be certain that I will keep this conversation to myself."

"Thank you, sir. If there is anything I can do to help, anything at all, please say the word." He bowed and left the room.

The colonel turned to the valet. "What do you have to say about all this? Do you agree with Philips?"

The young man snorted. "He's not telling you the half of it, sir, and that's all I'll say about that. I value my position here."

A few minutes later Georgiana was warming to the same theme. "He has not been the same since the two of you came back from Kent. He is abstracted, and sometimes I find that he is paying no attention to what I say. But the worst is when I come upon him when he is not expecting to see me, and he looks so bleak. I have tried talking to him, asking him if something is wrong, but he says that everything is fine, and it is so obviously *not* fine that I have no idea what to say. All I can think is that it must be something to do with me. It's been rather frightening. I haven't known who to turn to."

Colonel Fitzwilliam shook his head. "Do you have any idea what this may be about?"

She hesitated. "I know of nothing that can have caused such a change. I cannot think of anything that I would expect to bother him this much, anything *new*, that is, only the old things. There is no trouble with his friends, in fact he has been being rather unusually sociable, though he hardly seems to enjoy it. And I assume that there is not any financial trouble, because you would know about that, would you not? The kitchen talk is that there is a woman involved, but I cannot see what would upset him so much about that either." She paused, then added in a softer voice, "I have wondered if it has anything to do with last summer."

"I am quite sure it has nothing to do with that," he said reassuringly. "Not to worry, sweetheart; I will worm it out of him somehow. We shall get to the bottom of this."

After dinner the gentlemen retired to the study. Darcy poured out two glasses of port. Colonel Fitzwilliam sipped it appreciatively. "Now I remember why I come here: your wine cellar."

"Well, I would hate to think that it was for the company," Darcy replied.

"Unlikely. I have been told by a number of people that you have been rather poor company of late."

Darcy shot him a suspicious glance. "I'm honoured to know that I am so popular." . . . *your manners impressing me with the fullest belief of your arrogance, your conceit, and your selfish disdain of the feelings of others* . . . Swallowing a sizeable amount of port, he eyed his cousin warily.

"Something is obviously on your mind, Darcy. What is it?"

"Don't tell me Georgiana has you started on this, too. She has somehow decided that I am upset about something, and she has been like a bulldog about it. Pay no attention to her."

"You have always been a terrible liar. Now, tell Cousin Richard what the problem is."

"There is no problem, Fitzwilliam!" snapped Darcy.

"I am not an idiot, Darcy," he said amiably. "People are worried about you. I am worried about you. For God's sake, even you admit that it has affected Georgiana!"

Darcy, seeing the inquisitorial light in his cousin's eye, started to feel sympathy for cornered animals. He sighed. "Richard, leave it. There are some things that need to be private."

"There are some times when you need to turn to your family and friends. And stop guzzling that port as if it were water; it deserves better treatment than that." Silence was his only response. "Do not let your damned pride get in the way, Darcy. Pride goeth before a fall, and all that."

Darcy gave a harsh laugh. "Believe me, that is one lesson I have down very well, thank you."

"You cannot distract me that easily. Now, as your cousin, and your friend, and Georgiana's guardian, I am asking you to tell me what is wrong."

"For God's sake, stop it! If I need to talk, I promise, I will come to you."

Colonel Fitzwillliam stood up. For a moment Darcy thought that he had won the point, but then he saw his cousin was only going as far as the side table. Bringing the decanter of port and an unopened bottle of wine back to the desk, he refilled Darcy's glass. "If you want to do this the hard way, we will do it the hard way," he said in a voice the officers under his command would recognize instantly.

"And what exactly does that mean?"

"It means I plan to drink you under the table, cousin, and sooner or later you will be drunk enough to talk. Waste of good port, though."

"What makes you think you can out drink me?"

"I'm a soldier. It's one of the few useful skills we learn. Drink up, now."

Darcy, exhausted, rested his head in his hands. "Look, Richard, if I tell you what it is, will you leave me alone?"

In a somewhat gentler voice, Colonel Fitzwilliam replied, "Probably not."

They were silent for some minutes. Finally Darcy said, "It is the oldest story known to man. I fell in love with a woman, and she refused me. Are you satisfied?"

"She refused you? Darcy, I can't think of one woman in the world who would refuse you. Well, maybe the Duchess of ____, she has enough money and lands of her own, and no use for handsome young men, or so I hear. Of course, she is also old enough to be your mother."

"Very amusing, Fitzwilliam. Yes, there is a woman out there who would and did refuse me, for the very simple reason that she could not like or respect me."

Colonel Fitzwilliam sat back and pondered this information. Recalling his cousin's unusual behaviour at Rosings, an idea began to form in his mind. "Darcy, is it possible that we are speaking of the lovely Miss Bennet?"

Darcy drained his glass. "Touché, my friend. I applaud your deductive reasoning," he said with some bitterness.

"Well, I applaud your taste. If she only had money, I might have offered for her myself. I am surprised she refused you, though; I would have thought her more practical than that."

You could not have made me the offer of your hand in any possible way that would have tempted me to accept it. "You cannot be aware of how grave my sins are in her eyes, then."

"I know she found you high-handed. Are there other sins besides that?"

I have every reason in the world to think ill of you. "There are so many to choose from, it is hard to know where to begin. You could start with the fact that she received her information about my character from none other than our dear friend George Wickham. Then there is the small matter that I broke her sister's heart by discouraging Bingley from marrying her, and that I was unforgivably condescending and rude to her in my proposal . . . I think that covers the main points," Darcy said bitterly. "Let us not forget that I am arrogant and conceited as well."

"It was *her* sister that Bingley was in love with?"

"I thought she was indifferent to him, and apparently I was wrong." *Do you think that any consideration would tempt me to accept the man, who has been the means of ruining, perhaps for ever, the happiness of a most beloved sister?*

"What did she say when you explained it to her?"

Darcy stared into his wineglass. "I was too angry to explain at the time. I wrote her a letter afterwards, telling her the truth about Wickham, and my reasons for separating Bingley from her sister. If she believed it, if she did not tear it up without reading it, then perhaps she no longer thinks quite so ill of me, though that does me little good now."

"What—do you mean to tell me that you are giving up on her so easily?" asked Colonel Fitzwilliam.

"What other choice do I have? I have told her everything I can say in my own defense, and as for the rest, I can try to change my behaviour, but she will never see the results. I hardly think it likely that our paths will cross again."

"You could go to her and let her see you as you really are. Perhaps your letter did change her opinion, but you will never know unless you make the effort. It is not as if she can write to you, nor can she call on you or attempt to move into your social circles. You cannot expect her just to appear on your doorstep one day."

"You do not understand. I am quite resigned to never seeing her again," Darcy said wearily, his words causing a wrenching pain inside him. "She made it quite clear that she dislikes me, and frankly, I think she is right to do so. I do not deserve her love."

"Good God, if your father had thought the way you do, you would never have been born! How many times did he propose to your mother before she accepted him?"

"That is hardly the same. When she refused him, it was because she was already promised to another, not because he was the last man on earth that she could ever be prevailed upon to marry!"

"I still say your father would have told you to keep trying, if you love her that much."

Darcy ran his fingers through his hair. "I cannot," he said grimly. "She holds too much against me."

"You have defended yourself against whatever Wickham charged you with, and presumably Bingley and her sister have their chance to work things out now. Do you think she will not be able to see what you have done?" he challenged, increasingly frustrated with Darcy's self-pity.

"Bingley knows nothing of this."

"You haven't told him that you were mistaken? Why ever not?"

"Fitzwilliam, he would be justifiably furious with me."

"So you leave him suffering?" he said with some incredulity. "My apologies; you were right all along, and you should give up now. You certainly do not deserve her." He set his glass down carefully, and stood to leave. "And be careful with that port; you haven't the head for it. Good night, cousin."

Darcy reflected bleakly that he had not even told him his most dishonourable reason for not talking to Bingley. If Bingley married Jane Bennet, Darcy would perforce have at least occasional contact with her family, and would someday be subjected to the agony of seeing Elizabeth married to another man. He cradled his head in his hands, wondering if it were indeed possible to feel any worse than he did now.

Georgiana anxiously awaited the arrival of Colonel Fitzwilliam in the breakfast room the next morning, hopeful he would have some kind of information for her. When he finally arrived, she barely let him sit down before beginning her questioning. "Did he tell you anything?"

"Good morning to you, too, Georgiana. Please, I need some sustenance before tackling difficult discussions. And I would advise against trying to talk to your brother this morning. He should have the dickens of a headache when he finally wakes up."

"Actually, he has been awake for some time and has already gone out."

He looked at her in surprise. "Where would he go at this hour of the morning?"

Georgiana shrugged. "To see Bingley, apparently. I told him I thought it was a little early for social calls, and he said he thought it was actually rather late, whatever that may mean at seven in the morning."

"To see Bingley, eh? Good for him. Maybe there is hope for the boy after all."

Georgiana sighed dramatically. "Are you going to be mysterious as well?"

He laughed. "Afraid so, sweetheart. I did get him to talk, but I believe that what I heard is confidential. You are going to have to trust your old Cousin Richard to take care of it this time, at least insofar as your brother allows me to help."

"I hate it when you treat me as if I were still only eleven," she said with a scowl. "You can be even worse than William as far as that goes."

"Worse than William in what way?" asked Darcy from the doorway.

Georgiana jumped. "Back already? Was he not at home?"

"Oh, he was there, all right. What I had to tell him did not take long," Darcy said grimly with a sidelong glance at his cousin.

"I imagine that even Bingley has little to say this early in the morning."

"If you say so. Do you not have some business in town today, Fitzwilliam? Or even better, some that will take you very far away?"

"William!" Georgiana cried.

The colonel patted her hand. "No need to worry yourself, sweetheart. This is how your brother and I stay friends, now that we are too old for fistfights."

"Speak for yourself, *cousin*. Given how I feel this morning, you should feel fortunate that it is not pistols at dawn."

"I told you he would be grumpy, did I not?" the colonel asked Georgiana. "Never mind, I know when to retreat. It is one of the other things they teach us in the army."

She glanced from her brother to the colonel. "Will you be back for dinner?"

"I expect I will have to dine with the Major General, though the very idea is enough to make me lose my appetite. I should be back in the evening."

"If you live that long," grumbled Darcy.

Colonel Fitzwilliam smiled beatifically. "Glad to know you are feeling better, Darcy."

As he left, Georgiana turned to Darcy. "What was *that* about?"

He gave her an oblique look. The last thing he needed was a disagreement with his sister, given that she seemed to be the only person he cared about who still thought he had any redeeming features, now that Bingley had joined Colonel Fitzwilliam and Elizabeth in the ranks of those who were disgusted with him. "Ask me again when you are older—say, after your first grandchild is born."

"William, I worry about you," she said softly.

Her gentleness was more than he could handle. "I appreciate your concern, but you need not worry. If you will excuse me, I have some business I need to tend to."

She watched his retreating back, wondering if he would ever think her old enough to trust.

<hr />

Contrary to his expectations, Colonel Fitzwilliam was able to return to the Darcy home by early afternoon, although he could hardly claim that it was in the best interest of his regiment for him to do so. However, his words to Georgiana notwithstanding, he was worried about Darcy's state of mind, and felt it behooved him to be available in case matters deteriorated due to the apparent quarrel with Bingley. Thus he found himself penning a long overdue letter to his parents while surreptitiously eyeing his cousin, who was so deeply engrossed in a book as to have completely ceased turning its pages, when the arrival of Mr. Bingley was announced.

Without looking up, Darcy said, "Tell him if he wants pistols at dawn, he shall have to wait his turn behind you, Fitzwilliam."

"Why pistols? You have choice of weapons if he is challenging, and you could take either of us apart with a rapier."

"Who says I want to win?" said Darcy grimly.

"*Please* stop it, both of you," said Georgiana in a trembling voice. "It is not funny."

Both men looked over at her to see tears in her eyes. The colonel was immediately kneeling by her side. "Georgiana, sweetheart, this is just playing! Dueling is illegal, remember?"

"I *hate* it when you fight," she said faintly.

Darcy put his book down. "I apologize, Georgiana. My mood is beastly, and I have been taking it out on Richard, but no, we are not fighting. There is no need for you to worry. Look, we can be friends," he said, holding out a hand to his cousin.

"There is no need to patronize me, William!" she responded with a degree of defiance that startled both gentlemen.

"Mr. Bingley," Philips said from the doorway as Bingley entered with his usual eagerness, oblivious to the tension in the room.

"Colonel Fitzwilliam!" Bingley said with pleasure, advancing to greet him. "I had not heard you were in town! And Miss Darcy, how pleasant to see you again!" He turned to Darcy, whose demeanour suggested that he was expecting at the very least some form of violence, and rocked up on his toes. "Well?" he asked enthusiastically.

"Well what?" Darcy's voice was carefully neutral.

Bingley smiled broadly as if this were a foolish question. "Are you coming to Netherfield with me, or not?"

There was a minute of silence as Darcy carefully regarded Bingley, oblivious to his cousin's sudden attention. "Is it your wish that I come with you?" he asked stiffly.

"Of course!" Bingley said earnestly. "You really *must* come, you know."

Colonel Fitzwilliam whispered something to Georgiana that caused her to look at him in some surprise, but Darcy and Bingley were oblivious to the exchange.

"I suppose I could come for a short while," Darcy said slowly, as if the words had to be pulled out of him.

"Excellent, excellent!" Bingley was clearly delighted.

"May I come as well?" Georgiana's voice came timidly.

Darcy looked at her in surprise. It was rare enough for her to say anything in company, and making such a request in public was completely novel. "I am not sure that would be a good idea," he said, thinking of one particular member of the militia billeted at Meryton.

"Nonsense," said the colonel energetically. "It will do her a world of good to get out of London during the summer. I could hardly believe you planned to stay here through the hot weather. That is, if Mr. Bingley has no objections?"

"Of course not!" Bingley said. "It would be delightful if you would join us."

"Good, umm . . . I mean thank you," she said in a near-whisper, clearly having exhausted her store of courage. Darcy opened his mouth to speak, but then limited himself to a significant stare at Colonel Fitzwilliam.

"Wonderful!" Bingley said. "Shall we consider our plans?"

A fortnight after the removal of the regiment from Meryton, the normal good humour and cheerfulness that had disappeared from Longbourn with the departure of the officers began to reappear. The discontentedness of Kitty and Mrs. Bennet had waned, the families who had been in town for the winter came back again, and opportunities to display their summer finery were frequent. Elizabeth anticipated with pleasure her tour to the Lakes with the Gardiners, and could she have included Jane in the scheme, every part of it would have been perfect.

Mrs. Bennet was distracted as her querulous spirits were opened again to the agitation of hope, by an article of news, which then began to be in circulation. The housekeeper at Netherfield had received orders to prepare for the arrival of her master, who was coming down in a day or two. Mrs. Bennet was quite in the fidgets. She looked at Jane, and smiled, and shook her head by turns.

Elizabeth did not know what to make of the news, but found her mind traveling to the events in Kent and wondering what role Mr. Darcy might have played in the return of his friend to Hertfordshire. Had her information regarding the state of Jane's affections caused him to reconsider his interference, and perhaps even to take action to reverse it? She had studied every sentence of his letter, and her feelings towards its writer were at times widely different. When she remembered the style of his address, she was still full of indignation; but when she considered how unjustly she had condemned and upbraided him, her anger was turned against herself, and his disappointed feelings became the object of compassion. His attachment excited gratitude, his general character respect; but she could not approve him. Nor could she for a moment repent her refusal, or feel the slightest inclination ever to see him again. Yet should he be the instrument which reunited Bingley and Jane, such an effort could not but be rewarded by a certain warming of her regard. But when she recalled that effort would not have been required had he not interfered in the first place, her thoughts bent further towards resentment.

She did not consider it likely that she would encounter him again, except perhaps in passing, should Jane and Bingley someday be so fortunate as to mend their relationship and marry. She could not but imagine that he would avoid her diligently after her behaviour in Hunsford, and so did not consider the possibility that he might again accompany his friend to Netherfield. It was with the greatest of surprise and agitation, then, that she heard Kitty's intelligence that Bingley was coming to Longbourn to pay his respects, accompanied by none other than Mr. Darcy.

On hearing this news, Jane looked at Elizabeth with surprise and concern, feeling the awkwardness which must attend her sister in seeing him for the first time after receiving his explanatory letter. Both sisters were uncomfortable enough. Each felt for the other, and for themselves. Elizabeth sat intently at her work, striving to be composed, and casting about for an idea as to how to handle the forthcoming meeting. She did not dare lift up her eyes, till anxious curiosity carried them to the face of her sister, as the servant was approaching the door. Jane looked a little paler than usual, but more sedate than Elizabeth had expected. On the gentlemen's appearing, her colour increased; yet she received them with tolerable ease, and with a propriety of behaviour equally free from any symptom of resentment, or any unnecessary complaisance.

Elizabeth said as little to either as civility would allow, and sat down again to her work with an eagerness which it did not often command. She ventured only one glance at Darcy, and was more than surprised to see him entering into conversation with her mother, inquiring very civilly as to her health and recent events at Longbourn. Her mother, looking both startled and flattered by this unexpected attention, received him with a degree of warmth that embarrassed her daughter. Although Elizabeth barely dared to look up again, she followed with great anxiety his progress through the room to the point of neglecting to notice Bingley's approach of Jane. She was further surprised to see him engaging Mary on the subject of music, noting that his sister had recently begun learning a piece by Mozart that he remembered Mary performing when he had been in Hertfordshire last, and drawing a pleasing comparison between the devotion to practice of the two young women. Mary, sufficiently taken aback so as to be unable to afford a moral plati-tude appropriate to the situation, was driven to the extremity of actually responding to the subject at hand, and managed to make at least one intelligent comment regarding the music of Mozart.

Elizabeth's astonishment was extreme; and continually was she repeating to herself, *Why is he so altered? From what can it proceed? It cannot be for me, it cannot be for my sake that his manners are thus softened. My reproofs at Hunsford could not work such a change as this.* Her heart was racing with apprehension that he would approach her, and she knew not how to look or to behave when he, as she had feared, seated himself by her and addressed her directly.

"Miss Bennet, it is a pleasure to see you again," he said, in a voice that was perhaps not quite so calm as it might have been, yet with a civility that could not be denied.

She hardly knew how to respond. "You are most welcome back to Hertfordshire, sir. I hope you find it pleasing at this time of year." Bringing all of her courage to the fore, she forced herself to look up at him, and felt a slight shock as her eyes met his. Underneath the amiable look on his face, she could see that he was as nervous as she at this meeting, and she resolved to at least show she could match civility for civility.

"Yes, it is a most refreshing change from the airs of London. I must confess that I prefer the countryside to the city, but never more than during the warmth of the summer." Darcy inwardly cursed his inability to make intelligent conversation under these circumstances. He had done quite well, he thought, with her family, but those were comments he had carefully prepared in advance and utilized as if following a script.

"I cannot say that I have spent any significant time in town during the summer, but certainly I enjoy taking walks and admiring the summer scenery," she said, then wished she could retract her words as she realized that her reference to walks might be considered a reminder of their time at Rosings. She cast about desperately for a more neutral topic of conversation, and was amused when she realized that they were already discussing that safest of topics, the weather.

Relieved to see her smile, he continued, "Yes, I recall that you are a great walker, Miss Bennet. I would imagine that there would be many pleasant summertime rambles to be found, although certainly each season presents its own unique charms."

The ludicrous aspects of their strained conversation began to outweigh her anxiety, and she said slyly, "Yes, I would have to say, on reflection, sir, that summer is indeed one of my four favourite seasons."

He let out a startled laugh which he quickly covered with steepled fingers. "It is always refreshing to talk to a young lady of such decided preferences."

This time when she met his eyes it was with a distinct feeling of relief, that they had negotiated a difficult passage and established that they could indeed hold a conversation without hurling acrimonious insults and accusations at one another. She was glad of it, for certainly Bingley and Jane would have no chance at all if she and Darcy were in continual conflict. They sat briefly in a silence that was at first harmonious but became increasingly uncomfortable as the minutes passed, until Elizabeth took it on herself to break it by asking whether Mr. Bingley's sisters had accompanied them to Netherfield.

"I believe that they have plans to join us in some days, though there is one other person in our present company who more particularly wishes to be known to you. Will you allow me, or do I ask too much, to introduce my sister to your acquaintance during our stay at Netherfield?"

The surprise of such an application was great, but, while it was gratifying to know that his resentment had not made him think really ill of her, it added a degree of intimacy to their meeting that Elizabeth did not yet feel ready to accommodate. It was one thing to remain sufficiently civil as to allow necessary social intercourse, but quite another to further their connection. She was far from certain how she felt about such a plan, or what he might mean by it. However, she could see no grounds for objecting to the introduction, and thinking that more contact between Longbourn and Netherfield could not but improve Jane's chances with Bingley, she said, "I would be glad to make her acquaintance, if she wishes. I hope Miss Darcy is enjoying her visit to Hertfordshire."

"I believe she is, although she has not had much time to form an opinion. She has not gone far beyond Netherfield, but now that I am informed the militia is decamped from Meryton, I will feel more free to take her out." Darcy had noted her brief hesitation before agreeing to the introduction and, although disappointed by it, reminded himself forcefully that this new beginning would have to be taken very slowly and with great care if it were to have any chance of success, and God knew he wanted it to be successful. He had managed to keep some degree of reservation regarding this attempt right up until the moment when he walked into the room and saw her, with her fine eyes downcast and her cheeks covered with rosy blushes, and almost immediately he was more lost than ever, and prepared to do whatever it took to earn her affection.

"Yes, the departure of the militia was a relief to me as well." She wondered if he would hear the underlying message that she believed his words about Wickham, "I wish I could say that everyone in my family is in agreement with that sentiment."

Elizabeth took a moment to observe her sister deep in conversation with Bingley, whose face displayed such delight and pleasure that it was clear that his heart was as much hers as ever. She wondered how the gentleman beside her was feeling about the developments in that regard, and whether he would support Bingley's desires this time, or again seek to undermine the match.

"How long do you plan to stay at Netherfield?" she asked, then realized such a question could easily be misinterpreted.

"As long as necessary." Darcy reflexively responded with his true thoughts before realizing the extent to which his answer exposed him and might antagonize her. Again cursing his loss of coherent thought when confronted with Elizabeth Bennet, he watched in agony for her reaction, and stumbled to undo the damage. "That is to say, Bingley is hoping to stay, umm, probably through the summer, but there are a number of factors he has to take into consideration, and my plans are not completely fixed."

The effect of his words on Elizabeth was confusing; she felt a combination of an odd excitement and a certain distrust, wondering if he could possibly mean what she thought, or whether she might be misinterpreting his words. It was impossible to forget their last conversation: *You must allow me to tell you how ardently I admire and love you.* She was far from insensible of the compliment of such a man's affection, and the consideration that his regard for her could be sufficiently great as to overcome the natural resentment he must feel for her behaviour at Hunsford could not but inspire a certain degree of gratitude on her part, no matter how unequal she might feel in her response to him. Perhaps she was reading too much into a few simple words, and hardly knowing how to reply, eventually concluded that it was wisest to avoid any acknowledgement of his possible meanings. Fortunately, an appropriate distraction came to mind.

"I have had the good fortune to be invited to accompany my aunt and uncle from London on a tour of the Lakes this summer."

"That sounds like a pleasant prospect. The Lakes are very beautiful. I imagine that you will enjoy them greatly."

"You have visited them yourself, then, Mr. Darcy?"

"Indeed, I have been fortunate enough to have made that journey twice; once when I was young, and again some ten years ago in the company of my late father. It is, of course, a much shorter journey from Derbyshire than from here, so it was less of an undertaking. The scenery is quite as sublime as everyone says. I recall from my first trip that my mother was especially taken by the views; she was a passionate lover of nature in all of its wilder manifestations. I was still a bit young to notice it then."

"And when you were older—what did you think of it then?"

"By the time of my second journey, I was far more able to appreciate the beauties for myself, but perhaps less predisposed to enjoy them, as the trip was a difficult one for my father. It brought back memories of my mother's delight in the area."

"He must have been quite devoted to her," she said, touched by the personal nature of his recollections.

It was a moment before Darcy spoke. "Yes, their affection for one another was exemplary."

How had she allowed their discussion to touch on such private matters? Elizabeth's anxiety returned in full force. She fiercely renewed her attention to her needlework, with the unsurprising result that her needle promptly found its way into her finger. With a muffled exclamation of pain and embarrassment, she raised the injured finger to her lips, completely unaware of the effect that this simple gesture would have on Darcy.

"When is your journey due to begin?" he asked, desperately trying to distract his attention from her lips.

"We leave at the end of June," she replied, relieved to return to safer ground.

Almost three weeks, then, he thought. *Enough time to make a start, if all goes well.*

The gentlemen soon rose to go away, and Mrs. Bennet, mindful of her intended civility, invited them to dine at Longbourn in a few days time.

"You are quite a visit in my debt, Mr. Bingley," she added, "for when you went to town last winter, you promised to take a family dinner with us, as soon as you returned. I have not forgot, you see; and I assure you, I was very much disappointed that you did not come back and keep your engagement."

Bingley looked a little silly at this reflection, and said something of his concern, at having been prevented by business. They then went away, leaving Mrs. Bennet free to dissect every word of Bingley's during the course of the afternoon. She was very pleased with how things had gone off, and made many happy predictions for his future with Jane. Elizabeth, too caught up in her own thoughts to come to Jane's rescue, hardly attended until she heard Darcy's name.

"What I want to know," said Kitty, tossing her head with a laugh, "is who that pleasant, polite man who looked just like Mr. Darcy was. What could have caused such a change?"

"Perhaps he has studied the errors of his past behaviour, and sought to improve himself," responded Mary, who had clearly been quite won over by his recollection of her musical skills. "We should all admire such attempts when they are guided by reason, and look to him as an example that we all could bear to follow."

Chapter 2

As soon as she was able, Elizabeth walked out to recover her spirits, or in other words, to dwell without interruption on those subjects that must agitate them more. She puzzled over why he had come, first inclining to believe that it was to watch over Bingley, but then guided by her instincts to think it related more to her. But how could a man of such pride bring himself to approach her after her insulting behaviour? His changed manner towards her family seemed to suggest that he had taken her reproofs to heart, but she did not wish to assume too much.

Her own feelings were less a mystery to her. She was complimented, to be certain, that he apparently valued her opinion to the extent of heeding her reproofs and altering his behaviour, but she had previously felt no desire to see him again. But was his steadfastness a reason to change her estimation of him? There was so much which remained unknown. She resolved to think no more about him until she had a better sense of his intentions, but this resolution proved difficult to maintain for more than a short time at best, as thoughts of him kept intruding at odd moments.

She did not expect to see him again until Tuesday, when he and Bingley were engaged to dine with them, but was unsurprised when two days later he rode up to her as she was walking through the countryside. As she saw him approach, unable to avoid noticing the fine figure he cut on horseback, she resolved to meet him with composure and civility for Jane's sake, but found her pulse racing as he swung off his horse and drew near her.

"Mr. Darcy," she murmured as he bowed.

"Miss Bennet, this is indeed a fortuitous meeting. I was just thinking of consulting with you on a certain matter."

She smiled playfully. "One can hardly call it fortuitous, sir, to encounter me on a ramble on such a fine day as this one. It is more a foregone conclusion, I would say."

From the brief look that passed over his face, her attempt at light-hearted conversation had hit an unintended mark. She wondered whether he had indeed been looking for an opportunity to encounter her alone, and was conscious that her cheeks were warm.

"It does seem that we both have a propensity to enjoy the air. May I join you?"

"If you indeed wish to consult with me, it would seem a wise idea," she said gravely.

He glanced down at her, noting that she had neatly avoided stating an opinion on his presence, and wondering whether it was mere politeness that precluded her from refusing his company. The wrenching sensation this thought caused was almost enough to lead him to abandon the effort, but he forcefully reminded himself of his intention to show her that he had changed.

"I wished to speak with you regarding my sister," he said stiffly. "As I mentioned, she is anxious to make your acquaintance, but I am reluctant to bring her to Longbourn to make the introduction, as I am concerned she would find the situation difficult to manage."

Elizabeth felt a swell of disappointment. *I should have known better than to think he would truly change*, she thought. *He does not wish to expose his sister to the defects of my family and our intolerable social connections.* "Indeed, Mr. Darcy, I can suppose that she, like some others, might find me more appealing in the absence of my family," she said tartly.

Darcy turned to her in obvious distress. "Miss Bennet, I fear you have mistaken my meaning. I hope that Georgiana will meet your family very soon." Aware that he was stumbling badly in his attempt to convey himself, and fearing that he had already lost any ground he might have gained, he said, "May I speak frankly, Miss Bennet?"

"You may be as frank as you please, Mr. Darcy; I doubt that there can be worse than what I have already heard in the past," she said, growing more heated by the minute.

Darcy cursed himself silently. "Miss Bennet, I do not deny that I richly deserve your reproaches for what I have said in the past," he said with all the humility he could muster. "But I beg of you to listen to what I am saying now. My sister is quite painfully shy. She finds it extremely difficult to speak with people she does not know, and is accustomed to a very quiet life. If

I were to bring her to Longbourn, or any other household full of unknown lively people who are unafraid to speak their minds, I can guarantee she would be unable to say a word, and would leave convinced of everyone's dislike of her. I very much would like her to come to know you, but I cannot see any way to accomplish this unless I can find a more quiet setting for you to become acquainted." He forced himself to pause, aware that his words were rushing out of him with some desperation.

Her silence told him he had failed, and that his hopes of forgiveness were in vain. Sick at heart, he said, "I apologize, Miss Bennet, for my clumsy words. I have obviously made a misjudgment in broaching this matter. I assure you that no offense was intended, and I am sorry to have caused you any distress. I shall no longer disrupt your morning; please be assured that I shall not trouble you again." With a formal bow, he turned to leave.

Elizabeth was heartily ashamed of herself. To have jumped to such a conclusion could perhaps be understood, but to not allow the poor man a chance to explain himself before she began abusing him yet again—had she not learned anything from that humiliating experience at Hunsford? Was she forever to be mistaking this man? "Mr. Darcy," she said quietly, her eyes on the ground, "I am the one who needs to apologize, for the misjudgment was mine. I arrived at an unwarranted conclusion and should not have said what I did. If you are still willing, I would like to hear what you have to say."

Elizabeth could not bring herself to look up, but had she done so, she would have seen Darcy stop at her words, and a look of great relief come over his face. He took a moment to collect himself, and then said, "I would like that as well, Miss Bennet."

"Perhaps you could tell me the kind of setting Miss Darcy is most likely to be comfortable with," Elizabeth said in a somewhat subdued voice as they began to walk again.

"I hoped you might be willing to meet her at Netherfield," he said tentatively. "Then, perhaps, once she knows you better, I could bring her to Longbourn."

"I would be happy to come to Netherfield, sir. Would you care to suggest a convenient time?" Elizabeth's eyes were still downcast.

"Miss Bennet," said Darcy in a tone of emotion. "At the moment I would rather say how sorry I am to have distressed you, and to ask if there is anything I can do to relieve your discomfort."

Elizabeth looked up at him with a hint of a smile. "Your aunt, Lady Catherine, condescended to tell me on several occasions that I would never play the pianoforte really well unless I practiced more. By that measure, I must be developing true virtuosity in the art of feeling ashamed of things I have said to you, since I have had a great deal of practice at it."

"The difference, perhaps, being that I derive a great deal of pleasure in listening to you play pianoforte, and I would not have you berate yourself, especially since your response was understandable given the insufferable things I have said to you in the past. I have acknowledged to myself the truth of the reproofs you made in April and I have attempted to attend to those matters, but I realize you have no cause to believe that as yet."

Elizabeth could not begin to imagine how much those words must have cost a man of such pride. "There was also a great deal of untruth in the accusations I made that day, though I did not realize it at the time. I should apologize to you for believing without question the falsehoods of Mr. Wickham.

Ever since reading your letter, I have felt ashamed of my lack of discernment."

"Mr. Wickham's manners can be most persuasive when he so chooses. Had I told you immediately upon seeing him in Meryton what I knew of his past, the situation would not have arisen, but since I thought it beneath me to lay my private actions open to the world, I have no one to blame but myself for your misunderstanding."

"Sir, you are very harsh upon yourself, and seem to expect me to take no responsibility at all for making misjudgments of my own."

"Have I not reason to be harsh upon myself? Since you are apologizing for what you see as your errors, should I not express regret for my abominable condescension and ungentleman-like behaviour? I do not do so, Miss Bennet, not because I do not believe there to be cause, but because I do not believe any apology to be within my power, other than to demonstrate that I have seen the error of my ways."

"We had best not quarrel for the greater share of blame annexed to that evening," said Elizabeth. "The conduct of neither, if strictly examined, will be irreproachable; but I must and will hold myself responsible for the errors I have made, despite your generous attempts to exculpate me, sir."

"Miss Bennet," he said gravely, "perhaps we could demonstrate we have both improved in civility since that time by agreeing to begin anew and attempting to see one another without preconceptions." *If she refuses this, I know not what I shall do. Now that I have seen her again, how can I accept she will never be mine?* he thought, awaiting her response with trepidation.

Elizabeth could not but be aware of the significance of his request, but was unsure what her response should be. She was relieved to have cleared the slate by expressing her regrets to him, and would be pleased by a cessation of hostilities, for the sake of Jane and Bingley if nothing else. But did she wish to allow anything more? She could not imagine developing a tender regard for Mr. Darcy, and it would be cruel to raise any false hopes in him, yet refusing this overture which he had clearly come all the way to Hertfordshire to make would certainly be hurtful as well, and she was beginning to appreciate that he was a man of greater depth than she had realized. Glancing up at him, she saw a drawn look that clearly bespoke the tension that he was feeling, and discovered she had less capacity to disregard his feelings than she would have thought.

"I would be willing to entertain the possibility that we might yet be friends, sir, but as I do not wish to raise hopes for any future understanding that might come from it, I would ask you to reconsider whether this is a path you wish to tread," she finally said, gazing into the clouds in the distance, wondering how she would feel if he in fact demurred.

At least she did not refuse completely, he thought, *surely that must be promising*. Her statement was disappointing in its view of the future, but he could not forget that she had made an effort to resolve their earlier misunderstanding at some cost to her own pride, when it would have been far easier for her to simply let him go. He wondered whether her actions spoke louder than her words in this case, or whether they were no more than a manifestation of a sense of honour which would not permit her to leave him under a misconception. He could not be certain, but perhaps it was enough simply to be allowed to be with her for now. Yes, it was enough, more than enough. "I believe that I shall take my chances, Miss Bennet."

Elizabeth felt a not completely unpleasant sort of tension from his response. She had not thought he would be so open about his intentions. Any other gentleman of her acquaintance would have agreed to be friends, and not suggested a desire for more at this stage. What was it he had said at Hunsford? *Disguise of every sort is my abhorrence.* Clearly, she would need to accustom herself to a greater degree of frankness than she usually encountered. "I do not know whether you are brave, foolhardy, or both, Mr. Darcy," she said, attempting to lighten the atmosphere.

" 'Nothing ventured is nothing gained,' " he replied with a smile.

" 'Fools rush in where angels fear to tread,' Mr. Darcy," she said in lively retort.

" 'Fortune favors the brave,' Miss Bennet."

"Let me see . . . 'the fool doth think he is wise, but the wise man knows himself to be a fool.' "

Darcy smiled wickedly. " 'None but the brave deserves the fair.' "

Elizabeth, knowing she had been outdone, asked, "Was that Lovelace?"

He lifted an eyebrow. "Dryden, actually."

She laughed. "Well, sir, you have bested me for today. I shall have to retire from the field." *And I have made the startling discovery that the sober Mr. Darcy, despite all rumours to the contrary, appears to have a sense of humour.*

"I believe that I shall claim a penalty, then, and request that you come to Netherfield to meet my sister," he said.

She gave him a sidelong glance. "Right now?"

"Unless you are otherwise engaged."

She inclined her head with an arch smile. "No, sir, I am not. You may lead on."

"I could, Miss Bennet, but that would be *foolish*, since you no doubt know the route better than I."

"A fool who knows his own limitations, then," she said playfully.

"A fool that knows his own heart, at least."

Elizabeth coloured. "I believe the shortest route to Netherfield is that way, Mr. Darcy." *And fortunately it is not very far,* she thought. Thinking it was high time for a change of subject, she asked him to tell her about his sister, a subject that kept them occupied most of the journey.

Elizabeth felt embarrassed arriving at Netherfield in the company of only Mr. Darcy and then entering without a chaperone into a bachelor household. She knew this would likely occasion some talk among the servants, and hoped none of it would find its way back to Longbourn. She was relieved of these societal concerns when she finally encountered Miss Darcy in the music room, where she had been practicing the pianoforte. She seemed startled to be interrupted, but gave a quick, bashful smile when Darcy introduced Elizabeth to her.

Darcy had not overstated her shyness, Elizabeth decided. "I am delighted to meet you at last, Miss Darcy. Your brother has told me so much about you," she said with her warmest smile.

"I am sure he has been far too kind in what he has said," Miss Darcy said softly, "but I am very pleased to make your acquaintance, Miss Bennet."

"I have heard great praise for your musical abilities."

Miss Darcy glanced at her brother. "I fear he is prejudiced in my favour, but I do love music."

Elizabeth put aside her own sense of discomfort by expending all of her considerable abilities to put Miss Darcy at ease. She was pleased to discover that underneath her shyness lurked an intelligent young woman eager to have a friend. Elizabeth entertained her with stories about her sisters, and encouraged her to talk about her time at school.

Darcy participated but little in the conversation, seeming quite content to observe Elizabeth, who found his gaze more disturbing now that she understood its true nature than when she had thought he watched her only to criticize. As soon as civility would allow, she made her excuses, claiming that she would be needed at home. Miss Darcy stumbled through an invitation to call again soon, which Elizabeth warmly met with an invitation to visit at Longbourn. She stole a sly glance at Darcy to see how he bore the suggestion, but saw no evidence of concern or displeasure.

As she rose to leave, Darcy stood and said, "Miss Bennet, may I request the honour of escorting you back to Longbourn?"

Elizabeth, taken by surprise by this application, scarcely knew what to say. She would in fact much rather he did not, as she certainly had enough worry on his account already, but as there was no polite way to decline in front of his sister, she agreed to accept his company.

She felt distinctly nervous as they started off, and resolved immediately to behave as if nothing was out of the ordinary, which meant of course that it became completely impossible for her to behave in a natural manner. They walked in silence for some time, until Elizabeth, growing uncomfortable, decided that it was better to have conversation. "I enjoyed meeting your sister. She is quite charming, underneath that shy exterior."

"I was pleased that she opened up so much to you; it is not that common for her."

She stole a sly look at him. "But not, it seems, unheard of; Miss Bingley always claimed to have a close friendship with Miss Darcy."

He gave her an amused glance. "Do you believe everything that Miss Bingley says?"

"Implicitly," she said, looking up at him artlessly. "Doesn't everyone?"

Darcy laughed, delighted that Elizabeth was teasing him again. "Perhaps you should ask Georgiana about that. If she is feeling brave enough, she just might tell you what she thinks of Miss Bingley."

"I shall be fascinated, I am sure." *He should laugh more often,* she thought. *It quite changes his demeanour, and makes him look quite handsome.* "I will look forward to discovering what sort of student of human nature Miss Darcy is. I somehow suspect that there is more to her than meets the eye."

"When she is comfortable enough to speak freely, she has a great deal to say, and, although I admit to a certain bias, I believe she does have some good insights."

"When does she feel comfortable enough to speak freely?"

"More rarely than I would like, I confess; she has a rather short list of people she trusts—Colonel Fitzwilliam, her companion, our housekeeper at Pemberley, who practically raised her after our mother died, and one or two others. It is something of a worry."

Elizabeth had not meant to open up a delicate topic, and sought a way to change the subject, not realizing that Darcy, who had great hopes for her help in understanding his sister, was actually quite anxious to speak with her about his concerns about Georgiana. She took the opportunity to ask him about the health of his aunt and his two cousins whom she had met in Kent, which she was able to expand into an exposition of his extended family, but her patience and her ideas were nearly over by the time they approached Longbourn. With some relief, she said, "Well, Mr. Darcy, I thank you for your company, but I think it might be best for me to continue on by myself, as I do not particularly care to make explanations of your presence to my parents."

"By all means, let us not disconcert your parents," he said with a slight air of teasing.

She curtsied. "I will bid you good day, then."

"Until we meet again, Miss Bennet," he said. Catching her eyes with a serious look, he took her hand and raised it to his lips.

Elizabeth felt the shock of his touch linger even after he had departed. *What have I done?* she asked herself as she walked down the lane to Longbourn.

Elizabeth's impatience to acquaint Jane with the events of the day was great, and she related to her that night the chief of the scenes between Mr. Darcy and herself. Jane was less than astonished by these revelations, having already surmised that Darcy's presence at Netherfield suggested a continued partiality to her sister.

"I simply do not know how to handle his forwardness, Jane," exclaimed Elizabeth. "No sooner had I said that I could offer no more than friendship than he as much as said that he wanted more! Jane, what must I do to convince him that I do not wish for his addresses? Must I be as rude and unfeeling as I was at Hunsford?"

"He should, indeed, have respected your request, and not said so much as to make you uncomfortable with his intentions. But consider his disappointment, Lizzy. Are you not grieved for his unhappiness, which must be great indeed for him to venture to re-open your acquaintance? He must be very violently in love with you."

"Since you consider his disappointment so touchingly, dearest Jane, I shall consider myself free from the need to think of it at all, since I know that you will do it such ample justice! If you lament over him much longer, my heart will be as light as a feather."

"Oh, Lizzy, pray be serious. Does it truly mean nothing to you that he has altered his behaviour so strikingly? That he has acknowledged his errors in the manner of his previous proposal? It is not every man who would be willing to do so much."

"I did the same in apologizing for my misjudgments, without it meaning aught but that I dislike being in the wrong! Why should he not do the same?"

"Was it only disliking being in the wrong that led you to call him back when he was leaving? Truly, Lizzy, I think that you are not as indifferent to Mr. Darcy as you would like to believe."

Elizabeth thought of the indescribable sensation she had felt when he kissed her hand. Slowly she said, "I cannot claim that the compliment of his affections is unfelt, but how can it be more than that when I have always disliked him, and have no startling new reason to change that opinion?"

Jane sighed. "Lizzy, I have never understood why you thought so ill of him in the first place, and it certainly seems to me that his behaviour has been perfectly gentlemanly since his arrival if, as you say, somewhat forward."

Because I hold him responsible for destroying your happiness with his influence over Mr. Bingley. "Jane, since you can think nothing but good of everyone, his being in your good graces is not much of a recommendation."

"Can you think of nothing good about him? Come, I challenge you to find some positive feature in him. Even you, dearest Lizzy, must be able to find one or two!"

Elizabeth studied her reflection in the mirror. "He clearly cares a great deal for his sister. He appears to take his responsibilities seriously, even when it means visiting Lady Catherine, which is a cruel fate indeed. He is well-read. He is willing to admit when he is wrong, at least when sufficiently motivated to do so. There, that is four good features, and you asked only for one or two. But he is also ill-tempered, arrogant, condescending, controlling, lacking in social graces, and he values only wealth and social status. Like Miss Bingley, he is all too happy to obtain his pleasure by demeaning others. Is that not enough?"

"You are very harsh on him," said Jane with a smile. "I wonder which of us you are trying to convince. By the by, I would have to add that he is constant, honest, and valued highly by his friends. You will, of course, do as you wish, but it seems to me that perhaps you do not know him as well as you should if you are to make some sort of decision, and, since he seems determined for you to know him better, perhaps your best course would be to wait and let matters take their course. If, in time, you still feel about him as you do now, why, nothing is lost for you, and he can hardly claim that you led him on."

With a sigh, Elizabeth said, "You are, as always, annoyingly reasonable, and since I will be leaving with the Gardiners in little more than a fortnight, it would appear I am not risking much." *Then why do I have a foreboding that it will not be as simple as it sounds?* Her mirror provided no answers.

They did not see the gentlemen again till Tuesday; and Mrs. Bennet, in the meanwhile, was giving way to all the happy schemes, which the good humour and common politeness of Bingley, in half an hour's visit, had revived. On Tuesday there was a large party assembled at Longbourn, and the two who were most anxiously expected, to the credit of their punctuality as sportsmen, were in very good time. When they repaired to the dining-room, Elizabeth eagerly watched to see whether Bingley would take the place, which, in all their former parties, had belonged to him, by her sister. Her prudent mother, occupied by the same ideas, forbore to invite him to sit by herself. On entering the room, he seemed to hesitate, but Jane happened to look round, and happened to smile; it was decided. He placed himself by her.

His behaviour to her sister was such, during dinner time, as showed an admiration of her, which, though more guarded than formerly, persuaded Elizabeth that if left wholly to himself, Jane's happiness, and his own, would be speedily secured. Though she dared not depend upon the consequence, she yet received pleasure from observing his behaviour. It gave her all the animation that her spirits could boast, for she was in no cheerful humour. While her feelings on seeing Mr. Darcy were decidedly mixed, she could not help but be aware of him, and she was distressed to find that he was seated on one side of Mrs. Bennet and almost as far from her as the table could divide them. Observing closely, Elizabeth noted that he had lost none of his recent civility towards her mother, but was mortified to see her mother's flirtatious response to his consideration.

She wondered whether the evening would afford some opportunity of bringing Darcy to her, or whether the whole of the visit would not pass away without enabling them to enter into something more of conversation than the mere ceremonious salutation attending his entrance. The period which passed in the drawing-room, before the gentlemen came, was wearisome and dull to a degree that almost made her uncivil, yet she could not determine whether she most feared for or wished his appearance.

The gentlemen came, and she thought he looked towards her, but the ladies had crowded round the table, where Miss Bennet was making tea, and where Elizabeth was pouring out the coffee, in so close a confederacy that there was not a single vacancy near her which would admit of a chair. Darcy walked away to another part of the room, but followed her with his eyes, and she was unsurprised by his bringing back his coffee cup himself. She was determined to be composed, and said, "I hope your sister is well?"

"Yes, she is enjoying a quiet evening to herself. She was happy to make your acquaintance, and hopes you will visit again."

"It would be my pleasure; she is a very sweet girl." She could think of nothing more to say, and they stood in silence for some minutes.

"Miss Bennet, I recall when you were in Kent, you were par-tial to early morning walks. Is it a pleasure you continue at home?"

The memory of their meetings in the grove at Rosings, which she had thought to be accidental, made her blush. "When I am able, and the weather permits, I still enjoy an early ramble."

"Perhaps, since you know the neighbourhood so well, you could recommend some walks to me."

Her pulse fluttered in response to this evident request for an assignation, and she recalled her agreement to acquaint herself further with him. Certainly, it would be best if that were not done under her mother's eye; heaven itself could not protect her if Mrs. Bennet became aware that Mr. Darcy and his ten thou-sand pounds a year had intentions towards her daughter. Yet it should be nowhere too private; the warmth in his eyes when he looked at her did not predispose her to a sense of security regard-ing his behaviour. "The walk to Oakham Mount is pleasant at this time of year," she said.

His face warmed becomingly as he allowed himself a slight smile. "My thanks for the advice, Miss Bennet." She found her-self caught by his intent gaze, and had to force herself to look away. Clearly he had no intention of observing the fiction that he was interested primarily in her friendship.

When the tea-things were removed, and the card tables placed, she felt rather relieved by seeing him fall a victim to her mother's rapacity for whist players, and a few moments after seated with the rest of the party. They were confined for the evening at different tables, but his eyes were so often turned towards her side of the room, as to make him play unsuccessfully.

Mrs. Bennet had designed to keep the two Netherfield gentle-men to supper, but their carriage was unluckily ordered before any of the others, and she had no opportunity of detaining them. "Well girls," said she, as soon as they were left to themselves, "What say you to the day? I think every thing has passed off uncommonly well, I assure you. The dinner was as well dressed as any I ever saw. The venison was roasted to a turn—and every-body said they never saw so fat a haunch. The soup was fifty times better than what we had at the Lucases' last week, and even Mr. Darcy acknowledged, that the partridges were remark-ably well done, and I suppose he has two or three French cooks at least. And, my dear Jane, I never saw you look in greater beauty." Mrs. Bennet, in short, was in very great spirits; she had seen enough of Bingley's behaviour to Jane to be convinced that she would get him at last; and her expectations of advantage to her family, when in a happy humour, were so far beyond reason, that she was quite disappointed at not seeing him there again the next day, to make his proposals.

Elizabeth, meanwhile, was thrown into a discomfiture of spirits which kept sleep away for some time, and for every thought she had of Darcy's reformed behaviour, she thought even more of being able to escape this anxiety on her trip to the Lakes. Only two weeks, she reminded herself.

⁓❈⁓

By the end of the following morning, Elizabeth was fully convinced of the impossibility of becoming friends with a man whose every look bespoke desire for far more than companion-ship. No matter how innocent the conversation—and it ranged from books to music to nature—she found herself flushing alternately hot and cold, and excruciatingly aware of the nature of Darcy's interest in her. Instead of being invigorated by the walk, she felt on edge and nervous, and it was to this that she attributed her agreement on their return to pay a visit to Miss Darcy, when in fact she desired nothing more than to return home.

Nonetheless, she was able to enjoy her visit with Miss Darcy, and appreciated that her brother left them to themselves, instead of hovering protectively over his sister as Elizabeth had half-expected him to do. It would have been unnecessary, in any case; Miss Darcy brought out the protective instincts in Elizabeth as well, and she could readily understand why her brother worried as much as he did about her, and could see why she would have been an easy target for the likes of Mr. Wickham. When the conversation turned to how Georgiana liked Hertfordshire, she discovered that the younger girl had actually had little chance to see the area, having spent almost all her time at Netherfield.

"Well, I shall have to convince you to take some walks with me, so that you can see some of the local sights. Although they may not be as dramatic as what Derbyshire has to offer, they are still well worth the seeing."

Georgiana's face lit up. "That would be delightful! I have wanted to explore, but since I do not know the area, I have been afraid of losing myself."

"Why, it sounds as if Mr. Darcy has been quite neglecting you!" Elizabeth teased. "I shall have to have words with him."

"Oh, no!" cried Georgiana with a look of alarm. "He always does anything I ask; he is far too good to me. I just have not wanted to . . . trouble him. He is doing so much better than he was in London, and that is more than enough to make me happy."

"I assure you that I was only teasing, Miss Darcy; I am well aware of your brother's devotion to you," Elizabeth said with what she hoped was a reassuring manner, but inwardly somewhat amused by the gravity in which her charges had been taken. Perhaps seriousness was a Darcy family trait.

Georgiana looked relieved. "Oh, I am glad. I would not want him to feel guilty in any way, not now, not about me. I have been a great trial to him of late."

"I can hardly imagine that," said Elizabeth warmly. *After all, I believe that it has been my role to be a trial to him of late.*

"Oh, it is true. He has been so unhappy lately, and I have been so worried about him, and it is all my fault. You see," she hesitated for a moment, and then plunged ahead, "I did something, made a terrible lapse of judgment last summer, and it upset him a great deal, although he never said one word of reproach to me. But I can see that it weighs on him, and these last two months have been terrible. He has been so withdrawn, and so unhappy, so you see why I do not want to cause him any trouble, not now that he finally seems to have been able to forget it a little. But I am sorry, Miss Bennet, I should not be telling you all of my problems; please forgive me." She looked down, clearly most embarrassed by her confession.

Oh, dear, thought Elizabeth. *What a tangled web we weave!* She placed her hand over Georgiana's. "There is nothing to forgive, my dear. I am honoured you feel able to tell me your worries. But I think that you blame yourself far too much; I feel sure there are many things in your brother's life that might be disturbing to him of which you may be unaware, and whatever has upset him these last two months probably has nothing at all to do with you." She felt abominably guilty, as she suspected that she knew all too well the true cause of Mr. Darcy's distress.

Georgiana shook her head wordlessly, tears in her eyes.

Elizabeth sighed, deeply torn as to the proper course of action. "Now I am afraid it is my turn for a confession, and I hope that you will be able to bear with me, since it forces me to violate a confidence, and I must request that you not ask me questions about it so that I may protect as much of that confidence as I can. You see, as it happens I *do* know why your brother has been upset these last two months, and while I may not tell you what the cause is, please believe me when I say that it has absolutely nothing in the world to do with you."

Her face reflected hopeful disbelief as she turned to Elizabeth. "Truly?"

Elizabeth nodded, and, putting her arm around Georgiana as she dried her tears, offered what comfort she could until a few moments later when they were interrupted by the return of Mr. Darcy himself.

Darcy, somewhat stunned to find his tearful sister in Elizabeth's arms, opened his mouth to speak, then closed it again, and then finally managed a creditable, "Is something the matter?"

Elizabeth fervently thought that the Lakes could not be far enough from the Darcy clan to suit her. Drawing with an effort on her best playful and flirtatious manner, she said, "Why, Mr. Darcy, surely you know better than to ask such a question of two ladies who are in each other's confidence! We must have our secrets, you know." With her eyes, she implored him not to ask any further.

Happily, Georgiana took the lead by approaching Darcy and wrapping her arms around him. "Truly, William, everything is fine," she said, with an obvious note of truth in her voice that reflected the relief she had received from Elizabeth's earlier words. Elizabeth could not help but be touched by the tender embrace which Darcy gave his sister, nor but be amused by the baffled look on his face.

"Well, then, I am glad to hear it," he said. "I did not, in fact, come in to eavesdrop on your secrets, but to offer the use of the carriage to Miss Bennet, since I realize that we have kept you from home for quite a while, and your family must be wondering what has become of you."

"I will accept that offer gratefully"—*particularly if it takes me as far away from here as possible*—"as even I have had enough walking for the day."

The orders being given to prepare the curricle, it was only a short while until Elizabeth was bidding her adieus to Miss Darcy, while Mr. Darcy, who was clearly planning to drive her home, prepared to hand her into the carriage. No sooner were they on the road than Darcy expressed concern regarding his sister's behaviour.

Elizabeth was reluctant to enter onto the topic, but knew she would be doing Miss Darcy a disservice if she did not. "Mr. Darcy, there is indeed something I should tell you, but I do not expect that you will be happy to hear this." She felt him stiffen perceptibly, and a glance at his face showed a frozen look which did not go far to mask a feeling of devastation. Feeling quite out of patience with his single-mindedness regarding her, she placed her hand lightly on his arm and said with some exasperation, "No, it is not that. I am beginning to suspect that jumping to the worst possible conclusion is a Darcy family trait! This is something you will dislike, if I read the subject correctly, but it is not that. Pray forgive my bluntness; I seem to have exhausted my entire store of tact for the day with Miss Darcy."

The look of relief on his face told her she had guessed rightly. "Well, then, Miss Bennet, you may do your worst, and I will do my best not to jump to dreadful conclusions." He managed somehow to catch her hand in his before she could withdraw it.

She took a breath, prepared to protest the action, then decided instead to ignore it and save her energy for the conversation at hand, a conclusion which would have been more practical had his touch not proved to be significantly more distracting than she had anticipated. "Sir, Miss Darcy made several confessions to me, at least one of which I am sure you would have preferred that I not hear, but since I am concerned for her feelings I feel it appropriate to risk wounding yours by telling you the source of her anxiety, as it is one which you may wish to address."

"If it concerns Georgiana, I would prefer to know, even if I find it unpleasant," he replied unhesitatingly.

"She confided that you have been in a particularly black humour these last two months, and that this was her fault," she began.

"Where in God's name did she get that idea?" he exclaimed with more feeling than politeness. "I beg your pardon, Miss Bennet."

"She attributes it to a serious lapse of judgment which she made last summer. She did not give any details, although I assume that we both know to what she was referring. She has been blaming herself acutely for the situation and for being the cause of your distress, and apparently has been afraid to say anything for fear of making matters worse."

As she spoke, she saw his face set in grim lines, and suspecting that some of his annoyance must be directed towards her, she made a tentative attempt to withdraw her hand from his, only to have him tighten his grip. She subsided, and tried to calm herself with thoughts of leaving for the Lakes. No, she decided, the Lakes were not far enough away. Perhaps the Continent, or the frozen wastes of Russia would do. No one would have ever heard of the Darcys at the court of the czar. An involuntary smile curved her lips at the thought.

Darcy, having regained control of his temper, said, "If there is some humourous aspect of this situation, Miss Bennet, I would appreciate your sharing it, as I could certainly use some laughter."

"It was nothing at all," she hastened to reassure him. "I was thinking about the czar of Russia, in fact."

He stared at her in momentary disbelief. "I confess there are moments when you baffle me completely, Miss Bennet."

"Thank you," she said gravely. "I work quite hard at baffling you, and I am glad to know that my efforts are not in vain."

He could not help laughing. Despite all the difficulties Elizabeth presented, he could not fault his taste. There was no other woman like her. That she could on such a short acquaintance elicit from Georgiana something that had troubled her for months, tell him the unpleasant truth, and then make him laugh! And she was allowing him to hold her hand, albeit with some ambivalence, if he read her correctly. Thoughtfully, he allowed his thumb to lightly trace circles in her palm, and noted with pleasure that her colour was rising and her eyes dropped. At least she was not completely indifferent to him—surely that was something.

Elizabeth herself was unsure whether the sensations coursing through her were horrifying or pleasurable. How could she respond so strongly to his touch when she was wishing him half the world away? She schooled herself to offer no response that might give away the extent of his effect on her, and consequently forced herself to allow her hand to relax in his, with the unfortunate outcome of allowing his thumb even more scope for its exploration, and more latitude for wreaking havoc with her composure.

"Thank you for telling me about Georgiana," he said. "I apologize that it put you in a difficult position. I try my best with Georgiana, but there are times when the mind of a young girl is quite beyond my understanding."

"Sometimes a stranger has an advantage in these matters." What was wrong with her, Elizabeth wondered, that she was feeling throughout her whole body the effects of his attentions to her hand?

"If it is the right stranger," he allowed. "But I cannot and do not fool myself into thinking that I can offer her everything she needs."

"That would seem to be an impossible task. It appears to me that you have done admirably well, given the predicament inherent in the situation of a man of your years trying to raise a girl at the most difficult age." Elizabeth was surprised to realize that she meant it.

"It is a continuing challenge," he acknowledged. *It would be so much easier with you by my side.* Since they were nearing Longbourn, he asked, "May I have the privilege of seeing you tomorrow?"

He sounds almost humble, she thought, *but I cannot possibly bear to do this again so soon.* "I do not believe I can get away in the morning," she said, and then was shocked to hear herself continue. "Perhaps you and Mr. Bingley might call later in the day."

"Thank you," he said softly, and raised her hand to his lips to give it a kiss that was more a caress than a formality. The sensation was exquisite, much though she hated to admit it.

She felt enormous relief when she was able to take her leave of him. Drained by her efforts and the unfamiliar sensations he had induced in her, she decided to go straight to her room to refresh herself before facing her mother and sisters, but no sooner had she entered the house than Mrs. Bennet saw her.

"Lizzy!" she cried. "There is a letter from your aunt Gardiner."

Elizabeth took the letter with a smile, amusing herself again with the idea of the frozen wastes of Russia. Her amusement faded as she read the letter, which at once delayed the commencement of the tour and curtailed its extent. Mr. Gardiner would be prevented by business from setting out till a fortnight later in July, and must be in London again within a month; as that left too short a period for them to go so far, and see so much as they had proposed, or at least to see it with the leisure and comfort they had built on, they were obliged to give up the Lakes, and substitute a more contracted tour, and according to the present plan, were to go no farther northward than

Derbyshire. In that county, there was enough to be seen, to occupy the chief of their three weeks.

"Derbyshire," Elizabeth said numbly. She was excessively disappointed, having set her heart on seeing the Lakes, but the last place in England she desired to visit at present was the one place that would continually remind her of Darcy. And an additional fortnight before she could be free of him and his disturbing effect upon her—suddenly it was too much, and she made a hasty retreat to her room, where she could lament in private.

When the gentlemen from Netherfield arrived the following afternoon, Elizabeth was still feeling distinctly out of spirits and, apart from the pleasure it would give Jane, none too glad to see their visitors. She made little effort at conversation, but found this seemed to cause no distress to Darcy, who, as he had so often in the past, seemed to feel no discomfort at simply enjoying her presence in silence. Before long Bingley proposed their all walking out, and it was agreed to. Mrs. Bennet was not in the habit of walking, and Mary could never spare time, but the remaining five set off together. Bingley and Jane walked slightly behind, while Elizabeth, Kitty, and Darcy were left to entertain each other. Very little was said by either; Kitty was too much afraid of him to talk, and Elizabeth too dispirited.

As they walked past the road to Lucas Lodge, Kitty expressed a wish to call upon Maria, and as Elizabeth could think of no sensible reason to object, she agreed to allow Kitty to leave them. She pressed firmly onward without looking at her companion.

"Miss Bennet," he said after a silence of several minutes, "I cannot help but observe you seem somewhat out of spirits today. May I be so bold as to inquire if I have offended you in some manner?"

Elizabeth sighed, not wanting to explain herself, yet was still too fair-minded to take out her displeasure on an innocent—well, perhaps not completely innocent—party. "Mr. Darcy, I am in a prodigiously uncivil state of mind today, and you merely have the misfortune to be in my company at such a moment. I apologize for being such poor company; please do not construe my regrettable behaviour as in any way related to you."

"You have no need to apologize, Miss Bennet. I would not have you pretend to feelings you do not possess." He said nothing more for some time, and then asked, "May I ask if there is anything that is troubling you?"

Elizabeth, who had begun to feel irritated he had not asked this very question, discovered she was perversely annoyed he seemed to assume he had the right to ask it. "It is nothing of any concern to anyone beyond myself," she said shortly.

They walked on, Darcy struggling with a frustrating feeling of impotence that she would not allow him to help in whatever was troubling her, and an unhappy suspicion that he must be in some way responsible for her distress, despite her words to the contrary. Elizabeth, meanwhile, made the awkward discovery that, having gone to the trouble of pushing aside his concern, she now felt that she would like to tell him of her disappointment, and was further baffled as to why she would feel the desire to talk to him, of all possible people, about it. Finally, as she was not by nature of a sullen disposition, her wish to express herself won out.

"Sir, again I must regret my lack of civility. To be honest, I am merely sulking like a fractious child who has been denied an expected treat, and deserve no sympathy whatsoever."

With some relief at the change in her tone, he said, "My sympathy is not contingent on whether you feel it to be deserved, Miss Bennet."

"You are too kind, sir, but in fact I am being quite petty. I received news that my northern tour, which I have been much anticipating, is delayed, and that we will not be able to travel as far as the Lakes, which was a great wish of mine."

Darcy's first reaction was one of relief that he was not in fact the culprit, followed by a feeling of frustration that he had not the right to relieve her distress by offering to take her to the Lakes himself some day. "That must be a great disappointment; I recall how much you were looking forward to it."

She felt a surprising degree of relief after for having spoken of it, and resolved to be in kindlier spirits.

"I appreciate your thoughtfulness in telling me, and thus sparing me the need to jump to the worst possible conclusion," Darcy added.

She gave him a sidelong glance. Was he in fact making a joke at his own expense? "I will try to keep your frailties in mind."

"And speaking of frailties . . . " Darcy glanced over his shoulder at Jane and Bingley, who were a short distance behind them. Speaking noticeably more quietly, he said "Your sister is, I believe, concerned with observing the proprieties, is she not?"

Wondering where he could possibly be leading, she said cautiously, "That would be a correct assumption."

"Then I fear that she is determined to stay properly near us, which is unfortunate for poor Bingley, who was hoping for some time alone with her, as he has something very particular to discuss."

A delighted smile spread across her face as she realized what he meant. Remembering the last time the subject was raised between them, she said, "I . . . am pleased to hear it."

He glanced down at her. "Well, it remains to be seen if he will find the opportunity, given that we seem to be in the way. A pity, is it not?"

If he had been anyone else, she might have thought this a suggestion to take steps to improve the situation, but she found it hard to believe that he would approve either the sentiment or the lack of propriety. On the other hand, when she glanced up at him, she saw that he had an amused smile on his face. Perhaps she had misjudged him. "Mr. Darcy, I am beginning to suspect that you have some nefarious scheme in mind."

"No, in fact, I was counting on you to come up with the nefarious scheme, since you know better than I how to convince your sister, while Bingley will accept any excuse, no matter how weak, to steal away with her."

Elizabeth thought she might have to revise her opinion of him. "I will give the matter some consideration, sir," she said with a saucy smile. But separating themselves from Jane and Bingley would also have the effect of leaving her unchaperoned again with Darcy. Elizabeth felt a peculiar sensation at the thought of it, and knew that she must be blushing. She did not feel ready to be alone with him again, though no doubt he was desirous of the situation. She was willing to give him what he wanted in this case, though; if the price of allowing Bingley to propose to Jane was time alone with Darcy, she would pay it. After all, she had survived the previous day, and she could do so again, although she would need to take care given his increasing forwardness of the day before. She would be prepared this time, though. She would watch him closely and not permit any liberties. He might not be the easiest of men to refuse, but she had managed to do that before as well.

She considered how best to effect the separation of the couples. It needed to be something which Jane would perceive as temporary, yet capable of being extended to allow enough time for Bingley to say his piece. She decided to opt for a simple approach, and just as they reached a small thicket, without a word of warning to Darcy, she made a sudden exclamation of pain and caught at his arm as if to balance herself. He immediately turned and supported her arm, his face alive with concern, as Jane hurried up to help.

With a look of embarrassment towards Darcy, Elizabeth beckoned to Jane, and whispered in her ear that she had a stone in her boot, and if Jane would take the gentlemen on ahead, she would remove it and rejoin them in a few minutes. As she expected, Jane, conscious of her sister's modesty, immediately urged Bingley and Darcy to accompany her. Darcy looked momentarily confused, but after a moment said, "No, I cannot support leaving Miss Elizabeth Bennet by herself. I shall remain here in case she needs any further assistance."

Elizabeth hobbled to a fallen log, and said with a hint of annoyance in her voice, "As you wish, but I must insist that you remain where you are, sir, and turn your back."

"No, I must be the one to wait," said Jane.

In a voice rich with embarrassment, Elizabeth said, "Jane, please, just go on!" Her sister looked indecisive, but with Bingley's urging, eventually continued down the lane.

In the interest of verisimilitude, Elizabeth unlaced and removed one of her half-boots. Looking up to see Darcy watching her unashamedly with a slight smile on his face, she said dryly, "Why, imagine that! There appears to be no stone in my boot after all."

He raised an eyebrow. "Indeed?"

"However," she said judiciously, "I believe there is still sufficient pain that it is best to remain here until it improves."

"Certainly you must. And it would be unmannerly of me not to bear you company while you wait."

"Quite unmannerly," she agreed as he sat by her side, and she smiled at him in satisfaction at the success of her plot.

Her playful smile evoked a very different response in Darcy, whose eyes darkened as he gazed intently into her eyes. Elizabeth forgot to breathe, and as he dropped his gaze to her lips, felt a disturbing surge of sensation. She looked away from him abruptly, realizing that she was at a certain disadvantage as to avoiding his advances while she sat with one boot off and one on.

Darcy, seeing her discomfort, had rarely wished so fervently for that happy fluency of speech possessed by Bingley and Colonel Fitzwilliam. How in the name of heaven was he supposed to apologize for the way he looked at her, especially since he could hardly claim that he had not wanted to do more than look. Finally he said quietly, "I apologize, Miss Bennet. I shall endeavour to remember that I must be patient."

"I cannot argue with that conclusion," she replied, her eyes still averted. She hardly knew what to say or do; she was becoming uncomfortably aware that there was a rift between the distance she wished to establish between them and her response whenever he touched her or looked at her with those smoldering eyes. She could not but disapprove of herself for having such a reaction to a man towards whom she had no serious intentions. However, regardless of her inner conflict, she could hardly continue staring at the ground until Jane and Bingley returned, so with firm resolve but little self-confidence she looked up at him, only to find that he was now staring off into space.

"Do you suppose Mr. Bingley has realized yet that we have abandoned him?" she asked lightly.

The corners of his mouth turned up in a valiant attempt at a smile. "I would imagine so, since he was hoping for something of the sort. I suspect that he may have been surprised at your involvement, however."

"Well, you may tell him that I am prepared to injure myself on his behalf whenever the need arises."

He seemed to reach some sort of decision and turned to look at her. With a question in his eyes, he extended his hand, palm up, towards her. She looked at it, told herself that she would be out of her mind to be encouraging him, wavered, and, deciding that he was in need of the reassurance, placed her hand in his. A shock of sensation surged through her as he closed his hand around hers, and he rewarded her with an expression of unlooked-for warmth, leaving her full of unanswered questions about why she cared about reassuring him, why she was so warmed by his smile, and above all why having his hand on hers pleased her so.

After sitting in a companionable silence for some time, Darcy said, "You mentioned that your tour with your aunt and uncle is delayed. May I ask when you will be leaving?"

"In a month." She smiled at his transparency. Had it always been this simple to tell what he was thinking, and had she simply never given it a thought before?

"Georgiana will be pleased to have an opportunity to see more of you before you disappear into the wilds of the north."

"The wilds of the north, indeed," she said, then, recalling that she had not told him that the new plans involved Derbyshire, suddenly found the entire situation overwhelmingly amusing. She began to laugh, and found herself barely able to stop.

He raised an eyebrow. "Let me guess—it is the czar of Russia."

This only encouraged her, and she was wiping tears of laughter from her face when Jane and Bingley reappeared. Jane's face was shining with joy, and Bingley wore a rather silly smile. Elizabeth, having rapidly extracted her hand from Darcy's and restored her boot to its rightful location, immediately went to her sister and embraced her, and had the joy of hearing her acknowledge, with the liveliest emotion, that she was the happiest creature in the world. Elizabeth's congratulations were given with a sincerity, a warmth, a delight, which words could but poorly express. Every sentence of kindness was a fresh source of joy to Jane, while Bingley was receiving the equally warm congratulations of his friend.

Jane, desiring to go instantly to her mother with the news, and Bingley, equally anxious to obtain the permission of Mr. Bennet, quickly urged the party homeward. As they walked,

Darcy asked, "Someday, Miss Bennet, will you be so kind as to tell me what is so humourous about the wilds of the north?"

Elizabeth, too full of happiness for Jane even to object to the idea of Derbyshire, looked up at him with an impudent smile. "I imagine you would know far better than I, sir; after all, you live there and I have never been north of Hertfordshire."

He could come up with no response to this beyond a bemused smile.

Chapter 3

THE NEXT FINE DAY found Elizabeth en route to Netherfield, the arrangement having been made that she would call on Miss Darcy and take the opportunity to show her some of the natural beauties of the area. Bingley was a daily visitor at Longbourn by this time, coming frequently before breakfast, and always remaining till after supper, but Darcy, having gracefully, if not entirely happily, accepted Elizabeth's hint that she would prefer that he not be in such constant attendance, restricted himself to the occasional visit to Longbourn. Thus, it was not surprising to Elizabeth that he would choose to accompany his sister on their walk, nor was it completely unwelcome, as she had concluded it was best for them to spend time together in company rather than alone. The occasion was a generally successful one; though Miss Darcy was not as great a walker as either of her companions, she delighted in the company, and her brother tended to appear in his best light when accompanied by his sister.

Elizabeth was pleased to find that she enjoyed the time sufficiently to be willing to accept an invitation to dine with them, though she had trepidation regarding her departure, correctly suspecting that Mr. Darcy had some plans for that juncture. She was not surprised when he offered to drive her home in the curricle again, nor when he took her hand in his before they were even out of the drive at Netherfield, and his aspect changed from amiable gentleman and brother to that of the lover. She was able to accept his attentions with at least an external composure, and if internally her confusion remained great, at least her response was no longer as surprising as it had been at first.

This became a pattern as time went on, that every few days she would spend time with the two Darcys, usually walking or occasionally driving through the countryside, and then allow Mr. Darcy to claim his due on the road back to Longbourn. She could not explain why it was, but gradually anticipation began to replace her initial dread of the time alone with him. She grew to find more pleasure in the sensations his looks and the touch of his hand produced, once she saw that he asked nothing further of her on those drives, but her confusion continued regarding her feelings towards him. Her opinion of him had improved, but she still had a number of reservations about him. Although he continued in his civility towards her family, when they were in greater company, he became again the reserved and taciturn man she had known in the past; and although he no longer refused to converse when others approached him, he did not seek out these encounters. He could still be high-handed, and she found herself sometimes resentful of the assumptions he seemed to make about her availability to him. And while she appreciated his role in bringing Bingley and Jane back together, she still could not bring herself to forgive him fully for engineering their separation in the first place.

She felt fortunate that no one apart from Bingley, Jane, and perhaps Georgiana seemed to have realized his interest in her. Meryton society had seen no reason to reassess what was generally known as her dislike of him. The pleasant thought that the wealthy Mr. Darcy might have taken a liking to Elizabeth had crossed Mrs. Bennet's mind on occasion, but Elizabeth was able to divert her with misleading comments about her friendship with Miss Darcy and reminders that she was not handsome enough to tempt Mr. Darcy, and so her mother's fancies had instead turned to whether Miss Darcy could put Elizabeth in the way of any wealthy and eligible young men. On occasion she observed her father watching Darcy with a quizzical look, but if he had any suspicions in that direction, he kept them to himself.

Only a fortnight remained until her departure for Derbyshire when she went to Netherfield only to find Miss Darcy in bed complaining of a headache. After exchanging a few words with her friend, Georgiana admitted that she was not feeling well enough to enjoy company, but insisted that Elizabeth and Darcy continue with their plans of walking to Gadebridge Hill, an idea which clearly pleased Darcy, and Elizabeth could think of no real objection.

It was clear as they set out that Darcy was making every effort to observe decorum, to the point where he was failing to respond to some of Elizabeth's teasing, and her spirits were such that she could not resist a few barbed comments about his dignity.

"Personally, I do not associate an excess of dignity with brisk walks through the countryside," he said.

"Well, we shall see how you do when we encounter a muddy path or a recalcitrant cow, Mr. Darcy."

"I am aware that mud would not stop *you*, but how would you handle the recalcitrant cow?"

Elizabeth laughed. "Do you doubt, sir, that I cannot be even more recalcitrant than a cow when I set my mind to it?"

"No gentleman would dream of attempting an answer to such a question, Miss Bennet. I shall instead limit myself to pointing out that you seem to be maintaining a certain level of dignity as well."

"True, but only because I am, for your benefit, being far more proper and dignified than I should be were I walking by myself," she said archly.

"Indeed, and what improper and undignified behaviour would you be indulging in were you by yourself, Miss Bennet?"

She eyed him calculatingly, perfectly willing to see how much she could shock him. "Sometimes I like to run. It can be quite exhilarating."

His eyes widened slightly in surprise, but he mastered it well. "Far be it for me to keep you from any of your pleasures, Miss Bennet. Please feel free to run, if you so desire."

She judged he did not believe she would take up his challenge. If so, he underestimated her willingness to test him. With a teasing smile, she gathered up her skirts and set off at a fast run. She ran farther than she would usually have done to press the point, and eventually, on reaching the ruins of an old cottage, collapsed back against one of the standing walls, laughing and quite out of breath. Darcy appeared a moment later, and leaned an arm against the wall next to her.

Could she have seen the picture she presented, lips parted, eyes sparkling, and cheeks becomingly flushed from the exercise, she might have understood better where the look in his eyes came from, but knowing only that her shocking behaviour was leading him to the very thoughts she had hoped he would repress, she said in a lively manner, "Mr. Darcy, you are a difficult man to discourage!"

"Have you only just realized that?" He lightly ran a finger down her cheek, creating an exquisite sensation that left her even more breathless. "Surely you must know by now that I will do whatever I must." Elizabeth felt caught by the look in his eyes as he slowly bent his head towards hers until his lips gently caressed her own.

The unexpected shock of pleasure that ran through her astonished Elizabeth even more than the fact that she had not stopped him, nay, had not even wanted to stop him. What was happening to her, that she could not refuse that look in his dark eyes?

He drew back, a slight smile curving his lips, his eyes still fixed on hers. She was hesitant to meet his gaze while still moved by his kiss, but he would have none of it and tipped her chin up with his finger until she looked directly at him. Her heart pounded at his look of inquiry, and she wished she could give him the love he wanted, but enjoying his kiss was not the same as loving him. It ought to have been the loving that came first. She had never considered that her first kiss might come from someone to whom she was not at the very least promised, and despite the pleasure of his kiss, she was not altogether happy that it had not come in that context. It troubled her deeply that her thoughts seemed to have no impact whatsoever on her treacherous desire for him to kiss her again.

She knew that she must respond to him, and that she must be gentle but firm. "I believe that most people would say that you must *not* do that," she said, pleased to find that her voice did not tremble. She dropped her gaze again, not trusting her eyes not to betray her.

"There is only one opinion that matters to me," he said, his voice barely stable. He had not meant to kiss her; he knew only too well that she would likely take offense, but the sight of her looking up at him, laughing and so alive, had been more than he could resist. But now it was even harder, for kissing her had only exposed the well of need he felt for her—need which had grown through the long winter of trying to forget her, and had overrun him in those black months after Kent when he believed she could never be his, need that could only be sated by Elizabeth Bennet. Kissing her, even so briefly and lightly, was delicious beyond belief; he responded to it like a starving man in a waste-land, and he was desperate for more.

Elizabeth knew that she should not remain so close to him, that she should remove temptation by moving out of reach, but her body would not obey her. In an effort to rein in her errant thoughts, she forced herself to think of all the painful moments in their history, all the times she had hated and resented him. She remembered her fury with him after his proposal, and it suddenly struck her as amusing that she could have traveled so quickly from that point to one where she was aching for his kisses.

Humour, as it had so often done in the past, lent her the distance she needed, and she was able to free herself from the spell of the moment. She looked up with a smile, and made the fatal mistake of meeting his eyes again. The look of raw need in them caused all of her resolve to fail, and her wish to resist him melted into nothingness.

In his heart, Darcy knew he should go no further, that she had warned him, but he found himself helpless to ignore the desire on her face. If he could not have her love, he would settle for the moment for having her want him. He said softly, "But since I do care about that one opinion, I shall warn you that if you do not want me to kiss you again, you should take this opportunity to tell me so."

Elizabeth swallowed hard, searching desperately for the good sense that had deserted her the moment he touched her. Her lips parted as his hand gently cupped her cheek, a touch that reawakened the intoxicating feelings he had created in her, and she closed her eyes to savour the delightful sensation of his mouth meeting hers.

Darcy allowed himself to take his time with this kiss, tasting the pleasures of her lips, and, as he felt her unmistakable response, permitted a tiny fraction of the urgency he felt to express itself as he deepened the kiss.

Elizabeth had never suspected that such physical awareness could exist. The sensation of his kiss enveloped her, and she was achingly conscious that she wanted his arms around her, even as she acknowledged that she should not be permitting even this much in the first place. It took all her determination to keep herself from embracing him and pulling him closer. After what seemed far too short a time, he drew back, his breathing was ragged and his eyes dark with passion, and she suspected that she looked no different.

Darcy's struggle to master himself was at least as profound, but perhaps less obvious due to the extent of his practice at subduing his feelings for her. Elated that she had not only allowed him to kiss her, but had responded as well, it was all he could do not to renew his proposal immediately. He knew that it was too soon, and the expression crossing Elizabeth's face confirmed it. Instead of the look of warmth or affection he had hoped for, he saw her biting her lip and looking away.

Why? he demanded silently. She had wanted him to kiss her, he would have wagered a great deal that she had enjoyed his kisses, and she knew that his intentions were honourable, so why was she distressed? Could her dislike of him still be so intense, but if so, why would she have allowed him to take liberties with her? Were all the hopeful signs he had observed merely a figment of his desire to see them? She had never met any of his advances with clear evidence of pleasure, it was true, but recently, there had been some shy smiles when he caressed her hand, and once she had even actively slipped her hand into his in the curricle. He shook his head over the pathetic desperation of his thoughts, and stepped completely away from her, no longer able to tolerate seeing her distress.

Elizabeth wrapped her arms around herself as if she felt a chill, and with determination began to walk once more at a brisk pace, as if trying to escape from herself. Darcy fell in beside her silently, reassured that she was continuing on their journey, rather than insisting on returning. Now if only she would not look as if she were on her way to the gallows.

He tried to counsel himself to patience. He need not win her affection immediately, and she had made it clear that she preferred him to go slowly. Soon she would be leaving on her travels, and as long as the terms they parted on were warm, she would welcome seeing him again after her return. It would be a long wait. Georgiana had already indicated to him that she would prefer not to stay at Netherfield once Elizabeth was gone; the company of Bingley's sisters had as little appeal for her as for him. London would provide some distraction while they waited, perhaps, or they could even go to Pemberley. It was a long journey for that length of time, but then again, they need not return immediately, and it would raise suspicions if he timed his absence to coincide exactly with hers. It would be near the time of Bingley's wedding by then, and surely Elizabeth would be feeling pleased and happy about that event, and perhaps more welcoming to his suit.

He stopped in mid-stride as an excruciating thought lanced through him. Could the signs he had taken as warming of her regard instead be gratitude? Jane's happiness mattered so much to her; could she be rewarding his role in returning Bingley to Hertfordshire with the only currency she had? Did she see herself as purchasing her sister's happiness at the cost of her own? The thought was unbearable; he would rather never lay eyes on her again than take her at that price. Somehow he forced himself to keep walking.

He would have to leave. There was no possible way to live with the pain of seeing her if it was true; it was already a constant struggle not to take her in his arms. He would have to admit that the dream was ended. Yes, Pemberley, he would go to Pemberley and never again set foot in Hertfordshire, but even as he thought it he knew he would not be able to stay away for long.

When Elizabeth finally felt mistress of herself again enough to glance at him, she saw the disturbance of his mind visible in every feature, and his face set in the grim lines she had only seen once before, when she accused him at Hunsford of destroying Wickham's future. What had *he* to be distressed about? He had got what he wanted, after all; she was the one with the right to feel upset about what had happened. His assumption of her compliance reminded her of his proposal at Hunsford, and how he made his offer with the perfect conviction that she would accept him without question. Was it in fact any different now, apart from his going through the motions of courtship? He seemed to assume, at least until proven otherwise, that she would accept his caresses, his kisses, his familiarity—and no doubt his hand in marriage, in good time. And she had allowed it, one step at a time, allowed him liberties she had never expected to give anyone but her husband, and was beginning against her will to allow him inroads into her heart as well. He had changed his outward manner and made his admiration of her overt, and she had fallen into his hand like ripe fruit.

And now he had the presumption to consider himself the injured party! Well, this was as good a time as any to make clear that she would not continue to tolerate his forwardness. For once, though, she recalled her history of losing her temper with him before knowing all the facts, and forced herself to review the situation one more time before she spoke. In all fairness, she had to admit that she was to some extent responsible by her compliance, and that he likely would have respected her wishes had she told him to stop. Also, he did not, as a rule, have fits of the sulks without reason, though as often as not the reason existed only in his imagination. She was predisposed to being annoyed with him; at least it took her away from her own thoughts, but she had no wish to be unjust to him as she had in the past.

She stopped and turned to him, her arms crossed across her chest. "Please enlighten me, Mr. Darcy," she said, her impatience evident in her voice. "I have not the gift for leaping to the worst possible conclusion that you possess, so you perforce will have to explain to me whatever terrible possibility you have discovered this time."

He looked at her in shock. He was quite unaccustomed to being spoken to in such a manner, and he found his temper flaring. In an automatic effort to quell it, he said coolly, "Miss Bennet, I am afraid that the heat of the moment is leading you to flights of imagination."

He was quite mistaken if he thought that this would intimidate her from continuing her stand. "I am waiting, Mr. Darcy. I have no intention of walking all the way to Gadebridge Hill with whatever black beast you are carrying with you."

His complexion became pale with anger. "And what of your own black beast, Miss Bennet? If I am not mistaken, you are not best pleased yourself."

Ever able to see the humour of the moment, Elizabeth found the corners of her mouth twitching. "Mine is naught but a small grey creature of the night, sir. My question stands."

Darcy came to the disturbing realization that he did not understand the rules of this sort of skirmish where honesty was demanded, and anger was met with wit. He watched her through narrowed eyes for a minute, absent-mindedly noting how bewitching she looked with her eyes flashing in anger. "The thought had crossed my mind that you might be tolerating my attentions out of some mistaken sense of gratitude."

Her eyes widened. "That is, indeed, an impressively far-fetched conclusion. I believe, in fact, that I am insulted."

"Oddly enough, I am happy to hear that, although I had no intent to offend you."

Her gaze continued to clash with his for a moment, but Elizabeth found it difficult not to soften when she saw the obvious relief that he felt, and, as they managed to smile at each other, decided that just now she did not want to think any more about what had happened, but merely to enjoy his company and the beautiful day. Recalling his gesture after their conflict on the day of Jane's engagement, she held out her hand to him.

Although his face showed only a warming of his gaze, Darcy rejoiced at the step she had taken. Taking her hand, he drew her to his side, then raised it to his lips.

Elizabeth coloured slightly. "I daresay that your sister will be disappointed if you are unable to tell her of the view from Gadebridge Hill."

Not to mention that if we stand here any longer, I will end up kissing you again, and then we will be right back where we started, he thought, as they set off hand in hand. "She will be more disappointed when she realizes that this is likely our last opportunity to walk out before the arrival of Miss Bingley and the Hursts. I fear that it may not be the same afterwards."

"Perhaps if we select particularly muddy and long walks, we can fend them off, and it will not be so bad," Elizabeth suggested light-heartedly. "But that is easy for me to say; I do not have to stay in the same house with them. I must remember to rescue Georgiana when I can."

"She will appreciate it; she is often quite overwhelmed by Miss Bingley. In fact, I may need to be rescued as well," he teased.

"You, sir, are perfectly capable of handling Miss Bingley with no assistance from me," she replied, surprised by how content she felt walking so closely to him.

"Just as well, since you intend to desert us to her mercies soon enough. When are you planning to leave for your travels?"

"My aunt and uncle will arrive Monday and we plan to depart the next day."

"It seems you are quite fond of your aunt and uncle."

"Yes, I enjoy their company a great deal."

"I would like to meet them, if I may."

She glanced up at him, wondering if he realized that her uncle was in trade—she could not recall mentioning it—and if he would be so anxious to meet them if he knew. "If you wish," she said neutrally.

"I do not believe that you ever told me of your new destination. Do you know where you will go, apart from the wilds of the north?"

Elizabeth coloured, knowing that it was impossible to avoid the question once it was asked directly. "My aunt and uncle are setting the itinerary, and I do not know the details. My aunt has mentioned the Peaks, Matlock and Dovedale, and I believe she also plans for us to see Blenheim and Chatsworth. We will also be spending some time in a town in which my aunt spent her younger days. I believe you may be familiar with it; it is called Lambton."

That Darcy was startled by her response was clear, and she did not doubt that he realized that she had deliberately kept this information from him. "Yes, I know it well," he said slowly, "it is not five miles from Pemberley." His mind jumped ahead to further possibilities—*She will be at Pemberley!* He had dreamed so often about Elizabeth at Pemberley that he could picture her there without any effort—it was almost as if she were already in residence there, but the Elizabeth of Pemberley was the one who looked at him with passion in her eyes, who whispered words of love to him, who cried out his name as he made love to her in the great four-poster bed. The idea of bringing the real Elizabeth to Pemberley was enough to make his heart race.

She stole a glance at him, trying to gauge his response, but his expression was distant. She felt a sudden urge to apologize, though what she had to regret in travelling so near his home was not clear, but she was troubled by his apparent withdrawal. *Well,* she thought, *I do not need his permission to enter Derbyshire; I may visit it with impunity if I choose.*

She was determined to wait until he broke the silence, but as it went on and on, and she grew more and more uncomfortable to be walking hand in hand with a man who seemed to have forgotten her existence. Finally, she said, "Mr. Darcy, you appear to be miles away." She did not desire any further conflict, so to remove any possible sting from her words, she tightened her hand around his for a moment.

He came back to himself from his reveries of having her by his side at Pemberley, of awakening in the morning with his hand tangled in her hair, of kissing her sleeping lips until she returned to consciousness with a passion that matched his own. He turned to the real Elizabeth with a rueful smile. "You are absolutely correct, Miss Bennet; my mind was far away in Derbyshire. My apologies for neglecting you."

"And was your mind's visit to Derbyshire fruitful?" she asked, her eyes sparkling as she gazed at him, just as he had so often pictured.

Bending his arm, he brought her hand to his lips in a casual manner, and brushed a kiss across her knuckles. "That remains to be seen, my love," he said.

"Mr. *Darcy!*" she said with indignation, ignoring an odd sensation deep inside her. "That is quite enough, I believe!"

He looked at her in startled dismay. "What is the matter?"

"What is the matter? Mr. Darcy, if I have in some way led you to believe that I am willing to accept this level of familiarity, I do apologize, as it was not my intention to mislead you," she said vigorously, determined not to continue in the passive course she had set to date.

He released her hand immediately, his expression baffled and worried. "Miss Bennet, I deeply regret offending you in any way; it is my sole wish to please you, and I will certainly refrain from any behaviour to which you object. I . . . " He tried desperately to think of further ways to apologize before he lost all the ground he had gained, and then, recognizing that honesty was his only hope, said more calmly, "I cannot say that I completely understand, but if you do not wish me to kiss your hand, you may depend on it that I shall not."

She was quite surprised that he did not realize that his words were objectionable; in many ways it seemed more atypical of him to violate a social rule than to take liberties. "Mr. Darcy, my objection was to the overly familiar manner in which you referred to me," she said tiredly.

Darcy, taken aback, immediately began to review the conversation in his mind, and then paled abruptly as he realized what he had said. "Miss Bennet, I apologize, indeed, I ought to grovel at your feet; you are quite correct to upbraid me. It was a complete slip of the tongue; my mind was elsewhere, and I did not realize at all what I was saying. I do know better than that, and I certainly would not have intentionally have embarrassed either of us in that manner, and . . . "

"That is quite an adequate amount of groveling," Elizabeth interrupted with a smile, relieved by his obviously genuine embarrassment and regret. "I accept your apology, and shall not think on the matter again."

Darcy kept his eyes fixed directly ahead of him. This was not going well at all; every effort he made seemed to lead to disaster. It would be a miracle if she was still willing to speak to him at the end of the day. Perhaps he should revert to his safer, old patterns and hold his tongue as much as possible to avoid making a fool of himself again—but no, she would think him uncivil in that case. He certainly needed to control his fantasies of her.

Elizabeth, seeing his struggle, decided to take mercy on him. "Mr. Darcy," she said with laughter in her voice, "I fear that you are once again honing your skills at leaping to conclusions, and I must insist that you cease at once, and instead acknowledge that I am far too reasonable and pleasant a person to possibly dream up the sort of horrors you are capable of imagining."

His lips twitched. "Are you laughing at me, Miss Bennet?"

"I would be sorely distressed if I could find no source of humour in you, sir," she replied lightly. "And we are approaching our destination, and I hope we can remain friends long enough to climb the hill, so that we may save our breath for our exertions."

Darcy tried to match her light-hearted tones with fair success, and they were able to proceed in accord with one another as they tackled the ascent of the hill. Darcy took full advantage of the roughness of the path to have the pleasure of helping Elizabeth past obstacles, and by the time they reached the summit, his good humour was restored.

Darcy invited her to sit on a flat stone which afforded a view of the countryside. She pointed out various towns and holdings as they sat side by side, Darcy taking pleasure in holding Elizabeth's hand between his own and caressing it lightly from time to time. Elizabeth, feeling a combination of a warm contentment and an agitated excitement induced by his closeness and the remarkable sensations he seemed able to produce through his lightest touch of her hand, said, "Tell me something about yourself, something that I do not know."

"What shall I tell you about?"

"Whatever you like. Perhaps you could tell me about growing up at Pemberley."

He laughed. "Not Pemberley, please, or I will start having ideas you will object to again."

Puzzled, she said, "Because of Pemberley?"

"I have an excellent imagination, Miss Bennet, and I recommend we change the subject immediately."

Still mystified, she said, "As you wish. What shall it be, then? Tell me about going to university. Is that a safer topic?"

"Let me see, what can I tell you? I studied at Cambridge, and there were good times and bad. I missed home and my family intensely at first. It was my first time away since I had attended the first year at Harrow, about which the less said, the better. After that I had tutors at home, since my mother, once she became ill, was reluctant to have me so far away, and I supported her in that for my own selfish reasons. Once I became accustomed to being at Cambridge, though, my studies were fascinating for the most part, and I could think of nothing better than being expected to read all day long. Some other aspects of university life were a challenge given how reserved I can be. I could not enjoy most aspects of undergraduate social life, the fashionable set and the parties. I kept to myself until I found some activities which suited me better. I made several close friends then, men whose company was more congenial to me, and we have remained friends over the years since then."

"Which were the activities that suited you?"

He smiled in recollection. "I became a devotee of fencing, a practice I still continue when I am able, and which is well suited to me because I am not expected to talk while I am fencing. I also improved my expertise at billiards as well, for much the same reason, a fact which Bingley still has cause to regret."

"You make yourself sound quite misanthropic!"

"Hardly that; I enjoyed the company of those I knew well and trusted, but I had not yet learned to overcome my native shyness. I was much like Georgiana is now, which is why I do not like to force her to socialize, and instead encourage her to find friends in a way that is more tolerable to her. I cannot imagine that she will ever feel any more comfort or enjoyment than do I at balls and assemblies."

Elizabeth struggled to digest this information; of the many descriptions she could apply to Mr. Darcy, 'shy' had never once crossed her mind, yet he seemed earnest and straightforward. She decided that she would need to consider this revelation further when she had more leisure to reflect on it. "Georgiana is fortunate to have such an understanding guardian, then."

"Perhaps she is, but I am aware that I might be doing her a disservice in not forcing her to learn to cope with her shyness. I wonder sometimes if my protection makes her shyness worse."

She smiled up at him, and impulsively laid her head against his shoulder. "You worry a great deal, it seems."

Darcy forgot to breathe in the rush of pleasure that her affectionate gesture gave him, and wished that he could hold onto this moment forever. He longed to reciprocate, to pull her closer and to bury his face in her hair, but for once he remembered the need to subdue his own desires, that the most effective encouragement he could give her was not to frighten her away. The desire to touch her was more than he could completely suppress, however, and he found himself turning her hand in his so that he could stroke the soft skin of the inside of her fingers and her palm. As he bent his head slightly to observe it better, one of her curls brushed gently against his face with a sensation which left him achingly conscious of his need for her.

His response to her action had overwhelmed his attention to their conversation, and it was only with effort that he was able to recollect what she had been saying. "I admit that worrying is one of my failings. Does it come as a surprise to you, then?" He congratulated himself on having constructed an articulate sentence under these circumstances.

A smile crossed her lips. "I confess that I was beginning to catch an intimation of it, sir." Ironically, she was at that point doing an excellent job of worrying herself, wondering what capricious impulse had prompted her to lay her head against him, at a time when she knew full well that she should be avoiding even the appearance of encouraging him. How could she blame him for presuming too much when she persisted in behaving as if she wished for and encouraged his advances? He had caught her off-guard by expressing his insecurities about his behaviour, so different from his usual aggravating high-handedness, but there was no excuse for her improper behaviour.

It was past time for her to admit that her physical reaction to Darcy had gone beyond her control, a thought which both frightened and appalled her, since it went against her longstanding belief in her own ability to restrain herself. Yet it could not be denied; so small a cause as his caresses of her palm created such an ache inside her that she knew that, were he to try to kiss her again, she would put up no resistance, and would against her will welcome his touch. The realization that she was at risk of permitting sufficient liberties to feel obliged to marry was sufficiently alarming to override the temptation to continue to enjoy his attentions.

Without any outward sign of her distress, Elizabeth suggested it was time for them to return to Netherfield, and Darcy, though quite reluctant to end the enchanting interlude, managed to agree in an appropriately gentlemanly manner so as to allow them to begin the walk back in a harmonious manner that they managed to maintain until reaching their destination.

At Netherfield, Elizabeth expressed a desire to enquire after Georgiana's health before her departure for Longbourn, a request to which Darcy readily acceded, as he was happy for any excuse to prolong their contact. The patient turned out to have improved substantially in their absence, and was in fact out of bed and enjoying the sunlight through the sitting room window. Darcy warmly expressed his pleasure in her recovery, a sentiment which Elizabeth echoed with a bit more reservation, her suspicions being raised that Georgiana's illness might have been a ruse to put her brother and her friend alone together for an extended period of time.

"Georgiana, Miss Bennet revealed a most interesting piece of news to me today. It turns out that her forthcoming travels will be taking her to Derbyshire, and that she will be spending some time in Lambton," said Darcy.

"Really?" cried Georgiana, her eyes alight with enthusiasm. "You must come to Pemberley, then! I would much prefer to go to Pemberley than London; we have not been there since December. Could we not do that, William?"

"If that is your wish, we certainly may; I had not made a decision between Pemberley and London as yet, and we had originally planned to journey thither later this summer," Darcy said indulgently.

Elizabeth eyed him with amusement, thinking how neatly he had put that decision on his sister, knowing full well what she would suggest. She had known the subject of Derbyshire would not be dropped so easily as it had been on their walk, but she had not been expecting an ambush on the subject quite so quickly. "I must urge you not to base your plans on mine; I will be at the disposal of my aunt and uncle during our tour, and they have a busy itinerary planned already."

"Oh, but Pemberley would be an excellent location from which to visit so many of the sights of Derbyshire! Please, you must allow us to invite your aunt and uncle; I would so love to have you at Pemberley," said Georgiana.

This was rather stronger than Elizabeth had expected; she had thought they would be invited to call at Pemberley, not to stay there. She suspected that Georgiana did not understand about her connections—Darcy himself had learned to be polite to her family, but having some of them to stay at Pemberley was likely to be a different question. "Your invitation is very gracious, and I would certainly be delighted if the opportunity arose to see you while I was in Lambton, but I must insist that I have no say over the planning of our journey."

Georgiana, however, was not to be easily dismissed, and pleaded with Elizabeth to consider the possibility until Darcy, who had managed to stay out of the discussion, rescued her by offering to drive her home.

They set off in their usual manner, and as they drove off Elizabeth, following their ritual, slipped her hand into his. Darcy looked down at her with a smile that warmed his features becomingly. "Do you have any idea how much pleasure you give me by doing that?" he asked quietly.

Elizabeth, who had much rather not hear about it at all, especially when her insides seemed to give a very peculiar lurch at his words, tried to avoid serious discussion by responding playfully, "Hopefully enough to compensate for a small fraction of the trouble I cause you!"

He looked at her seriously. "I would not wish to be anyplace else."

Her cheeks warm, Elizabeth dropped her eyes. "Mr. Darcy, I would prefer not to enter into this discussion at this point," she said in a voice barely above a whisper.

"As you wish, then," he said, as neutrally as he could. He wondered if she had any idea what this was like for him, waiting for days for nothing more than the chance of a few hours with her, and then only a little time alone. How was he to stay sane when he was forced to hope for her to allow him to hold her hand, when what he wanted was to take her in his arms and kiss her in such a way that would brand her forever his—what it was like to love her so desperately, to dream each night of taking her in his bed, and to need her affection and approval so badly, yet to receive only ambiguous signals regarding her feelings about his attentions. She had taught him the hard way about humility, and, by God, now she was doing the same thing with patience, and he hated this lesson just as much as the one before it.

Perhaps this was becoming too intense. Perhaps he needed to remember he had other responsibilities in life besides wooing Elizabeth Bennet. A little perspective might help him through this. If she held to her usual pattern, it would be two, or more likely three days until he saw her again. Perhaps a night or two in London was what he needed. Certainly he had enough business piling up there that required his attention. And then, if he could get her to Pemberley, even for only a few days, where he could see her every day, every morning over breakfast, every evening, where he could take her for walks through the gardens and the park without having to worry about what her parents would think, or who would see them . . . *If you do not stop thinking this way instantly,* he told himself sternly, *you will end up doing something rash that you are certain to regret later. Think about London. Think about anything else at all.*

Elizabeth had noted his withdrawal following their earlier conversation. She was initially glad he had heeded her request to discontinue the discussion, but was now less happy with the result, as his behaviour was no longer what she expected under these circumstances. They never spoke much on these rides, but he had always used this brief time alone to look at her with a warmth that was hidden at other times, and to take every possible advantage in caressing her hand. Now he seemed more withdrawn, but perhaps that was only because they had already had a great deal of time together that day. She was beginning to have enough of a sense of him, though, to suspect that this was not the case, and she wondered what the cause might be.

Perhaps he was more discouraged by her earlier request not to speak of his feelings than she had thought, or perhaps it had been one refusal more than he felt prepared to bear after she had also avoided the invitation to Pemberley. They had certainly done their share of quarrelling earlier in the day, and that she had needed to limit his familiarity on more than one occasion might also be construed as discouraging. Well, if he was disturbed by her decisions, his position was indefensible, since she had been more than justified in each of her refusals, and without question should have taken those refusals much further than she had. As she began to feel irritated, she reminded herself that he had not in fact made any complaint about her actions, nor was he acting in an angry manner; and if his *feelings* were ones of disappointment or discouragement, well, certainly the poor man was entitled to whatever feelings he chose, so long as he did not attempt to impose them on her. No, she had no cause for complaint in his reaction; she simply did not like to see him unhappy.

With an impulse that she did not wish to inspect too closely, she spoke his name, and, when he turned to look at her, reached up and brushed her lips very quickly and lightly against his. She had never seen him look so startled, and she looked down with a small satisfied smile.

With a feeling of incredulous delight, he reined in the horses, and, as the carriage came to a stop, said, "Well, Miss Bennet, if your parents ever told you that you should never distract the driver, I am certainly glad you chose not to heed their instructions."

She stole a quick glance at him, too embarrassed to look at him directly. "Your horses seem well trained enough to manage to stay on the road for a moment."

"My horses are admirably trained. However, now that you have my full and complete attention, I cannot help but wonder if there is any chance of persuading you to consider a repetition of your action."

"And you claim to be shy!" she teased.

"With sufficient motivation, I can overcome it, and I believe that I am more than sufficiently motivated at the moment."

She still could hardly look at him, but managed to comply with his request, despite her burning cheeks. It was so swift that she felt a response more to her daring than to the brief contact.

Darcy was managing the near-impossible by appearing calm and pleased despite feeling far from calm. Again he had been more successful when he allowed Elizabeth to set the pace and did not demand more than she felt ready to give, and he was determined to give her no reason to regret her action. He was resolved not to make the mistake of asking too much again, and made no effort to move beyond the brief, feather-light contact she had initiated, despite his strong impulse to capture her lips with his own and to drink his fill of her. He saw how embarrassed she was, and thought it best to keep his response minimal, but could not stop himself from leaning down and stealing one more kiss from her, of no more duration or depth than the ones she had freely given him. With an effort, he steeled himself, picked up the reins, and set off again, only then allowing himself to glory in the fact that Elizabeth had kissed him of her own free will. God, but she was full of surprises! Just when he thought that there was no progress, too. He tightened his hand on hers, and was delighted to feel her return the pressure.

All too soon they were approaching Longbourn. Darcy stopped just out of sight of the house to take a moment to kiss her hand, and on impulse turned her hand over to place a kiss in her palm, and then one on the delicate skin inside her wrist. He heard her sharp intake of breath with the greatest of pleasure. She was looking at him again, with confusion but neither displeasure nor fear. "Thank you for today," he said softly before bringing the carriage up to the door.

"Good day, Mr. Darcy," she said with more equanimity than she felt.

"Good day, Miss Bennet," he replied. He watched her until she went in the door, then drove off, full of elation.

That night, as Elizabeth sat at her vanity brushing her hair, she thought back on the events of the day with some agitation. She could no longer say with any honesty that she had no feelings for Darcy. If nothing else, he affected her powerfully on the physical level, more, in fact, than she had thought possible. That it troubled her when he was in distress, and that she wished to protect him, was indubitable; she felt a real interest in his welfare, but still doubted the wisdom of allowing that welfare to depend on herself.

Her chief disturbance lay in the cause, or lack thereof, for her change in sentiments towards him. She enjoyed his company more than she had in the past, and his caring behaviour towards his sister was a testimonial in his favour, but the fact remained that he was a man accustomed to being in control of all around him. He was accustomed to making arrangements as he pleased, including making decisions on the behalf of others, and he was managing to do the same with her to a disturbing extent. He did not hesitate to let her know what he wanted, or that he intended to persist until he got it. Try as she might, she was unable to recall any instance in the whole of their acquaintance when he had submitted to another's will. Nor, apart from his obvious concern for his sister, could she recollect any clear instance of goodness or benevolence to further establish his character.

Some of the appeal of his company at the moment lay in her own vanity and desire for companionship. Since Jane's engagement, she had but little time to bestow on her sister, for while Bingley was present, she had no attention for anyone else, and in his absence she talked of nothing but him. Thus was Elizabeth deprived of her closest confidante and friend, and, with

Charlotte long gone, little other source of congenial company. How could she but be pleased to have a man of Darcy's sensibilities at her disposal with no goals but to please her and to attend to her whenever she wished? A romance based on her loneliness and his availability would hardly seemed destined for success, and suggested the disturbing idea that Elizabeth was taking advantage of Darcy's feelings for her own purposes.

Why could she not have fallen in love with someone like his cousin, Colonel Fitzwilliam, who was amiable, interesting, and calm, someone without the tendency to withdraw and the capacity to brood, who was not always such a mystery? She had watched each step of the way as Bingley fell in love with Jane, and she had seen admiration, affection, thoughtfulness, and delight in her company, but never the frightening intensity which Darcy often displayed towards her. And there really was no question, she finally admitted to her reflection in the mirror, that she *was* falling in love with him. The idea terrified her.

She had always scoffed at the heroines of the romantic novels who fell in love with the wrong man, yet how else could she characterize this? What sort of basis for a marriage was physical attraction and fondness for a lover's attention? Courtship was brief and marriage long, and while he was most attentive now, what might happen when the wooing was over and she was won. Would there be a return to days of his silent observation of her?

This is unbearable, she thought. She wanted to be with him, to feel the pleasure that only his touch could bring her, and at the same time, she feared the outcome. She would never tolerate being controlled, and he already seemed to have far too much power over her feelings. She knew what she *ought* to do—to follow the advice she would herself give to those romantic heroines, which was to put a stop to it now, before it went any further, by telling him his hopes were in vain; to try to recover herself while she still had the power, so that someday in the future she might have the opportunity to love a man more suited to her. But it had already gone too far for her to give him up. She could try to slow the pace of their romance, though she would have no cooperation whatsoever from Darcy in that regard, and she could try to contain the intensity; she could see him less often, avoid spending time with him alone, limit the liberties she allowed him, as she certainly should in any case. And she should stay away from Pemberley and any suggestion of a future for her in his home, on his terms.

Georgiana was not looking forward to the day for more reasons than one. She had come to enjoy Elizabeth's lively company, but she had not been able to see her for several days owing to a succession of rain. It did not help that William had been pacing the halls of Netherfield like a caged lion for the same period of time, and had hardly been pleasant company. It was starting to annoy Georgiana that he insisted nothing unusual was happening and Elizabeth was no more than an acquaintance. Did he think her so blind? She smiled as she thought of how her brother looked whenever he saw Elizabeth. If only he would work up the courage to propose to her! When she sent them off together to Gadebridge Hill, she hoped the walk would give him his chance, but that had proved to be a disappointment.

But William's irritability and the lack of Elizabeth's company did not trouble her as much as the prospect of spending the day with Miss Bingley, who had arrived, along with the Hursts, the previous day. Miss Bingley would, as always, be most attentive to her, and she would have to tolerate her insincere compliments, which were as troublesome to her as Miss Bingley's demeaning remarks about everyone who was neither a Bingley nor a Darcy. She was not blind as to the true intention of Miss Bingley's civility to her; she had lived in fear for some time that William would fall into her snares, and had been much relieved when one day he had made his opinion of his friend's sister clear in a conversation with her. Now she had no worries whatsoever on that regard, apart from how Miss Bingley would react to William's attentions to Elizabeth.

She gathered herself together to go downstairs. She had delayed as long as she could by having breakfast brought to her room, but William would think something was wrong if she did not appear soon. Perhaps she could escape quickly to practice her music, preferably for a long time.

"My dear Georgiana!" came Miss Bingley's honeyed tones as soon as she entered the room. "I am so pleased to see you. I was beginning to fear that you might be unwell. How charming you look this morning!"

"Thank you," she said softly. "I am well." Her eyes darted around the room, but she did not find William. Had he already made an escape? "Is my brother here? There was something I wished to tell him."

"He and Charles have deserted us, I fear. They have gone to Longbourn with the intent of inviting *dear* Jane to dine with us today."

Georgiana did not miss the mild venom in Miss Bingley's voice when she spoke the name of her future sister, nor the scorn when she mentioned Longbourn. She opened her eyes wide, and said, "Oh, I am so sorry to have missed them! I love calling at Longbourn. Everyone there is so lively and pleasant." She hoped neither William nor Bingley would see fit to mention that on the one occasion she had visited Longbourn, she had been too nervous to say more than five words to anyone but Elizabeth.

Miss Bingley looked taken aback, but recovered quickly. "I am so glad to hear that you have found friends here. I have worried that you might be lonely, given how limited the country society is."

"Oh, I have not found it limited at all! It reminds me of Pemberley. But if Miss Bennet is coming to dinner, I had best go practice now. I promised William I would work faithfully every day on my Mozart." Georgiana hastened to depart, but was forced by politeness to listen to several rounds of compliments on her musical abilities and dedication to practice before she could retire to the peace of the music room.

Dinner was made more agreeable for Georgiana by the addition of Elizabeth to the party, a change which clearly had not been communicated earlier to Miss Bingley, to judge by the look on her face when the guests arrived. Georgiana stayed close by Elizabeth's side as much as she could, despite frequent efforts by Miss Bingley to draw her off into conversation. Elizabeth appeared not the least intimidated by either Miss Bingley or Mrs. Hurst, but instead met their sneering civilities with pleasant discourse, showing her more truly well-bred than the others.

Darcy was less satisfied with the progress of the evening. He had grown accustomed to spending time with Elizabeth either alone or with only Georgiana present, a situation in which her wit and teasing were allowed full rein, to his delight. She was more subdued in this company, no doubt due to the need to fend off the comments of Bingley's sisters. It was clear he would not have her to himself for so much as a minute, a situation that was not to his liking, especially after their last meeting.

His frame of mind would have been improved had he known that Elizabeth shared some of those sentiments. Overall, she told herself firmly, Miss Bingley's presence would be helpful, since she would do everything within her power to prevent Darcy from being alone with Elizabeth. But she could not help missing his warm, intent look and his touch. The only moment of relief came when Darcy and Bingley attended them to their carriage, and, while Jane and Bingley bid one another a prolonged adieu, Darcy took the opportunity to hold her hand longer than necessary when handing her into the carriage.

When the gentlemen returned inside, it was to discover Miss Bingley, who had carefully noted where Darcy's attention lingered during the evening, venting her feelings in criticisms of Elizabeth's person, behaviour, and dress. "For my own part, I must confess that I never could see any beauty in her. Her face is too thin; her complexion has no brilliancy, and her features are not at all handsome. Her nose wants character; there is nothing marked in its lines. Her teeth are tolerable, but not out of the common way, and as for her eyes, which have sometimes been called so fine . . . "

"I think she is lovely," Georgiana interrupted, her heart pounding so loudly she was sure it could be heard at Longbourn.

The attention of the entire party turned immediately in response to this novel behaviour on her part. Darcy looked at her as if she had suddenly turned into a stranger, though not in a displeased way.

Miss Bingley recovered quickly, and, though she should have recognized that she was not recommending herself to either Darcy or Georgiana, angry people are not always wise. She continued, "I remember, when we first knew her, how amazed we all were to find that she was a reputed beauty; and I particularly recollect your saying one night, Mr. Darcy, after they had been dining at Netherfield, 'She a beauty! I should as soon call her mother a wit.' But afterwards she seemed to improve on you, I believe."

Georgiana's eyes turned on her brother full of shocked reproach, hardly able to credit he could have said such a thing, but when he did not deny it, she said, astonished by her daring, "Miss Bingley, Elizabeth is a dear friend of mine, and I will thank you not to speak of her in such a way in my presence. I find her pleasant, witty, generous, and altogether too well-bred to make these kind of derogatory comments." As soon as the words stopped pouring out of her mouth, she realized she had gone too far. With a stricken look, she whispered a good night to the room and turned and fled.

Bingley recovered first. "Well, Darcy, your little sister is growing up! You are going to have your hands full with her soon."

"I am indeed," said Darcy thoughtfully.

Miss Bingley could not stop herself. "Judging from her behaviour, I cannot say that I believe Miss Elizabeth Bennet is an altogether good influence on Georgiana, Mr. Darcy."

"Quite the contrary," he said with a smile, thinking of how much he would enjoy telling an edited version of this tale to Elizabeth. "I believe she is just what Georgiana needs." He then went away, and Miss Bingley was left to all the satisfaction of having forced him to say what gave no one any pain but herself.

Chapter 4

THERE WAS NO RESPONSE when Darcy knocked at the door of Georgiana's room. Suspecting that she was hiding, he said, "Georgiana, it is William. I know you are in there; please open the door." A moment later his sister appeared and let him into her sitting room. She did not meet his eyes, and looked as if she were expecting a scolding.

"I wanted to see if you were well; you looked upset when you left," he said awkwardly.

"I am well," she responded quietly. "Are you angry with me?"

"Far from it. I was proud of you for speaking up to Miss Bingley."

She did not reply. Darcy shifted in his chair uncomfortably, wondering what in the world to say to her. *Elizabeth would know,* he thought, and indulged in a brief fantasy of riding to Longbourn and telling Elizabeth he needed her to talk to Georgiana for him. Then, while he was bringing her back, he would take her in his arms and show her all the passion that he had been hiding. He pushed those thoughts away firmly.

"Why did *you* not say anything when she was being so horrible about Elizabeth?"

Darcy sighed. "That is a perfectly reasonable question. I imagine I would have said something sooner or later, but I have developed a tolerance for Miss Bingley's remarks, and I pay little attention to them. Also, the more jealous Miss Bingley becomes of my regard for Miss Bennet, the more offensively she treats her, so I protect Miss Bennet by saying nothing."

"I never thought about that part. But did you really say that horrible thing about Elizabeth and her mother?"

He swore to himself that if he ever managed to convince Elizabeth to marry him, she would have to handle all the serious conversations with Georgiana. She had never before questioned his behaviour, and certainly not in this manner. "Yes, I did, or something much like it. I have said a great many ill-judged things in my life which I regret, and that would be high on the list."

Georgiana bit her lip, wondering if she truly dared to ask the question she most wanted the answer to. "Are you going to propose to Elizabeth?"

Darcy was back on solid ground now. "Miss Bennet and I are just friends."

"There is no need to treat me like a child. I have seen how you look at her."

"This is a private matter, Georgiana," he said in a voice that declared the subject closed.

Georgiana subsided, not yet ready to openly defy him. Perhaps she would ask Elizabeth.

Darcy could not recall any instance in which he was as annoyed with his sister as he was when she began Elizabeth's next visit by announcing that she was looking forward to visiting with Elizabeth alone, and promptly took her off to her rooms. He tried to console himself with the knowledge that he would have been unable to converse with her in private in any case, much less follow up on the delightful finish to their recent day together, but he was at the point of feeling such a degree of deprivation of her company that his irritation remained unchanged. It had been over a week since the day she had kissed him, and he had not been one minute alone with her since. It was enough to drive a man to distraction, or at least to contemplate kidnapping.

Elizabeth gave him a sympathetic glance in response to his obvious disgruntlement before she and Georgiana went out, but it provided little comfort. Darcy was obsessed with the many things he was denied at the moment: he longed for time alone with Elizabeth, he wanted the opportunity to kiss her again, he needed to know what she was feeling about him, and above all, he desired her love. He hated being so mystified by the state of her regard for him; she obviously felt *something*, but how much was attraction and how much was affection baffled him. At times, he thought he detected her concern for him, but then again, she never seemed particularly pleased to see him, and was more likely to greet Bingley or Georgiana with a warm smile than him. He had seen desire in her eyes, but not a look of tenderness or affection. It was ironic; when he proposed to her in Kent, he had not been particularly concerned about whether she cared about him—as long as she was willing to marry him, the reason was unimportant. Now it was the caring that concerned him most, and it would be a bitter ending indeed to win her for any reason but love. He shook his head and decided that if he could not be with Elizabeth, he might as well be productive, and retreated to the room he was using as his study to tackle the enormous pile of papers his steward had sent him.

Elizabeth was not in the least confused about how Darcy was feeling at the moment, since he had done an abysmal job of hiding his frustration. She was inclined to sympathize, as she had missed his company as well, but she was also amused at Georgiana's unusual assertiveness, and curious as to why she would not want Darcy present, especially as she was of the opinion that Georgiana wanted to throw the two of them together as much as possible. She suspected Georgiana wished to confide in her, but that was far from the truth.

Georgiana, tired of being left in the dark, was in fact preparing to interrogate Elizabeth, and her only uncertainty was how direct to be about her intentions. She eventually elected to be straightforward, mostly out of doubt in her own ability to be subtle, but also feeling that this might suit Elizabeth better. She felt it best, though, to start with the relatively simple questions. "Have you thought any further about coming to Pemberley?"

Elizabeth sighed. Every time she saw Georgiana, this subject arose again. Darcy, on the other hand, carefully avoided any mention of Pemberley with her. "There truly is nothing for me to think about, since, as I have said, the decision is not mine."

"It seems as if you would prefer not to visit us," she said somewhat plaintively.

"Georgiana, I would be delighted to visit you, but this particular visit is problematic. You have never met my aunt and uncle, and they move in very different circles than you. I think it would be preferable if we merely called on you."

"I would like to meet them, and I am certain they would be more congenial company than Miss Bingley and the Hursts!"

"I confess that I would think them so, but that hardly matters."

"Of course it does! I feel certain that William would enjoy their company as well." She paused, then asked, "May I ask if you are promised to someone else?"

Elizabeth looked at her in great surprise. "No, I am not promised to anyone. Why do you ask?"

"It was just a thought. When my cousin, Colonel Fitzwilliam, wrote to me last, he said I should tell you the story of my parents' courtship, and that made me wonder, because my mother had been promised to another man."

"And what, pray, is the story of their courtship?" Elizabeth wondered what role the Colonel might be playing, and whether he was speaking on Darcy's behalf or his own.

"Well, I do not know all the details, because everyone stopped talking about it after my mother died, and it is much more amusing when my uncle tells it. So you should really ask William, or Richard, or my uncle."

"But you must know the outlines of the story, at least."

"Oh, yes. Well, when my father met my mother, he announced that he was going to marry her, and he proposed to her every day for a long time, and then somehow it was settled with her betrothed to end the engagement. It was more complicated than that, but as I said, I do not know the details."

"An interesting tale," said Elizabeth, amused by what she assumed to be the moral of the story regarding the persistence of men of the Darcy family. "Do you remember your mother well?"

"Only a little; I was five when she died, and she was ill all my life, or at least never well. She never completely recovered from my birth. She and William were close, though; it was hard for him when she died, I think."

"It must have been hard for all of you."

"I hardly understood what was happening, but I know that my father was devastated. He and William had some problems after that."

"Oh?" Elizabeth found that she was very interested in hearing about Darcy's earlier years.

"As I understand it, my father had a difficult time being around William for a while, because he reminded him so much of our mother. And then there was . . . a person, a favourite of my father's, who tried to turn him against William for his own benefit. After that there was never the same trust between them, which grieved William, who wanted very much to please him. I believe that it was a little better at the end, when my father was dying, and William came home to take over the management of the estate, and he could see how serious William was about it." Georgiana risked a glance at Elizabeth, wondering what she thought of this.

"I imagine he would be very serious about it."

"Oh, yes, and after my father died, William had no time for anything but managing Pemberley for the longest time. There had been some mismanagement in the last year of my father's life, after his steward had died, and of course William had so much to learn. I remember that whenever I wanted to see him, he would either be out on the estate or buried behind a huge pile of paper in the study. But he always found time for me, anyway."

"An ideal elder brother."

"Oh, yes! There could not be a better one. Are you in love with him?"

Elizabeth could not help smiling at the abruptness and earnestness of the question. It reminded her of Darcy's behaviour, but what seemed demanding in him was more endearing in his sister. "That is a very personal question," she said gently.

Georgiana looked crestfallen. "I apologize. I . . . it is so frustrating watching William, and not knowing what is happening, or why he doesn't just propose to you . . . . I am sorry, I should not have said that either."

"It sounds as if you need to be asking him these questions, not me."

Georgiana made a face. "Yes, and then he starts acting as if I were still eleven years old, and tells me that you are just friends in his 'don't ask any more questions' voice. And I think that *he* is the reason you are avoiding coming to Pemberley, though I am at a loss as to why."

Elizabeth could not help laughing at this characterization, which seemed very apt to her. She could well imagine how frustrating it must be for Georgiana—even more frustrating than Georgiana's persistence on the question of Pemberley was becoming. "Your brother and I are both strong-willed, and this means we have a number of difficulties to work out between us before we could even begin to discuss marriage. We are also prone to rather explosive and hurtful quarreling. So you must not be too hard on him for not proposing; I am sure that he wishes it were that simple."

"I do not see why he has to make everything so complicated!" she said petulantly.

Elizabeth laughed, feeling rather sorry for Darcy if his sister was faulting him for failing to propose to her. "Georgiana, dearest, did it ever occur to you that I might be the one who is creating difficulties?"

"You?" Georgiana said in disbelief. "Why in the world would you not want to marry him? There is no better man to be found anywhere!"

"Even if he still treats you like a child?" Elizabeth said with a smile.

"Elizabeth! That is not what I meant!"

"Well, as it happens, I do not like being treated like a child either. But have patience with us, my dear, and try not to be too hard on your brother."

A knock came at the door, and in response to Georgiana's call to enter, the door opened to reveal a roguishly determined-looking Darcy. "Miss Bennet, I have come to abduct you."

"To abduct me! Where, pray tell, are you planning to take me, sir?"

"Almost anywhere will do," responded Darcy in a mock growl.

"I have always wanted to see Italy," Elizabeth said thoughtfully.

" 'Tempt not a desperate man,' Miss Bennet."

" 'Beware of desp'rate steps,' Mr. Darcy!"

Darcy gave a wicked smile. " 'Peace! I will stop thy mouth.' "

Elizabeth opened her mouth to protest the obvious conclusion, but Darcy was too quick for her, and bent to press a firm kiss on her lips. Astonished at this behaviour in front of his sister, Elizabeth fixed a stare on him that had little effect on his very satisfied look. " 'O, what men dare do!' " she retorted.

"Remember, Miss Bennet, that I am desperate." He took her by the hand and tugged her towards the door. "Please excuse us, Georgiana," he said to his stunned sister.

Elizabeth, amused by this unexpectedly playful and unrestrained side of him, followed cooperatively if not without apprehension of being observed. Fortunately, he managed to lead her as far as his study without interruption, and then released her only to close the door behind them and lock it. When he turned to face her, she allowed a raised eyebrow and a severely doubtful look to speak for her.

Darcy had the grace to look slightly guilty, and stood away from the door. "You are welcome to leave whenever you wish, Miss Bennet; but this house is full of people who seem determined to keep us apart, and I do not want to be interrupted." He had not in fact planned beyond this point when the thought had occurred to him that his initial idea of kidnapping had some merit.

"Well, Mr. Darcy," said Elizabeth, a smile lurking about her lips, "what is it that you want? No, wait, I withdraw that question; I shall ask instead whether there is a particular purpose to this abduction."

"A purpose to this abduction? Perhaps I should start instead with your first question, which addressed what I want," he said, fully aware that this was the first time he had been alone with her in a week, and of how simple it would be for him to take her into his arms, and damn the risk of being caught.

Elizabeth recognized the look in his eyes, and her own reaction was enough to give her doubts about the wisdom being behind a closed door with him. She was sufficiently sensitive to her desires after so long without his touch to respond to no more than a look, and realized the necessity of a distraction.

"I had an enlightening visit with your sister," she said with a playful smile. "Since Georgiana usually says so little, I had not realized that, when she chooses, she can be almost as persistent as certain of her relations."

"That she can," he said, his eyes hungrily devouring her. "And what was she after today?"

"Among other things, she is persisting in her invitations to Pemberley." She was beginning to find it difficult to think about anything apart from her body's treacherous demands for his touch, her desire to run her fingers through his hair and find his lips with her own. In an effort to clear her mind, she walked to the window and stood looking out. Having her back to him was an improvement; she still felt tingly all over, but at least she could concentrate. "It is becoming difficult to continue to decline without risking hurting her feelings."

"Then why not accept the invitation?" he asked.

Her heart began to pound as she heard him moving closer. "Even if I had the right to make such plans, which I do not, I have doubts about the wisdom of bringing my aunt and uncle to Pemberley, as I have no desire to have my relatives be an embarrassment to you. Given that you have been silent on the subject of the visit, I suspect that you have reservations as well."

"You would be far from correct in that supposition. I have strong feelings on the subject, and they are not reservations."

"I am aware that such a visit would excite the scorn of many of those in your social circle, and your relatives would be appalled." She could feel him close behind her, and she was beginning to find it difficult to breathe.

Unable to resist temptation, he put his hand on her shoulder. The nearness of his fingers to the uncovered skin of her neck made him almost dizzy. "If they feel that way, they are no loss to me." Images of Elizabeth at Pemberley led him to those possessive and passionate feelings he tried so hard to keep in check—images of her face across the table from him, the warmth and softness of her in his arms as he made love to her, of her lying in his bed, her dark hair spread across the pillow, her inviting smile for him alone. His hand almost involuntarily slid the short distance across the neckline of her dress to caress the skin of her shoulder. She was even softer than he had imagined.

The touch of his hand on her sensitive skin ignited a fire in Elizabeth that was impossible to ignore. She found herself leaning her head away from his hand to allow him greater access. As he accepted the invitation by stroking his fingertips along the line of her shoulder to her neck where he continued his caresses, she felt flooded with sensations of excitement and pleasure. Slipping his free hand around her waist, he drew her back against him, and slid his other hand slowly down her arm to join it. She felt enthralled by the feeling of his strong body against her back, and she arched her head back to claim even more of him. The sensation of being enclosed by his arms was beyond her imaginings. It spoke both of safety and fierce desire, love and yearning.

He spoke softly in her ear. "Regardless of whether you choose to come to Pemberley, Pemberley already belongs to you, and has for many months now." His lips grazed her neck, sending shivers through her. "Elizabeth Darcy has been gracing the halls and rooms of Pemberley since my first stay at Netherfield. While I have been passionately admiring Miss Elizabeth Bennet," he paused to trail a line of kisses along her neck, "every night in my dreams she has been walking by my side at Pemberley, and she will always haunt me there, no matter what choice you make." With every phrase he allowed himself to explore her softness further, placing kisses in the hollows of her shoulders, the sensitive skin behind her ear, and every point in between. "Yes, I want you to come to Pemberley; I want to show you every nook and cranny, to take you through every part of the grounds, until it means as much to you as it does to me."

She was deeply moved by the intensity of feeling in his words even as she found herself almost unbearably aroused by his caresses, each touch causing such sensations of delight and desire to course through her that she felt she could hardly bear it. Needing more, she turned her head and sought his lips with a hunger that could not be disguised. The shock when their lips met stirred her further, and the kisses that followed, unlike the gentle and testing ones he had given her before, were filled with urgency and need. She wanted to relieve his distress, she yearned for his touch, and she longed to surrender herself completely to him.

"Will you come to Pemberley?" he asked against her lips, before exploring them again with a thoroughness that devastated her defenses, leaving her so aroused that she felt she could deny him nothing.

"Yes," she whispered, as his fingers traced lines of fire along her sides, and she knew that, had he asked her at that moment to marry him, she would have agreed to that as well.

Darcy, intoxicated by the feel of her, the taste of her, and most of all by her response that was passionate beyond all his hopes, was risking losing himself in her as he had done so often in his dreams, but knew not how to stop himself from slaking his incredible thirst for her. He tried to focus on the thought of her anger at his behaviour that was sure to follow, but as she pressed herself against him and sought more of his kisses, he lost all ability to care for anything beyond the moment.

Elizabeth felt equally lost, but as his lips traveled from hers down to the nape of her neck, where they wrought complete havoc on any remaining self-control that she might have, she opened her eyes for a moment and found herself looking through the window straight into the shocked face of Caroline Bingley.

Her gasp of horror and sudden stiffening caught Darcy's attention even before she managed to speak his name, and he looked up, fearing to find that she was angry with his attentions. Only someone who knew him well would have recognized the slight shift in his face from desire to quiet fury when he met the eyes of the source of her distress, or recognized that he was acting on that anger when he followed the course of action which he knew would upset the interloper more than anything else, which was to resume scattering kisses across Elizabeth's face and neck.

As Miss Bingley turned her back with an obvious sneer and walked off, Elizabeth pulled away from him and covered her hands over her face. When word of this reached Longbourn, her father would have no mercy; she would find herself married to Darcy before the end of the week. She should return home right away, and try to control the damage with a confession before the news arrived. But such an outcome would be the last thing that Miss Bingley would desire. No, she would keep her peace about what she had seen in order to keep her own options with Darcy open, rather than risk forcing him into a marriage with Elizabeth.

"I suppose that I should say thank heaven that was Caroline Bingley," she said shakily, struggling to regain her equanimity. "She is the one person who has more to lose than we do if word of our behaviour were to spread, so in this circumstance, there is no one on whom I would rather depend."

Darcy gave a somewhat ragged laugh. "Do you know, I do not believe that I have ever heard anyone say that of her before." *I have nothing to lose*, he thought, *and I could only wish that you felt the same.* He ached to embrace her again.

The shock and fear had initially driven all feelings of desire from Elizabeth, but as she looked at Darcy, she wished to be back in his arms. "We should find Georgiana," she said determinedly.

"Perhaps so," he acknowledged, reminding himself that it was a success that she did not appear angry with him. He unlocked the door and held it open for her, and as she walked past, he caught her by one hand and kissed her lightly, looking for some kind of reassurance. He was relieved to see that she smiled in return, albeit worriedly.

⁂

Darcy spent a long night alternately lost in recollections of how it felt to have Elizabeth in his arms, and worrying how she might react to what had occurred between them. There had been no further opportunity for them to speak privately, and although she had seemed calm enough, during dinner she seemed to become more withdrawn. When he walked her out to the carriage, she did not meet his eyes, although she was perfectly pleasant to him. Yet again he cursed his difficulty in ascertaining her feelings.

He resolved to call on her the next morning. She did not want any attention drawn to the time he spent with her, but he could not bear worrying about it for another day. Accordingly, he found Bingley before he managed to steal off to Longbourn, and engaged his cooperation to help him have a few minutes alone with Elizabeth.

The plan went smoothly; although Elizabeth seemed surprised to see him, she readily agreed to walk out with Jane, Bingley, and him, and Bingley was only too happy to take care that he and Jane lagged well behind the other two, and eventually struck off on a different path. Darcy lost no time in taking Elizabeth's hand and drawing her to his side as they walked, and he smiled at her with a warm look.

She acknowledged him with a restrained smile of her own, but seemed disinclined to make conversation, leading Darcy to believe she was disturbed by the events of the previous evening. He debated how to begin, and finally said, "I owe you an apology for my behaviour yesterday."

Elizabeth coloured. "I would prefer not to speak of it, sir." Indeed, she had spent much of the previous night chastising herself for her failure to stop his advances and worrying about possible complications. She still agreed with her initial assessment that Miss Bingley would likely not expose them for her own reasons, but it had occurred to her that Miss Bingley was capable of seeking revenge in other ways. She was concerned how Darcy might have reacted to her shameless behaviour. Would it not reinforce his concerns about the inappropriate conduct of members of the Bennet family?

Darcy was at a loss. How was he to beg her forgiveness if she would not hear his apology? "I have no desire to cause you any distress, so I shall say only that I would far rather hear your chastisement than have this come between us."

"I am in no position to chastise anyone," she replied in a low voice.

He looked at her sharply, then stopped and took her by both hands. "Are you concerned that *I* might be upset with *you?*" he said with incredulity.

She forced herself to look him in the eye. "My behaviour was far from irreproachable."

With a wordless exclamation he put his arms around her and held her tightly. "My dearest, when you give a man exactly what he has been longing to receive for many months, the last thing that would occur to him is to reproach you for your behaviour!"

His endearment and apparent assumption of an understanding between them was more than she could manage after a mostly sleepless night, and she found tears coming to her eyes. The harder she tried to suppress them, the more they threatened to overflow—*just like my feelings about this man*, she thought, and began to cry in earnest.

Darcy, who was quite enjoying holding Elizabeth in his arms, did not immediately realize she was in tears, and then experienced a moment of panic not dissimilar to what he had felt recently with Georgiana. He should somehow understand what was upsetting her, but had no idea what was the matter, having thought he just reassured her. Clearly it was his fault in some way, and his guilt for causing her distress was great. Unsure as to the best course of action, he tried to comfort her by whispering endearments in her ear and holding her close to him, which unbeknownst to him had the unfortunate effect of fueling the fire of her distress. If only she would share her feelings with him! "My sweetest, please tell me what is troubling you," he pleaded.

Elizabeth was attempting desperately to think of nothing beyond that he was comforting her. She could never say what was disturbing her without hurting him deeply—how could she tell him how much against her better judgment her attraction to him was? Once she stopped crying, she would need to tell him to cease referring to her in the affectionate manner which he was using. Exhausted with both her constant inner struggle against her feelings for him and the more outward struggle not to accede to the liberties he tried to take, she wanted nothing more than to give up the battle and agree to be his simply to conclude the matter, but she knew full well how quickly she would come to rue such a cowardly decision. Finally she calmed herself enough to respond. "I am simply not ready for this."

Darcy thought carefully before replying. He could not afford a misunderstanding now. "If I take your meaning correctly, this is happening too quickly for you. Is that it?"

She nodded, her face still buried in his chest.

He kissed her hair, savouring the softness and the sweet scent of roses in it. "We can go more slowly, then; we have all the time in the world before us. I will not rush you."

She could not help laughing through her tears at his words. "Mr. Darcy, I do not mean to suggest that you are not a man of your word, but I strongly advise that you refrain from promising the impossible. I am afraid that I do not believe you constitutionally capable of not rushing me."

Her characterization forced a smile from him. "There is perhaps some truth to that. Perhaps I should promise instead to do my best not to rush you, and to listen when you tell me otherwise."

"That is more credible, sir." As she calmed herself, she allowed herself to enjoy the feeling of resting her head against him and the comfort of his arms around her.

This lasted only a brief time, though, as Darcy, while far from wishing to give up his current desirable position, was cognizant that he had just agreed to slow down his demands, and forced himself to release her. He consoled himself with the thought that she had, by asking him not to rush her, implicitly acknowledged that she had accepted that they were headed towards further intimacy.

"I appreciate your understanding, Mr. Darcy," Elizabeth said softly as they began walking again. He looked at her, and their eyes caught in a long gaze.

"I do not ever wish to distress you in any way," he responded. After several minutes, he added, "There is one matter in which I will need your assistance, Miss Bennet."

"And what is that, sir?"

"I do not wish to offend you, but in order to keep my word, I stand in need of your advice as to what constitutes rushing you, and what does not."

Elizabeth blushed scarlet. It was a reasonable question, but she could think of no modest way to answer it, nor, even could she answer, could she have produced a consistent response. On some occasions, one of his intent gazes felt like more than she could bear, but at other times, her tolerance was quite different.

Darcy had to admit that she looked exceedingly appealing when she blushed. Recognizing the impossible position in which he had put her, he sought to obtain the needed information without forcing her to state directly which liberties she would accept. Thoughtfully, he took her hand in his as they continued to walk. "I believe that this is not rushing you; am I correct in that assessment?" She nodded. "Nor this?" He raised her hand to his lips and kissed it, then held it close to his chest, and she nodded again. "How about this?" he asked, placing a series of light kisses in the palm of her hand. She dropped her eyes, but still nodded infinitesimally. "Your pardon, Miss Bennet; I am afraid my question was not clear. Do you mean to say yes, that is rushing you, or yes, that is acceptable?"

"No, that is not too much," she said quietly, though not without doubts about the accuracy of her answer, given the strength of her reaction.

Tread lightly, now! he cautioned himself. Stopping, he stepped closer to her and allowed his lips to caress her hair. "Is that too much?" She shook her head, eyes still downcast. Taking a deep breath and reminding himself of the necessity of self-control, Darcy tipped up her chin with one finger and permitted his lips to touch hers for the briefest moment.

She closed her eyes at the moment he kissed her, feeling the impossible sensations of pleasure lance through her, and then reopened them to look up at him. "Sometimes," she said.

He raised an eyebrow. "Sometimes?"

"Sometimes," she repeated with a smile, then added with an air of impudence, "I never said it would be simple."

"No, it never is simple, is it? Very well, sometimes then." He kissed her gently again, but more lingeringly this time, and allowed himself to taste the pleasure of her lips before pulling back. "Too much?"

She looked at him with some hesitancy. "Yes," she said softly.

He inclined his head. "My apologies, Miss Bennet; I shall attempt to keep that in mind."

Her hand crept up and touched his cheek. His response to her touch was instantaneous and electrifying. "But please do it again," she whispered.

He searched her face trying to clarify this contradictory request. There was a look of tenderness in her eyes that had never been there in the past, and he could not resist it. "Elizabeth," he whispered, and reclaimed her lips, struggling to keep his hunger in check, and as she responded, he drew her gently and slowly into his arms, prepared to release her if she hesitated in any way.

Elizabeth, trembling from the intimacy of hearing him use her name, found her hands stealing up around his neck, and she surrendered into the fullness of his embrace as his lips tantalized hers. But Darcy felt his control begin to slip. Determined not to go beyond the limit she had set, he stepped back. Her hands slid to his chest, where they paused a moment before dropping, only to be caught by his. She smiled at him tentatively, and he tugged on her hand and began to walk once more, knowing all too well what would likely happen if they remained as they were.

A change of subject seemed in order. "I am looking forward to meeting your aunt and uncle. Are they aware of my presence here?"

"Yes, I wrote my aunt and mentioned your interest in making her acquaintance, so she should not be surprised." She smiled briefly. "I also told her that we were on rather more cordial terms than the last time that you were in Hertfordshire." She decided against mentioning the friendly conversations that had taken place between her aunt and Mr. Wickham when the Gardiners had visited Longbourn last, but she had also written a warning regarding Wickham's unreliability, lest Mrs. Gardiner be inclined to hold his information against Darcy.

"She knew something of your past opinions, then?"

"Yes, when they visited last December, Mr. Bingley was still a topic of conversation, and you were often mentioned in conjunction with him," she prevaricated, since it had been Wickham who most frequently raised Darcy's name. "But both my aunt and uncle are eminently sensible people, and unlikely to make judgments based on hearsay."

They continued to talk pleasantly on what became a long ramble, since neither felt an inclination to lose the company of the other. As they finally approached Longbourn, Darcy, unable to help himself, asked, "May I have the privilege of seeing you tomorrow?"

She looked at him with a teasing smile. "I might be able to steal away for an early morning walk, if that would be of interest."

"You know perfectly well it would be of great interest, madam," he said, making no attempt to hide his pleasure that she had not only agreed, but had for the first time suggested a way to allow them to be alone.

Looking up, she saw the familiar intent look enter his eyes, and felt an immediate rush of desire for his touch, but their location on an open road prohibited any action. She gave an amused smile as she saw him reaching the same conclusion with a degree of annoyance.

"Tomorrow is a very long time away, Miss Bennet," he said persuasively.

She gave him an arch look. "I suppose you will say next that no one has taken the time to show you the wildflowers that bloom behind the churchyard wall."

"Are they very private wildflowers?"

"They never share their secrets with anyone," she assured him gravely.

"Have I mentioned, Miss Bennet, that wildflowers are a particular passion of mine, and that I hope that they are *very* nearby?"

"I would not want to keep you from one of your particular passions, sir," she said provocatively. Gesturing down a path by the church, she added, "They are this way, if you would care to see them."

Afterwards, Darcy would have been hard pressed to recall anything at all of the wildflowers.

Chapter 5

DARCY STOOD IN THE *doorway of the room which had been Elizabeth's during her stay at Netherfield, gazing on her sleeping form, covered only by a revealing nightdress. As he watched, she opened her eyes and saw him, an inviting smile growing on her lovely face. He crossed the room and sat on the bed beside her, tracing his finger down her cheek, and then down her neck and further along her body. When his hand reached her breast, he saw her eyes darken with desire, and she reached up her arms to welcome him. Wordlessly he sank into her arms, capturing her lips with a kiss which demonstrated the depth of his need for her. The feeling of her body beneath his sent his desire spiralling out of control, his hands exploring every intimate inch of her as his mouth devoured hers. He pressed his hips against hers as she writhed beneath him and whispered, "Please, William, make me yours." Without hesitation he pulled away everything which stood between them and poised himself to plunge into her. She raised her hips to meet him, and with a powerful thrust he took her, glorying in the feeling of his possession of her. As she moaned beneath*

*him with each intensely pleasurable stroke, he thought to himself,
'Mine, she is mine, she is mine . . .'*

Darcy regretfully surfaced from his dream on the morning of
his rendezvous with Elizabeth in a haze of arousal and desire.
The responsiveness she had shown to his attentions in the last
two days had caused an intensification of his dreams, both sleeping and waking, and his imagination had proved remarkably
adept at recalling how it felt to kiss her. *Restraint!* he cautioned
himself. *You are incredibly fortunate that she seems inclined to give
you what you desire—let her do it in her own time!* He dressed with
unusual care, whistling all the while, to the bemusement of his
manservant, Wilkins. At last satisfied with his appearance, he
set off.

Elizabeth, having awoken to the same thoughts and medita-
tions which had at length closed her eyes the previous night, was
contemplating the possibility that love was incompatible with a
good night's sleep, a proposition Darcy would have seconded,
had he been aware of her opinion. Dreams of a Pemberley that
was an even grander and more pretentious version of Rosings
were interspersed with confusing sensations of kisses where she
felt a longing for something more, but knew not what, leaving
her embarrassed by her desires when she finally awoke. She was
anxious to see Darcy, yet worried by her wishes and the notice-
able softening in her feelings towards him. She reminded herself
that it would be difficult to feel unkindly towards a man after the
intimacy of crying in his arms, but she could not credit this as
responsible for the change.

She felt a certain pleasurable kind of anxiety as she walked
out, and wondered how the time with him would go. Her heart
skipped a beat when she spotted a dark form ahead in the grove

where they had agreed to meet, and she hurried forward until she could see the look of passionate welcome in his eyes.

Accustomed to subdued greetings from Elizabeth, Darcy experienced a burst of pleasure when she smiled on seeing him. God knew he never had a clue as to what she was thinking of him, but surely this had to be a good sign. Advancing towards her, he took both of her hands in his and pressed a kiss on each one. "Good morning, Miss Bennet."

"Good morning, Mr. Darcy," she said, with a hint of her impudent smile.

If you keep looking at me like that, my love, I am going to disgrace myself by trying to make my dreams a reality, he thought. "Have you a destination in mind for us today?"

She hesitated a moment before nodding. The place she had in mind was secluded, but he seemed to be in a relatively restrained mood, so she thought it would be safe enough. She led him along little-used footpaths to a small wood, which they skirted briefly before following what appeared to be a deer trail between the trees. As Darcy ducked under low-hanging branches, he wondered if she knew what she was about in taking him to such an isolated spot. Part of him believed that she had not given the matter a thought, but another part insisted on hoping that her desires matched his.

She stopped when they came to a small clearing where a stream ran beneath two large willows. He saw her glance at him as if to gauge his reaction, and wondered if this was a test of some sort. Stepping towards the stream, he parted the boughs of one of the willows to discover a sheltered space, and just beyond it, a grassy bank leading down to the water's edge. Looking back at her, he said, "This is a lovely hideaway. Did you discover it?" He was gratified to see a pleased smile on her face. Evidently his reaction was satisfactory.

"It is my retreat."

"Thank you for sharing it with me," he said softly, noting a look of warmth in her eyes which made his resolutions that much more difficult to keep. In search of a distraction, he noticed the ribbons of her bonnet blowing gently in the wind. Almost without thought he reached over to her and untied them, noticing that she lifted her chin to permit his action. He raised his hands to her temples and gently removed the bonnet. He noted that her hair was looped up in a simpler style than usual. Presumably she had left Longbourn before the servants were available to style it. His fingers itched to discover what it would take to make it come down. Tracing a line down her cheek with his fingers, he was delightfully startled when she turned her face into his hand and kissed it lightly.

Elizabeth found the silence mesmerizing as he looked at her intently, apparently waiting to see what she would do next. *How could the simple act of removing my bonnet move me so?* she asked herself. Already she had exposed more of herself than made her comfortable by bringing him to a place so special to her, and her present reaction to him only increased her uncomfortable sense of vulnerability. Not trusting herself to speak, she took his hand and led him to the bank of the stream. When she came to the edge where there was a bit of a scramble to reach the water, he held her back while he went ahead, and then lifted her down.

She laughed as she looked up at him, his hands still resting on her waist. "Mr. Darcy, I have managed to do this on my own for many years!"

"Are you trying to deprive me of excuses to hold you?"

With a playful look, she freed herself, and, with the ease of long practice, held up her skirts and began to cross the shallow stream, stepping gingerly from rock to rock. Part way across, she reached down and ran her fingers through the cool water, then, with an impudent smile, flicked her fingers to send a spray of droplets in his direction. At the look of feigned outrage on his face, she continued her journey at a more rapid pace as he set off in pursuit of her, his long legs giving him an advantage out-weighing her greater knowledge of the route. Just before she reached the opposite bank, he caught her hand, causing her to reel precariously to keep her balance.

"I believe that I have you at a disadvantage, Miss Bennet," he said mischievously.

"How so, sir?"

"Why, in that my boots are higher than the water is deep, whereas yours are not," he said, with a challenge in his eye. Elizabeth, unable to resist, pulled sharply at his hand, causing him to stumble into the water. He continued, "See, I am com-pletely protected. You, on the other hand, have placed yourself at grave risk."

Laughing, she tried to pull her hand away, but with a firm tug, he caused her to overbalance, then swept her up in his arms before she could fall. "And now, Miss Bennet, I have you at my mercy, since if you try to escape from me, you will certainly end up wet."

Elizabeth, already feeling completely at his mercy owing to the overwhelming flood of sensation from the way he was hold-ing her, said archly, "And what do you intend to do with me, then, Mr. Darcy?"

He bent his head to trace kisses along her neck, so conveniently available to him in this position, and caressed her leg with the fingers of his hand supporting her knees, causing exquisite feelings of pleasure to run through her. "I am certain that I can think of something," he murmured as he moved his mouth to capture hers.

"And what will happen if I refuse to cooperate in your nefarious schemes?" she retorted between breathtaking kisses.

"Then it is into the water with you," he said, making as if to toss her. She shrieked and wrapped her arms tightly around his neck.

"You would not dare!"

"Actually, Miss Bennet," he said, finding her close embrace to be vastly appealing, "I think that you would look remarkably fetching when wet. Of course, then I would feel obliged to find some way to keep you warm so you would not take a chill, and naturally it would take some time for your clothes to dry, but I am certain that I could think of some way to pass the time . . . "

"Mr. Darcy!" Elizabeth exclaimed, her cheeks scarlet at his forwardness, but he resumed kissing her with an ardour that left her with no desire to resist him.

"In fact," he murmured roguishly, "I find the idea so appealing that perhaps I should seek out deeper water to allow greater efficiency." He started to walk upstream.

"No!" she cried. "I surrender, I surrender!"

"Sweeter words have never been spoken," he said, kissing her enticingly. "Now, since you are my prisoner, I believe that it is my right to demand a ransom before setting you free."

Elizabeth's breath caught at the idea of what he might

request, even in jest. "What did you have in mind, sir?" she said, pleased that her voice did not tremble.

Thoughtfully, he allowed his eyes to sweep slowly over her from head to foot, his possessive, examining look sending tingling sensations of excitement throughout her body, then met her eyes with a slight smile on his face. "I demand that you let your hair down," he told her, a rakish smile playing across his face.

He had chosen well, he thought. It was an intimate request, and it would fulfill one of his favourite fantasies, yet was not overly compromising. He watched the reaction flow across her face until she returned his gaze with a challenging one of her own. "Done, sir," she said. "Now pray return me safely to dry land."

"At your service," he said, fulfilling her request. She immediately scrambled up the bank, and sat in the soft grass at the top. He did not remove his eyes from her for a moment, and when she paused, he added, "I am waiting, Miss Bennet."

With a look that expressed a certain air of challenge, she reached her hands back and slowly removed several pins from her hair, aware of his fixed gaze through every inch of her body. She shook her head several times, causing a cascade of unruly dark curls to tumble down her back.

He caught his breath at the captivating sight. *Surely she would never have done that if she did not intend to accept me,* he thought with a rush of pleasure. The combination of the intimacy of her appearance and her provocative gaze stimulated a sense of unreality which allowed him more control over his reaction than he might have expected, but he would have to guard his behaviour to retain her trust.

"Well, sir?" she said with a teasing defiance.

"*Very* satisfactory, Miss Bennet," he replied. He could be happy indefinitely just looking at her.

"Do you plan to stay down there all day?" she asked.

"Your wish is my command," he said, climbing the bank to sit by her side. He admired the sight of her hair blowing in the breeze, and longed to run his hands through its enticing richness, but if he began to touch her now, the likelihood was that he would not be able to find the strength of will to stop. He leaned back on his elbows, thus keeping his hands out of harm's way.

"You are suddenly very quiet, Mr. Darcy," she said with a raised eyebrow.

He gave her a look which assured her of the content of his thoughts. "Sometimes, Miss Bennet, it is best to admire without comment."

His reaction had surprised her; she had hardly expected after his earlier forwardness that he would suddenly revert to being the perfect gentleman, and it left her feeling somehow frustrated that he could stimulate such feelings of abandon in her, and then withdraw. She gave him an unconsciously seductive glance, and noted with satisfaction his heightened colour. "I hope I have not done anything to offend you."

"Hardly, Miss Bennet; you are merely testing my self-control, and I believe it wisest to keep my hands to myself at the moment, lest I succumb to overwhelming temptation." He glanced at her, noting that her amused look verged on repressed laughter. "Are you so heartless as to laugh at my predicament, Miss Bennet?"

"Yes, indeed; why should I not? After all, if I am both 'heartless' and an 'overwhelming temptation,' you have no one to blame but yourself for starting it," she teased. Her laughter served to break the tension, and he reached to take her hand. "Oh, no, sir, you must keep your hands to yourself!" she said sportively.

Willing to play her game, he placed his hands on the ground, and leaned over to kiss her, but at the last moment she pulled away. "I refuse to be a temptation, Mr. Darcy!" She looked at him expectantly, wondering how he would respond to her teasing refusals.

"Let me see, then," he said thoughtfully, his eyes mischievous. "No hands, no kisses; what does that leave me?" Before she could protest, he shifted his position to allow him to rest his head in her lap. He smiled up at her engagingly, causing a delightful ripple of laughter from her. She found this playful, relaxed, and flirtatious Darcy quite appealing, if difficult to fit together with the proper and reserved public man. She ran her fingers through his thick hair, then smoothed it away from his face. He closed his eyes in order to better enjoy her ministrations. He looked younger and somehow more vulnerable, and she felt a rush of affection for him.

She held back a sigh, thinking how very confusing her feelings about him were. Which was the real Darcy—was it the man with the perpetually serious mien, or the one who delighted in verbal jousting? Proud and reserved, or shy? Always careful, never violating the proprieties, or lighthearted and forward? Sometimes it seemed that the only thing she could be certain of was what he wanted from her, and sometimes even that seemed to shift. She wondered if he would be content with her eventual acceptance, or whether he would continue to demand more and more of her private self. At times like this, it seemed that all he needed was someone to care about him for himself, not for what he could offer in terms of support or protection. Apart from his cousin, she could think of no one who treated him with affection and as an equal. He had been taking care of other people for so long. Who did he turn to when *he* needed support? He seemed so independent, needing nothing and no one—*except you*, a voice inside her said.

A smile curved her lips as she considered the hubris it would require to take on the responsibility of taking care of Fitzwilliam Darcy. Continuing to stroke his hair, she let her eyes trace the lines of his face, wondering at her sanity in allowing herself to love this complex and often difficult man—as if she had *allowed* herself to love him; the truth was closer to what she had said of him at Hunsford, that she loved him against her will, against her reason, and even against her character. It was certainly poetic justice.

He opened his eyes at that moment, catching the unguarded look of affection on her face. *Well, if he was unsure before this how I feel about him, I have just betrayed myself*, she thought uneasily. Retreating behind a mask of humour, she said, "I was beginning to wonder if you were asleep, sir, you appeared so comfortable."

Answering her in kind, he retorted, "And if I had, it would merely be because thoughts of you keep me awake at night."

She raised her eyebrows. "It seems I have many sins to answer for in your mind!"

"And many more I hope you will commit, as well," he said softly, wishing that he could see that caring look in her eyes again. Sitting up, he took her face between his hands and kissed her slowly and deeply, and slid his hands gradually back into the depths of her hair, allowing himself to be enveloped in complete sensation. He continued to kiss her until he deemed her ardour the equal of his, then pulled back to look at her. The warmth of desire in her eyes amidst the becoming dishevelment of her appearance left him both aroused and gratified by his ability to give her pleasure.

"You look very pleased with yourself," Elizabeth teased.

"Oh, I am," he murmured enticingly. "Almost as pleased as I am with you." Wrapping his hand in a lock of her hair, he pulled her towards him in such a way that she ended up in his embrace when their lips met again.

The exquisite sensations of delight that coursed through her in response to his touch seemed more than she could bear, and she knew in the deepest fibers of her being just how much she wanted him. His lips began to roam freely, and she gasped in shock and unforeseen pleasure as his hand rose to cup her breast. She could feel the touch of his hand through her entire body, and as she found herself seeking more of it by arching her body against his fingers, she realized how near she was to the point of allowing him anything. Somehow she forced herself to say, "My family will be wondering what has become of me."

Gently caressing her breast as he let his lips drift downward to the neckline of her gown, he whispered, "Tell them that I was making love to you in a secluded glen."

In the instant before reality intervened, all she could think of was how much she wished she could allow him to do just that, and it was only her fear of how vulnerable her feelings were to him already that permitted her to remember the reasons why she must not. Even as she was responding to and reciprocating his demands, she said, "Please, sir, I cannot make you stop, but I beg you to do so anyway."

"It will be weeks before I see you alone again," he pleaded, hardly knowing what he was saying. She moaned as his thumb drifted across her breast with an intimacy she had never imagined, her need for him growing by the minute.

"Even so," she whispered, her lips meeting his again and again, until he pulled back and, with an obvious effort to control himself, ran his hands over his face.

It was several minutes until he had the self-possession to speak calmly. "My love, you are a delightful menace to my peace of mind." He wondered how on earth he could allow her to leave with her aunt and uncle. Standing, he held out a hand to her. "I think that it is past time for us to leave here." His resolve would fail if they remained there, and his body was demanding with every fiber to discover what further intimacies she would allow him.

"Yes," she said, smiling lest he think her angered with him. She was grateful for his hand, uncertain of her own strength at that moment. As in the past, she felt oddly weak when he called her 'my love,' and this time she was in no position to take exception to his familiarity. "But you will need to give me a moment, sir, or we shall certainly cause talk." She gathered her hair and twisted it into a more presentable form. He fetched her bonnet as she restored the hairpins to their proper position. She reached her hand out for it, but instead he settled it on her himself, his fingers lingering on her neck as he tied it in place.

On the return journey they attempted to distract themselves with a lively debate on the relative merits of Coleridge and the newly published *Childe Harold's Pilgrimage* of the scandalous Lord Byron, leading Darcy to contemplate the interesting reading material which Mr. Bennet thought fit for a young woman, until they reached the point where they would go their separate ways. Darcy was unsure how far he could trust himself, and limited himself to touching her cheek. "Miss Bennet . . . "

"Yes?"

He was about to speak when he recalled his promise not to rush her, and he shook his head with an expression of regret. "No, not yet," he said, as much to himself as to her. "I will see you tomorrow, then, at Longbourn."

She tried to speak to his uncertainty with her eyes. *Surely he must know after today that he has won,* she thought. "I shall look forward to it, sir."

"For the sake of my sanity, I hope that you persuade your aunt and uncle to come to Pemberley."

"Only time will tell on that," she said.

"Just remember, Miss Bennet, that I know where the Lambton Inn is, and you already know I am not above kidnapping when it suits my purposes."

She laughed. "I shall keep that in mind. Until tomorrow, then."

He kissed her hand lingeringly. "Until then." He watched as she walked towards Longbourn, not moving from his position until she was long out of sight.

Bingley appeared in the door of the billiard room, where Darcy had retreated after dinner for some much-needed peace and an opportunity to reflect on the events of the day. "Bingley!" his friend exclaimed. "This is the earliest I've seen you back from Longbourn in days. Would you care for a game?"

"How could you?" his friend said in a low voice.

"How could I what?" Darcy began to rack the balls.

"I seem to have played the fool here. When you did not want to talk about your interest in Lizzy, I assumed it was because you were not yet sure of your feelings. It never occurred to me, not once, that your motives could be less than honourable," Bingley said, his voice full of anger and hurt. "She is going to be my sister soon, for God's sake, Darcy!"

Darcy looked up at him sharply. "Bingley, what are you talking about? Of course my intentions towards Eliz . . . Miss Bennet are honourable—why would you think anything else?"

"Because I have heard what everyone is saying!"

"And what, pray tell, is that?" Darcy asked with a hint of sarcasm in his voice.

"Every servant here is talking about the compromising situations you have been seen in! By tomorrow, the word will be all over Meryton, if it is not already, and Lizzy's reputation will be in tatters, thanks to you!"

Darcy rolled his eyes. "Calm yourself, Bingley! I am not denying that we have had . . . tender moments, but good God, man, the only reason I am here in the first place is to try to convince her to marry me!"

"If that is the case, then why have you not proposed to her?" Bingley demanded.

Gripping the edge of the table tightly, Darcy said in a quiet but dangerous voice, "I have, and she refused me, and I am attempting to convince her to change her mind. If you have any doubts about the value of my word, I suggest that you apply to your future sister, who will confirm this in every particular."

Bingley seemed to deflate in response to his words. "Really? I mean . . . everyone is saying that you have no intention of . . . "

"Bingley, I assure you that I am the only expert on what my intentions are, and if it will reassure you I will promise to make them absolutely and publicly clear tomorrow, although God only knows if Elizabeth will ever forgive me for it. Will that satisfy you?" Darcy spat out the words.

"Darcy, I . . . I'm sorry . . . I should not have doubted you, but when I heard what they were saying . . . "

"Please do not tell me what they said." He stalked out of the room before he said anything worse.

On reaching his rooms, he threw himself down in a chair and pulled off his cravat. *Damn it!* he thought. *Just when things were going so well. How could I have been such an idiot as to not have been more discreet?*

Wilkins emerged from the dressing room. "Good evening, sir. May I be of any assistance?"

Darcy tipped his head back and closed his eyes. "Yes, Wilkins. You can tell me what they are saying down in the kitchens about me."

"If you wish, sir. There are some wild rumours that you have taken a mistress here, and that you have been found with her in compromising situations on several occasions, and that you will be marrying Miss de Bourgh. I have, of course, stated categorically that this is untrue in its entirety, and apparently one young woman who also works at Longbourn on occasion has also said that she does not believe a word of it."

Darcy winced. "I assume the young lady in question is Miss Elizabeth Bennet?"

"That would be correct, sir. I have taken the liberty of making some inquiries regarding these rumours, if that is of interest to you, sir."

Darcy opened his eyes and scrutinized the ever-reliable and discreet Wilkins. "Pray continue," he said.

"The original report seems to have been that you were seen emerging from the churchyard with Miss Bennet, who was flushed and too close to you. However, there are various embroidered versions of this that are more . . . compromising."

Darcy ran his fingers through his hair. So the wildflowers had not been so very private after all. "Wilkins, I applaud your initiative, as ever," he said tiredly.

Wilkins allowed himself a brief pleased smile. "Thank you, sir. Will there be anything else, sir?"

"Not at the moment, Wilkins," Darcy said. "No, on second thought, Wilkins, please look in that second drawer there. Yes, that one, on the right. Do you see a small box there?"

"Yes, sir." He picked up the box and brought it to Darcy.

Darcy waved him back. "No, I do not need it, Wilkins, but I would like you to look in it." The puzzled Wilkins opened the box. "Now, if you would, please read the engraving inside the ring."

Wilkins broke into an uncharacteristic broad smile as he obeyed. "May I offer you my congratulations, sir?"

"Not until the lady accepts it," Darcy said. "However, I wanted to be sure you knew of its existence in case you ever needed to start a rumour of your own."

"Yes, sir. I understand perfectly. In fact, sir, I was just thinking that you might be getting hungry later, and that this would be a good opportunity for me to stop by the kitchens to bring you a bite to eat."

"A capital idea, Wilkins."

Wilkins bowed and left. Darcy dropped his head into his

hands. Elizabeth would be furious. He could only hope that the stories had not yet reached Longbourn. Not that this could make any difference in what he needed to do to protect her reputation, but if he could just have a few minutes alone with her to explain why he had to do this, perhaps her anger might be mitigated. But it seemed hardly likely that he would; he would not see her until after the arrival of her aunt and uncle the following day, and then she would be leaving on her journey. Well, there was nothing to be done for it, except to hope for a chance to explain himself. With a deep sigh, he walked over to his writing desk and drew out a sheet of paper.

Mrs. Gardiner's suspicions had been raised against Elizabeth after receiving her letter, and those suspicions were now compounded by the warning that her niece had given her almost immediately after their arrival at Longbourn regarding the shyness of Miss Darcy and the need to be patient with her. She therefore watched most attentively when the Darcys arrived, and did not miss the small blush on her niece's cheeks, nor the look in the gentleman's eyes when they landed on Elizabeth.

Elizabeth made the introductions, and Darcy quickly engaged the Gardiners in a discussion of Derbyshire, Lambton, and their proposed travels. Mrs. Gardiner looked over at her niece, wondering why Lizzy had ever described this polite and unassuming young man as so proud and disagreeable. After some extended conversation, Darcy announced that his sister had a request to make.

All eyes turned to Miss Darcy, who said hesitantly, "Mr. and

Mrs. Gardiner, my b—brother and I would be honoured if you and Miss Bennet would consent to be our guests at Pemberley for the d—duration of your stay in the area."

The Gardiners glanced at each other in surprise. Mrs. Gardiner said warmly, "That is a very generous offer, Miss Darcy, but we could not presume to impose on you on such short acquaintance."

"Nonsense," said Darcy. "It would not be the least imposition. Miss Bennet is an acquaintance of long standing, and my sister and I would enjoy the opportunity to show you some of our favourite sights, and we are of course but a few miles from Lambton. Mr. Gardiner, if you enjoy fishing, there are several excellent locations on the grounds where you might like to try your hand."

Mrs. Gardiner glanced at Elizabeth to attempt to ascertain her view of this invitation. Although clearly not surprised, her niece was making no attempt to participate in the discussion, and was sitting with her eyes averted. Presuming, however, that her studied avoidance spoke rather a momentary embarrassment, than any dislike of the proposal, and seeing in her husband, who was fond of society, an interest in accepting it, she said, "Well, this is an unexpected opportunity, Mr. Darcy. Perhaps you would allow us a moment to discuss the possibility?"

"Of course," Darcy said warmly.

Georgiana surprised both her brother and Elizabeth by adding a few words of her own. "Please, I would like it very much if you would consider it."

The conversation had by this point drawn the attention of a surprised Mrs. Bennet, who felt the need to comment with excessive warmth on the great civility of the invitation, and all the fine things she had heard of Pemberley, to the embarrassment of her daughters. Jane tried in vain to steer the conversation to safer subjects.

The Gardiners returned after a few minutes. Mr. Gardiner said, "Miss Darcy, Mr. Darcy, we have considered the matter, and we would be honoured to be your guests during the week we had planned to spend in Lambton."

Georgiana's eyes lit up. "That will be wonderful!" she said.

"Excellent," agreed her brother. After discussing the arrangements at some length, he asked, "Will your travels be taking you to Matlock as well?"

"Yes, indeed," Mr. Gardiner replied. "We are looking forward to seeing it, and walking in the Peaks."

"Perhaps I might impose on you and join you briefly while you are there, as my own aunt and uncle have expressed an interest in meeting Miss Bennet, and it would seem to be an excellent opportunity for that to happen, if you would be willing to join me in paying a call on them."

Elizabeth turned to stare at him in shock. Did he not realize that he might just as well have announced his intentions to the room at large? "I am afraid they might prove to be too exalted company for the likes of us," she said quietly, her voice barbed.

Darcy turned to her with an unreadable look in his eyes. "My aunt and uncle are quite amiable, Miss Bennet; I feel certain you would like them."

Mrs. Gardiner, sensing the sudden tension between the two, as well as the complete silence of the rest of the room, decided to intervene. "Your aunt and uncle live in Matlock, then, Mr. Darcy?"

He looked back at her, grateful for the distraction, but before he could respond, Elizabeth said in a flat voice, "Mr. Darcy's uncle is the Earl of Derby."

"Well," Bingley jumped into the sudden silence these words left behind, "this does sound like a marvelous trip! I have only been through the Peaks briefly, but you will find Pemberley to be truly delightful. The grounds are some of the loveliest I have ever seen, and I have spent many a happy hour there." He rubbed his hands together, and smiled boyishly at the company.

"Yes, I remember your sister telling me about a trip you took there," Jane said, with a worried glance at her sister. "When was that?"

"That would have been last spring, would it not, Bingley?" said Darcy.

Elizabeth sat seething as the conversation continued between the Gardiners, Darcy, Bingley, and Jane. How *dare* he go against her express wishes in this way? How could the man she had allowed to hold her, to kiss her, to caress her, then turn on her in such a way? The look on her mother's face showed the damage had indeed been done, and she could foresee precisely what would happen the minute Darcy left. If this was his idea of not rushing her, she had a great deal to say to him on the subject. *Why did I allow myself to trust him? I knew perfectly well how much he likes to have things his own way, and how readily he will disregard the wishes of others; why did I think that he would treat me any differently? Why was I so foolish as to allow myself to care for him?* She felt ill as she considered the position in which she now found herself.

Darcy attempted to address her several times, but she responded with as few words as civility would allow, leaving him in an agony of distress. She was clearly as furious as he had feared, and he could not see any way to find time alone with her to explain, nor had he found an opportunity to give her his letter.

When Darcy announced that it was time for them to take their leave, Mrs. Bennet, with a level of civility which would have embarrassed Elizabeth had she not been so preoccupied by her hurt and her anger with Darcy, invited the guests to stay to dinner, but Darcy declined graciously, saying that he and his sister had preparations to make, as it turned out that they would be leaving Netherfield earlier than expected owing to some business matters. He then made a point of circulating through the room to bid his adieus to her family, and he paused for some time to speak with her father. Elizabeth was not able to make out the conversation, but when Mr. Bennet glanced at her with a raised eyebrow several times during the exchange, and then the men shook hands at the close of it, she had some strong suspicions of the content of it. When Darcy and Georgiana made to leave, she made no efforts beyond those of basic civility in bidding them adieu.

"Lizzy!" Mrs. Bennet said. "Won't you see your guests to their carriage?" Elizabeth winced, the demanding tone of her mother's words making it clear that she was already planning the wedding.

She made a point of walking out with Georgiana, who was pleased and excited both by Elizabeth's forthcoming visit to Pemberley and her brother's intimations, and spoke her farewells to her in as warm a tone as she could manage. She did not turn to Darcy until his sister was already in the carriage. "Mr. Darcy," she said coolly, her eyes flashing dangerously.

"Miss Bennet, I understand that you are unhappy with the

steps I have taken, and I regret the necessity, but once you understand the reasons, I am sure you will agree I had no other choice. Knowing we would be unlikely to have time to speak privately, I wrote this to show my reasoning." He held out the letter to her.

Elizabeth pointedly folded her hands behind her back. "Mr. Darcy, I would be surprised if we are not being watched at this moment, and if you believe that I will take a letter from your hands under these circumstances, you are mistaken."

Worry began to show in his eyes. "Please, I beg of you, this is a matter of no little importance," he said quietly, to avoid Georgiana's ears. "There is gossip of a damaging nature regarding us, and it must be quelled. Please, read the letter."

"My apologies, sir, but I will not. I am sure that you find it as unpleasant as I to have your wishes disregarded. Good journey, sir." Elizabeth curtsied and turned away, leaving Darcy with the letter in his hand. Behind her, she heard his muttered imprecation, and at the door, turned to give him a long, serious look before entering the house.

She wished nothing more than to escape to her room, or to disappear on a long walk, but since avoidance was impossible, she straightened her shoulders and returned to her family. Her mother, as she had expected, was in raptures, and immediately threw her arms around her. "Oh, my dearest Lizzy!" she cried. "Why have you never said anything? Good gracious! Lord bless me! Only think! Mr. Darcy! Who would have thought it! Oh, my sweetest Lizzy! How rich and how great you will be! What pin-money, what jewels, what carriages you will have. I am so pleased—so happy. Ten thousand a year! Oh, Lord! What will become of me? I shall go distracted!"

Elizabeth allowed Mrs. Bennet's effusion to wind down somewhat before venturing to interrupt. "I am sorry to disappoint you, madam, but I must inform you that there is in fact no agreement between Mr. Darcy and me. I believe that you have taken his words for far more than was meant!"

Mr. Bennet laughed. "Come, Lizzy, you are not going to be *Missish*, I hope, and pretend to be affronted! Unless, perhaps, you are not the daughter that he meant when he said that he wished to speak with me about my daughter on his return—I do have three other daughters who are unspoken for, but he could not have meant Kitty or Lydia, since he does not wear a red coat. Mary, have you been stealing off to conduct a romance with Mr. Darcy?" He spoke the last with mock severity.

"Father!" Mary spluttered. "That kind of joke is most unsuitable!"

Elizabeth was horrified to hear that Darcy had been so direct with her father—she would not have thought it of him, but she could hardly disbelieve her father. Recognizing the pointlessness of arguing at this juncture, but still seething in helpless fury, she said, "I will only repeat that I am *not* engaged to Mr. Darcy, regardless of what *he* may think, and that I will not discuss reports of this any further!"

Her mother, however, was not to be subdued, since Darcy's intention was more than enough to satisfy her, and Mr. Bennet could not resist a little more teasing. Jane and Mrs. Gardiner watched Elizabeth in concern, clearly perceiving that she was most unhappy with this turn of events, until the point where Elizabeth realized that her composure was in jeopardy, and retired to her room. Her mother made to follow her, but was nimbly distracted by Mrs. Gardiner's efforts, while Jane quietly slipped out and went to comfort her sister.

She found her lying on her bed in tears, and put a consolatory hand on her shoulder. "Lizzy, I am so sorry that our parents are reacting in this way. I know it must be very embarrassing; although they do mean well, I wish that they could express their approval of the match more suitably."

"The match?" asked Elizabeth angrily. "At the moment, I have no wish to see him again after what he did today."

Jane was feeling somewhat perplexed. "What did he do today?"

"We had agreed that we would conceal his intentions from the family. He had promised just a few days ago not to rush me. But apparently it no longer suits him, so here he is, placing me in a situation that will make it extremely difficult to refuse him, and betraying his word to me! I knew it, Jane, I knew better than to allow myself to be led to this position, I knew perfectly well he would attempt to rule me the way he does everyone else, and I let myself disregard it, and believed that he had changed. What a fool I was! As soon as he felt confident of my regard, my opinion no longer mattered."

"Lizzy, dearest Lizzy," Jane said soothingly. "Surely there must be a misunderstanding; I am certain Mr. Darcy would not disregard your wishes. Allow him a chance to explain himself. Perhaps there is a logical explanation."

"His *explanation* is that it is to avoid gossip," Elizabeth said scornfully. "Jane, how could I have been so foolish as to let myself care for him?"

Jane continued to try to comfort her sister, but Elizabeth was disconsolate. Eventually, she felt it necessary to return to Mr. Bingley, but promised Elizabeth she would return shortly. In fact, she returned far sooner than expected, long before Elizabeth had reached any conclusions on how to manage the damage.

"Lizzy, Charles says he must speak to you, that he has a con-fession to make," Jane said hesitantly. "Will you see him? He is waiting by the back stairs."

Elizabeth wanted to refuse, feeling that Bingley would only support his friend, but the pleading look on Jane's face, and her desire to avoid any conflict between Jane and Bingley, caused her to change her mind. After drying her tears, she accompanied Jane to where Bingley was pacing nervously.

"This is all my fault!" he exclaimed. "Lizzy, Jane has told me how distressed you are, and I simply must tell you I was the one who insisted that Darcy declare himself today. He did not want to do so, and he said you would be angry, but I did not believe him. Please, though, believe me when I say that the blame is mine, not his. There has been some very disturbing talk among the servants, and I was concerned about its impact on you. I only meant to protect you."

Feeling rather like she was facing an apologetic puppy, Elizabeth said, "Pray do not disturb yourself, Mr. Bingley. I fear that you take too much responsibility; Mr. Darcy does exactly as he pleases, and if he acted on your request, it is simply because it suited him, not because of anything you said."

"Lizzy," Jane said worriedly, "Mrs. Phillips is here, and she says everyone in Meryton is saying that . . . oh, I cannot even say it. Mr. Darcy *was* trying to protect you, and it seems to have worked. Our mother seems not disturbed at all by the gossip, and says only that you are to be married, and it is all to be disre-garded. I cannot imagine how she would have responded had he not spoken this morning."

"Of course, I had forgotten that Mr. Darcy is never wrong," said Elizabeth bitterly. "It is a shame that he has to suffer the responsibility of making these important decisions for everyone else. Please excuse me, Mr. Bingley; I fear that I am not civil company at the moment."

Jane and Bingley looked after her retreating back with consternation.

Darcy could not decide if he was angrier at himself for not handling the situation better or at Elizabeth for refusing to hear him out. He had expected it to be difficult, but not disastrous; unfortunately, it would appear that he had been incorrect in that regard. The look on Elizabeth's face when he left haunted him—the coolness, the anger, the rejection of it. What a way to start their separation! By the time she reached Pemberley, who knew if she would be thinking, or if she would even follow through on the agreed-upon visit. God, how could it have gone so badly so quickly?

He went directly to his rooms upon their return to Netherfield, not trusting himself in the event of meeting Miss Bingley. Throwing himself down in a chair, he drummed his fingers on the arm as he tried to decide on a course of action. He had to find some way to speak to Elizabeth before her departure, but would she even agree to speak with him? Perhaps he could see her early the next morning before she and the Gardiners departed.

An image of her from the previous day rose before him, of the smile on her face when she first saw him, then changed into the cool look she gave him from the door at Longbourn. He dropped his head into his hands.

He knew one thing only. He must make peace with her before she left.

"Lizzy, my child, sit down," said Mr. Bennet when Elizabeth appeared in the library in response to his summons. "I have just been subjected to a most dramatic rendition of the current news from Meryton, which I fear is mostly concerning you. It appears that there is general agreement that you and Mr. Darcy are on intimate terms, with what are said to be several examples of times that he has been seen kissing and embracing you. Would you care to tell me the truth of this matter?"

Elizabeth felt that there was little point in denying it; although no doubt much of the gossip was fiction, there was certainly truth enough to it, and the behaviour of Darcy and Bingley only supported it. "No, sir, I have nothing to say on the matter."

With a deep sigh, Mr. Bennet removed his glasses. "I am now completely mystified. If I am not mistaken, last autumn your pointed dislike of Mr. Darcy and his complete indifference to you were well known to everyone. Half a year later he returns, apparently with some kind of interest in you, and this seems to surprise you not at all, and in fact you seem to choose to spend considerable time with him. Then, today, he announces his intentions, and you become angry and deny that you have an understanding. Then we are given to understand that the entire neighbourhood is talking about the compromising positions you and he have been caught in, and you make no attempt to refute it. Now, this would seem to be an excellent plot for a comic opera, but I would be most appreciative if you could make some sense out of it for me."

"You seem to have the facts well in hand, sir. I assume that you have something more to say to me than to recite history."

"Lizzy, I am not seeking to anger you. I would like, for the sake of my own comfort, to ascertain the state of your affections towards Mr. Darcy, but I have no doubt that you see as clearly as do I that under the circumstances I have little choice as to my course of action."

"And what would that be, sir?"

Mr. Bennet massaged his temples. It distressed him more than he could say to see his favourite child in this state, and not to be allowed to offer her comfort or understanding. "You will have to marry him, Lizzy. I can only hope that this is more palatable to you than it seems at the moment."

She looked him in the eye, having already reached this conclusion on her own. "Is there anything else, sir?" she asked levelly.

Standing, he sighed, and walked over to her and placed a kiss on her forehead. "No, there is not, except to say that I am always available if you would like to speak further of this, and that I do want the best for you, Lizzy."

She softened slightly, sorry to see his pain for the position in which she had put herself. "I know," she said quietly.

Chapter 6

Elizabeth declined to join the family for dinner, pleading a headache and the need to complete her preparations for her departure on the morrow. Although her natural high spirits were beginning to reassert themselves somewhat, she felt unequal to the challenge of being the focus of everyone's attention, especially her mother and her aunt Phillips. She was also embarrassed to be the subject of a scandal, and would prefer not to know any further details of the rumours. Her hope was that she could learn to make the best of an unfortunate situation, and she reminded herself firmly that although her marriage to Darcy was destined to be conflictual, at least there was a basis of affection underneath. She now regretted refusing to hear him out that afternoon. It was not a promising beginning to what was bound to be a long series of compromises, and, if she were to be completely honest, she found it upsetting that they had parted on such a hostile note.

Mrs. Bennet did not appear to miss her daughter, since her presence was not necessary to a discussion of the wonderful match she had made, and how every mother in the district would be envious. If Elizabeth wished to hide in her room rather than to display her conquest, it was of no importance to her mother.

However, it was a different matter entirely after dinner when Mr. Darcy chose to call, requesting to speak with Elizabeth despite the unseemly hour. After all, he had apparently not actually proposed yet, and Mrs. Bennet was certainly not going to permit any possible opportunity for that to be bypassed, regardless of headache or heartache. She appeared at her daughter's door, demanding her presence to speak to Mr. Darcy, fussing over her hair and gown, all while insisting that she make haste and not keep the gentleman waiting. Elizabeth could not but be amused by her mother's machinations, especially when she discovered that, in complete disregard for propriety, her mother expected her to meet Darcy in the rear sitting room rather than joining the other guests.

Darcy was standing by the window, looking serious, and twisting the ring on his finger. Elizabeth, feeling it would be beneficial to set a more positive tone, said lightly, "You appear to have an ally, sir. I believe that had I not cooperated in coming down immediately, my mother would have used a horsewhip!"

Relaxing slightly at this evidence that her anger had abated, he said, "I am sorry to hear that you have been feeling unwell."

She shook her head. "I am well enough. I did not feel the inclination to be in company this evening."

"I am sorry then to disturb you." He felt unequal to exchanging these distant pleasantries with her after reliving her rejection for hours. He could not bear to face the withdrawal of her affections. If he lost her now, he did not know how he would survive it. He crossed the room and took both her hands in his. "I came to beg your understanding and forgiveness. I do not wish to part as we did."

Elizabeth hesitated. She had to explain her need to be involved in decisions, and her intent was to be pleasant and calm with him as she clarified her problems with his behaviour and her future expectations. She had not anticipated, however, how painful it would be to be in his presence with a quarrel between them, nor how much she would long for a resolution of the sense of betrayal she still felt. She wanted more than anything else to throw herself into his arms, but was resolved not to continue their past neglect of proprieties given the difficulties it had already caused. "Nor do I, and I am glad that it is important to you as well."

"There is nothing more important to me than you," he said softly.

She cast her eyes down in embarrassment. "I . . . "

"And I deeply regret that my actions led to this outcome."

"Mr. Darcy," she said uncomfortably, "I appreciate your apology, but I believe that we must discuss the matter somewhat further, as I fear that otherwise we may face ongoing difficulties. I would prefer to resolve the matter now, if you are willing."

"As you wish, of course," he said cautiously, an element of fear beginning to settle in him. "What do you wish to discuss?"

"I fear that we have differing understandings of why the events of today were upsetting for me, so I would ask for clarification of the reason for your apology."

His heart sank. "For upsetting you, and for being sufficiently lacking in self-control that there could be grounds for these rumours in the first place."

"But not, apparently, for what you said."

His pride reasserted itself. "I am sorry that it upset you, and that it put you in a difficult position. I do not see that I had any choice—at least any honourable one—but to say what I did."

She took a deep breath. "Had you seen fit to consult me, I might even have agreed, but you did not see fit to consult me. Please bear in mind in the future that I expect to be involved in decisions which concern me to this extent, whether or not you see any choice in the matter."

The rush of relief he felt at her reference to the future was great. "I . . . will endeavour to do my best, because I do value your opinion, Miss Bennet. Had there been an opportunity in this case, I certainly would have informed you of my plans."

"You would have *informed* me of your *plans*. Mr. Darcy, you seem to be in the habit of making decisions for other people, and expecting them to bend to your will. You will have to make an exception for me, however, because I will not tolerate it. This, more than anything else, is what upset me today." At the look on his face, she feared that she had gone too far.

He turned away and walked to the window, where he stood in silence and looked out. Her words had angered him, and he knew better than to answer her when he was angry. Did she not realize he was constantly expected to make decisions for others, and how hard he strove to act in their best interest? She clearly had no understanding of his responsibilities. He willed his breathing to slow. He could not afford to be irate with her right now; too much was at stake, and any hold he had on her affections too tenuous. God, if he lost her now . . . there could be no repetition of his furious lashing out at Hunsford. Of course, at

Hunsford she had been in the right, although he could not admit it for some time.

Was it possible she could be correct again? Clinically, he looked at her complaint. He could still see no fault in his behaviour, but if he looked at it from her position—yes, he could see that he would not have liked it either. Perhaps he had fallen too much into the habit of making decisions by himself, and that would indeed need to change if he married. Yes, that much he could accept, but he could not bring himself to face her accusing look. First he needed to find a way to tell her that he understood, but he was paralyzed by his fear that her warmth of the previous days would be a thing of the past, regardless of his actions now.

Elizabeth was discovering that Darcy in a rage, even a silent one, was a frightening thing, and that, having unleashed the tiger, she had no idea of how to rein it in. Yet another fear underlay that one. What if she had finally pushed him too far? At what point would he decide she was not worth the struggle? She gathered all her courage and forced herself to approach him. Bracing herself physically as well as mentally, she reached out and put her hand lightly on his arm.

He looked down at her hand as if puzzled where it had come from, and then abruptly crushed her into his arms. She let out a half-sobbing breath of relief as she laid her head against his chest, grateful beyond words not to be rejected. Her desire to believe that they could work this out, that they could go back to the previous day and begin again, was overwhelming.

Burying his face in her hair, Darcy said a silent prayer of gratitude. He could accept anything as long as he had Elizabeth, but he could no longer bear this constant uncertainty of her regard. The doubt had become more than he could stand. "Elizabeth," he pleaded, with an edge of desperation, "for God's sake, please tell me that you care, even if only a little bit."

She reached up and took his face in her hands. "Can you not tell?" she asked with a catch in her voice.

"No, I cannot. I have misread you so badly and so often that I no longer believe that I can judge."

"Mr. Darcy," she said with some amusement, "I hope that you do not believe I give my favours this freely to men I do not care about!"

There was a pause as he took this in. "Miss Bennet, I do believe that you are teasing me."

"Do you not deserve it, sir?" she asked archly.

"And this is what *you* deserve for even teasing about giving your favours to other men." He took possession of her lips demandingly. His fiercely possessive kisses kindled a need she had not known that she had, as his hands, claiming the right to explore the curves of her body, engendered in her a desire that made her wish she were his in truth. Gratified by her response, he deepened his kisses. By the time he was satisfied, Elizabeth found herself clinging to his shoulders for support. "I feel it only fair to warn you, Miss Bennet, that I am a very possessive man."

With a shaky laugh, she said, "That hardly comes as a surprise!" Her plan to insist on observing the proprieties was turning out to be less than successful.

"Good," he said, returning to plunder her mouth again. "Pray do not forget it."

Elizabeth, somehow able to recollect through the passionate haze he had induced in her that Darcy tended to be in need of a surprising amount of reassurance regarding the obvious, said, "Mr. Darcy, you have no cause for concern. I have always assumed that my husband would be the only man I would ever kiss, and I have seen no reason to revise that opinion."

His eyes kindled. "Perhaps we should make that official." He watched closely for her reaction. He had no intention of making a proposal this time until she was ready.

Elizabeth looked at him, willing her pulses to slow. *Yes, let us get past this,* she thought. *I would have rather waited until I had fewer reservations, but since I have no choice in the matter, we may as well have done with it. And there is no reason for him to know that I have doubts; certainly it was only a matter of time until I was ready to accept him, and he deserves the happiness of believing that I accept him with no qualms.* "What did you have in mind, sir?" she asked with a knowing smile.

With a feeling of exultation, he took both of her hands in his. He pressed the lightest of kisses inside of her wrist first on one hand, then the other, leaving Elizabeth feeling barely able to think, much less to be coherent. "Miss Bennet, will you do me the infinite honour of agreeing to be my wife?"

She took a deep breath. "The honour would be mine, sir."

There was a moment of stillness, then he said, "Say that again."

She smiled at him impishly. "Yes. Yes, I will marry you. Yes, I will be your wife. Yes, I will spend my life with you. Yes, I will be the mother of your children. Yes."

"Please feel free to continue, Miss Bennet. I could listen to this for a long time."

"Such vanity! No, sir, I believe that it is your turn to speak; I have upheld my end of the conversation."

His eyes, lit by heartfelt delight, locked with hers. "There are no words for how I feel at this moment, my love." He brought out of his pocket a small box, from which he removed a sapphire ring that he slipped onto her finger.

"It is beautiful," she said quietly.

"I am glad to finally have it where it belongs," he said. Their eyes met, and the sheer joy in his melted any last bits of resistance she might have had. "Kiss me, Elizabeth," he whispered.

With a raised eyebrow and a mischievous smile, she freed her hands from his and wound them around his neck. Allowing her body to touch his lightly, she pulled his head down to hers and deliberately put into practice everything she had learned from his kisses. She ran her fingers into his unruly curls, delighting in the manner in which her action clearly aroused Darcy. Enjoying this sense of power, she tested it further by trailing her fingers down his neck along the edge of his cravat, and was rewarded by a clear increase in his response.

"Dear God, life with you is not going to be dull," he said feelingly when she finally released him.

"I should hope not!" she said with a sparkle in her voice. She felt inordinately pleased with herself.

"I must speak to your father now, and then we will tell the rest of your family."

"Mr. Darcy," Elizabeth said a bit sharply. "Did we not have a recent discussion on the subject of consulting me on decisions?"

He had the grace to look slightly embarrassed. "Ahh . . . yes, we did. My apologies, my dearest. I can see I will require some retraining."

"Your apology is accepted."

"How shall we inform people of our engagement, then?" He stole a quick kiss out of sheer pleasure over being able to say those words.

"With all the present fuss, I would almost prefer to wait."

He opened his mouth to tell her that was impossible, and then thought better of it. "I would have some concerns about leaving your family to deal with these rumours in our absence without knowledge of our engagement to present in response."

"Your point is well taken. Very well, we can tell them now. Would you be willing to consider, however, delaying announcing the news at Pemberley? I would feel more comfortable coming there first as a guest, without all the expectations that would accompany me if I were to be known as the future mistress."

"I would prefer not to delay it long, but I see no harm in a few weeks," he conceded.

"Thank you." They smiled at one another in accord. "While you are speaking with my father, perhaps I will join the rest of the family, which should allow my mother to get through the worst of her effusions before you arrive."

"I had thought that we would tell your family together."

She laughed. "Do you think that once you walk out of this room and into the library that there will be anything left to tell? But that is only fair; I shall await you here."

"I will return as soon as I may," he said, but found that he had to give her one more lingering kiss before he could face the brief separation.

"Mr. Bennet, I am certain that you have little doubt as to why I am here this evening," Darcy began.

"On the contrary, young man, I have a great number of questions as to why you are here this evening," said Mr. Bennet.

"You do?" asked Darcy in surprise, then recalled himself. "Pardon me; I meant to say that I would be happy to answer any questions you may have, sir."

"Good, good, I am glad to hear it. Then perhaps you can explain to me how it has come to pass that you and my daughter have been caught in clandestine assignations when, the last any of us had heard, you found her not handsome enough to tempt you, and she had a healthy dislike of you. I have heard Lizzy's version of the story; now I would like to hear yours."

Darcy winced. Was that ill-fated remark at the Meryton Assembly to haunt him for the rest of his life? "Sir, I can understand that your opinion of me may have suffered owing to recent talk; I have no doubt that I would feel the same were I in your place. However, I assure you that my intentions towards your daughter have always been strictly honourable."

"Indeed." Mr. Bennet's voice was sharp. "Mr. Darcy, I do not claim to understand the situation. I know that Lizzy is unhappy and angry, I know that she has expressed in the past some reason to distrust you, and I know that for reasons that are unclear, she has been choosing to spend time with you and apparently to accept your attentions. Under the circumstances, I have no choice but to give you my permission to marry her, just as I told her that I had no choice but to insist that she marry you, but I do not feel under any obligation to be happy about it."

Taken aback by this unexpected burst of anger, Darcy hardly knew where to begin. He had not expected hostility, and while his initial thought was not to discuss this further until he had a better chance to understand Mr. Bennet's position, he considered how important her father's opinion was to Elizabeth, and determined to swallow his pride and persist. "Sir, I believe you are under some misapprehension. Certainly Miss Bennet and I have had misunderstandings in the past, but after I, that is, after *we* furthered our acquaintance in Kent, we were able to clear up a great deal of confusion, including the truth behind the lies she had been told. We have been on more cordial terms since then. I would encourage you to speak further to her, sir. I do not believe that she is unhappy about anything except the circumstances of our engagement, and it is my goal, sir, to make her happy in everything."

Mr. Bennet sat back in his chair. "So you feel that it was the time you spent together in Kent that made a difference, then."

"In a way, yes," Darcy said cautiously.

"*What* time that you spent together in Kent?" Mr. Bennet said, his voice like a whip.

Wondering if this was some sort of trick, Darcy said, "In April, when Miss Bennet was visiting her friend Mrs. Collins, and I was visiting my aunt, Lady Catherine de Bourgh."

Mr. Bennet looked suddenly tired. "Lizzy has never seen fit to mention seeing you there."

"You did not know, then?" Darcy said in surprise. "So you have not heard about . . . " He trailed off, realizing that Elizabeth must not have wanted her father to know about their interactions in Kent. "Or about Wickham, either?" He had rarely felt so completely inarticulate.

"Sit down, Mr. Darcy. This is clearly going to take some time. Perhaps you can tell me now about all the things I have not heard," said Mr. Bennet icily.

"Perhaps we should ask Miss Bennet to join us to give her point of view."

"Perhaps not. Now, you were about to tell me about Kent, I believe."

Feeling like a schoolboy called onto the carpet, Darcy summarized the events of April in a clipped voice, omitting only the venom of their disagreement the night he proposed, and briefly reviewed his history with Mr. Wickham. "When I returned to Netherfield last month, Miss Bennet, no longer being under a misapprehension regarding my feelings towards her, was kind enough to allow me to begin to court her anew."

"Odd, I had thought it traditional to ask the permission of the father of the young lady involved, Mr. Darcy, but perhaps I was mistaken."

Darcy had not been Master of Pemberley for five years to accept this sort of insult lightly, even from the father of his beloved. "Perhaps you misunderstand my position, Mr. Bennet. In the interest of future understanding, let me make myself clear: given a choice between protecting your daughter and pleasing you, I will always choose your daughter."

"Do you believe that she needs protection from me, then?" Mr. Bennet said silkily.

Darcy fixed a steady stare on him, a tactic that worked well on recalcitrant tenants. "That is not what I said, as you are well aware, sir. But if it satisfies you to be angry with me because your daughter has chosen for her own reasons to keep certain facts from you, please feel free to do so. It does not disturb me."

The corners of Mr. Bennet's mouth twitched. "I am glad to hear it. If you plan to marry Lizzy, it will be to your benefit to be imperturbable."

"I *am* going to marry her, Mr. Bennet, and for her sake, I hope that we can be on better terms in the future." Darcy laid his challenge out smoothly.

"Treat her well, Mr. Darcy, and we will have no problems."

"Sir, you need have no concerns in that regard." Darcy stood and bowed formally. "I believe she is waiting for me, so I shall take my leave."

Mr. Bennet waved his hand in dismissal, thinking that Lizzy might not have done so badly for herself after all.

Elizabeth had assumed that the interview with her father was a formality, given his words to her earlier, but was beginning to worry as time went on. When at last Darcy rejoined her, she said, "I had begun to wonder if you had forgotten me."

"Hardly, my sweet. But your father had a number of questions. I am sorry to say that he does not seem to look favourably upon me," he said, sitting next to her. "I made an important discovery, though, which is that if my flaw is to tell everyone else what to do, yours is to tell them nothing at all. I had not realized that you had left your father completely in the dark about everything that has happened between us."

"It . . . has been very confusing; for some time I have hardly known what to say, and I am afraid that when I spoke with him earlier today I was rather . . . distressed," she admitted.

"He did not seem to think me a welcome suitor," said Darcy, looking at her thoughtfully. He had always assumed that

Elizabeth's tendency to keep her thoughts private reflected a certain lack of confidence in him, and having made the startling discovery that she had not even told her beloved father of his interest in her was causing him to rethink this conclusion. Could it be that she was so reticent about her personal affairs even with those to whom she was closest? She was certainly skilled at turning aside serious discussion with witty repartee in such a way that one hardly noticed her failure to respond. He wondered how much she told Jane of her private affairs.

Of course, Georgiana would probably make the same accusation of slyness about him, and he recalled what it had taken for him to confess his situation to Colonel Fitzwilliam in London. But he had never, once he determined that his interest in her to be a lasting one, tried to keep his feelings secret from Elizabeth. Although she had not understood his interest in the past, it was not because he failed to try to express it in his own way. He did not want to keep her at a distance, as he had so many other people, and more than anything he wanted her to feel that she could share anything with him. Perhaps he would have to take the lead in this regard until she felt more able to trust him with her feelings.

"I will tell him that is not the case," Elizabeth said softly. "I would not want him to think you unwelcome." She held out her hand to him. "Shall we go to my family?"

Taking her hand, he pulled her gently towards him, and she slipped into his arms as if she had been made expressly for that purpose. "Perhaps first you could show me that I am not unwelcome," he said with a slight smile.

Elizabeth, experiencing that pleasurable sensation of coming home that the familiarity of a lover's embrace can bring, raised her lips to his without a second thought. As their mouths met, she surrendered to the blissful sensations that only he could arouse in her. Experiencing the heady delight of accepting the pleasure he could give her without the feelings of guilt which had haunted her in the past, she moaned softly as he deepened the kiss and she felt the full force of her passion answering his.

When he lifted his head just enough to be able to gaze into her eyes, she said, "Do you feel welcome yet, sir?"

"I feel so welcome that I may never let you go," he responded fervently, proceeding to feather kisses along the side of her face and down her neck, deeply gratified by his ability to give her pleasure. That his Elizabeth could be so amazingly and delight-fully responsive to him gave him a satisfaction he could not deny, and he reveled in his sensation of ecstatic pleasure as he felt her surrendering control to him. Deeply aroused, he kissed her with a thoroughness that left her breathless and longing for more. Beyond the ability to restrain himself, and somehow knowing that she would not find the will to object, he slid the edge of her gown just off her shoulder. Pressing passionate kisses along the newly exposed flesh, he heard her gasps of pleasure and felt her arching against him with a thrill that only aroused him further. *If only we were truly alone*, he thought, desperate for more of her.

No sooner had the thought crossed his mind when he heard footsteps outside. He released her abruptly and straightened her gown, but there was nothing he could do about the half-drugged look of passion in her eyes, and he suspected that his appearance was at least as obvious.

Mr. Bennet appeared in the doorway, a look of amuse-ment on his face. "There you are, Lizzy. I believe we have an announcement to make, if the two of you can spare a moment for the rest of us."

"Yes, we were just saying that we should join the others," Elizabeth managed to say.

Mr. Bennet, whose first approach to the room had been quiet enough to remain unnoticed under the circumstances, raised an eyebrow but said nothing. Any dismay he might have felt about the behaviour he had witnessed was outweighed by his relief in realizing that his Lizzy was clearly not as opposed to this match as he had feared. "Shall we, then?"

<hr />

The bustle of departing travellers filled Longbourn early the following morning as trunks were loaded and reloaded, the Gardiner children taking the opportunity again and again to bid their parents farewell, and Mrs. Bennet instructing Elizabeth repeatedly how she should behave while at Pemberley in order to continue to please Mr. Darcy. Elizabeth herself was bemusedly recalling how, just a few weeks before, she had been eagerly anticipating this journey as an escape from Darcy's attentions, whereas now the idea of missing him was of much greater concern. A feeling of delight filled her as she spotted the object of her thoughts himself riding towards her. She had not expected to see him; they had said their farewells the previous night.

He dismounted and came straight to her, his warm gaze upon her. As he kissed her hand, she was conscious of having a special smile for him as well. "Good morning, my love," he said quietly, for her hearing only.

"Good morning, sir," she replied with a slight blush, aware from his look that he would rather have been kissing her lips than her hand. "It is an unexpected pleasure to see you this morning."

"You overestimate my ability to stay away from you. It looks as if your departure is imminent; I am glad that I arrived in time."

"Yes, I believe we will be off shortly."

"May I beg a moment to speak with you separately first?"

"Of course." She led him away to a distance that would not allow easy eavesdropping.

"Since we have but little time, I will refrain from remarking on how you look lovelier every day and how much I missed you last night, and limit myself to mentioning how passionately I adore and admire you—and how much I hate it when you wear gloves," he said, touching the offending article.

Elizabeth coloured, suddenly cognizant that their engagement would open the way for a new kind of courting that could be as demanding as his kisses. "Well, sir, my mother has instructed me to please you in all matters, so I will risk shocking my family," she said with a smile, and removed her gloves.

He immediately took her hand and raised it to his lips again. "Much better," he murmured, his eyes dropping to her mouth. "You are a delightful and charming temptation, Elizabeth, and you are distracting me from what I came to say."

She raised an eyebrow, impressed with his ability to make her name sound like an intimate endearment. "And what, pray tell, is that?" she asked, her lips tingling as if he had in fact kissed them.

He drew a letter from his pocket and held it out to her. "I wrote this for you to take with you, hoping that you might find time to read it tonight."

She smiled at him warmly. "Thank you. I am glad that I may safely take it this time!"

"There are advantages to being engaged. *Many* advantages."

"When we have more time, sir, I shall make you enumerate them all for me," she said playfully. She was beginning to consider the possibility that she was destined to spend their entire engagement blushing.

"It will be my pleasure to do so, my love. But I would not wish to make a poor impression on Mr. and Mrs. Gardiner this early in our acquaintance by delaying them simply so that I can enjoy a few moments more in your presence, so perhaps I should return you to them."

"Perhaps so." As they were walking back to rejoin the others, she said, surprising even herself, "I shall miss you."

The startled look on Darcy's face could not hide the delight he felt. He was painfully aware that Elizabeth had neatly avoided ever saying anything that would indicate the state of her affections regarding him, even when accepting his proposal, and he had suffered occasional moments of distress since then when he remembered Mr. Bennet telling him that he had instructed Elizabeth to accept his proposal, and wondered what role that may have had in her acceptance. "You will be in my mind constantly," he said quietly.

She looked up at him with a sober gaze, unsure how best to respond in a serious interchange of this sort with him. She had worked to keep their conversations in the past light-hearted, and was more intimidated than she cared to admit by the prospect of a serious discussion of their feelings. In fact, she found the idea terrifying. Fortunately, rescue was at hand in the form of her family.

Darcy paid his respects to the Gardiners, who were already seated in the carriage, and to Mr. and Mrs. Bennet before taking the liberty of handing Elizabeth in. After a brief but heartfelt farewell, they drove off. Elizabeth turned to watch him as they departed, trying to memorize his features, and marveling at the amazing sight of Darcy ensconced among her family.

<hr/>

The travellers stopped for the night in Oxford, arriving with enough daylight left to wander the streets and see the sights before settling in at their inn. Elizabeth duly admired the beauty of the ancient buildings of the colleges, and the newer, but equally striking, Radcliffe Camera. She had looked forward to visiting Oxford, but now she found that her mind tended to wander from their surroundings to a certain dark-haired gentleman. Climbing the tower of the magnificent University Church provided some physical relief for her agitated spirits, and she managed to enjoy the spectacular view over the spires of the town for some minutes before her thoughts drifted to the letter Darcy had given her, wondering what it contained.

She waited to read it until she had some privacy at the inn after dinner, while her aunt and uncle went out to enjoy a twilight stroll along the river. She held it in her hands for several minutes before opening it, and finally broke the seal with the Darcy crest—*Soon to be mine, as well!* she thought with a sense of unreality.

My dearest Elizabeth,
   I hope that your first day's travels have gone well, and that this finds you comfortably situated and enjoying your

surroundings. I have no doubts that by the time you read this, I will be fully engaged in mourning your absence and treasuring the memories of our last weeks together to assist me through the days to come.

There was so much that I would have liked to have the opportunity to say to you today, so many thoughts I would have liked to share with you on the long hoped for occasion of your acceptance of my hand. But it was not to be, given the circumstances, both joyful and distressing, which distracted us from the important business of communicating to one another our thoughts and feelings on this time of change. I know that your interest in considering marriage to me is very recent, but it is no less dear to me for that.

I was surprised, nay, astonished in Kent to discover that you were ignorant of my interest in you—in fact, I must confess that I went so far as to wonder if you might have feigned lack of knowledge of it for reasons of your own, until I recalled that such deception would not have been in your character, and that had you known of my interest, you would have no doubt found some method to preclude matters reaching the point they did. But my admiration of you was real, and had been powerful since the first days of our acquaintance, and all my time away from Hertfordshire had not been sufficient to put you out of my mind for a single day. Yet I must confess with some shame that from where I stand today, I can see there was something lacking in my regard for you at that point, a quality that would have advanced it from the point of fascination and ardent admiration to the kind of devotion and respect that I have always felt—based on the example of my own excellent parents—should exist between a man and his wife. It was not until I thought that I had lost you completely and irrevocably that I came to recognize all of your admirable qualities which had promoted the depth of my attraction to you. I cannot tell you of the power of my despair in those days as I gradually grew to comprehend that you had been right to refuse me, and to acknowledge that I had caused my own downfall. Your reproof, so well applied, I shall never forget: "had you behaved in a more gentleman-like manner." You know not, you can scarcely conceive, how those words tortured me; though it was some time, I confess, before I was reasonable enough to allow their justice. I did not expect ever to encounter you again, yet as I recognized my failings, my first desire was to make myself into a man of whom you could be proud were you ever to meet me again. I cannot tell you how deep was my trepidation when I decided to lay my heart at your feet once more, but by that time I had come to realize how necessary you were to me, and how little I could conceive of any sort of future that did not include you at my side.

I cannot tell you the joy it gives me that you have consented to be my wife. You have taught me so much already, my beloved Elizabeth, for which I am eternally grateful, and the knowledge that we shall face the future together is of great comfort to me. To know that I will have the privilege of seeing your smile each day is to feel gifted with the greatest delight imaginable.

I would continue at length on this subject, but my time is growing short if I am to deliver this to you in the morning. I look forward to your arrival at Pemberley with the greatest of anticipation. Until then, be assured that you will be in my thoughts and my heart always, and that I am, as ever, yours in every way,

Fitzwilliam Darcy

Elizabeth had tears in her eyes as she finished reading the letter. His words of love, which were so difficult for her to hear when she was in his presence, could touch her in a different way through his writing, and his eloquent description of the pain he experienced after her refusal of his first proposal told her more of the depth of his affection than his endearments ever could. She felt undeserving of so deep regard as his, and could not help but feel that her affections were not the equal of his own. *But nor have they had the chance to stand the test of time as his have, and love can grow,* she told herself. *He has placed his faith in me, and I must try to deserve it, yet without giving myself up to him.*

She held the letter to her cheek for a moment before settling to read it again, and by the time she retired for the night, she was in a fair way of knowing it by heart.

Elizabeth and the Gardiners devoted the following day to visiting Blenheim. It is not the object of this work to give a description of that remarkable palace nor its grounds, but to attend to the spirits of Elizabeth, which remained in some disarray; and by the time they reached the picturesque Grand Cascades, her silence had drawn the attention of her aunt, who had been hoping vainly that Elizabeth would unburden herself to her of her own accord. As it appeared that she would not do so, Mrs. Gardiner felt that her lack of spirits at this point justified inquiry.

"Lizzy, you are very quiet. Are your thoughts more of Blenheim or a certain gentleman from Derbyshire, I wonder?" said Mrs. Gardiner gently.

"I am just in awe of all we have seen."

"Is that so?" her aunt asked, doubt apparent in her voice.

If my flaw is to tell everyone else what to do, yours is to tell them nothing at all. Elizabeth recalled Darcy's words, and his implication that her strong sense of privacy stood in the way of close understanding between them, and wondered why she was avoiding telling one of her most trusted confidantes of her struggles. With some hesitancy, she finally said, "I am trying to make sense of my engagement to Mr. Darcy, and I find it resists analysis."

"In what manner does it lack sense? He clearly loves you ardently, and it is apparent that he has engaged your tender feelings as well, has he not?"

"Oh, he has," said Elizabeth with a sigh, "although it was barely more than a month ago that I told him that I could offer him nothing more than friendship, and I hardly know what to trust anymore."

"I assume you must trust *him*, to have accepted his proposal."

"Yes, I do, but sometimes I am not sure what I trust him for is what I want!"

"Why, whatever do you mean, my dear?"

"I trust that we will argue regularly, I trust that he will be persistent in trying to have his own way, I trust that I will have to struggle for my own autonomy . . . he is very predictable in some ways!"

"Hmmm, my dear, it sounds as if he has a will strong enough to stand up to you. I would not be so certain that is unfortunate. I think it would be far too easy for you to find a man who would let you have *your* way all too often! You are not Jane, after all. I believe that you may require a man of strong will if you are to be happy."

Elizabeth pondered this novel idea. Perhaps there was some truth to it. When she did not respond, her aunt added, "And are there not reasons for you to like him, as well?"

With a smile, she replied, "Oddly enough, Jane asked me much the same question when he returned to Netherfield, and I could come up with very little. I imagine that I could do better now."

"And what would you say now?"

"I would say that he is well-educated, enjoys a good debate, has an amusing sense of humour and a sharp wit when he cares to exercise it, and can be enjoyable company. He is honest, responsible, and devoted; he can be depended upon to take what he perceives as the honourable course, and he will try to be in charge of it."

"So, he can stand up to you, and challenge you intellectually, and you can rely on him . . . and what was it that was giving you doubts?" asked her aunt slyly.

Elizabeth drew a breath to retort, then laughed, realizing that she had left herself no ground to stand on. "I take your point, aunt, but I still think he is far too persuasive when he sets his mind to it!"

"And do you mind so much being persuaded?"

"No, perhaps not," she admitted.

"Lizzy, you have grown up to be self-reliant, which is hardly surprising since both of your parents, in their very different ways, cannot always be relied upon. It can be difficult to give up such self-reliance, even when it is no longer necessary, but I do not think it mere chance that you have chosen for your husband a man who is eminently reliable and responsible. You might consider allowing yourself to rely a little more on your Mr. Darcy."

"I did not choose him, the fact is that he chose me, and that I have been persuaded to be so chosen," Elizabeth retorted.

"Perhaps he is sensible of needing a wife with a will of her own, on whom he might rely from time to time!"

Elizabeth cast an amused gaze on her aunt. "Well, I can tell whose side you favour, aunt!"

"And that, my dear Lizzy, is the side of your eventual happiness," her aunt said, satisfied with the results of their conversation, and now ready to turn her attention to the site of their pleasures. "Now, what think you of the grounds here?"

Chapter 7

THEIR TRAVELS CONTINUED TO the north, and the following week they reached the vicinity of Pemberley. Elizabeth, as they drove along, watched for the first appearance of Pemberley Woods with some perturbation, and when at length they turned in at the lodge, her spirits were in a high flutter. She had been envisioning the look that would be in his eyes when they met, and the image made her skin tingle. A flicker of anxiety underlay the thought; she could give no sensible reason, but there was a fear that he might not be pleased to see her. She tried to regard it as a manifestation of the general apprehension about their meeting, and not as further evidence of her vulnerability to him.

She had taken up pen and paper more than once during their travels to write to him, but found herself incapable of composing anything more than a mere travelogue, which would be trivial in comparison to his letter to her. She had spent endless hours pondering the dilemma of how to allow herself to love him while maintaining her independence and critical facilities, and was no closer to an answer than when she left Longbourn.

Her mind was too full for conversation, but she saw and admired every remarkable spot and point of view. The park was very large, and contained great variety of ground. They entered it in one of its lowest points, and drove for some time through a beautiful wood, stretching over a wide extent. They gradually ascended for half a mile, and then found themselves at the top of a considerable eminence, where the wood ceased, and the eye was instantly caught by Pemberley House, situated on the opposite side of a valley, into which the road with some abruptness wound. It was a large, handsome, stone building, standing well on rising ground, and backed by a ridge of high woody hills; in front, a stream of some natural importance was swelled into greater, but without any artificial appearance. Its banks were neither formal, nor falsely adorned. Elizabeth was delighted. She had never seen a place for which nature had done more, or where natural beauty had been so little counteracted by an awkward taste. They were all of them warm in their admiration.

They descended the hill, crossed the bridge, and drove to the door, where they found Darcy and Georgiana already outside to meet them. *He must have had servants watching for us every minute!* thought Elizabeth, and her spirits fluttered as she caught his gaze. His smile was barely perceptible, but the warmth in his eyes could not be missed as he stepped forward to hand her out of the carriage. Without releasing her for a moment, he raised her hand to his lips. "Miss Bennet," he said softly. "Welcome to Pemberley." Recalling his other guests, he turned to greet the Gardiners, but remained standing so close to

Elizabeth that it was difficult for Georgiana to find room to give her a sisterly embrace.

Georgiana invited them inside and offered refreshments. As they entered, Elizabeth found that she could hardly spare a glance for her future home; her attention was taken by the gentleman at her side, whose mere presence seemed to be sufficient to cause feelings of desire to course through her. They were shown through the hall into the saloon, whose northern aspect rendered it delightful for summer. Darcy led Elizabeth to its windows which, opening to the ground, admitted a most refreshing view of the high woody hills behind the house, and of the beautiful oaks and Spanish chestnuts which were scattered over the intermediate lawn. Under the guise of showing her the prospect, he whispered, "Dearest Elizabeth, I thought this day would never come. I cannot tell you how much I have missed you."

She looked up at him, and the intensity of his gaze was such that for a moment she feared he would kiss her right there in front of their families, but he did not. "I am glad to be here," she said breathlessly.

On their being seated, Darcy taking care to be next to Elizabeth, the discourse began immediately with discussion of the travels each party had undertaken. Mr. and Mrs. Gardiner had a great deal to say of Warwick, Birmingham, and Kenilworth, with Georgiana managing to interpose a shy question from time to time. If Darcy and Elizabeth, being more involved in exchanging glances, spoke less than the others, none saw fit to comment on it.

After they had an opportunity to take refreshment of cold meat, cake, and a variety of all the finest fruits in season,

Georgiana, with a glance at her brother, gathered her courage and offered to show the Gardiners their rooms, a suggestion which they gratefully accepted, and an arrangement was made to reconvene in an hour. They had no sooner passed the door than Darcy with the greatest of relief took Elizabeth into his arms and kissed her with a fervor that confirmed how strongly he had felt her absence.

She had forgotten how powerfully his kisses could affect her, and had not the experience to recognize the degree to which her own desires had built up during their separation, and so was taken by surprise by the intensity of the sensations that overcame her as his lips met hers. Shivers of pleasure danced through her as he tasted the delights of her mouth, and she ran her fingers deep into his thick curls.

Darcy, intoxicated by the touch of her, the scent of her, the taste of her, could not quench his desire, and ran his hands demandingly down her back, then lifted her into his lap. He could not get enough of her, and he trailed kisses across her face as if he needed to stake a claim to every inch, but even more important than satiating his need to touch her and to kiss her was his desire to arouse her to the same level of passion that he was experiencing. Nothing in his life had the power to excite him so much as when he managed to evoke a passionate response in Elizabeth. Craving evidence of her desire, he continued to place kisses along the lines of her neck, seeking out each crevasse until he reached the sensitive hollow at the base of her neck. His wishes were fulfilled as she leaned her head back in encouragement of his exploration and moaned softly.

Emboldened and inflamed by her response, Darcy stroked his hand down her arm, and then slowly and seductively began to trace his fingers along her leg, first down the outside of her thigh, then exploring inward. The powerful and exquisite sensations this evoked in her caused her to turn her body towards his, craving more and closer contact, and he responded to her unspoken need by sliding his hand up over the curves of her hips until he encountered the temptation of her breast. Her softness aroused him fiercely, and his desire to make her his almost overpowered him. Impulsively he began to caress her through the cloth of her dress, causing her to shiver. The depth of the pleasure his touch gave her only made Elizabeth long for more, and she slid her hands down his back passionately. She felt that she could not bear it; she had missed him so much, had missed his touch so much, that now she could hardly control her need.

Darcy, aware that he was exceeding the limits of his self-control, but so stimulated by her arousal that he no longer cared, returned his mouth to hers, demanding and receiving a response that matched his own. He had to have more, and as his tantalizing touch on her breast grew more demanding, he felt the involuntary movement of her hips against him in a way which magnified his desire yet further.

Clinging helplessly to his shoulders, Elizabeth felt the burning sensation of his mouth traveling across her jaw and down her neck, but this time as she leaned back, he did not stop at the base of her neck, but continued downward towards her neckline. As he reached the tender flesh which swelled there, she arched herself forward as if to demand even more. He was only too glad to oblige, and his other hand began to pull down the sleeve of her gown, gradually revealing her bare shoulder. The sight of it begged for his exploration, and he could not sate himself on the taste of her exposed skin. The fact that she was allowing him this degree of license, that she was making small and inarticulate sounds as he explored and surveyed her lovely body, that she seemed beyond the ability to ask him to cease what he was doing all combined to push him over the edge, and he began to run his fingers inside the neckline of her gown as he had promised himself he would not do, ready to plunge his hand in to explore the oft-imagined tenderness of her breasts. He knew that there would be no stopping then, that once he had gone that far, he would not rest until she was his in every way, and he knew he had no right to take such advantage of the reaction he had deliberately provoked in her.

"Elizabeth," he groaned. "Merciful God, please stop me, Elizabeth!" He did not know whether he hoped that she would heed him or that she would not.

A debilitating sensation of longing ran through her as she took his meaning, and she wanted nothing more than for him to slake the desires that were racing through her, but she heard the desperation in his voice, and somehow was able to force herself to return to her senses. It was almost a physical blow to him as she moved out of his arms and away from him, straightening her gown with embarrassment, her body still trembling with the desires he had roused in her.

His arms felt bereft without her. He closed his eyes for a moment, struggling to regain command of himself. Looking into her lovely, passion-filled eyes, eyes he could easily drown in, he said incoherently, "God in heaven, Elizabeth, I never meant to let it go that far." The remorse in his voice was unmistakable.

"I . . . " she said, her mouth dry, shocked both by what had almost happened, and by how much she still wished that it had. She closed her eyes and took several deep breaths until she felt a modicum of calm within her. "I know you did not, nor did I, and perhaps it is best to leave it at that."

"As you wish," he said almost automatically, then added, "Elizabeth, I have always prided myself on my self-control, but the moment I am near you, one glance from you and it all vanishes as if it had never existed."

Elizabeth's mouth curved in an amused smile. "It is a good thing, then, that we plan to marry!"

He was momentarily taken aback by her humour, then saw the value of it. "Indeed, madam, it is a very good thing." He forced himself to stand and to ring for a servant. "I shall have someone show you to your room. I dare not take you there myself at the moment," he said dryly.

"I think that is wise."

A young woman came to the door and bobbed a curtsey. Darcy said, "Please show Miss Bennet to her room, Nan."

"Yes, sir," she responded. "Right this way, miss."

"Miss Bennet," he said as she was walking out the door. When she turned to look at him, he added, "I *am* pleased to have you here."

She gave him an impish smile. "Thank you, sir. I had somehow managed to receive that impression already. Until later, then, Mr. Darcy."

<hr />

It took Elizabeth some time to restore her fraught spirits to their normal state after her encounter with Darcy. She could not believe it; she had been at Pemberley not even an hour, and already matters with him were running out of her control. Her vulnerability to him had not lessened with time or distance—if anything, it had increased. How was she to retain any sense of herself when her attraction to him ran unchecked? She needed to recall that despite their obvious physical compatibility, they were prone to virulent disagreements in other areas. It was critical that she retain her independence, or she would find herself being dominated by his forceful personality in all regards. She needed to retain more of a reserve with him, and to keep in the forefront of her mind that her response to his touch need not govern her behaviour towards him. How to balance this restraint with her love for him and their eventual marriage was more confusing; now that they were engaged, she could no longer reasonably draw back from him or refuse to be alone with him as she had in the past. She vowed to herself she would find a way, and thus fortified in spirit and resolve, she felt at least capable of rejoining the others.

On her return downstairs, she was met by Georgiana, who informed her that there would be time to take a tour of the house before dinner if she so desired. In easy agreement with the idea, the Gardiners joined them as well. They found Darcy ensconced in his study where he was engaging himself in some business to take his mind from thoughts that were best suppressed. Elizabeth surprised herself by blushing when she saw him, and having some difficulty meeting his eyes, but fortunately the tour offered her sources of neutral conversation to help her past her initial embarrassment.

Elizabeth took great pleasure in discovering the admirable taste of her future husband as she viewed his home. The rooms were lofty and handsome, and their furniture suitable to the fortune of their proprietor, but they were neither gaudy nor uselessly fine, with less of splendor, and more real elegance, than the furniture of Rosings. She was delighted to discover that from every window there were beauties of nature to be seen. Every disposition of the ground was good; the hill, crowned with wood, from which they had descended, receiving increased abruptness from the distance, was a beautiful object. She looked on the whole scene, the river, the trees scattered on its banks, and the winding of the valley, as far as she could trace it, with delight. She could not have been better pleased, and could barely credit that she would someday be mistress of all this.

She was interested to notice that Darcy, in his interactions with the servants, showed none of the pride or reserve that she had observed at Netherfield, and seemed overall to be of a gentler disposition than had been the case in the past. Never in her life had she seen his manners so little dignified, and when he introduced her to his housekeeper, a respectable-looking, elderly woman by the name of Mrs. Reynolds, the affection between the two was apparent. His attentions to her aunt and uncle were all that was civil, and they clearly enjoyed his conversation. All in all, she felt that she had never before been so pleased with his behaviour in company. She hardly knew what to make of the change, which made it all the more difficult to maintain her reserve as she tried to demonstrate her pleasure in his conduct through the warmth of her manner.

After dinner Darcy suggested a twilight stroll through the gardens, an idea which appealed to Elizabeth very much. She had seen enough of the beauty of the park through the windows to make her anxious for a chance to explore it, but she was willing to settle for the gardens for today. The Gardiners and Georgiana considerately declined the invitation, so the two set off on their own. Elizabeth was of two minds about being alone with him again, finding that she both desired and feared it.

"So, what think you of Pemberley, my love?" he asked.

"It is everything that is delightful and charming, and lives up to all the praise it has received. I cannot make a single complaint so far," she said warmly.

"Then it pleases you? Will you be content to live here?" There was a certain eagerness in his voice, like a little boy anxious to please.

She was tempted to make a teasing response, but a look at his face suggested that this was not the moment for it. "I believe that I shall be very happy here, provided, of course, that you are here as well."

His look of satisfaction showed how well her words had pleased him, and she was glad to have discovered an indirect means to indicate her affection, since she could not yet feel comfortable expressing open affection and using endearments as he did. "I believe, my love, that it will be difficult to tear me from your side once we are married. That reminds me, however, that we do have an obligation to discuss our wedding plans."

Elizabeth laughed. "Well, we can *discuss* them all you please, but I have a suspicion that I have ceded all of my choices by leaving for a month immediately after becoming engaged. My mother will no doubt have everything arranged to her satisfaction by the time I return. At least I had a say in choosing the bridegroom!"

Darcy looked in doubt as to how seriously he should take her remarks; clearly there was little he would not put past Mrs. Bennet. To relieve his uncertainty, she added, "Do you have particular thoughts about the wedding?" She found that she still was not quite prepared to say "our wedding."

"Bingley suggested to me that we consider a double ceremony, which seems a pleasant notion, and would certainly save a good deal of work," —not to mention making the occasion a good deal sooner than it would otherwise be— "if you do not think six weeks too soon." It was far longer than he would like.

Six weeks! Elizabeth thought. I am still having trouble believing that I am marrying at all, though after what happened today, it is perhaps best not to wait too long. She tried to imagine walking these paths in six weeks as the Mistress of Pemberley, and failed completely. "I suppose it would make sense to do so, if you are willing. I could write to Jane to suggest it, and if she is agreeable, she could propose it to my mother."

"Unless your mother has already decided on it by herself," he said, with just a hint of a smile. Reaching over, he tidied a tendril of her hair which had come loose. "I am not certain I wish to spend time among the gossiping people of Meryton at the moment. I fear that I am not forgiving towards people who try to hurt you, my love."

She looked up at him affectionately. "I would imagine not. Your sense of loyalty is something I have always admired, even when I disliked you—or perhaps, in the interest of marital felicity, I should say before I realized that I liked you."

"I think I would prefer that," he said in a teasing manner, "but so long as you do not change your mind again, you may say whatever you like."

"Though we both have reason to think my opinions not entirely unalterable, they are not, I hope, as easily changed as that implies."

"I believe you; but then again, I know what it took to change your mind the first time. I am glad not to have to do that again."

She glanced up at him flirtatiously. "It seemed to me that there were at least a few moments along the way which you enjoyed. Some of your, umm, *arguments* were quite persuasive."

"I will not deny that I enjoy . . . *persuading* you," he said, his gaze intent, but then he seemed to withdraw for a moment. He had spent a good deal of time since that afternoon establishing strict criteria for his behaviour with her. His loss of control earlier had shaken his faith in himself. "Elizabeth," he added, his voice serious.

"Yes?"

He chose his words carefully. "You would perhaps be wise not to offer me any encouragement during your stay here."

She was initially puzzled by his words, but as she took his meaning, her cheeks flushed with shame. She was under no illusion that her behaviour earlier in response to his kisses had been anything but discreditable, but had been of the opinion he was pleased by it; certainly it had seemed as if he had encouraged it, on this as on past occasions. Apparently, though, he had different standards for propriety at Pemberley, where he had an image to uphold—or perhaps it was lingering doubts from the rumours in Hertfordshire—and obviously felt she had failed to take responsibility for preventing such occurrences. She felt ill even thinking of it—*well*, she decided, *if he wants proper behaviour from me, he will certainly get it now.* She did not think she could bear to have him touch her, knowing what he thought of her.

She had her pride as well, though, and straightened her shoulders before she spoke. "Very well, sir; you shall have no cause for concern, I assure you," she said in a voice well suited for a social occasion. *Why, why, why do I keep letting down my defenses to him? I cannot believe that I have allowed this to happen again.* She could feel the first stirrings of anger at him, but knew she must protect against that as well.

He smiled, unnoticed by Elizabeth whose eyes were fixed firmly ahead, and said, "I appreciate it."

"Mr. Darcy, I find that I am feeling somewhat fatigued. Perhaps we could return to the house?" She wanted nothing more at the moment than to escape his presence and the utter humiliation she felt at his rebuke.

His brow furrowed in concern. He had never heard her complain of fatigue on a walk before, certainly not on such a short one; perhaps she might be falling ill. He took her hand in his and asked, "Are you well, my love?" He was startled when she pulled her hand away, rather ungently, he thought. "What is the matter?"

The temptation to make an angry response was great, but Elizabeth forced herself to remain cognizant of the need for her to learn the arts of compromise and peacemaking. She took a deep breath to calm herself, then said, "I am not pleased by your implication that I am at fault for encouraging you."

Darcy looked at her in bewilderment. How had she come upon the idea that he was criticizing her? Aware that their disagreements had a tendency towards escalation, he sought to find common ground. "I fear that we have somehow misunderstood one another, then, since I did not intend to make any such implication, and it would be unjust if I did."

Unsure whether to believe him, she asked, "May I ask, then, what you did intend to say?"

It was his turn to look away, his cheeks tinged with red. "My intention was to ask your assistance in curbing my behaviour lest it become out of hand."

"Oh." Elizabeth's colour rose. "I did misunderstand you, then. My apologies, sir."

"What did you think I meant?"

"I . . . assumed that you disapproved of *my* behaviour."

"Elizabeth, the next time you believe that I disapprove of something you have done, please ask me, because I assure you it is unlikely to be true. In this case, you have touched on something of which I am so far from disapproving as to be somewhat of an embarrassment, so please, do not trouble yourself."

She could think of nothing to say to that, and so kept her peace.

"One of the advantages of being at Pemberley," he said, leading her around a corner into a walled formal garden, "is that here *I* am aware of all the pleasantly secluded locations where one is unlikely to be interrupted."

Elizabeth raised an eyebrow. "And how precisely do you propose that I help you curb your behaviour? Perhaps you could be so kind as to lend me a pistol for the duration of my stay, though I should need some instruction in its use."

He smiled at her roguishly. "Perhaps you could forget that I ever made such a foolish suggestion."

"Mr. Darcy, I am hardly that forgetful!" she replied in mock disapproval. She felt her lips tingle in anticipation as he drew her into his arms.

"But please remember this: discovering that you are so responsive to me was a most delightful surprise. Pray do not ever change it."

She gave him a challenging smile. "In that case, sir, are you planning to converse with me or to kiss me?"

Darcy made the only possible reply.

⤞✦⤝

The next few days afforded Elizabeth the opportunity to acquaint herself further with Pemberley and its environs. She immediately fell in love with the park and grounds, and never tired of walking out to discover new delights, either with her aunt and uncle or with her decidedly amorous betrothed. They visited some of the finer sights of the area, and Elizabeth began her acquaintance with the town of Lambton where her aunt had spent her youth.

More importantly, the time gave her an opportunity to observe Darcy, and she rapidly reached the conclusion that he was a different man when he was at Pemberley. Gone were the pride and distance that she had once thought his main characteristics, and in their place, she saw more of the relaxed, warm, and appealing man she had glimpsed when alone with him in Hertfordshire. His actions were caring and concerned, his generosity obvious—and clearly a byword with his staff—and his civility warming. She was hard put to explain to her aunt and uncle why she ever had a negative impression of him. The difference astonished and fascinated her, and she thought more than once that, had she met Darcy first at Pemberley, they would have reached an understanding earlier and with far less difficulty than they had.

She commented on it once to Darcy when they were alone. He responded, "This is where I am at home; I am never so comfortable as when I am at Pemberley. Here I know everyone I see, and they know me, and we both know what to expect of each other. I have never been at ease among those I do not know well."

"But you know Bingley and his family well; why would you be ill at ease at Netherfield?"

He looked surprised that she need ask the question. "I did not know the servants, nor the neighbours, and I knew that they were all drawing opinions of me. I dislike the feeling. Here I know what people think of me, and I know that their opinion is unlikely to change if I should make a mistake or accidentally offend someone."

"And what do people think of you here?" she asked with a smile.

He put his arms around her. "They think I am the Master of Pemberley, and when they discover that you are to be my wife, they will think me the luckiest man alive," he said, and kissed her with such passion that the subject was dropped for some time.

Darcy was also well pleased by the constant presence of Elizabeth. Knowing he would see her frequently each day, if not spend the entire day with her, put him in high spirits, and her gradually increasing comfort with him added to his delight. After their conversation on the first day of her visit, he found it easier to maintain his self-control with her, and enjoyed each and every opportunity they had to explore the pleasure they could give one another without feeling the acute hunger for more than he could have.

His nights were a different matter. The days between their engagement and Elizabeth's arrival at Pemberley had afforded him his first good nights of sleep since he had met her. It was an unpleasant surprise to discover that her visit brought a return of his sleepless nights, though for a very different reason. His day-time ease in her presence disappeared once she retired for the night, and he became painfully aware not only of her absence, but also of the permeability of the barriers that stood between them. His imagination presented to him the picture of that of which he was deprived, and the image of Elizabeth, dressed in nothing but a nightgown, with her hair loose upon her shoulders and an inviting smile on her lovely face haunted him. The knowledge that this temptation resided under his roof with only a few feet of hall and a door between them did not leave him for a moment, and for the only time in their acquaintance he had moments of wishing she were not quite so passionate in her responses to him, so that he could be more certain she would throw him out in disgrace if he ever tried to breach that one barrier. Unfortunately, he knew from experience that it was possible for him to take advantage of her responsiveness to go further than she might choose at a saner moment, and his imagination ran wild with ideas of what might happen if he found his way into her bedroom. He knew himself well enough to be certain he would not act on his impulses, but the mere presence of the possibility kept sleep at bay until late into the night.

Elizabeth, unaware of his nighttime battles, was enjoying her ability to be more at ease with Darcy each day as she came to understand him better. She was finally beginning to comprehend what he had meant when he said that he was shy, and that she had misinterpreted the results of that shyness as arrogance and incivility. When she felt mystified by the changes in

Darcy, she need only look at Georgiana, who also blossomed at Pemberley, though not to the degree her brother did. It was enough, however, to reveal a rather sly sense of humour and some of the excitement typical to a girl of her age, and Elizabeth was pleased to discover that her future sister could chatter away as well as Kitty or Lydia could when the circumstances were right.

Unfortunately, several days into their visit, Georgiana became ill with a bad cold, and after making a valiant attempt to ignore her symptoms in an effort to be a good hostess, retired to bed. She insisted, however, that her guests go about their business, and Mrs. Gardiner proposed that it might be a good time for her and her niece to visit her Lambton acquaintances, which would also allow Mr. Gardiner and Mr. Darcy to enjoy an often-discussed day of fishing. The party did not gather again until dinnertime, when the ladies were regaled with tales of the sport the gentlemen had found. Darcy had found the day a pleasant one, but, as he far preferred the company of Elizabeth to that of fish, and this had been the longest daytime period he had been deprived of her company since their arrival, felt that it could have been improved upon. A brief evening tryst in the garden helped appease his feelings of deprivation, but not without exciting urges he preferred to forget as nighttime drew near.

When Elizabeth retired for the night, she could hear Georgiana's laboured coughing from the next room, and found it difficult to sleep thinking of how she must be feeling. Remembering how she had sat with Jane when she was ill at Netherfield, on impulse she made her way to Georgiana's room, careful to avoid notice as she was dressed already for bed.

Georgiana was in fact very grateful to have some distraction from her ailment, and Elizabeth ended up spending several hours with her in the kind of sisterly conversation that Georgiana had always craved before she finally fell into a restless slumber.

On returning to her room, Elizabeth found that she was now too alert for sleep. She picked up the novel that she was reading, but decided that it was too engaging for her current needs; what she required was some dull sermons or some such that would bring sleep quickly. There would certainly be something to fit the description in the extensive library below.

She debated dressing, but dismissed the idea as too much bother. It was well past midnight, and no one would be up and about to see her, and even if they did, her dressing gown was quite modest. Taking her candle, she slipped out of her room, down the stairs, and to the library. Once in the door, she stopped to find her bearings in the extensive space, recalling from her earlier explorations that there had been some religious books along the far wall. Passing behind a series of chairs, she had just turned the corner to reach them when a light to one side caught her attention, causing her to bring her hand over her heart in surprise.

"Very fetching, Miss Bennet." Darcy's familiar voice came from out of the shadows.

She could barely make out his form, lit only by a small candle. She blushed furiously as she recalled her current improper attire, but told herself firmly that she was every bit as covered as she would be by her normal apparel, and, after all, he had the opportunity to see her with her hair down before, so there should be no reason for concern—at least so long as no one knew of this encounter. "Mr. Darcy! I did not expect anyone to be about at this hour."

"Nor did I," he replied. He had been drinking in the sight of her, illuminated by the candle in her hand, since she stepped in the door, taking in the glimpses of her nightgown beneath the clinging dressing gown, and her long dark curls in disarray just as he had pictured. Though good manners required that he stand when she entered, he stayed seated, knowing that if he moved at all, he would move much further than he should. They could not be more alone, and he had been sitting here for hours longing for her; his need to take her in his arms and make her his was almost more than he could bear. "What brings you to burn the midnight oil?" he asked, knowing that if she said anything at all about thoughts of him, he would be completely lost.

"Georgiana could not sleep—her cough was keeping her awake—and we sat up together talking," she said, feeling as if she were babbling. "Then I could not fall asleep, and I thought something to read . . . " she paused, swallowing hard, as her eyes adjusted enough to make out that he was wearing nothing more than shirt and breeches, " . . . something to read might help me sleep." Her mouth felt dry, and her feet seemed rooted to the ground.

"I believe you might be able to find one or two books here," he said dryly. "Please help yourself." *Or you could come here to me, and I will happily ensure you do not mind being kept awake, my love.*

Far too aware of his presence, she turned and selected a book almost at random—it had 'Sermons' in the title, at least. She could feel his eyes running over her. The tension palpable in the air, she said, "I think that this should do." Her gaze was drawn again to the shape of his shoulders, undisguised by waistcoat and tailcoat.

He could see the look of awareness in her eyes. "Go to bed, Elizabeth, while I can still call myself a gentleman," he said, keeping the tone of his voice lighter than his words would suggest.

She could not help smiling impudently in response. "Good night, William," she said obediently, a touch of mischief in her voice as she dropped a formal curtsey before turning to leave. She had not gone more than a half dozen steps before she felt her hand seized by his. Slowly she turned to face him, her heart pounding.

"Say that again," he commanded.

Her breath caught. He looked even more devastatingly attractive from only an arms-length away. *It is time for the coward's way out,* she thought. "Good night, Mr. Darcy," she said sedately.

With a slight smile, he hooked his fingers through the belt of her dressing gown. "Not quite right. Try again, Elizabeth."

She ran her tongue over her dry lips before finally allowing herself to meet his eyes, knowing full well that he would be able to read in hers how much she desired him. "Good night, William," she said softly.

"Not yet, my love," he said. Dropping her hand, he took her candle from her and set it on the mantle behind her, his eyes never leaving hers. Very slowly he bent his head towards hers, and just before their lips met, she gasped as she realized that while she had been distracted, his hands had been untying the belt of her dressing gown, and were now sliding inside. The warm touch of his hands on her waist through the thin fabric of her nightgown made her forget everything beyond the rush of heat running through her as he captured her mouth in a kiss that seemed to demand her very soul.

She felt as if she were melting as his hands caressed her, slowly traveling around to her back in a thorough exploration of her curves. She moaned, her mouth still against his, as he traced up the line of her spine to her neck where his fingertips crept under the neckline of her nightgown. Unable to control the wild sensations traveling through her, she put her hands to his chest, savouring the shape of his muscles beneath his shirt, and slid them up to his neck, for once unencumbered by a cravat, where the feeling of his warm skin under her fingers excited her yet further.

Darcy tried to focus his attention on her kisses, tasting the passion that was clearly sweeping between them, but the rest of his body remained all too aware of how little stood between them, and as he finally pulled Elizabeth to him, the sensation of her softness molding itself to him stole away any remaining rational thought. He slid his hands down over her ribs to take possession of the curves of her hips, and as he pressed her against him in an urge as old as man, his fingers made the stimulating discovery that she seemed to be wearing nothing at all underneath the nightgown.

He was lost, and he knew it. He could not wait for weeks; he had to have her. Knowing that she could feel the evidence of his arousal, he began to spread kisses down her sensitive neck in the way that he knew inflamed her, tasting the skin of each hollow as she arched herself against him. He caressed her hips, discovering how this made her writhe against him in a most pleasurable manner. If only he could be sure that she would not refuse him . . .

Elizabeth felt almost wild from the currents of desire that were racing through her; she felt cravings she could not comprehend trying to take control of her body. She knew her danger, but could not bring herself to stop. She sighed with pleasure as his hand rose to cup her breast through the thin fabric. His fingers caressed her softness, then she felt a sharp burst of impossible pleasure lance through her as his thumb stroked her nipple. She moaned, wanting the delicious feeling to return, and he fulfilled her need by rolling her nipple between his fingers as he reclaimed her mouth and drank deeply of her.

He exulted in her response, and, sensing her growing inability to remain upright, swept her into his arms and carried her to a loveseat where he settled her across his lap in a position that left him well able to continue the attentions that were causing such overwhelming pleasure to her. As she whimpered and writhed in response to his touch, he commanded softly, "Tell me you want more."

She did not want him ever to stop. "More," she whispered helplessly, and he was only too happy to indulge her need. This was every fantasy he had ever had come to life. After a minute, however, his fingers paused in their attention to her breast, and she looked at him in mute, bereft longing, unable to understand why he had stopped. She saw that he was beginning to undo the top ties of her nightgown; for a moment, sense began to return to her, and she whispered, "William . . . "

"Shhh," he soothed her as he slipped his hand into the opening to reclaim her breast. The feeling of her soft skin and the hardness of her peak excited him beyond what he believed possible. "Let me give you pleasure, my love." His lips followed the course set by his fingers until he pushed aside the flap of fabric to expose her breast. She froze for a moment, but the sensations ignited as his tongue explored her nipple quickly stole away her senses, and as he finally drew it into his mouth and suckled her, she found herself overwhelmed by her need and surrendered herself up to him.

He placed his hand lightly over the heart of her desire as he continued his attention to her breast, and when she began to press against him as her hips moved involuntarily, he finally took the risk of letting his hand travel under her nightgown to caress her legs.

His delicate, tantalizing touch drove her even closer to the edge, and as he moved his hand upward to explore her thighs, she instinctively parted her legs to allow him access. When his fingers finally slipped into her wetness to find her most sensitive spot, she felt her need for him rise to an unbearable peak. Continuing to stroke her where she most needed him, he whispered, "Elizabeth, please let me love you."

Her only coherent thought was that she might not survive if he did not continue what he had started. She managed to nod slightly, and he exultantly picked her up in his arms again and carried her out of the library, through the hall and gallery until they reached his bedchamber. He closed the door behind him and placed her gently on his bed, then lay down beside her and resumed the activities which had so pleased her earlier. As he sensed her desire rising to a crest again, he paused and said, "I want to see all of you, my love."

He slipped her dressing gown off her shoulders, taking a moment to caress the sensitive areas of her neck as he did so. Feeling lost in her passion, she allowed him to untie her nightgown, and as he lowered it over her shoulders, his lips followed the same route as he tasted the delights of her newly exposed skin. Finally he slid the nightgown off, and the heat of his gaze as he took in her appearance made her forget any shyness. He found the sight of her in his bed as he had so often imagined unbearably arousing. "You are so very beautiful, my love," he said reverently, running his hands down the length of her. Transfixed by the breathtaking vision before him, he stripped off his shirt before returning to her.

Elizabeth drank in the sight of him. The beauty of his bare torso only made her want even more, and she ran her hands down his back, desirous of bringing him closer to her. Overwhelming feelings of desire and love overtook her. She could never have enough of him. She longed for the completion that she instinctively knew only he could bring her.

Darcy moaned her name, knowing that he could wait no longer, and began to tear at the buttons on his breeches until he was able to remove them as well. He lowered himself onto her, and as her legs parted to make room for him, he sought out the place he most desired. "Elizabeth, dearest, darling Elizabeth, are you ready for me?" he asked softly, covering her face with kisses.

Although uncertain as to precisely what she was agreeing to, but knowing that she needed something from him, she breathed, "William, oh love, please, yes." She clutched him to her, entranced by the sensation of his skin against her own, and kissed him in such a way as to assure him of her acquiescence.

His feelings on hearing her words were overpowering. Barely able to contain himself, he whispered, "My love, this may hurt, but only for a moment," before sliding himself deep inside her. He closed his eyes in ecstasy at the sensation. She dug her fingers into his shoulder as the brief pain came, and he forced himself to stop until she relaxed again, distracting her with deep kisses full of longing as he waited. "God, I adore you so, my dearest, dearest love," he murmured, stimulated by the feeling of her flesh surrounding him and the knowledge that she at last was his.

The pain was sharp, but Elizabeth found that it was soon overwhelmed by the pleasure of having him inside her. Exquisite sensations overtook her as he slowly began to move within her. She wrapped her legs around him, seeking to bring him into her even further, and as he established a regular rhythm, she felt wave after wave of delicious pleasure take her until finally she was swept away on an astonishing crest of pleasure that convulsed her body. As Darcy felt her reach her climax, he found his own release and, moaning her name, collapsed into her arms.

As rationality slowly returned to him, his first thought was for the remarkable and stunning event that had just occurred; his second was the realization that in pursuit of this same event, he had just seduced his beloved Elizabeth, and she had every reason to be furious with him. A sense of guilt and panic began to wind its way through him.

Elizabeth was still reeling in astonishment at the fulfillment she had found in Darcy's arms. She knew instinctively that she had given herself to him utterly, not just in body but in spirit as well. Comprehension of what had occurred was slow in coming, and as it crept into her mind, she struggled to push it away. She distracted herself by winding her hands into his hair and kissed him deeply, an offering which Darcy accepted with gratitude and relief, and returned with interest, until, realizing his weight must be oppressive, he rolled off her and pulled her into his arms, shifting the bedclothes to cover them both. With a sigh, Elizabeth rested her head on his shoulder, feeling she was at last in the place intended for her, and let herself relax in contentment, setting aside for the moment the knowledge that there was going to be a price to pay.

As she nestled against him, Darcy felt a moment's hope that all might yet be well. He stroked her hair and held her close, willing her to understand his love for her. "Elizabeth, my dearest," he said at last, "I must beg your forgiveness, even though I know that I do not deserve it."

She kissed his shoulder, then his neck, and then his lips. Stroking his cheek gently, she gazed at him with her eyes full of the love she could no longer disguise. "William . . . is that what you would like me to call you? Or would you prefer Fitzwilliam?"

He could not but smile at the moment she had chosen to ask that question. "My love, just now you could call me anything you like, and I would think it delightful." His relief that she did not appear to be angry, or even worse, horrified, was great, and he could not stop himself from dusting her lips with light kisses. God, there was no possibility that he could ever get enough of this woman!

"William, there is nothing to forgive. You did nothing that I did not allow you to do, and what regrets I have must go on my own shoulders. But at present I would rather not think about misgivings; they will come soon enough, and for now I would rather just . . . " she paused, lost for words.

"Just what, my love?" he asked with some anxiety.

"I would rather appreciate this time with you, and think of the consequences later." She hoped that she was not shocking him, but her feelings at the moment seemed far too precious to waste on recriminations.

"Elizabeth, dearest, darling Elizabeth, this is all I want, to be with you like this," he said, aware he was being incoherent, but so overwhelmed by love for the woman in his arms that he felt the need to express it somehow. He stroked her cheek tenderly, and then ran his hand along her body, treasuring the feel of her next to him, and the knowledge that she was his at last.

She would not have thought it possible, but his touch aroused new desires in her. As his hand continued to caress her, finally coming to rest cupped possessively around her breast, the ache in her loins began anew. She communicated her need to him by deepening the kisses they shared, and the mere sight of the look of desire in her eyes stimulated a similar reaction in him.

As his arousal became evident to her, she tried to bring him to her, seeking the release he had given her earlier, but was held back by the touch of his hand. "Not so quickly this time, my love; allow me to enjoy taking you there slowly," he said, a warm, intent look in his eyes as he shifted her to lie back on the bed. Previously he had been focused on assuring her cooperation; now he wanted to take pleasure in watching her respond to him. Raising himself on one arm, he kissed her slowly, tantalizingly exploring her mouth until he felt her gripping at his shoulders. Running his fingers unhurriedly down her neck, he held her eyes with his as he began to stroke her breast in gentle circles, gradually moving inward until his fingers lightly caressed her nipple. She gasped, and a smile of satisfaction grew on Darcy's face as he repeated the action again and again, watching her desire grow. He kissed her again, more demandingly this time, and she thrust her fingers into his hair and held him to her as she sought to sate herself with his mouth. She released him only when his hand wandered lower to stroke her inner thighs, leaving her hot with desire.

But she had been passive long enough; she began to run her hands down his chest, glorying in the feeling of his skin beneath her fingertips. "Show me how to please you," she whispered to him.

He laughed softly. "If you please me any more, my love, I may not survive the experience!" he said, but he guided her hand downward. His eyes closed as she stroked him, and he hardened even further in her hand as she explored the ways to give him pleasure. His moans gratified her as she saw that she could indeed create in him those feelings which he did in her, and she was disappointed when he removed her hand.

"Love, you do not know what you do to me!" he exclaimed. His resolution to set a leisurely pace had vanished, but he took time to caress her in her most sensitive spot slowly, and then more quickly, until he could see her approaching the pinnacle. He entered her then, and teased them both with slow strokes, resisting her unspoken demands for more, but as her sweet whimpers of pleasure increased, he could hold back no longer, and sought his own oblivion as the waves of satisfaction overtook her.

As Elizabeth gradually returned to her senses, she could think of nothing but her love for him. His lovemaking was so far from her expectations of the duties of the marriage bed that she did not know how to comprehend it, but she had never before felt so close to another person. All of her fear left far behind, she whispered to him as he lay sated in her arms. "I love you so, William."

His arms tightened convulsively around her at the words he had so longed to hear from her. "Elizabeth, my own Elizabeth," he murmured, his heart full of a happiness that could not be spoken, just as the bliss she had given his body was beyond any description. "You are so much more than I deserve. I only wish I had the words to tell you what you mean to me."

They remained entangled together, whispering endearments to one another. Elizabeth was in such a perfect state of contentment that she felt as if she were floating; Darcy, although at least as elated as she, could not keep his mind from inevitably turning to the practicalities of the matter. "Dearest, I believe we had best not wait six more weeks to marry."

"It might be difficult to do it sooner," she replied vaguely.

"Yes, but there could be consequences from tonight, and, to be completely honest, I cannot imagine that I could stay out of your bed for that long after what we have shared tonight."

"Mmmm. What would you propose, then?"

"We could marry here, in the next few days. I could ride to Matlock tomorrow to obtain a license. Or, if it is important to you to marry from home, we could plan to have the ceremony just after you return to Longbourn in, what, three weeks' time."

"That would seem a long time," she said drowsily, the long sleepless night beginning to catch up to her.

He smiled. "I agree, and I do not know how I could possibly let you leave with your aunt and uncle when your place is here with me."

She nestled in even closer to him. "Whatever you wish, William. You may decide."

He paused, not knowing what to think of this sudden submissiveness, but he was willing to take advantage of it. "Then I will speak to your uncle in the morning, and we will marry as soon as we may."

She smiled affectionately at him. "Very well," she said softly. Closing her eyes, she relaxed into his embrace.

He watched her with pleasure, thinking of how many of his dreams had been fulfilled tonight, and how he would not trade this night for anything in the world. Soon he noted that her breathing had slowed, and a wave of tenderness rushed over him when he realized that she had fallen asleep in his arms. It was far too pleasant an experience to end quickly, although he would have to wake her soon in order to return her safely to her own room before anyone could discover them.

The next thing he knew he was being roused from a sound sleep by a knocking at the door. Momentarily he was disoriented, wondering why Wilkins did not come in to wake him as usual. Awareness of the warmth of Elizabeth's body against his brought memories flooding back, and panic struck at the idea of her being found in his room. Leaping out of bed, he pulled the curtains around the bed to disguise her presence. "I am coming!" he called, seizing his dressing gown and tying it around himself. Taking a deep breath, he opened the door and stepped through to his sitting room, where he found a flustered looking Wilkins.

"Sir, I am sorry to disturb you, but there is a problem. There is a fire at the Wheelers' cottage; there is some fear of it spreading, and Mr. Dawson is asking for you."

Darcy swore under his breath, raking his hand through his hair as he tried to think. "Very well, I shall come as soon as I am dressed. Are they saddling a horse for me?"

"Yes, sir," he said, not meeting Darcy's eyes.

Darcy had never seen his valet look this ill at ease before, and suddenly realized Wilkins must have come into his bedroom as was his custom, and discovered Elizabeth's presence, hence his retreat to the sitting room. Well, there was nothing to be done for it now. "Wait here," he instructed tersely.

Turning back into his bedroom and closing the door behind him, he went over to the bed and sat down. Elizabeth's eyes were open wide, whether in distress or surprise he could not tell. He leaned over to kiss her. "I must leave, my love. There is an emergency, a fire on the estate, and I must go at once. I am so very sorry to leave you right now; I know that the timing could not be worse."

Feeling suddenly shy as she realized her state of undress, she said, "Of course, I understand."

Recognizing her embarrassment, he took her nightgown and robe from where they had fallen and handed them to her. "I will return in a minute," he said, heading for his dressing room. He emerged shortly wearing a workman-like outfit of shirt and trousers. She was already out of bed, as decent as she could make herself, and he took her into his arms. "I am so very sorry to leave you like this, Elizabeth. My man Wilkins is without, and I will ask him to assist you in returning to your room. He already knows you are here, and he is the soul of discretion." Seeing her blush furiously, he added, "Not to worry, he approves of you. Please remember that I love you more than life itself." He stole one last kiss.

"Please be careful." She touched his cheek.

"I will," he replied, and departed.

Elizabeth kept on a brave face until he was out of the room, and then sank back onto the bed, her head in her hands. Her sangfroid of the previous night had completely evaporated, and shock, horror, and embarrassment had taken its place. What had she done? She felt ashamed and ill at the thought of what had occurred. How could she have allowed this to happen? How could she step out of that door and face Darcy's manservant, knowing that he knew what had transpired that night? She had never been so mortified in her life. A flush of humiliation filled her, but recognizing that she needed to be out of his bedroom as soon as possible, before anyone else discovered her, she resolutely went to the door and opened it.

The ever-efficient Wilkins stood outside, his eyes firmly averted. "Miss Bennet, I took the liberty of fetching some items from your room. I cannot claim any expertise in the matter of ladies' dress, but I hope this is satisfactory. If there is anything else you require, please do not hesitate to ask." He handed her a stack of items which included a dress, petticoats, shoes, stockings, and a hairbrush.

"Thank you, Wilkins," she said shakily. Retreating into the chamber, she dressed herself as well as she could. She looped her hair into a simple knot at the back, thinking with the ghost of an amused smile that Wilkins would never succeed as a lady's maid unless he remembered hairpins.

Darcy had not been completely correct in stating that Wilkins approved of Elizabeth, although he no doubt believed it himself. Wilkins in fact had no opinion of her. He had little direct contact with Miss Bennet up until this time, though he knew who she was, of course, and had carefully noted all available information about her. He was a man of powerful loyalty and deep admiration for his employer, and he saw his job as one of simplifying and improving Mr. Darcy's life. He had strong opinions on the clothes Mr. Darcy wore, the rooms Mr. Darcy stayed in, and the food Mr. Darcy ate. He withheld judgment on his master's friends and activities; if they made Mr. Darcy happy, Wilkins approved, if not, he did not. He did not see a need to have an opinion on the air Mr. Darcy breathed, for it was simply a necessity, and having observed his master closely during the last year in Hertfordshire, London, and Kent, he had come to the conclusion that this was the category in which Miss Elizabeth Bennet belonged. Mr. Darcy was happy when he was with her, and deeply unhappy when he was not, so there was no need for Wilkins to develop an opinion on her. She was simply necessary.

He was, however, pleased to see that she could conduct herself with appropriate dignity in the embarrassing situation in which she found herself, and he even went so far as to have a few unkind thoughts for Mr. Darcy regarding the position in which he had put her. When she emerged from Darcy's room, he asked her to wait in the sitting room until he indicated to her that the hallway was clear, and when he was finally able to usher her out safely, she gave him an amused, if somewhat embarrassed, smile with her thanks. Having successfully negotiated that task, his next goal was to find fresh linens for the beds, so that he could strip off the current sheets before the arrival of the housemaids, lest any gossip follow Mr. Darcy. He shook his head over the whole matter.

Elizabeth returned to her room only long enough to correct the details of her dress and to put up her hair. The last thing that she wanted at the moment was to sit alone with her thoughts, and sleep would be a hopeless proposition, and so she went downstairs even though it was far too early for breakfast. Although servants were busy throughout the house, none of the family were yet awake, so she elected for a brisk walk through the gardens to distract herself. Unfortunately, the slight soreness between her legs proved a constant reminder of the events of the night, as were the words that insisted on echoing in her mind, no matter how much she tried to stop them—*I am his mistress.* The words would not listen to any of her arguments that they were engaged, that this made no difference in the long term, that no one need know. She brooded over how they were to explain to her aunt and uncle why they wished to marry so quickly, with none of her family present, and she discovered no convincing answers.

Chapter 8

At breakfast, Mr. Gardiner informed her that Darcy would be unable to join them on their trip to Haddon Hall that day, as some urgent estate business had arisen. Elizabeth did her best to appear surprised and disappointed by this intelligence, and thought she had been fairly convincing. As the day progressed, however, it became apparent that Mrs. Gardiner at least had noticed she was somewhat out of spirits, asking several times if anything was troubling her, questions which her niece attempted to avoid by making reference to a sleepless night. Meanwhile, Elizabeth was busy trying to answer her own uncomfortable questions, which related to how this had come to pass, and her feelings about her premature loss of virtue. *His mistress.* That she was embarrassed and discomfited was obvious, and that she felt shame over her inability to refuse him was true as well, but she tried to remind herself that they had merely advanced the date of the event, and wondered why it should make such a difference to her. The truth, she finally recognized, was that she missed Darcy terribly. If she could only have been with him and had his reassurance, her distress would be significantly lessened.

On their return to Pemberley, she was exceedingly disappointed to find that he was still away from the house, and the servants seemed to have no news of him, apart from saying that he was expected to return in time for dinner. She eventually attempted to settle with a book, but found herself glancing out the window every few minutes to watch for his return. At one point, she saw two workmen approaching across the grassy hill, but the next time she looked out, she realized that one of them was Darcy himself, his shirt torn and filthy, his face streaked with soot, and with a companion who looked no better than he. She flushed as thoughts of the previous night filled her mind. As they came closer, she recognized the second man as his steward, and she watched in shocked fascination as Darcy clapped him on the back before walking off to the house.

She walked rapidly towards the front hall, and was half-way down the long staircase when she spotted Darcy being accosted by one of the footmen. "Mr. Darcy, sir, begging your pardon, but I wondered if you had any news. Mrs. Wheeler's sister Ann works in the kitchen, and we have all been worrying, sir."

"I assume you have already heard about the children?" Darcy asked somberly. At the footman's nod, he added, "Give me a quarter hour to make myself decent and I shall come to the kitchens myself to tell them what I know."

"Thank you, sir. They will appreciate it."

Darcy paused a moment, and then said, "On second thought, perhaps I should go there immediately." Part way across the hall Darcy spied Elizabeth on the steps. Their eyes met and held for

a minute, and the warmth in his went a long way towards soothing Elizabeth's nerves, as she saw his lips shape the word 'later.'
The relief that she felt, just knowing that he was in the house,
was both great and seemingly inexplicable.

When she returned downstairs for dinner, she found the
Gardiners and Georgiana, who was feeling somewhat better,
already present. Darcy joined them a little later than was his
wont, restored to his usual well turned-out self, his hair still
damp. Apart from lines of fatigue around his eyes, he looked no
different from usual. As he sat on the loveseat next to Elizabeth,
he leaned over to whisper in her ear, "I adore you." She looked at
him with gratitude and a blush, feeling a surprising sensation of
pleasurable completeness at his presence. Returning his attention
to the party at large, he asked after their travels, and seemed
interested in hearing of the splendors of the rose gardens of
Haddon Hall. When Mr. Gardiner asked about his day, he replied
only that he was attending to some business with his tenants.

He was as attentive to her as was possible in company, giving her warm glances and addressing questions to her whenever
possible, but eventually it occurred to her that all was not well.
He seemed on edge and uncomfortable. She wondered and worried as to the cause; whether it could be the events of the day, or
those of the previous night, and if so, what he was thinking. Her
stomach churned anxiously. She wished they could be alone so
that she could ask him, and seek his reassurance.

She found herself watching him carefully, almost obsessively,
and saw that he seemed to wince occasionally, and, just before
they were to go in to dinner, she observed that he was holding
his glass in a peculiarly stiff manner. Concerned, she waited until

the others were distracted, and reached over and took his hand. To her surprise, he tried to pull it away. She felt a sharp pang of rejection before recognizing that he was not avoiding her, but attempting to prevent her from seeing his hand, and her concern for him rose. Eyeing him suspiciously, she said quietly, "I would like to see your hand, Mr. Darcy."

"Miss Bennet, it is nothing to worry yourself over, merely a scrape," he responded rather shortly.

"Mr. Darcy," she said, her tone a warning. Their eyes locked in a brief battle, then Darcy, with an exasperated roll of his eyes, turned his hands so that she could see them. She bit her lip to stifle a gasp when she saw the burns, blisters, and scrapes that scored much of his palms and the inside surfaces of his fingers. After a first moment of shock, she reassured herself that they did not look deep, though certain to be very painful, and asked, "Have you put anything on them?"

"No need," he said in a voice that declared the subject closed.

"I beg to differ," she said. "Those require care. Excuse me, sir, I shall return shortly." She stood and exited before he could protest, as she was certain he would, then paused out in the hall, realizing that she had no idea where to locate the items she needed at Pemberley without creating more commotion than Darcy would wish. Finally she asked a servant to help her locate Mrs. Reynolds.

The housekeeper seemed surprised to see her. "How may I help you, Miss Bennet?"

"Mrs. Reynolds, I am looking for some oil of lavender, or perhaps oil of chamomile. Would you have something along those lines that I might use?"

Mrs. Reynolds promptly sent off a servant for the required items, then asked, "Is there a problem, miss?"

Elizabeth debated the suitability of telling her, then, recollecting the obvious affection between the two, elected frankness. "Mr. Darcy burned his hands today, and I believe that oil of lavender will be beneficial to his burns."

The housekeeper's respect for the young lady increased as she noted that Miss Bennet was not only concerned about the master, but knew remedies as well. "Will you be requiring bandages as well, then?"

Elizabeth paused. "It would be a good idea, if he accepts them."

A brief smile crossed Mrs. Reynolds' face. "Just a moment, miss. Let me see what I can find." She returned several minutes later, followed by a girl with a basin, towels, and strips of clean linen. Leading the way to a small room near the dining-parlour, she laid out the supplies, and asked conversationally, "May I ask, miss, how you convinced him to accept this? He is usually reluctant to be cared for."

Elizabeth hid a smile without complete success. "I did not offer him a choice."

With a shrewd look, the housekeeper said, "Then perhaps you should bring him here; he may listen better to you than to me."

Accepting this directive, Elizabeth returned to him and quietly asked, "Mr. Darcy, would you be so kind as to accompany me for a moment?"

Looking somewhat displeased, especially since they seemed to have garnered the attention of the others, he replied, "I do not believe it necessary, Miss Bennet."

Her eyes narrowed. Leaning towards him, she whispered in his ear, "If you do not cooperate, sir, I shall be forced to take desperate action."

A slight smile crossed his lips. "And what would *that* entail, Miss Bennet?"

"I am sorry to resort to vile threats, but if you do not join me, I will tell your sister what you have done to your hands," she whispered.

"That is blackmail!"

"I am glad to see that you do not underestimate me, sir!"

He sighed deeply. "Very well, Miss Bennet, I am at your command." He followed her to the prepared room. His eyes narrowed as he took in the presence of Mrs. Reynolds, but obediently complied with her instructions to seat himself and hold out his hands.

"Oh, Master William," the housekeeper said reproachfully as she surveyed the damage, and shook her head disapprovingly. "We shall need to clean those off before anything else. I cannot believe that Wilkins let you out like this without a word to me!"

Elizabeth had to press her hand against her mouth to hide a smile at this interaction and at the distinctly sulky look on Darcy's face at that moment. "There is no need for all this," he insisted. "Miss Bennet's concern is touching, but this is hardly serious."

"Miss Bennet has twice the sense you do, Mr. Darcy!" Mrs. Reynolds said tartly. "Now, hold still while I clean them. However did you do that?" She pointed to a line of raw flesh across his fingers.

"Bucket line," he said succinctly. "I have altogether the wrong sort of calluses."

Seeing the obvious flash of pain cross his face as the process was begun, Elizabeth, thinking that he might like some privacy, said, "Perhaps I should rejoin the others now."

He looked up at her. "Oh, no, Miss Bennet. You forced me into this; you will have to stay to comfort me." He grimaced at a particularly painful sensation.

"I fear Mr. Darcy has never been the best patient," Mrs. Reynolds said in a soothing voice.

"I am hardly surprised. I have noticed he prefers to take care of others, rather than of himself," Elizabeth teased, hoping to distract him from his discomfort.

Mrs. Reynolds glanced at her shrewdly, noting the looks that she and Darcy were exchanging, and it occurred to her that perhaps there were other things Wilkins had failed to report to her. She smiled to herself as she applied the remedies, then pulled out the bandages.

"No bandages," Darcy said definitely, pulling his hands away.

"Sir, they need bandaging. This hand, at the very least," Mrs. Reynolds argued.

Elizabeth rested her hand lightly on his shoulder for a moment. He looked up at her and sighed, seeing the determined look in her eye. "Very well. But just this hand," he said resignedly. "Do you plan to always be this insistent, Miss Bennet?"

She gave the matter a moment's consideration. "Yes, I do," she said with certainty. "Do you plan to always be this recalcitrant, Mr. Darcy?"

"You may count on it, madam!" he retorted.

"Well," she said with a playful smile, "I am glad that we understand one other, then."

Darcy looked back at Mrs. Reynolds in time to catch a broad smile on her face as she tied off the bandage. "You need not agree with her so easily, you know, Mrs. Reynolds. You are supposed to be on *my* side, after all!"

"Not to worry, sir; I can tell already that Miss Bennet and I will get along very well indeed," the housekeeper said significantly. "Now, we should change those tomorrow. I shall speak to Wilkins about it, and I shall give him some laudanum for you as well; you may need it tonight to sleep."

"That will *not* be necessary," he stated firmly.

"Nonetheless, he will have it if you need it," Mrs. Reynolds said as she gathered her supplies.

Darcy offered Elizabeth his arm, but as they departed, he did not turn towards the dining-parlour, and instead led her into his study. For a moment Elizabeth worried that he was angry with her for her insistence, but as he caught her to him, she realized that he had a different agenda in mind. She went into his embrace with a sigh of heartfelt relief, leaning her head against his chest, comforted by the sound of his heart beating. This was what she had needed all day.

"Are you well, my love?" he asked gently, kissing her hair. She nodded, not calm enough for words. He added, "I must apologize again for leaving you today; I would have much preferred to spend it by your side. I hope it has not been too difficult?"

"Now that you are here, all is well."

"And before?" he asked perceptively.

She shrugged, and evaded his question. "I missed you."

Her words were sufficiently sweet to Darcy's ears to cause him to overlook any other meanings to her response. "I missed you as well," he said warmly, "and I worried about you." When she made no response, he added, "I plan to speak to your uncle tonight, if you have no objection. I apologize that my plans in that regard were delayed."

She looked up at him with a smile. "I understand some things are unavoidable."

He held up his bandaged hand. "I can see that there are going to be an increasing number of unavoidable things in my life!" he said with rueful good humour.

"I am glad you recognized its inevitability. You were very well-behaved about it," she said in as grave a manner as she could manage.

He looked down at her with a teasing smile. "Well, Miss Bennet, I *was* quite cooperative; now I believe that I deserve to be distracted from my pain."

"There are any number of excellent books that I can recommend to you, sir," she said playfully, "or perhaps I could ask your sister to play for you."

"That was not precisely what I had in mind."

"I thought you wanted me to avoid encouraging you."

His smile was devastating. "How much trouble can I cause when I cannot use my hands?"

"True enough." With a mischievous smile, she took his arm with the unbandaged hand carefully by the wrist. Lifting it to her face, she brushed the back of his hand lightly against her cheek, then began tormenting him by covering it with feather-light kisses from the line of his sleeve to his uninjured fingertips, to which she gave a little extra attention. "Is that better?" she asked impishly.

"Much more effective than laudanum," he responded in a somewhat strangled voice. He bent to kiss her, but she ducked away from him, standing on her toes to touch his neck with her lips, teasing him as he had so effectively done to her in the past.

"Elizabeth, please . . . "

Taking pity on him, she pulled his head down to hers and allowed him to claim her lips. His kiss was passionate, but it also seemed somehow distracted. She pulled back and looked up at him, a concerned look on her face. "I can tell that something is the matter, but not what it may be."

He gathered her to him somewhat clumsily, avoiding the use of his hands, and buried his face in her hair. He was silent for a moment, then said heavily, "It was a difficult day, and parts of it have stayed in my mind."

"Will you not tell me about it?"

He sighed. "Come sit with me, then." He settled himself in a large armchair, and opened his arms to her, and with a slight blush, she sat on his lap and leaned her head against his shoulder. "It was dreadful, naturally," he began. "The family lost everything they owned, and there was so little that I could do to help them. They were devastated, and . . . " His voice trailed off.

"And what?" she asked softly.

"Are you certain that you wish to hear this? It is not pretty, I must warn you."

"If you had to see it, then I want to hear about it."

"Their two youngest children were still in the house," he said, his voice tired and strained. "We could not reach them until the flames were mostly doused; their father's leg was crushed when he tried to go in too soon. Thank heaven there was no wind! I found one of them when we finally went in—that was when I did this." He opened his hands. "There was nothing that could be done; he had hardly been touched by the fire, but the smoke must have been enough. I carried his body out to his parents." He paused. "I did not know him, but I remember when he was born; it was shortly after I took over managing the estate."

She felt a wrenching sensation as he first spoke, realizing that he had placed himself in danger, and then her feelings shifted to sympathy for his pain. She held him close, knowing that there was nothing she could say, but wanting to comfort him. He permitted her to stroke his hair for a minute, then turned his head to kiss her hand absently. "I know that it is foolish, but I feel as if somehow I ought to have been able to prevent it," he said, his tone closer to his usual one.

"That *is* foolish," she said gently, "but I understand that you might feel that way. Is there anything that can be done for them now?"

"I believe that it is all in hand. They are staying with family, and I had some clothes and other necessities sent down to them. Some of the other tenants will work their fields until they can manage again. I have told them that we will rebuild, but that will take time—there will be enough work just clearing the site. There is little else that can be done at present. I will ask Georgiana to call on the family tomorrow."

"If you wish, I can accompany her."

"She would appreciate that, I know; she finds these duties somewhat uncomfortable. It is kind of you to offer."

"It will be *my* responsibility soon enough."

He glanced at her in surprise. "So it will be," he said slowly. "I had not thought of it that way." Oddly, he had given little thought to the idea of Elizabeth as Mistress of Pemberley, and he felt a twinge of jealousy at the thought of having to share her attention.

"I see that you have some doubts about that; I know that I am inexperienced, but I will learn, and I am not afraid to ask questions."

"Now you are the one jumping to conclusions. I have no doubts about your ability; I was merely contemplating the sad fact that I will not be the sole focus of your attention. I am a very selfish soul, you know."

She kissed him affectionately. "You are the one I love; responsibility for Pemberley simply happens to come with you."

He caressed her cheek with the back of his hand. "Do you have any idea how much it means to hear you say that you love me?"

"You may hear it any time you wish," she said lightly, again finding discussing her feelings for him to be difficult. "But do you suppose that the others are still waiting for us to begin dinner?"

"Let them wait," Darcy said, sounding every inch the high-handed Master of Pemberley she had once thought him. "I have had to do without you all day, and I need a little time to hold you and tell you how ardently I love you before I have to return to calling you 'Miss Bennet' and keeping my hands to myself."

Elizabeth had no desire to object to this idea, and settled herself comfortably in his arms. A thought occurred to her. "William," she said.

"Yes, my love?"

"I would like to point out that while I have considerately remained composed during our discourse, I do have strenuous objections to you taking risks such as walking into burning buildings."

"Dearest, I appreciate your concern, but I also have responsibilities which sometimes you will not like," he said tenderly.

"You also have responsibilities to me now, and someday to our children, and they include keeping yourself safe," she said firmly. "I would like you to think for just a minute how *you* would feel if I were putting myself in that sort of danger."

Darcy, who had his own worries about the dangers Elizabeth faced which were unfortunately triggered by her choice of words, tightened his arms around her and buried his face in her hair. "Your point is taken," he said, his voice muffled, seeing images of his mother's near-fatal illness after Georgiana's birth, and her death five years later along with her newborn son.

Elizabeth felt his tension, and without fully understanding its source, said, "Perhaps that was a poor example; I am forgetting that you are far better at the art of worrying than I am. But you are too dear to me to risk, so please take care."

"I shall," he said, deliberately putting aside the images of the past. "You may count on the fact that I want to be with you." Unwilling to continue in this vein, he changed the subject definitively by capturing her mouth with a kiss with an eloquence spoke of his love for her, and it was some time before either of them gave further consideration to anything besides the other.

They eventually did rejoin the rest of the party for dinner, where Darcy was required to recount some of the day's events when his bandaged hand was noted. Georgiana, who was acquainted with the family from various estate events, was much concerned by the news, and relieved that Elizabeth would accompany her on her call to the family.

Once the ladies had withdrawn after dinner, Darcy poured out generous helpings of port for himself and Mr. Gardiner. It had been a very long day, and this was not an interview he was anticipating with any sort of pleasure.

"Mr. Gardiner," he began, "I am glad we have a few minutes here, as there is a matter I would like to discuss with you. It would be better if I could broach it with Mr. Bennet, but in his absence, I believe you to be the appropriate person to whom to address this."

"Well, this sounds serious! I shall be happy to help however I may."

Darcy swirled the port in his glass, and watched it as if fascinated. "As you know, Miss Bennet and I did not have an opportunity to discuss a wedding date before we left Longbourn. We have been considering the matter, and have come to the conclusion that we would like to marry as soon as possible."

"Well, I certainly see no problem if you wish to have the wedding as soon as we return to Longbourn. I daresay that Mrs. Bennet can manage most of the arrangements, although she may be disappointed by the lack of frills!"

"In fact, sir, when I said as soon as possible, what I meant was immediately, or at least, as soon as I can obtain a license. I would propose that I ride to Matlock tomorrow; if the bishop is in residence, I should be able to arrange it quickly. Otherwise I will have to send to London, which would delay matters by a few days." He looked up wearing his calmest demeanour to meet Mr. Gardiner's puzzled gaze.

Mr. Gardiner took a sip of port. "Why the hurry, Mr. Darcy?"

"I spent quite some time today trying to devise answers to that question, ranging from why we would want the ceremony to be at Pemberley to the strength of my devotion to your niece, but the facts of the matter are these: something happened last night that should not have, and I am anxious to regularize matters as soon as may be."

Darcy's anxiety rose as there was no immediate answer from Mr. Gardiner. Finally he said, "I suppose that you realize, Mr. Darcy, that you are fortunate to be confessing this to me rather than to Lizzy's father."

"I have no doubt of that, sir," Darcy said carefully. "I also doubt there is anything that you can say to me on the subject that I have not already said to myself."

"So I would imagine." Mr. Gardiner had already drawn his own conclusions regarding Darcy's sense of responsibility. "Well, you have my consent, for what that is worth; it sounds like the most reasonable course under the circumstances. Do you plan to write to Mr. Bennet, or to present this as a *fait accompli?*"

Darcy grimaced. "Frankly, sir, between telling him to his face and giving him weeks to become more angry with me before I face him, I would choose the former."

Mr. Gardiner laughed. "I suspect that is wise of you. I shall try to put in a good word for you there, and point out that you at least deserve credit for your honesty. I must say I am beginning to feel some trepidation for when my own children reach this age!"

"I fear it can begin much earlier than this," Darcy said, thinking of Georgiana at Ramsgate.

"I hesitate to imagine. Perhaps we should join the ladies, then, as it seems we will have much to discuss," said Mr. Gardiner, which sentiment Darcy heartily endorsed.

The ladies took the intelligence of the wedding plans in good grace when Darcy and Mr. Gardiner rejoined them; Georgiana was delighted that she would have her new sister so much sooner than expected, and Mrs. Gardiner, having had ample opportunity to observe the attraction between the young couple, thought only that they were most eager to marry. Elizabeth said little beyond concurring with the plans.

Darcy was beginning to feel decidedly on edge. He was weary in mind and body from the events of the day, but it was his conduct of the previous night that was troubling him most. Since being back in the comfort of his home and away from other distractions, he was growing increasingly disturbed as he considered what he had done. During the day he had used the danger and horror of the fire to shield himself with limited success; feelings of shame and self-loathing kept intruding. He was not unaware that part of the reason he was the first into the burning cottage was to prove to himself that even if he had been untrustworthy, uncaring, and self-seeking the night before, he could at least still manage to be brave and responsible. But even that was a cowardly act. He had without question violated almost every principle by which he lived his life for a purely selfish and unworthy motive, without a thought as to how it would affect anyone else. He could not even make the excuse of having been out of control; no, he knew very well that there had been a moment when he made an active decision to proceed with seducing Elizabeth. True, he had not been in the clearest frame of mind at the time, and his desire for her had been such as to cloud his thinking, but that was no excuse. He had behaved despicably. Elizabeth might be inclined to forgive him, but he was nowhere near forgiving himself. She had always been generous with her forgiveness of his faults, a fact he appreciated, since he had been in need of it so often, but even Mr. Gardiner had let him off without the tongue-lashing he so richly deserved. He felt oddly grateful for the pain in his hands. He ought to suffer in some fashion, and without that discomfort he would feel even worse.

He did have a good idea who would be likely to give him what he deserved, though, and so it was not without a certain amount of trepidation that he asked Mrs. Reynolds to join him in his study later that evening.

"Mrs. Reynolds, there is an upcoming event for which I will need your assistance in planning."

"Certainly, sir. What would you like me to do?"

"First there is something I must tell you, which is that two weeks ago Miss Bennet did me the honour of agreeing to become my wife. We agreed not to announce the engagement immediately, since she wished to have an opportunity to experience Pemberley without all the expectations that would be put upon her as the future mistress."

Her face lit up, although this intelligence was not completely unexpected; she had never before seen such warm behaviour on his part towards a woman. She was very pleased with the tidings, as she had long been hoping to see him settle himself at Pemberley and produce some young Darcys to fill the hallways. "That is joyful news, sir. She is a delightful young lady."

He cleared his throat, recalling her siding with Elizabeth against him in the matter of treating his burns, and suspecting that it would not be the only time he would face such an alliance. "We have decided that we prefer to have an immediate wedding, and it is with this that I will need your assistance in making arrangements. I believe that the day after tomorrow will suit admirably."

She looked at him in some confusion, uncertain how to interpret this information. Finally, she decided that he must not be serious, and smiled. "Is that a jest, sir?"

"Not at all, Mrs. Reynolds. Now, I realize that there are certain arrangements that must be made. I will be away most of tomorrow, and I would like you to consult with Miss Bennet as to . . . "

"Mr. Darcy," she interrupted, an obvious measure of her distress. "We cannot possibly manage your wedding on such short notice! What of the guests who must be notified, what of Miss Bennet's family? And she must have an appropriate gown, and Lord knows what else!"

"We do not plan to invite any guests other than Georgiana, Mr. and Mrs. Gardiner, and possibly my aunt and uncle, if they are available. No trimmings are necessary, and if Miss Bennet is not satisfied with her own apparel, perhaps one of my mother's gowns could be altered to fit her; her height is much the same, I believe."

She made one more attempt. "Sir, surely she deserves to have a fine wedding, with her family at her side, rather than a patched-together affair!"

She certainly does, he thought, *and it is my fault that she will not have it.* He leaned back in his chair, his face unreadable. "Nonetheless, that is the plan."

Her eyes narrowed as they waged a brief silent battle. There was an obvious shift in her voice from the respectful family servant to the strict disciplinarian of his youth as she asked sharply, "Mr. Darcy, is there some reason why this must occur so quickly that would compensate for all the difficulties involved?"

"The matter is decided. That will be all, Mrs. Reynolds."

Her voice was filled with suspicion. "Did you compromise the young lady?"

His only response was to look at her with the gaze that had withered the arguments of many a difficult opponent.

"Fitzwilliam Darcy, if you were not too big, I swear I would put you across my knee and give you what you so richly deserve! How *could* you? What would your mother have said? I can tell you what your father would have said, and you would have had worse than a beating there! You were raised better than that. This is behaviour I would have expected from George Wickham, not you! And you call yourself a gentleman—I am most thoroughly ashamed of you!"

He made no response, nor did his face change, apart from a brief wince at the mention of Wickham. She continued to glare at him furiously until he finally closed his eyes in a well understood signal of defeat. She allowed him to suffer for a few more moments before she spoke again, her voice somewhat softened. "Well, there is nothing to be done for it now, I suppose. It will have to wait another day at least, though; the services for the Wheeler children will be the day after tomorrow, and it would be disrespectful to have your wedding the same day. And we must have a reason . . . " She paused for a moment before continuing, "We will put it about that the Bishop is set upon officiating at your wedding himself, so it has to be done while you can both be at Matlock; that also means that the ceremony will be held at the cathedral, which will draw away any attention from the lack of attendance by Miss Bennet's family. We can arrange a celebration here as well—yes, I believe that is the best idea. Does that suit, sir?"

"Admirably," he said quietly.

"I shall consult with Miss Bennet in the morning, then, sir." She rose to her feet somewhat stiffly.

"Thank you, Mrs. Reynolds. I leave it in your capable hands." Once she had left, he leaned back in his chair, running his fingers through his hair. Oddly enough, he felt more relief than anything else at their discussion, and was thankful to have handed off the responsibility for planning the event. He had been racking his brain all day in an attempt to invent a reasonable excuse for marrying so soon, and Mrs. Reynolds had solved that dilemma inside a minute.

Feeling more relaxed than he had all day, he returned to the drawing room, in hopes of finding Elizabeth still there. He wished to speak with her privately, to inform her of what had been decided, and that she need not worry about a similar loss of control on his part again. However, when he arrived, he discovered that she had already retired for the night. Disappointed, he joined the Gardiners briefly for conversation, before making his own excuses.

Elizabeth was preparing for bed when a not completely unexpected knock came at the door. She opened it to find Darcy on the other side, and quickly moved to allow him to enter before he could be seen by anyone. She had wondered if he planned to come to her, and had been unable to decide whether she feared or wished for his appearance more, and how she would behave if he did come. Now that it came to the moment, though, a smile came naturally to her face, and she felt breath-less, but to her surprise he did no more than touch her face lightly in greeting.

"I have been making arrangements this evening, and I wanted to inform you of them tonight since I plan to ride to Matlock at first light," he said. This was his opportunity to prove he had mended his ways, that he could be trusted in the most challeng-ing situation possible, and challenges certainly did not come any greater than being alone with her in her room while she was in her nightclothes. He forced his thoughts away from her lovely form, and determinedly focused upon the conversation.

"And what do your arrangements entail?"

"I have spoken to Mrs. Reynolds regarding plans for our wedding, and she has decreed that it is to be in three days' time, assuming that I have no difficulty arranging matters with the Bishop and obtaining the license. I believe she plans to consult with you regarding it in the morning. I also wanted to mention, in case you were planning to write to anyone in your family, that your uncle agreed that it might be wisest not to inform your fam-ily of our plans until we can do so personally, though . . . " he paused to smile endearingly, "if you are of a different opinion, we can certainly review that decision."

"Well done, sir," she replied with a laugh. "For a moment I feared you had forgotten our agreement regarding consulting me."

He looked slightly uncomfortable. "I am trying to learn, though it may take me some time, but I will point out in my own defense that you did say last night that I could make the decision regarding when we married."

"True enough, although I could argue that you were taking advantage of me in a defenseless moment," she retorted cheerfully.

The colour drained from his face at her words, and a look of deep guilt came over him. "I know that only too well, Elizabeth, and if I felt that there were anything in the world that I could do to make up for it, I would do so without hesitation, but as it is, all I can do is to say that I recognize my fault, and apologize from the bottom of my heart, and hope that someday you will be able to forgive me."

The distress in his face pained her deeply. "William, you misunderstand me completely," she said gently. "My joke, and it was obviously a poor one, was that I offered to let you make the decision on the wedding *when I was half asleep*, and thus not at my best. I bear you no anger over what happened last night. As I said then, you did nothing which I did not permit, and I take responsibility for my own actions."

"You may have permitted it, but only after I intentionally did everything within my power to make it difficult for you to refuse," said Darcy, feeling honour bound him to confess the full degree of his fault.

"You may have attempted to persuade, but you did nothing to force me. It may have been poor judgment on both our parts, but I refuse to dwell on what might have been," she said, less than comfortable with the course of this conversation.

He looked at her in unhappy bafflement, leading Elizabeth to the conclusion that he would prefer to have her rail at him than to refuse to blame him, but she could recognize that his distress would not be alleviated by any amount of reassurance. A smile touched the corners of her lips as she conceived of a suitable revenge for his stubbornness, but she debated whether she had the audacity to follow it through. She could hardly believe she was considering it, though it would certainly relieve some of his anxiety and distress. Impulsively, she stepped up to him and began to untie his cravat.

"Elizabeth, what are you doing?" he asked in a strained voice, looking down at her tempting form, clad only in the night attire which he knew so well how to remove.

She dropped the cravat on the floor, and proceeded to his coat. "I am undoing the buttons of your coat, sir."

"I am aware of that; my question is why."

Elizabeth hid a smile. "My proximate goal is to remove your clothing. Following that it is my intention to seduce you, sir." She paused briefly in her endeavours to kiss his neck lightly.

"Elizabeth, it was *my* intention in coming here tonight to demonstrate to you I can be trusted not to take advantage of you again, and you are making it extremely difficult!"

She finished with his coat and began on his waistcoat. "I cannot see why. You have made your point admirably, and now the question is whether *I* can be trusted not to take advantage of *you*, and I fear the answer to that question is no." Realizing that she would need at least minimal cooperation from him if she were to have any success in removing his coats, she slipped her hands inside them and tried to tempt him by caressing his chest through the fine lawn of his shirt. Moving to press her body against his, she felt the evidence of his arousal as she opened the collar of his shirt and kissed the exposed hollows of his neck.

"Elizabeth," he groaned. She continued to spread kisses across his neck while she pressed her hips against his provocatively until, with a moan, he captured her mouth with his in a kiss that spoke of undeniable hunger. She took advantage of the moment to slip his coats off his shoulders, letting them drop to the floor.

The process of seducing him, she was fascinated to discover, was at least as exciting to her as the known delights of his touch. In the past, he had always taken the lead in touching her, and she was finding this reversal a heady experience. She ran her hands lightly across his shoulders, and drew them tantalizingly slowly down his back before beginning the process of extricating his shirt from his breeches. She had just managed to slide her hands onto the warm skin of his waist when he raised his mouth from hers. "Well, my love, if you are bent on this process of seduction, perhaps I should mention to you that removing your own clothes would be at least as effective in that regard as removing mine," he said.

"I appreciate the intelligence, sir," she said teasingly as she explored the warmth of his chest. "Perhaps I should investigate the truth of that hypothesis, once I have had a chance to enjoy myself with this." Although somewhat reluctant to give up the pleasure of touching him, she removed her hands and stepped back. With a seductive smile playing across her lips, she untied her dressing gown and slipped it off, allowing it to fall to the floor in a pile of silk. Aroused by the expression on his face as he watched, she undid the ties of her nightgown one at a time, making the discovery that he seemed even more affected by the process as she proceeded more slowly. Finally she slid first one shoulder, then the other out of her nightgown, so only her fingertips were holding it up, and then she let that drop as well.

It was beyond understanding, she decided, how he could excite her so much simply by looking at her. "Pray do not forget your hair, my love; that is a very effective tool in seduction as well," he said, his voice hoarse. She obligingly undid the braid she had made for the night, and shook her long curls loose with a beguiling smile, looking up at him as she touched the tip of her tongue to her lips enticingly.

Darcy had reached the end of his endurance for this delightful game. He strode towards her, his hands going to tear at the buttons of his breeches until, with a muffled curse, he discovered just how extraordinarily painful the process of dealing with buttons was likely to be for him for the next few days. Elizabeth, recognizing his difficulty, pushed his hands away, and said with a flirtatious smile, "Please allow me." She undid the buttons, though at a far slower pace than he would have chosen, and had the inspiration of interrupting that activity periodically to stroke the bulge in the front of his breeches, enjoying the sense of power she felt when he moaned her name pleadingly.

"I am simply doing everything within my power to make it difficult for you to refuse me, William," she teased him provocatively.

"Believe me, I could not refuse you if I tried at this point." He kissed her neck and nibbled at her ear. "And you have me at a distinct disadvantage, madam, since I am unable to use my hands as effectively as I would like to make you suffer as much as I am suffering at the moment."

She smiled wickedly at him as she continued the process of removing his breeches. As soon as he was free of them he said with a roguish look, "There is, however, nothing wrong with the rest of my body!" He propelled her backwards to the delightful accompaniment of her laughter until she was forced onto the bed. Holding her shoulders down with the backs of his hands, he kissed her greedily, then sought her nipple with his mouth and suckled her until she writhed and moaned beneath him. Once he was certain she was ready for him, with a passionate demand quite different from the gentleness he had shown the previous night, he thrust himself deep inside her, and possessed her with hard, rapid strokes that demonstrated the strength of his desire and drove her to the peaks of arousal until she was engulfed by waves of exquisite pleasure. Triggered by her moans of ecstasy, his release followed almost immediately.

When he at length surfaced from the oblivion to which she had led him, he said with concern, "I apologize for my loss of control, my love. I hope that I was not too rough with you?"

She shook her head. "I found it very . . . exciting," she said, smiling with the memory. "I believe I enjoyed seducing you, as well."

"You, my love, are a menace!" exclaimed Darcy.

"Is that a complaint, sir?"

"Not at all! I am quite content to have been seduced so effectively. And, as Shakespeare says, 'Therefore 'tis meet that noble minds keep ever with their likes; for who so firm that cannot be seduced?' "

"Sir, I cry foul; learning quotes on seduction is not a part of a young lady's education. You shall have to choose another topic."

"Perhaps it should be part of their education—there are many gentlemen who would think it a good cause." He caressed her cheek.

"Then seduction, perhaps, is one of the skills a truly accomplished young lady must possess, along with a thorough knowledge of music, dancing, and singing?"

"I would say so," he said with mock gravity, "though I might point out that if you wish to truly excel at seduction, you will need, as my aunt Catherine would say, to practice it quite constantly."

She nipped his shoulder affectionately. "I will have to consider how to obtain my practice, then."

"Solely in the interest of furthering your education, I will volunteer to be the subject of any further experiments you choose to undertake."

"That is one of the many things I admire about you, William— your constant attention to the improvement of my mind."

" 'Let me not to the marriage of true minds admit impediment,' my love."

"A much fairer subject, sir. 'Young men's minds are always changeable.' "

"But hardly a kind response! Let me see—'Nature that framed us of our elements, warring within our breast for regiment, doth teach us all to have aspiring minds.' "

Elizabeth smiled mischievously. " 'Beauty stands in the admiration only of weak minds led captive.' "

"Unkind again! I shall refrain from continuing this battle, and kiss you instead."

Elizabeth had no objection to this plan. "I wish that I could stay with you like this forever, and never have to leave to face the world."

"I believe that I could find it in my heart to share that sentiment, but is the world so difficult to face?" He stroked her hair, enjoying the fine texture of it, and wound a curl around his finger, thinking of all the nights he had dreamed of tangling his fingers in her tresses. He still could hardly believe that she was his.

Elizabeth coloured, not wishing to burden him with her daytime distress, especially as she could hardly claim any lack of responsibility tonight. "Not so difficult, no," she said. In the silence that followed, she realized that some of her comfort had been lost with her misleading words, and thought of her resolve to share more of her thoughts and feelings with him, as she wished he would for her. Before she could think better of it, she divulged the truth. "But I had a difficult time of it today. When you are with me, this feels so right, so . . . predestined, but when we were apart today, I felt . . . " She could not quite bring herself to say the words.

He caught the serious intent in her voice. "What did you feel?" he asked gently.

Tears pricked at the corners of her eyes, and she turned her face into his shoulder, shaking her head in response.

Worried, he said, "Please, Elizabeth, tell me. Do not shut me out, I beg you."

She took a deep breath. Her voice was quiet, and somewhat muffled by his body, as she said, "It is uncomfortable to feel I am your mistress."

Her words were like a sudden wound in his side. He caught her face in his hands, ignoring the pain of his burns, and forced her to look at him. "Do not *ever* think that way again! You are not my mistress; you are my . . . please bear with me; what I say may disturb you, or even seem heretical, but it is how I feel . . . you are my wife, Elizabeth. It has not yet been blessed by the church, but last night you and I took one another as husband and wife. Every word I will say during our wedding is already true, and as God hears prayers, he knows that my commitment to you is every bit as solemn and holy to me now as it will be when we kneel before the altar; and he knows that in my heart I have already taken you to have and to hold from this day forward, for better for worse, for richer for poorer, in sickness and in health, to love and to cherish, till death us do part." He came to a sudden halt; he was not accustomed to revealing his private beliefs, and he was afraid that he might have shocked her.

She looked searchingly at him, considering his words. She would never have thought of it that way, and was surprised to discover that he held such radical ideas, but could see how it was consistent with his attitudes, values, and sense of honour. She could see this was an issue of some solemnity to him, and wondered what other depths he had yet to reveal to her. Slowly she nodded; she could accept what he had said.

He let out his breath in relief that her reaction was so temperate. Yet he was still concerned regarding her worries. "Do I shock you?"

Her face lightened with the playful smile that he loved so much. "No, I am not shocked, though I had not known that I was marrying a closet Anabaptist!"

"Hardly that!" he said with a laugh. "No, I value the worth of the Church in our society, and I believe in the importance of public ceremony and blessing. Why are you smiling at me like that?"

She laughed, nestling close against him. "This is an unusual setting for a theological discussion."

"I cannot argue your point. It is, however, an excellent setting for telling you how much I love you, my dearest, loveliest Elizabeth."

She allowed her kisses to speak for her in reply, and enjoyed holding him close to her until the fatigue of sleepless nights overtook them both.

Darcy had, as planned, ridden off at first light, shortly after Wilkins had hunted him down in Elizabeth's rooms, much to the lady's chagrin. She took the opportunity, however, to steal a few more hours sleep before she rose for the day, finding herself in the unusual position of being last to the breakfast table. Once she was finished, she found Mrs. Reynolds anxiously awaiting meeting with her, to which Elizabeth readily consented.

"Miss Bennet," the housekeeper said, "I would just like to give you my personal best wishes, as well as those of the staff. I was delighted to hear that Mr. Darcy has finally chosen a bride, and I must say that I do not think that he could have done better." And *what a relief that he did not choose that Bingley woman—we would have lost half the staff!* she thought.

Elizabeth thanked her, and assured her that she was looking forward to working with her, and that Mr. Darcy had told her that she could do no better than to rely on Mrs. Reynolds.

"Well," said Mrs. Reynolds briskly, visibly pleased with this praise, "I understand that we have a wedding to plan in very short order."

Elizabeth hid a smile. "I am afraid that Mr. Darcy has his mind quite made up on this."

Mrs. Reynolds shook her head. "Do you know, he told me first that he wanted to have it *tomorrow*? Well, I set him straight on that, so we have a little time. But tell me, Miss Bennet, about what you would like for your wedding."

"Well," said Elizabeth somewhat hesitantly, "It will obviously be quite small, with no one outside immediate family—such family as I have in Derbyshire!—in attendance, and I believe that it can be quite simple, as well."

Mrs. Reynolds' skeptical face said very clearly that Miss Bennet had no idea of what marrying the Master of Pemberley involved. "Well, Miss Bennet, I appreciate that you are concerned with limiting demands on the staff in such a short period of time, but we must recognize that a certain degree of formality is to be expected on such an occasion. I assume that the Bishop will be wanting to officiate, so it will need to be held in the cathedral at Matlock, of course."

"I have no reason to think he would make any such request of the bishop," Elizabeth demurred.

Mrs. Reynolds cocked her head and looked at her in a puzzled manner. "Has Mr. Darcy spoken with you about this at all?"

Elizabeth laughed. "No, in fact, apart from soliciting my agreement to the date, we have not discussed it in the slightest. Apparently there is some information that I am missing. Perhaps you could help me understand?"

Shaking her head disapprovingly, Mrs. Reynolds said, "That boy will be the death of me! How can he expect you to plan a wedding under these circumstances? Miss Bennet, Mr. Darcy is the Bishop of Matlock's godson—the bishop is Lord Derby's cousin—and there is a lovely chapel attached to the cathedral which would be delightful for a small wedding. I assume Lord and Lady Derby will attend as well."

"Ah," said Elizabeth with a smile. "Yes, I can see that he neglected a few details. Perhaps it might make sense to include Miss Darcy and Mrs. Gardiner in this planning, as they might understand the implications of all this better than I."

"Of course, Miss Bennet, if you wish; but do keep in mind that this is *your* wedding, and you may make the choices you wish!"

"Mrs. Reynolds, I am extremely particular about one aspect of my wedding, and that is the bridegroom; as long as Mr. Darcy is there, the rest is of little importance to me, and I am happy to take advice from you and Miss Darcy on the rest."

She could not have pleased the housekeeper more. She believed Miss Bennet was no fortune-hunter, but evidence of devotion to the master was always welcome.

Once Georgiana and Mrs. Gardiner joined them, planning began in earnest, with Elizabeth looking on in some bemusement. Questions arose about a celebration for the tenants, but Elizabeth vetoed the idea of any sort of wedding breakfast, given the distance from Matlock. A final issue was a dress for Elizabeth; there was an immediate unanimous conclusion that her traveling clothes were simply unsuitable for such an occasion, and that it would be near impossible to have anything new made to order in so short a time. Fortunately, Mrs. Reynolds seemed to have a solution in hand for this as well, producing as if by magic a lovely and elegant cream-coloured gown of an older style decorated with the finest of lace and adornments. Georgiana, obviously recognizing it, announced it to be the perfect solution.

"I believe that this would be close to your size, Miss Bennet, and it would take only a few minor alterations of the sleeves and waistline to bring the style up to date."

"Whose is it?" Elizabeth asked, fingering the folds of fine material.

"It belonged to Lady Anne; it was a favourite of hers for balls," Mrs. Reynolds said proudly.

Elizabeth looked at the dress in silence for some moments, considering how Darcy would respond. Finally she said slowly, "I will discuss it with Mr. Darcy, and if he feels it to be appropriate, I would be honoured to wear it, but without any alterations as to style; if I am to wear his mother's gown, it should be as she wore it."

Mrs. Reynolds nodded, her eyes suspiciously shiny. "Mr. Darcy suggested that you wear one of his mother's gowns, and this is the obvious choice. Perhaps we should try a fitting to see if it will suit?"

Not an hour later, Elizabeth was once more feeling slightly overwhelmed as she was surrounded by three seamstresses taking measurements and pinning the hem of the lovely dress. It was far richer than anything she had ever worn in the past; she could see that she would have to ask Georgiana if she could borrow some jewelry to wear with it, as what little she had with her would look foolish next to such elegance.

"A gusset here, I think, Mrs. Reynolds," said one of the seamstresses, "and the hem will need to come up, of course, but otherwise I believe that it will suit quite well."

The housekeeper negotiated the arrangements to ensure it would be ready by midday the following day, as a somewhat bemused Elizabeth looked on, wondering what Darcy would say to all of this.

Chapter 9

Elizabeth discovered quickly just how much interest a new Mistress of Pemberley could generate. Although Darcy had only acknowledged the engagement the previous evening, the news had spread astonishingly quickly; when she accompanied Georgiana in calling on the bereaved tenant family, dozens of other tenants found a need to visit just at that moment as well, and at the later church service, she questioned whether anyone had heard a word of the sermon, given that every eye seemed to be fixed on her. Mrs. Reynolds pronounced her officially not at home to callers, pointing out that if she spent her time satisfying the curiosity of all the neighbours, she would have no time to prepare for the wedding.

Darcy managed to return by afternoon, having succeeded in his quest to meet with the bishop and obtaining the license, and slightly shamefacedly admitted to the truth of Mrs. Reynolds' assumptions that the ceremony would be in Matlock. "I did not invite my aunt and uncle, though; there will be sufficient confusion without introducing them into the midst of it," he paused to kiss her lightly, "and we can return here immediately afterwards, if that suits you, my dearest."

"I believe that I can manage that," she said playfully, "so long as other surprises remain at a minimum!"

She thanked him for his thought about his mother's dress, attempting to ascertain if he favoured the idea, and was pleased to discover that he did. "There is something I must give you to complete the ensemble, though," he said, bringing her to his study, where he unlocked a drawer and drew out a long box. He handed it to her, and when she looked questioningly at him, said, "It is yours. Open it."

Raising the lid, she gasped as the sight of a diamond and sapphire necklace, obviously an heirloom, and exquisite in its simplicity. Speechless, she touched it lightly with one finger, and then looked up to find a pleased smile on Darcy's face. "William, I . . . I hardly know what to say," she eventually said. She had never received such an extravagant gift—nor even dreamed of receiving one—and did not even know how to express her thanks.

"This was my mother's as well, and I remember her wearing it with that gown. Most of her jewels are Georgiana's, but she left me this to give to my wife. It matches the ring I gave you," he said somewhat shyly.

She looked up at him, thinking of how much he enjoyed giving Georgiana gifts, and recognizing he likely would derive the same enjoyment with her. "Thank you, William," she said, feeling words were inadequate. "I shall be proud to wear it."

He lifted it out of its case and placed it around her neck, then stepped back to admire the sight. He had long pictured her wearing it; since he associated it so strongly with the woman he would marry, it was almost a badge of possession in his mind. He smiled, thinking of her wearing it in public after they were married, when he would have the right to have her always beside him.

Seeing the warmth of his look, Elizabeth slipped her arms around his neck and kissed him, a gesture which he returned and deepened. She sighed happily as he clasped her to him, and set to enjoy the taste of his lips, stirred by feeling his strong body against hers. When they paused for breath, she said, "I do love you so."

God, she has no idea what she does to me! he thought as his body responded to her touch, his mind returning to her seductive behaviour the previous night. A surge of urgent desire took him in its power, and he ran his hands down her back to her hips demandingly. He recaptured her mouth and ravished it thoroughly, then hungrily pressed kisses along the line of her jaw and down her neck. "Dearest Elizabeth," he groaned, struggling to restrain himself as his body demanded immediate gratification. Trapping her between himself and the desk, he pressed his hips against hers demandingly as he devoured her kisses. His every instinct told him to take her, right there in the study.

"William," she breathed, astonished and more than a little aroused by his unexpected passion. "Someone could walk in . . . "

"I know," he growled, pressing heated kisses along down her neck and shoulders. "That is the only reason you are still wearing your clothes."

The exhilarating passion of his kisses excited her, and she could hardly keep her own response in check as he began to caress her breast, but her fear of discovery was even greater. "William, not here!" she whispered fiercely, catching his face between her hands.

It took more than a moment for him to reassert control over himself. "May I come to you tonight?" he asked, his voice rough.

How could he make her desire him so much? "Yes," she breathed, her eyes caught in his heated gaze, and their mouths met hungrily as if drawn together by a power greater than theirs. She shivered with longing as she felt the proof of his arousal against her, wishing that they need not wait. She forced herself to break off the kiss, and buried her face in his shoulder until she could look up at him with some degree of restraint. "Am I to expect this reaction whenever I wear this necklace?" she said playfully.

He smiled in spite of himself. "You are to expect this reaction *constantly*, madam."

Elizabeth was amused by the whirlwind of activity around her for the rest of the day. Georgiana felt that Lord and Lady Derby would be offended if they were not invited; Mrs. Reynolds supported her on this, but Darcy remained firm that he wanted no one else present. There were two more fittings for her gown, and a long discussion with her maid as to how her hair was to be done; several styles needed to be tried and opinions sought from Mrs. Gardiner and Georgiana. The Gardiners had decided that it would be best for Elizabeth to travel to Matlock with them the following day, spending the night there before the ceremony, at which time they would be met by Darcy and Georgiana. Plans needed to be set for the celebration for the tenants, but fortunately Elizabeth needed only to observe this part, as she had little to offer at this point. From time to time she would see Darcy with a look on his face that suggested that his mind was on their interrupted activity in the study rather than on wedding plans, and she would give him a mischievous smile.

By suppertime she was beginning to be of the opinion that Gretna Green would have been a better option, but she remained sensible of the fact that the demands she faced were really quite modest in comparison to all the commotion that would have occurred if they married at Longbourn. "Not to mention that my aunt is more helpful and far less frantic than my mother would be," she told Georgiana in good humour. Still, she occasionally found herself looking around and trying to imagine that in two days she would be Mrs. Darcy and the Mistress of Pemberley; it still seemed far from real to her.

She did not intend to try to stay awake until Darcy arrived that night; she knew that he would not be able to come to her until the household was all abed, and after two very short nights, she thought it would be beyond her ability to remain wakeful that long. She had whispered as much to him when they said goodnight, and the look of desire in his eyes afterwards left her with a warm, excited sensation that did not fade as she prepared for bed.

She had thought that, tired as she was, she would fall asleep immediately, but no sooner was she abed than she began to feel uneasy. It took several minutes for her to realize that she was missing her lover, and that even after just two nights of falling asleep in his arms, her bed seemed very empty and cold without him. She missed his warmth beside her, his arms around her, his light kisses to her head as they talked, the endearments he whispered to her. If she buried her face in the pillow, she could just catch a whiff of his scent from the previous night, and it made her long for his presence even more. *Tomorrow night will be even more difficult,* she thought ruefully. *At least I know that he will be here sometime tonight.*

※

Their parting the next day was more difficult than Elizabeth had anticipated; in her practical way, she had thought that one day apart should present no great difficulty, but when the moment came, it was only her sense of decorum that kept her from throwing herself into his arms. Amused by her own irrationality on the subject, she said softly to him, "Sir, I should be embarrassed by how sadly I shall miss you until we meet again tomorrow."

He gave her a telling look. "I promise you, Miss Bennet, that I shall be feeling your lack every moment of the time," he said meaningfully, his words leaving a sensation of anticipation inside her. "But after tomorrow, there shall be no cause for separation."

Glancing over her shoulder, Elizabeth saw that the carriage was ready. "I shall look forward to it, Mr. Darcy."

He kissed her hand before handing her in, then watched until the carriage was out of sight. With a sigh, he returned to his study, where he hoped to make good use of the time to attend to neglected business, but it was not long before his mind was more agreeably engaged in meditating upon an absent lady. This agreeability did not last long, however, as his thoughts moved from Elizabeth herself to her absence, and by dinnertime Georgiana was ready to chide him for his dolorous appearance. The night was indeed a long one for him as he discovered just how accustomed one could become to the presence of a loved one in a few days, and his only comfort was knowing that it was their last night apart. When dawn came, he was only too glad to make an early start for Matlock and Elizabeth, and as he joined a sleepy Georgiana in the carriage, his thoughts rode ahead of them.

A little later that morning, one of the footmen sought out Robbins, the butler. "The post has come, sir," he said, "and there are two letters for Miss Bennet. I was wondering where I should put them."

Robbins thought for a moment; the new mistress had not yet set up a sitting room of her own, yet it would hardly be appropriate to leave them in her new chambers for her wedding night. "You may leave them with me for now," he said. He looked at the letters, noting that they seemed to be in the same handwriting, but one had apparently been misdirected. Finally he decided that the best idea was to leave them on Mr. Darcy's desk with his post; that way she would receive them soon enough after their return.

⚬⚛⚬

Matlock proved to be a charming town set on the side of a steep hill, with an attractive river running through the valley under the shadow of a large cliff. As they drove into town, Elizabeth could see the imposing spires of the cathedral on the top of the hill dominating the vista; a shiver went down her spine at the inspiring sight, thinking of what was to happen there on the morrow. The inn recommended by Mr. Darcy was not far from Cathedral Close, and after they were settled in, Mrs. Gardiner suggested to Elizabeth that they walk out to explore the town. Mr. Gardiner pleaded fatigue, leaving the ladies to set forth on their own.

"It has been some time since I have had the opportunity to spend time alone with you, Lizzy," said Mrs. Gardiner.

"Yes, the pace has been rather hectic," Elizabeth admitted with a rueful smile. "I feel as if my affairs have quite dominated your tour, no doubt to the detriment of your plans."

"I would not have missed this for the world," her aunt reassured her, "though I wonder at how calmly you have taken all these changes in plans."

Elizabeth said dryly, "Is there any point in not being calm? After all, I agreed to this."

"Does it not trouble you that you will not have your wedding at Longbourn, with your family and friends in attendance? I have wondered if you might feel disappointed in not having the wedding of your dreams."

Elizabeth laughed. "You are confusing me with Jane, I fear. She is the one who has always dreamed of the perfect wedding; my focus has always been to marry for love, and the ceremony itself does not mean so much to me as the life that follows. But yes, I admit that I had never considered that I might marry without my father to give me away, and Jane by my side—I wish they could be here, although I do recognize that it may be just as well that the rest of the family is not! I could, after all, have insisted that we wait until my return to Longbourn to hold the wedding, but I think this may be for the best in many ways."

"And in what way is it the best for you, my dear?"

An amused smile spread slowly over Elizabeth's face. "It gives me very little time to think and worry about what I am undertaking; I believe that may be a great advantage!"

Her aunt looked at her in concern. "You have second thoughts, then, Lizzy?"

"Hardly second thoughts, but I must admit that I did not quite realize what I was taking on when I agreed to marry Mr.

Darcy. I knew that he was wealthy and that he owned a fine estate, I knew of his relationship to Lord Derby, but I did not quite appreciate how far removed his social sphere was from mine until we started to plan the wedding. When we settled on an immediate wedding, I had pictured a simple ceremony at the parish church; it was a shock to discover that everyone at Pemberley assumed that a simple ceremony was one that took place in a cathedral, presided over by a bishop, and the major conflict being whether to include a peer of the realm in the guest list—no, I had not realized at all the extent of the differences, and I wonder what it will be like when we are in London, or entertaining at Pemberley—I can hardly conceive of it! There will be a great deal that I shall need to learn."

"When we were at Blenheim, Lizzy, you seemed worried that he would try to control your actions. I have recently had some concerns in that regard of my own," Mrs. Gardiner said carefully.

Anxiety coursed through Elizabeth; she had counted on the Gardiners' good opinion of Darcy to help sway her father towards acceptance of her marriage. "What concerns have you had?"

Mrs. Gardiner was silent for a minute. "Your Mr. Darcy was apparently quite frank with your uncle about why he wished to marry you so soon."

Elizabeth coloured and looked away. "Yes, I had assumed that he might be; it is very like him. He does not care for disguise or dishonesty."

"It seems rather out of character for you, Lizzy, which makes me wonder how he came to obtain your . . . cooperation, or whether in fact you did cooperate."

Elizabeth turned to her aunt in shock. "You cannot think . . . No, in no way did he force me. He was only . . . very persuasive, and I seem to be susceptible to his form of persuasion. My susceptibility is out of character, aunt, nothing else."

"I am relieved to hear it, Lizzy," said Mrs. Gardiner. "Although I cannot but disapprove of what happened, I am not without understanding of the position in which you find yourself, and I believe that mistakes are to be learned from rather than dwelt upon. I do have a concern, however, about this sudden wedding raising talk."

With a sigh, Elizabeth said, "There will no doubt be talk; there is *already* talk, but I assume that it will die a natural death when I do not produce an heir to Pemberley in seven months. There is no reason for anyone outside the family to know just how quickly this occurred, and my mother will be happy to assume that we were following the London fashion by being married by license in a cathedral chapel; it will be a tale she can tell to all of her friends for years to come." She paused, and her face became more somber. "I do not look forward to telling my father, however."

"No, I would imagine not," her aunt replied. "Have you and Mr. Darcy made your peace about this? I am still concerned that you may feel forced into this wedding."

"Yes, we have made our peace," Elizabeth said, glad that she did not have to tell her aunt precisely how that peace had been achieved. "And the truth is, aunt, that I have felt powerless over this situation for much longer than the last few days; I am becoming accustomed to it, and I have learned that my judgment and discernment are by no means so flawless as I would like to think them, and that some of those very things into which I have been forced have proven to be for the best."

"I am reluctant to guess at what you may mean, Lizzy."

"My entire history with Mr. Darcy is one of events proceeding against my will. I did not want Mr. Darcy to fall in love with me, yet he did; I did not want him to court me, yet he did; I did not want to fall in love with him, or even like him, yet I did; I did not want to become engaged so quickly, yet we did—there has been no part of this that has felt voluntary to me, but I would not change anything. So a less than voluntary wedding hardly comes as a shock, I fear." It was fortunate, Elizabeth thought, that her sense of humour was so inclined as to see sport in everything, as otherwise she might feel quite resentful.

"You are not dissatisfied, then?"

"I believe that I would have preferred to follow a more typical course, but no, I am not dissatisfied."

"I am glad to hear it," Mrs. Gardiner said. Pointing to a large building of white limestone, she asked, "Do you suppose that is the Bishop's palace?"

Elizabeth responded playfully, "You could ask him tomorrow. I must say, I still cannot quite credit any of this."

The following day began with an air of unreality about it to Elizabeth; it seemed almost as if she was play-acting at being a bride. The richness of her gown, accentuated by the sapphire necklace, felt wildly extravagant, and when Mrs. Gardiner finished the ensemble by draping a lace veil she had purchased in Lambton over her niece's hair, as she insisted was the latest romantic vogue at London weddings, she felt that she could barely see plain Elizabeth Bennet of Longbourn any longer.

Elizabeth felt surprisingly little anxiety regarding the wedding itself, but a great deal about how she would handle herself.

She had never met a bishop; she was not completely certain that she understood the proper etiquette for the situation, and hoped that Georgiana would set an example which she could follow. She wished above all for a few minutes with Darcy before the ceremony, but understood that this would be an unacceptable violation of tradition.

Darcy himself was sharing the same longing. He had never realized that it was possible to miss someone as viscerally as he did Elizabeth, and knowing that she was nearby but out of reach was difficult to bear. It was a great relief when the deacon informed him that it was time for him to approach the altar, as it meant that he would soon be in her presence again, but his self-possession took something of a blow when he entered the chapel and saw a jovial-looking Lord Derby and his elegant wife sitting beside Georgiana in the box pew. He cursed inwardly, wondering who had seen fit to violate his express request that they not be informed.

Once he reached the altar, though, his mind bent back to Elizabeth as he awaited her entrance. Finally she appeared on her uncle's arm, haloed by the bright sunlight streaming through the chapel windows, and it was not until she was half way down the aisle that he could see her clearly. He caught his breath at the vision of elegance before him, and a wave of possessive love flowed through him. To see her coming towards him, wearing his mother's gown and the jewels he had given her, put all else from his mind; he had so long ago given himself to her, and now they were to be made one.

As she came forward to stand at his side, their eyes met for a long moment, communicating the pleasure and relief that each felt. Darcy had to struggle to turn his eyes forward again as the bishop, a splash of colour in his white, red, and purple vestments, began the familiar words of the ceremony in a sonorous voice.

" . . . duly considering the causes for which matrimony was ordained. First, it was ordained for the procreation of children, to be brought up in the fear and nurture of the Lord, and to the praise of his holy name." Darcy tensed for a moment at the mention of the one part of marriage about which he had some second thoughts, then forced the thought away. "Secondly, it was ordained for a remedy against sin, and to avoid fornication; that such persons as have not the gift of continency might marry, and keep themselves undefiled members of Christ's body." He tried to glance unobtrusively at Elizabeth, hoping this did not distress her, but she seemed to be looking straight ahead in a calm manner. He longed to take her in his arms. "Thirdly, it was ordained for the mutual society, help, and comfort, that the one ought to have of the other, both in prosperity and adversity. Into which holy estate these two persons present come now to be joined." Elizabeth looked up at him at this point and smiled; the look in her eyes warmed him to his soul.

Their eyes held as the service continued, and a wave of feeling began to take Darcy as the moment of the occasion became real to him, that this was when Elizabeth would be formally bound to him for life. The bishop continued, "Fitzwilliam, wilt thou have this woman to thy wedded wife, to live together after God's ordinance in the holy estate of matrimony? Wilt thou love her, comfort her, honour, and keep her in sickness and in health; and, forsaking all others, keep thee only unto her, so long as ye both shall live?"

Darcy's heart was light and his voice firm as he responded, "I will."

"Elizabeth, wilt thou have this man to thy wedded husband, to live together after God's ordinance in the holy estate of matrimony? Wilt thou obey him, and serve him, love, honour, and keep him in sickness and in health; and, forsaking all others, keep thee only unto him, so long as ye both shall live?"

Elizabeth looked up to meet the bishop's eyes for the first time as she said, "I will." The bishop took her hand from her uncle and placed it over Darcy's, and as he began to repeat his vows, she gazed up at his beloved face, knowing that he was thinking, as was she, of the night he had already spoken those words to her. The slightest of smiles crossed his face as she took him to be her wedded husband, her voice clear as she repeated the bishop's words, " . . . to have and to hold from this day forward, for better for worse, for richer for poorer, in sickness and in health, to love, cherish, and to obey, till death us do part, according to God's holy ordinance; and thereto I give thee my troth."

His dark eyes held such warmth for her that she could feel her love for him rising within her as he slid the ring upon her finger. It might have been only the two of them in the world as he said, meaning each word with every fiber of his being, "With this ring I thee wed, with my body I thee worship, and with all my worldly goods I thee endow: in the name of the Father, and of the Son, and of the Holy Ghost. Amen."

They knelt for the prayer, and suddenly it no longer mattered to Elizabeth that the marriage had been rushed, that her family was far away; all that mattered was the man at her side. The bishop joined their hands again, and said the words over them, "Those whom God hath joined together let no man put asunder."

It is done, thought Darcy. *After all this time, after all the pain, it is done.* He had never before appreciated how difficult it could be for the newly wed couple to wait patiently through the prayers, blessings, and psalms, while their feelings ran so high. He wished he could carry her off to Pemberley right at that moment, not knowing how he could bring himself to make the social conversation necessary at the end of the service. When it was finally concluded, as they walked together down the aisle, he bent his head to whisper to her, "At last, Mrs. Darcy." The pleasure it gave him to say those words was beyond measure.

She turned her lively eyes on him. "At last, Mr. Darcy."

At the chapel door their families came to meet them, and Darcy made the introductions, almost slipping once when he presented the Gardiners to Lord and Lady Derby as "Miss Be—Mrs. Darcy's aunt and uncle." She smiled up at him mischievously.

Lord Derby shook his nephew's hand with gusto, offering his congratulations. Darcy said, "I am of course delighted to see you, uncle, but I do wonder how you were informed of the proceedings."

Lord Derby laughed heartily. "Let me see—I was informed by my cousin the bishop, and by your sister, and by your housekeeper. I am, in fact, an extraordinarily well-informed man, except, perhaps, by you."

"The notice was very short, sir, and I did not wish to cause any inconvenience," Darcy said smoothly.

"William," said Lady Derby, "might I have a word with you?" She drew Darcy apart from the others, abandoning Elizabeth to the company of Lord Derby.

"So, Mrs. Darcy, I need your help to settle an argument between my wife and me," he said jovially.

Elizabeth raised an eyebrow, a shock still running through her at the sound of her new name. "I would be happy to be of assistance if I may, Lord Derby."

"Tell me, then, when did you and my wayward nephew meet?"

She blinked in surprise at the question. "I believe we first saw one another in mid-October of last year, but it would have been another week or more before we were formally introduced."

"October!" he snorted in disbelief. "October—I cannot believe it!"

"I assure you that I remember it clearly," Elizabeth said smoothly, *though I do not think that I shall tell you what your nephew said on that memorable occasion.* "I am not sure why you find it quite surprising; I believe that October is as fine a month as any other to meet."

He laughed at her pertness, and said, "Well, we both lose the argument then. My wife guessed that it was a month ago; I thought no more than two weeks. Who would have thought October?"

Both of Elizabeth's eyebrows rose in response to this. "Two weeks! That hardly seems likely."

"Well, you would know best, I suppose," he allowed, "but we have always said that when young William finally made up his mind, he would nab the young lady in question and marry her without further ado, and when we heard about today, it seemed only logical to think that our predictions had been correct. I am seriously disappointed." He shook his head.

"You seem to assume, Lord Derby, that the young lady in question would consent to be nabbed," replied Elizabeth with spirit.

"Oho!" he exclaimed. "So that is the way the land lies, then! Gave him his comeuppance, did you? Good for you—he was certainly overdue. Too many beautiful women throwing them-selves at him for years, you know," he said with a confidential air.

"Well, if it makes you happier, we have only been engaged for two weeks," Elizabeth allowed.

"That is a relief—that is more the William we know! So he did not propose to you the first time he saw you?" he asked, sounding like a child denied a long-expected treat.

Elizabeth smiled in great amusement. "I am sorry to disap-point you, but I cannot think of anything that would have been further from his mind on that occasion."

He shook his head again, as if mystified by the behaviour of the younger generation.

Darcy approached them at this point, and Elizabeth linked her arm through his. "Mr. Darcy," she said mischievously, "it seems that I am a great disappointment to Lord Derby."

"I am sorry to hear that, Mrs. Darcy, since I have just agreed that we would join him for a brief wedding breakfast at Derby House," he said in like manner, clearly unsurprised to find her already teasing his uncle.

"Not at all, Mrs. Darcy," said Lord Derby urbanely. "I find you uniformly charming. My nephew is another matter entirely; he is indeed a disappointment."

"For failing to inform you of my wedding? I knew that if you were invited, you would take the opportunity to tell my bride terrible things about me."

"Did I do anything of the sort?" he demanded of Elizabeth, but without giving her a chance to respond, he continued, "William, this lovely lady tells me that you met her *last October* and that you are only now getting around to marrying her! What sort of example are you setting?"

Darcy gave Elizabeth an ironic look. "I see nothing wrong in keeping her in suspense about my intentions," he said. "Mrs. Darcy, have I thought to mention to you that some members of my family run to an excess of character? Of course, you have met Lady Catherine, and as you know, a more gentle and circumspect soul never walked the earth, but some of our relations are rather more difficult than she."

"You introduced her to Catherine, and not to us? Now I *am* offended!"

"I must confess, Lord Derby, that I managed to find Lady Catherine completely on my own, with no assistance from Mr. Darcy," Elizabeth intervened, but stopped short of mentioning her cousin. She was still uncertain of how much Darcy intended to tell his family about her connections. Mr. and Mrs. Gardiner could easily be mistaken for people of fashion, after all, and she did not know if he intended to disillusion his illustrious relations.

"Mrs. Darcy's cousin is the recipient of a living from Lady Catherine," Darcy explained. "She had the opportunity to dine at Rosings on several occasions during a visit to him."

"And lived to tell the tale? Mrs. Darcy, I am indeed impressed."

Shortly thereafter they departed from the cathedral en route to Derby House, which proved to be an imposing edifice of the same white limestone as the cathedral lying a short way outside of town near the river. Lady Derby had arranged a sumptuous wedding breakfast—Elizabeth could not help but wonder what would have happened had Darcy not agreed to attend it—that outstripped her expectations by far; it was clear that Lady Derby was a gifted and experienced hostess. The bishop was announced shortly after Darcy and Elizabeth arrived; Elizabeth followed suit behind Lady Derby in curtseying and kissing his ring. Darcy stayed close by her side as the bishop spoke to her, asking her questions about her impressions of Derbyshire and Pemberley. It seemed a somewhat stilted conversation to Elizabeth, and she was relieved when he moved his attention to Georgiana, giving Elizabeth the opportunity to offer her thanks to Lady Derby for her attentions.

Lady Derby was a very genteel lady of understated but direct opinions who was quite curious as to the mettle of the young woman who had captured her nephew's heart. It was clear to her from observing them both that it was a love match; she would not have expected Darcy to settle for anything less, but she had in the past few years felt some concern as to whether he would ever meet someone to suit his needs, surrounded as he was by fortune hunters and flatterers.

Elizabeth brought up her acquaintance with Colonel Fitzwilliam, and the two conversed on that subject briefly before Lady Derby turned her attention to the subject of her nephew, mentioning that Elizabeth seemed rather different than many of the young ladies of Darcy's acquaintance.

"Yes, I remain convinced that the reason he first noticed me was that I showed no interest in him whatsoever," said Elizabeth with a laugh. "It is my impression that he was quite tired of the constant attention he received."

"Yet somehow he seems to have gained your interest," Lady Derby suggested.

With an amused smile, Elizabeth said, "He can be very per-suasive—and persistent—when he sets his mind to it."

"Yes, he is very like his father in that way, though he does not have his father's easygoing disposition. He is more complex; he will not be the easiest of men to understand, I expect."

"I would be hard put to disagree with you, Lady Derby," responded Elizabeth, "though I prefer to think of it as his having great depth."

Lady Derby smiled gently. "That is one way to put it, I suppose. He has been through trying circumstances over the years, and although he generally does not admit to their extent, they have left their mark on him."

Elizabeth wondered what message she was being given. "I imagine that I shall learn more about that over time; as you say, he tends to be private about the past."

"I certainly hope that we shall see more of you in the future; you should not let my nephew hide you away at Pemberley."

Wondering at the shift of subject, Elizabeth was about to respond when a voice came from over her shoulder, "You will allow me, I hope, a bit of time alone with my bride before you begin to carry her off on social obligations," Darcy said smoothly. "And while I am on the subject, it is past time for us to depart; we are expected at Pemberley."

"I hope you will allow us to keep Georgiana for a few days, William. We hardly get to see her these days," said Lady Derby.

"If she would like to be kept, I see no objection," he allowed. Lady Derby approached Georgiana, who initially seemed reluctant, but on further persuasion from her aunt, appeared to change her mind.

"She has agreed to stay, but only tonight; she wishes to return to Pemberley with the Gardiners tomorrow, if that suits."

With an amused smile, Elizabeth thanked Lady Derby for the wedding breakfast, and implicitly for her tact in separating out Georgiana to allow them privacy on their wedding night. She and Darcy bid their adieus and were soon en route to Pemberley.

They had barely left before Darcy moved from his proper position sitting opposite Elizabeth to the decidedly improper one of sitting by her side, and augmented his impropriety yet further by pulling her close to him. "At last I have you to myself, Mrs. Darcy," he said.

The pleasure of having his arms around her after a day of deprivation brought an immediate smile to her face. "Just you and I, Mr. Darcy, and, of course, the driver and the footman. It was very thoughtful of your aunt to keep Georgiana."

He laughed and kissed her lingeringly. "It was, indeed, which is why I may forgive them for ambushing us at our own wedding."

"I know that you had not invited them—was it so disturbing that they were there?" she asked. Lord and Lady Derby had seemed quite pleasant to her, and she had been wondering why he had so steadfastly avoided informing them of the wedding.

"No, not disturbing. I did not wish to add to the stress of the occasion for you by bringing them in, and thought it wiser to allow you to meet on a less momentous occasion. They can be, in their own ways, somewhat challenging to deal with, but today seemed to bring out the best in them, so I cannot complain."

"Challenging? How so?" Elizabeth succumbed to temptation and slipped her hand inside his coat.

He gave her an amused look. "It is a long way yet to Pemberley, madam!" he said. "Well, my uncle can tease mercilessly. Lady Derby, well, she is invariably pleasant, charming company, and she never makes any demands, but for some reason after speaking with her, one ends up doing whatever it is that she wishes, regardless of how one might feel about the matter. I suspect my uncle was quite taken by surprise when he found himself proposing to her. It is an astonishing talent; were she a man, I am convinced that she would be running the country, not just Derby House and all her relations, but it is all with the best of intentions."

"Fortunately for you, I have a great deal of experience at being teased. As for your aunt, we shall have to see. Today she seemed primarily concerned that I care for you adequately, and I can hardly fault her for that, and since I have every intention of caring for you very well indeed, she could not change my mind on the matter," said Elizabeth.

He kissed her hair, taking pleasure in simply knowing she was his wife, and that nothing could part them now. "So long as you are with me, my love, I shall have no complaints," he said. "I will be forever grateful that you saw fit to give me a second chance, despite your reservations."

She blushed, recalling how distressed she had initially been by his attentions on his return to Hertfordshire. "Well, the truth is that I had no intention of allowing you much of a chance at all, but it seems that my efforts were for naught."

"Well, then, I am grateful that you stopped fighting me long enough to begin to like me," he said teasingly. He slipped his fingers into her hair, caressing the silky strands until he encountered hairpins, which he began to remove.

"You are incorrigible, sir!" she said.

"Because I like playing with my wife's hair? I so rarely get the opportunity, for it seems that whenever I have access to your hair, I tend to be distracted by your other charms. It seems just the thing for a long coach ride," he said, kissing her neck.

Enjoying the sensuous feeling of his hands exploring her hair, she said, "I should have known it was hopeless by how hard I had to fight. I had an inkling of it already on the day you introduced me to Georgiana."

"That soon? How did you know?" he asked, continuing his collection of hairpins.

She blushed. "What worried me was the way I reacted when you kissed my hand. Other men had done the same in the past, had handed me into carriages, had danced with me . . . "

"That is *quite* enough on that subject," Darcy interrupted.

She smiled at him wickedly. " . . . but, while pleasant enough, the experience had never particularly affected me. But as soon as you touched me, it was different. Even when I was still firmly decided against you in my mind, still I was not able to forget how I felt when you kissed my hand."

He caught her cheek and turned her face towards his, kissing her possessively, feeling all the satisfaction of her admission that she did not respond to others as she did to him. A jolt of the carriage pulled them apart, and they smiled regretfully at one another.

Elizabeth, the sensation of his kiss still fresh on her lips, could not help recalling her anger with what she had perceived as the treachery of her body when she had responded to his early advances, and it was ironic that the same reaction that caused her such distress could now bring her such pleasure. Darcy had returned to his enjoyable task of demolishing the careful arrangement of her hair, and, as it tumbled down around her shoulders, she nestled against him in contentment.

They spent a long while in this manner, Darcy playing gently with Elizabeth's hair as she leaned against him. He could not recall feeling as peaceful in a very long time, merely from sharing her presence and knowing she loved him. It was the culmination of his dreams since he had met her, and he could still barely credit it was true, and had to fight the feeling that she could still somehow be snatched away from him. His eyes traced the line of her profile, trying to memorize the moment.

Elizabeth, reveling in the pleasure of feeling him beside her, closed her eyes to better savour the experience. It seemed impossible to believe that she had fought against this so long, and she could barely remember being the girl who had taunted Darcy at the Netherfield ball about his relations with Wickham. Now she could hardly imagine how she had lived without him, and the realization of her need raised a small spectre of fear within her. She had never allowed herself to need anyone in this way before; she had always been careful to keep her heart safe, and made sure that she could not be affected by the changes in someone else's fancy. She had kept parts of herself secret even from Jane, but she was beginning to realize that she might find it harder, if not impossible, to do so with Darcy, that part of a love and desire as intense as his was an equally intense need and hunger for its object that might not allow for that distance. To need him so in face of this was disturbing, and unlike anything she had faced in the past.

It is a sad statement, she thought, *that I sit here recognizing my fear of losing the man who has just promised before God to spend the rest of his life with me!* With an amused smile, she looked up at him, and when he noticed her regard, she said from her heart, "I love you, my husband."

His hand drifted from her hair to the back of her neck

where his fingers began to caress her. He smiled slowly as he bent his head to claim her lips. He tasted the pleasures of her mouth as he drew from her the passion that he knew lay under the surface, passion that was now his to explore and enjoy at his leisure. In an unhurried manner he continued to tantalize her with his mouth, sliding his hand onto her back and just underneath the neckline of her gown, until he felt her surrender to her desire and cling to him in return. "I have waited so long to call you my wife, my beloved, adored Elizabeth," he murmured, "and I shall continue to show you how much I love you every day of our lives."

Elizabeth was discovering to her dismay how much more difficult it was to satisfy herself with his kisses when she knew what more pleasure could be had than when she had remained innocent of the possibilities. It was going to seem a very long time until they retired for the night. Darcy, thinking likewise, decided that a change in subject was much required, and said, "We must consider how to inform your family of our marriage."

Elizabeth rolled her eyes. "Perhaps we could hope that they just never notice," she suggested lightheartedly.

"I believe that it might strike them that something is amiss when I carry you off to my bedroom each night," he said with a smile. Realizing that he had managed to bring the conversation back once more to exactly the point which he wished to avoid, he added, "I assume we should tell them in person?"

"I would think that best. Presumably we shall have to reach Longbourn no later than my aunt and uncle; we can certainly not leave them to explain why I have failed to return with them."

He laughed. "That would indeed put them in an uncomfortable position. Well, then, I assume we should travel to Longbourn when they leave Pemberley. We will no doubt need to remain there until Bingley's wedding—do you think that your parents would be offended if we stayed at Netherfield instead of Longbourn?"

"Well, if they are, the reduced stress for us will no doubt out-weigh the offence! We can always present the argument that Netherfield has more space, especially as the wedding approaches."

He wound his hand in her hair again. "I am sorry that this has made matters so much more complicated," he said.

"You are worth it," she said with an impish smile. "I believe you may have been right, sir, when you suggested that our ability to wait longer may have been overrated."

"Mine certainly was," he growled in her ear before nibbling on it. "My ability to wait until we reach Pemberley is coming into further question by the minute."

She raised an eyebrow as she blushed. "I am not of the opinion that a carriage is a pleasant or safe place for such endeavours, sir."

"While it is tempting to try to convince you otherwise, unfortunately I suspect that you are correct, madam," he replied.

Chapter 10

THE WEDDING CELEBRATION THAT night was quite the opposite of the solemn, quiet ceremony of the morning, and it brought home to Elizabeth full force what it would mean to be the lady of the manor. It began at sundown with dancing by torchlight to the music of fiddle and flute, followed by food on a grand scale for all the tenants—Elizabeth was astonished to see what the Pemberley kitchens could produce on such short notice, and when she saw the gathered masses, she realized for the first time just how many lives depended upon her husband's management. She and Darcy had shared a light dinner earlier, which was fortunate, since they were quite busy throughout the feasting, Darcy distributing gifts to the poor, and Elizabeth presenting small nosegays of flowers to the children, who bobbed shy curtseys and bows in acknowledgement. The house was completely decked with flowers—she wondered if she would find the gardens stripped bare the following morning—and filled to the brim with revelers.

She found herself feeling unaccountably shy when Darcy introduced her to the crowded masses, and blushed when they cheered her heartily, which only encouraged some of the lewd comments which flew back and forth among the tenants. Darcy had warned her of this aspect—"This is still the North, my love," he had said—and she tried to keep her composure, but to the delight of the crowd, one or two of the comments clearly embarrassed her thoroughly, and they were all the more pleased to discover that the new Mistress of Pemberley had the capacity to laugh at herself when this occurred. Darcy, who was not such a tempting target for heckling, escaped more lightly, staying at Elizabeth's side throughout.

After the formal festivities finally drew to a close, Elizabeth and Darcy retired to her room, where they stood at the window as a group of villagers sang ballads and made music below them. When they came to the chorus of one of the songs, Elizabeth felt Darcy's eyes on her.

> O farewell grief and welcome joy,
> Ten thousand times therefore
> For now I have found mine own true love,
> Whom I thought I should never see more.*

He murmured in her ear, "There are cakes and ale in the village, but I fear that they will not leave until they see me kiss you. May I?"

She looked up at him with an amused smile. "Well, if I must tolerate your attentions, Mr. Darcy, I suppose there is nothing to be done for it. I shall strive to bear it with equanimity."

---

*The Bailiff's Daughter of Islington, traditional

The corners of his mouth twitched, and he pulled her into his arms for a kiss perhaps slightly more thorough than the circumstances required. Her cheeks were scarlet as they called their thanks to the cheering singers.

"Now, my love," he said as he drew her away from the window, "about this matter of tolerating my attentions . . . "

Elizabeth was feeling quite satisfied with married life the next morning, when, after having the pleasure of awakening slowly in her husband's arms, she sat with him at breakfast, knowing that no one was expected beside the two of them, and that this could no longer be seen as improper. The warmth with which Darcy's gaze rested on her brought a smile to her face, and she was not above seeking his hand under the table merely to celebrate the fact that she could do so.

After breakfast, they planned to part briefly as Mrs. Reynolds had offered to introduce the staff to Elizabeth and begin the first stages of her education in the workings of Pemberley, which Elizabeth hoped to embark upon before they took their necessary trip to Longbourn to acquaint her parents with the news of their marriage. They had hardly had a chance to start the discussion before Darcy reappeared with letters in hand. "Mrs. Darcy, I have just discovered that the post brought these letters while we were in Matlock; I believe they are from Longbourn, and I thought you might wish to attend to them immediately," he said.

"Oh, yes," responded Elizabeth eagerly. She took the letters, and, discovering they were both from Jane, asked Mrs. Reynolds to excuse her until later. With a smile for her husband, she settled herself in the parlour to read her letters. She had been a good deal disappointed in not finding a letter from Jane on their first arrival at Pemberley; and this disappointment had been renewed on each of the mornings that had now been spent there; now her sister was justified, as one of the letters was marked that it had been missent elsewhere. Elizabeth was not surprised at it, as Jane had written the direction remarkably ill.

The one missent must be first attended to; it had been written five days ago. The beginning contained an account of all their little parties and engagements, with such news as the country afforded, as well as her sister's raptures over her dearest Mr. Bingley; but the latter half, which was dated a day later, and written in evident agitation, gave more important intelligence. It was to this effect:

Since writing the above, dearest Lizzy, something has occurred of a most unexpected and serious nature; but I am afraid of alarming you—be assured that we are all well. What I have to say relates to poor Lydia. An express came at twelve last night, just as we were all gone to bed, from Colonel Forster, to inform us that she was gone off to Scotland with one of his officers; to own the truth, with Wickham!—Imagine our surprise. To Kitty, however, it does not seem so wholly unexpected. I am very, very sorry. So imprudent a match on both sides!—But I am willing to hope the best, and that his character has been misunderstood. Thoughtless and indiscreet I can easily believe him, but this step (and let us rejoice over it) marks nothing bad at heart.

His choice is disinterested at least, for he must know my father can give her nothing. Our poor mother is sadly grieved. My father bears it better. How thankful am I, that we never let them know what has been said against him; we must forget it ourselves, though how you are to broach the matter to Mr. Darcy I can make no suggestion. My dear Bingley has been everything that is kind, and I am most thankful that he is here. They were off Saturday night about twelve, as is conjectured, but were not missed till yesterday morning at eight. The express was sent off directly. My dear Lizzy, they must have passed within ten miles of us. Colonel Forster gives us reason to expect him here soon. Lydia left a few lines for his wife, informing her of their intention. I must conclude, for I cannot be long from my poor mother. I am afraid you will not be able to make it out, but I hardly know what I have written.'

Without allowing herself time for consideration, and scarcely knowing what she felt, Elizabeth, on finishing this letter, instantly seized the other, and opening it with the utmost impatience, read as follows—it had been written a day later than the conclusion of the first:

By this time, my dearest sister, you have received my hurried letter; I wish this may be more intelligible, but though not confined for time, my head is so bewildered that I cannot answer for being coherent. Dearest Lizzy, I hardly know what I would write, but I have bad news for you, and it cannot be delayed. Imprudent as a marriage between Mr.

Wickham and our poor Lydia would be, we are now anxious to be assured it has taken place, for there is but too much reason to fear they are not gone to Scotland. Colonel Forster came yesterday, having left Brighton the day before, not many hours after the express. Though Lydia's short letter to Mrs. F. gave them to understand that they were going to Gretna Green, something was dropped by Lieutenant Denny expressing his belief that W. never intended to go there, or to marry Lydia at all, which was repeated to Colonel F., who, instantly taking the alarm, set off from B. intending to trace their route. He did trace them easily to Clapham, but no farther, for on entering that place they removed into a hackney-coach and dismissed the chaise that brought them from Epsom. All that is known after this is that they were seen to continue the London road. I know not what to think. After making every possible enquiry on that side London, Colonel F. came on into Hertfordshire, anxiously renewing them at all the turnpikes, and at the inns in Barnet and Hatfield, but without any success; no such people had been seen to pass through. With the kindest concern he came on to Longbourn, and broke his apprehensions to us in a manner most creditable to his heart. I am sincerely grieved for him and Mrs. F., but no one can throw any blame on them. Our distress, my dear Lizzy, is very great. My father and mother believe the worst, but I cannot think so ill of him. Many circumstances might make it more eligible for them to be married privately in town than to pursue their first plan, and even if he could form such a design against a young woman of Lydia's connections, which is not

*likely, can I suppose her so lost to every thing?—Impossible.
I grieve to find, however, that Colonel F. is not disposed to
depend upon their marriage; he shook his head when I
expressed my hopes, and said he feared W. was not a man
to be trusted. My poor mother is really ill and keeps to her
room. Could she exert herself it would be better, but this is
not to be expected, and as to my father, I never in my life
saw him so affected. Poor Kitty has anger for having con-
cealed their attachment, but as it was a matter of confidence, one cannot wonder. I am truly glad, dearest Lizzy,
that you have been spared something of these distressing
scenes; I do not know how I would manage it, though, were
it not for the aid and support of my dear Bingley, who has
been everything one could possibly ask in this time of trouble. Adieu. I take up my pen again to make a request,
because the circumstances are such that I cannot help
earnestly begging you all to come here as soon as possible. I
know my dear uncle and aunt so well that I am not afraid of
requesting it, though I have still something more to ask of the
former. My father is going to London with Colonel Forster
instantly, to try to discover her. What he means to do, I am
sure I know not, but his excessive distress will not allow him
to pursue any measure in the best and safest way, and
Colonel Forster is obliged to be at Brighton again tomorrow
evening. In such an exigence my uncle's advice and assistance would be every thing in the world; he will immediately
comprehend what I must feel, and I rely upon his goodness.
I can only rely on you, Lizzy, to determine what is best done
regarding Mr. Darcy; I know this must be a blow to him, but*

*if he has any advice or thoughts on how W. is to be found, I
beg of you to send word to my father immediately.*

Elizabeth's distress on reading this was great, and she scarce
knew what to say or how to look. Lydia and Wickham! She
grieved for her lost sister, she feared for the well-being of her
family, and she could only be horrified by the prospect of Darcy's
response to this news. His sister-in-law, not only ruined, but by
Wickham! The mortification would be nigh unbearable, and
such proof of the weakness of her family must make him regret
their alliance. How were they to explain what could not be hidden to Georgiana?

She could not hide this intelligence, however, and despite
her fear over her reception she knew she must go to him immediately—but how could this not come between them in the most
hurtful manner? Was one day of marital happiness all they were
to have? She caught her breath on a sob, and before her courage
could fade away, she took herself to his study, where she found
him working behind his desk.

He looked up as she appeared at the door, and, seeing her
look so miserably ill, he said with more feeling than politeness,
"Good God, what is the matter?"

She looked at his beloved face and burst into bitter tears.
He strode to her side immediately. "Elizabeth, what is it? You
must tell me, dearest. Is it news from Jane?" Wordlessly she
handed him the letters, and then sat down, unable to support
herself any longer.

Darcy, torn between reading the letters and comforting
Elizabeth, who was clearly beyond any explanation of the matter,

compromised by kneeling beside her and taking her hand while he scanned the letters. His face was fixed with astonishment as he read the first, and when he came to the second, a few words unsuited to a lady's presence escaped him. She burst into tears on seeing his contracted brow, and she covered her face with a handkerchief, not wanting to see his face when he looked up at her with knowledge of her sister's disgrace.

His shock and horror was great, but his concern for Elizabeth was even greater. He put his arms around her compassionately, wishing for something he could say that would comfort her.

"When I consider," she said in an agitated voice, "that *I* might have prevented it! *I*, who knew what he was. Had I but explained some part of it only—some part of what I learnt, to my own family! Had his character been known, this could not have happened. But it is all, all too late now."

"It is too late to stop it, but not too late to mend it, dearest. They shall be found, and he shall be made to marry her," he said in what he hoped to be a reassuring manner.

She shook her head in distress. "Nothing can be done; I know very well that nothing can be done. How is such a man to be worked on? How are they even to be discovered? I have not the smallest hope. It is every way horrible!"

He took her face between his hands and forced her to look at him. "Elizabeth, there is nothing easier in the world than working on Wickham—all it takes is money. If I know Wickham, he will not be hiding so much as waiting to be discovered so that he can make his demands. You must have faith in me, my dearest; you know that I have dealt with him before, and I can do it again."

She looked at him with eyes filled with pain. "I cannot ask it of you—you cannot take on the mortification of this; it is a matter for my family."

"Good God, what do you think *I* am? You married me yesterday, Elizabeth, and I *am* your family, and, if I may venture a guess, I am the ultimate cause for this dreadful affair, and it lies to me to remedy it," he said forcefully.

"How could *you* be the cause? It is Lydia's weakness, Lydia's folly, and my wretched, wretched mistake of failing to explain what I knew when my eyes were opened to his real character."

Taking a deep breath, he said, "Elizabeth, please listen to me. Does Lydia know of our engagement?"

"I cannot say—I suppose she must, that my mother must have written her with the news; she no doubt sent it to everyone she could," she said hesitantly.

"And Lydia would no doubt have reported it to Wickham, knowing his opinion of me. You cannot suppose that she was the true inducement—she has no money that can tempt him, but she has that connection to me. No, Elizabeth, this has everything to do with me; this is just what he attempted last summer with Georgiana, but now he is trying to strike at me through you."

She stared at him in horror—she had not thought so ill, even of Wickham, as to think that his vengeance would extend so far. Darcy, misinterpreting the look on her face, leaned his forehead against hers, and whispered sorrowfully, "Can you ever forgive me, my dearest, for bringing this upon you?"

"You have done nothing to cause this," she said fiercely. "You are not to blame for Wickham's behaviour, nor for Lydia's, and I will not have you fault yourself for it!"

He held her close to him, wishing that he could take this grief from her. "Elizabeth, I need to consider what must be done. Is there nothing I could bring you for your present relief? A glass of wine, shall I get you one?"

"No, I thank you, nothing but you," she said none too fluently.

He removed himself to the chair beside her, where he could continue to hold her hand while he considered matters. Finally he said, "The Gardiners will return here tonight; even if I sent a messenger to Matlock now, it would not bring them back in time to leave today, and there is no point in worrying them before anything can be done. You and I shall leave for London tomorrow morning, where we will meet your father and begin efforts to discover them."

"Jane asks me to return to Longbourn, and I have no doubt she needs my help and support in dealing with my mother," she said tentatively.

Darcy shook his head decisively. "Jane does not know the full situation, and she has Bingley with her for support. I will need you with me to deal with Lydia; I doubt she would listen to anything I have to say—and I will need you myself, I have no doubt. Perhaps the Gardiners could go to Longbourn instead."

It will take me some time to accustom myself to the idea that my first loyalties must now go to him, and not to my family, she thought. *I must remember that I am his wife now, as unconventional as our wedding may have been.* With an unpleasant shock, it came to her how their abrupt marriage would look to her family in light of these new events, and what her father would feel faced with another daughter who had been rushed to the altar.

The day seemed interminable to Elizabeth. She would have preferred to be taking some form of action, but apart from overseeing the packing for the trip to London, there was little she could do but wait and worry. Her mind kept flying to Lydia, fretting over her safety as well as her future, for what future could there be for her, either as Wickham's wife or as a ruined woman? Wickham would never be able to provide for her in any sort of acceptable manner—her lot would be continual poverty and the misery of a marriage to a liar and wastrel, and *this* was to be the best possible outcome. The humiliation and misery that Lydia was bringing on her family also pained her; not only would it materially affect the marriage chances of Kitty and Mary, and delay, possibly indefinitely, the wedding of Jane and Bingley, but its effects on the Darcy family must be considered as well. She could only imagine the extent to which Darcy would be mortified by the continued connection to Wickham, and there was no question that the news would be hurtful to Georgiana. Darcy had been clear that he did not wish to blame her in any way for it, but Elizabeth could not help but worry whether his ability to keep separate his feelings about Lydia and about her was strong enough to keep this affair from contaminating his affection for her.

Her anger and shock at Lydia's behaviour led to further unpleasant thoughts as she considered her own conduct in recent days and weeks. She was appalled by Lydia's choices, yet how were they so very different from her own? Was it not mere good fortune on her part that her lapses, though every bit as grave as Lydia's, were to go quite unpunished while her sister suffered irreparable damage? She had begun to feel less troubled by her permissive behaviour as it became clear that the conse-quences would not be severe, but this situation could not but bring back to her awareness the gravity of her own errors.

The Gardiners and Georgiana returned in the late after-noon, and after Darcy had taken a few minutes to greet his sis-ter, he asked the others to join him in his study, where Elizabeth was awaiting them. One look at her face was enough to convince Mr. and Mrs. Gardiner that all was not well, and after they had perused Jane's letters and heard an explanation from Darcy detailing his connection with Wickham, as well as the past behaviour of that gentleman, they readily offered any possible help in resolving the situation. While in general agreement with the plans drawn up by Darcy, Mr. Gardiner felt that his presence in London could be useful, and after some discussion it was resolved that he would travel to town with Darcy and Elizabeth while Mrs. Gardiner proceeded to Longbourn, accompanied by servants from Pemberley for her safety and the sake of propriety. She would stay there as long as required before returning to London with the children, and it was agreed that she would not reveal Elizabeth's marriage at present, given the apparent level of distress already present in the household.

After the Gardiners left to refresh themselves before din-ner, Elizabeth remained with Darcy, drawing comfort in her distress from his presence. She was still there when Georgiana came in to tell her brother about her stay at Matlock. Seeing Elizabeth's tear-stained face and her brother's grave counte-nance, Georgiana immediately inquired as to the cause of their distress.

"It is nothing of any import, Georgiana, merely a minor difficulty," Darcy said reassuringly. "You need not trouble yourself over it."

Georgiana looked unconvinced, knowing well the extent to which her brother strove to keep unpleasantness from her. "If it is not so serious, please tell me then, else I shall continue to worry about it."

"Georgiana," her brother said with a warning in his voice.

She gave him a pained look. "You cannot keep me a child forever, William," she said softly, turning to leave them.

Elizabeth said, "Georgiana, wait. I believe that she has a point, William. She cannot be protected from this for long, and it is my belief that she has the strength to handle it."

"I hardly think that this is the time . . . " Darcy fell silent as he noted the look on Elizabeth's face. "Well, if you think it best, I will trust your judgment."

Elizabeth gave him a grateful look and took Georgiana's hand. "We received some bad news from Longbourn today, and I fear that it will prove particularly distressing to you. It seems that my youngest sister, Lydia, who was in Brighton while you were at Netherfield, has eloped, or perhaps more accurately, has run off, with none other than Mr. Wickham."

Georgiana's face froze, and then took on a look of concerted control that Elizabeth found strikingly similar to that which she had observed on Darcy's face on like occasions. "I see," she said quietly.

"Elizabeth and I will be leaving for London in the morning, as will the Gardiners, in an attempt to discover them," Darcy said gently. "I will, of course, send you word as soon as we have any news."

She was silent for a moment, and then said, "I will keep you in my prayers." She turned to leave, causing an anxious look to pass over her brother's face. "Thank you for telling me, William," she said before departing hastily.

"Perhaps I should go after her," Darcy said worriedly.

"Give her a little time first," said Elizabeth. "Had she wanted to talk, she would have stayed." Although she was also concerned about Georgiana's reaction, she had greater faith than Darcy in his sister's ability to take care of herself.

It was at a rather subdued dinner that evening that Georgiana announced her intention to accompany them to town. Taken off guard, Darcy said, "I hardly think it necessary for you to undertake so long a journey. This is not a particularly pleasant time of year to be in town, after all."

"Nonetheless, I would like to go," she said in a voice just above a whisper.

Darcy looked at her, perplexed. It was unlike Georgiana to argue with him, and that she would do so in front of others was quite startling. He did not wish to hurt her feelings at a time when she must already be feeling quite sensitive, but the last thing he wanted was to have to worry about Georgiana's feelings when he was trying to deal with Wickham.

Elizabeth said, "You sound as if this is quite important to you, Georgiana."

Georgiana glanced at her in relief. "Yes, it is," she said, her voice a little steadier.

"I doubt that there will be any time for outings or pleasurable activities," said Darcy.

She took a deep breath. "I do not require anyone to amuse me, William. I assure you that I can take care of myself."

Darcy thought to himself that he would never understand the workings of his sister's mind, and certainly not the moments when she chose to assert herself. "Elizabeth, what are your thoughts?" he asked.

Elizabeth folded her napkin. "If she wishes to come, I see no objection," she said, her eyes meeting her husband's, hoping to communicate to him the need to recognize Georgiana's steps towards independence.

He sighed. "Very well, then, Georgiana, you may come if you wish."

Later, when Georgiana was able to speak to Elizabeth privately, she thanked her for her support. "It is not that I think that there is anything I can do to help, but I do not want to spend the rest of my life trying to avoid whatever part of the country he might be in. This seems as good a time as any to face my fears."

Elizabeth embraced her. "I am glad that you have the courage to face it now. That is the first step to healing."

"I cannot help but think that it could have been me, but for the chance of William's arrival," she said softly. "I was such a fool. You would never have been taken in so, Elizabeth."

"I beg to differ, I spent a good deal of time in Mr. Wickham's company, and I was quite taken with his amiability and manners. I even believed lies that he told me about your brother," Elizabeth said ruefully.

"I find that hard to believe!" Georgiana exclaimed, then, realizing what she had said, timidly retreated, saying, "I do not mean to doubt your word, Elizabeth; it is only that it surprises me."

Elizabeth shook her head. "It seems we are all vulnerable to having our hearts lead us astray from what is right," she said, thinking of the principles she had violated in her behaviour with Darcy.

When Darcy came to her that night, she was curled up in the window seat looking out into the starlit darkness. He was aware that Elizabeth had been out of spirits since reading Jane's letters, and had been somewhat at a loss as to how to comfort her. His belief that his presence in her life had been the cause of Wickham's choice of Lydia made it difficult for him to approach her; he could not help but think that she would consider any joy that they had to have been purchased by the misery of her sister, and that she would resent him for it. The idea that she might withdraw from him was like a knife wound, sharp and intense, and it took all his courage to draw near her.

It was something of a reassurance that she immediately put her arms around him, laying her head upon his shoulder. She had been longing for the comfort of his embrace and the forget-fulness she could find in his arms, even as her sense of shame over her lack of self-control with him continued to increase.

He held her close, awash in the paradoxical feelings of free-dom that he felt only at her touch, and, unable to keep his feel-ings inside him, murmured, "I love you so very much, Elizabeth; I cannot imagine my life without you by my side." He could feel some of the tension leave her body at his words, but as she remained silent, his anxiety grew. "Dearest love," he said finally, "please say something, or I shall be leaping to the worst possible conclusion again."

She looked up at him in surprise, hearing the seriousness of his words beneath the apparently playful tone. Having been caught up in her own concerns, she had given little thought to what his might be. "And what would that conclusion be?" she asked.

He looked into her eyes, and not without anxiety said, "That you could not forgive me for what has happened to Lydia."

"William, I remain in awe of your ability to concoct reasons for me to be angry with you. Should I ever desire to have a fit of pique, I will certainly come to you to obtain an appropriately far-fetched justification. No, I do not blame you in any way; you have been everything that is kind and supportive, and I have no complaints whatsoever."

He could not help but smile at her look of amusement. "I am relieved to hear it. It worries me when you are out of spirits and reserved as you have been today."

She wished for the ability to express her anxieties to him as easily as he seemed to do with her. "I . . . " she began, but found herself unable to continue, and responded instinctively by reaching up to kiss him in a way that left him without doubts as to her intentions. Surprised, but by no means averse to such a notion, he returned her attentions with interest, tasting the pleasures of her mouth and running his hands down to her hips.

She did not pull back until she was breathless with desire, her body clamouring for the pleasure and release that only he could give her. Feeling their closeness, she was finally able to voice her fears. "I am afraid of this coming between us," she confessed, her voice uneven.

"No," he said strongly, taking her face in his hands. "Nothing is going to come between us again—I will not allow it." He kissed her passionately and deeply, as if branding her with his truth. "My love," he groaned, his mouth traveling along her jaw and down her neck. "Never think such a thing, never!"

Elizabeth was too caught up in the pleasure of his kisses to respond. When he finally raised his mouth, Darcy said, "I hope you are convinced, my love, that this matter of Lydia will not come between us."

She smiled, affectionately caressing his chest. "You made yourself quite clear on the subject, William," she responded.

"That is not quite the same as saying that you are convinced," he said suspiciously.

Nestling against him, she said, "Perhaps it would be more accurate to say that some issues remain unresolved for me."

"May I ask what those would be?"

She had to kiss him before finding the courage to answer. "I find that I am quite unhappy with Lydia's behaviour, and, at the same time, I find it to be not particularly different from my own, and this is a source of some dissatisfaction."

He frowned. "Is this because we anticipated our marriage vows?"

"That, and . . . well, I did permit a great deal before that, as well."

"Not as much as I asked."

"Nonetheless."

It was only a short step in Darcy's mind from distress over her behaviour to anger at the one who provoked and encouraged that behaviour. His anxiety rose, despite his efforts to quell it.

She would hardly be in my arms if she were angry with me, he thought. *For God's sake, do not try to read more into her words than is there; she needs support, not conflict.* Carefully, he said, "While there are superficial similarities, I believe that your situation was quite different from Lydia's."

"Yes, in that it is my good fortune not to pay a price for my errors."

He sighed. "Elizabeth, you once thought highly of Wickham. If he had asked you to elope with him then, would you have done it?"

"No, of course not!"

"Why not?"

"Well, it would have been an imprudent match, and if I chose to ignore that, why elope? There would have been no reason not to follow the normal course, and it would have made me suspicious if he did not wish to do so."

"Would you have let him kiss you?" Darcy hoped fervently that his question would not be answered in the affirmative.

She flushed. "Of course not."

"But you let me kiss you," he said, and followed his words with action.

When he released her, she said mischievously, "You were more tempting."

"A very attractive answer, my love, but I doubt that temptation would be your only consideration."

"Mmm . . . it would depend on how tempting it was. Very well, I shall be serious, if you insist. You had made your intentions clear, and I knew that you would not shirk your responsibilities. I accept your point, sir."

"And when I took you to my bed, we were formally and publicly engaged, which is not to say that it was acceptable on either of our parts, but it is a far cry from running off with a man for no good reason! But I do have one question for you."

"What is that?"

"How tempting was I?"

She smiled, and traced the line of his jaw with her finger. "Very, very tempting," she said. "Tempting enough to make me love you when I was determined not to."

"Thank God for that!" he said, gazing into the eyes that had so bewitched him when he had been equally determined not to care, and kissed the woman who had become the source of all his happiness.

They set off early the next morning in the Darcy traveling carriage, a luxurious conveyance which would make excellent time on the trip to London. At first, conversation amongst the travelers was somewhat stilted, as the topic on everyone's mind was not one suitable for discussion in front of Georgiana. After a time, however, Elizabeth was able to find an interest in the new countryside through which they were passing. Darcy, who was naturally quite familiar with the route, was happy to point out sights along the way.

They traveled as expeditiously as possible; and after sleeping one night on the road, reached Gracechurch Street the following evening. When they reached the outskirts of London, Elizabeth's mind turned to upcoming events. Her anxiety grew as they approached Gracechurch Street; she knew that her concern should all be for Lydia at this point, but she could not help but wonder if her father would be at the Gardiners' house, and if so, how he would react to the news of her marriage. It was certainly not the setting in which she would have chosen to inform him of it, and she dreaded the idea of discussing the circumstances leading to it.

Her fears were realized when they arrived; Mr. Bennet came downstairs to greet them when informed of their coming. He appeared exhausted, and there were new lines around his eyes. Elizabeth felt all the attendant concern one would expect for her father, and worried about how her news would affect him.

Mr. Bennet had not anticipated seeing Mr. Gardiner for a day or two yet, since he had expected him to stop at Longbourn; the arrival of Darcy, Elizabeth, and Georgiana was a complete surprise. Nonetheless, he greeted them all warmly, with an embrace for his daughter, and thanked Darcy for bringing Elizabeth and Mr. Gardiner to the city so promptly.

Darcy glanced at Elizabeth, then at Mr. Gardiner, who made a motion with his eyes. "Mr. Bennet, may I speak with you privately?" he asked.

"Now?" inquired Mr. Bennet, not having failed to notice the interaction.

"Yes, sir," said Darcy determinedly.

"I believe that I shall join you as well," said Mr. Gardiner. "Lizzy, will you entertain Miss Darcy in our absence? Our cook can no doubt provide some sort of refreshment for you."

"Of course," she said, wondering whether she should ask to participate in the discussion, but it seemed that Darcy and her uncle felt it better that she did not. She watched after them with concern as they withdrew to the study.

"Well, Mr. Darcy," said Mr. Bennet as he seated himself. "What can I do for you?"

"There are two matters which I need to broach with you, Mr. Bennet," said Darcy, nervously twisting his signet ring. "The first is regarding the reason I came to London, which is that I know some of Wickham's connections in London as well as his habits, which I hope will be of assistance in discovering him."

"Any assistance will be welcome," Mr. Bennet said.

"Perhaps we could meet in the morning to discuss this further," Darcy ventured.

Had he been in a better state of mind, Mr. Bennet would have found Darcy's tentativeness and obvious disquiet entertaining, but his patience and tolerance had suffered a great deal over the past days. "As you wish," he said briefly.

The easy part over, Darcy braced himself for the storm. He had hoped that his offer to find Wickham would at least warm Mr. Bennet towards him, and his demeanour became more distant and cool as he tried to disguise his anxiety. "The other matter of which I need to inform you will no doubt come as something of a surprise; it is that Elizabeth and I were married Tuesday last in Matlock."

Mr. Bennet's face registered shock. He folded his hands quietly in front of him as he stared intently at Darcy. "*What* did you say?"

"Your daughter and I are married," Darcy said, his voice inflexible and reactionless.

"Without a word to me?" Mr. Bennet said in a conversational tone which was belied by his affect.

"Yes," Darcy said briefly. "We had intended to travel to Longbourn later this week to acquaint you with the matter, but events have interfered with those plans."

"Did it occur to you, Mr. Darcy, that I might be less than

pleased with this development?" An element of disbelief entered Mr. Bennet's voice.

"I did not expect you to be pleased, sir." Darcy began to worry that Mr. Bennet's reaction was going to be even worse than he had feared.

"And yet you went ahead with it anyway."

"Yes."

"May I ask why you decided to completely disregard what you knew to be my wishes and the plans of my family?" Mr. Bennet's voice was beginning to rise, an almost unheard of occurrence in a man who had always employed humour to defuse difficult situations.

Darcy, feeling that his father-in-law had every reason to be angry, and aware that his reply was likely to make him angrier still, said in what he hoped to be a calm voice, "It was necessary."

"It was *necessary?*"

Mr. Gardiner, concerned by the escalation of the situation, decided it was time to intervene. "He had my agreement," he said gently. When Mr. Bennet's eyes turned to him in furious disbelief, he added, "I did not see any better alternative under the circumstances."

Mr. Bennet could not believe, would not believe what his brother-in-law was implying. "Under what circumstances?" he asked slowly, as if the words were being dragged out of him. Not his Lizzy . . .

Darcy's eyes were carefully focused on a point in midair, as if close attention to some imaginary detail there would cause the question to evaporate into nothingness. Finally Mr. Gardiner said, "Under the circumstances that they needed to marry as soon as possible."

The silence this produced was profound and long-lasting as

Mr. Bennet considered the implications. Elizabeth was already married, she was no longer of his household, but was mistress of Darcy's; he had not given her away, but rather she had been taken from him. His lively, witty, clever Lizzy was no longer his, and now she belonged to the oft-disagreeable man in front of him, who had seduced her and won her unfairly. He eyed Darcy with a deep fury. "Do you have anything to say in your own defense, Mr. Darcy?"

Darcy refocused his gaze on Mr. Bennet. "Nothing at all, sir," he said evenly.

Mr. Bennet exhaled sharply. Biting out his words, he said, "I should have expected this after what happened in Hertfordshire. Of all the irresponsible, heedless, selfish . . . "

Mr. Gardiner's hand clamped down tightly on his arm. He said mildly, "I am glad to say that Lizzy does not seem to be distressed by the circumstances of her marriage, and were I to venture a guess, I believe that she finds it to be something of a relief, although she has been quite concerned about your reaction."

The thought of Elizabeth's worry softened her father slightly, forcing him to recall that alienating Darcy would only interfere in his closeness to her. "Lizzy has taken this well, then?" he asked Mr. Gardiner.

"Were it not for the situation with Lydia, I would say that she is very happy," replied Mr. Gardiner.

Mr. Bennet could have found it in his heart to wish that she would be a little more unhappy about leaving her home and family, but he knew Lizzy's nature well. "Well, as there is little I can do about this, perhaps the less said, the better," he said grudgingly.

Darcy inclined his head silently in acknowledgment.

The lines of exhaustion showed more prominently in Mr. Bennet's face as he quelled his anger. He stood, saying, "I would like to speak with Lizzy now."

Darcy forestalled him. "I will bring her in, then. My sister is not aware of the circumstances of our wedding, and I prefer that she not be involved in this."

Mr. Bennet could not resist a final knife thrust. "You would not care to have your sister follow your example, then."

"Mr. Bennet, if you wish to label me irresponsible, reckless, and selfish I shall not argue with you, but I am not a fool," snapped Darcy, having reached the end of his tolerance. He regretted his show of temper almost instantly, and as he put his hand to the door, said, "I hope that you understand that I love your daughter very much."

"Not enough to respect her, apparently."

"Look at it as you will, then, sir," Darcy said with finality as he exited.

Mr. Bennet dropped his head into his hands. Looking on with concern, Mr. Gardiner said, "While you are considering what he has done, do not neglect to think of what he has *not* done—he did not make an attempt to hide what happened from either you or me, he did not simply hope that there would be no consequences of the event and proceed with the plans, and he did not attempt to justify himself."

"Oh, yes," said Mr. Bennet with a bitter humour. "Compared to the other young man who seduced one of my daughters, his behaviour is admirable, but you will have to forgive me if I bear a grudge that it happened at all."

"I understand completely. However, I do think that he is

doing the best he can with a difficult situation, and that he has made every attempt to take responsibility for what he has done. And although I cannot excuse it, the fact of the matter is that the attachment between them is as passionate a one as I have ever seen, and being in such close proximity did put them in a certain amount of peril."

Another thought occurred to Mr. Bennet, and he looked at Mr. Gardiner with displeasure. "And where were you when this was happening?" he asked sharply.

Mr. Gardiner looked at him with some sympathy. "I was asleep, as is my habit during the night."

Mr. Bennet closed his eyes, and said tiredly, "My apologies, Edward. I should not have implied that this was your fault in any way. I just cannot believe that Lizzy would behave in this way. Lydia, certainly, or Kitty, but Lizzy? And what can she possibly see in him?"

"He can be very pleasant and charming," said Mr. Gardiner earnestly, "and he does appear to love Lizzy beyond all measure. Surely you can find something in common with him there."

Chapter 11

AFTER THE GENTLEMEN HAD disappeared into the study, Elizabeth and Georgiana had retreated to the sitting room, which was somewhat chilly as a fire had not been lit yet. Her agitation could not be masked; she knew that her father was going to be made unhappy, and that it should be through her means, that she, his favourite child, should be distressing him through her behaviour, should be filling him with fears and regrets, was a wretched reflection. Georgiana, unaware of Mr. Bennet's ignorance of recent events, assumed that her sister's disquiet sprang from concern over Lydia, and attempted to cheer her with conversation, but Elizabeth sat in quiet misery until Darcy appeared again.

His slight smile reassured her to some extent. "Come, my dear, your father wishes to speak with you before we depart," he said. He followed her into the hall, where he caressed her cheek lightly. "He did not take it quite so badly as he might have; I think that we, or at least you, shall be forgiven, though perhaps not immediately."

"Perhaps you should wait with Georgiana while I speak to him," she said worriedly.

His eyes flashed for a moment. "Elizabeth, I am your husband, and if you think for a moment that I would allow you to go in there without me, you are quite mistaken."

She smiled anxiously but with good humour. "You are right, of course; I fear that I am not yet accustomed to being wed. Perhaps I shall be used to it in a fortnight or two."

"You shall have many years to become accustomed to it, my love." He took her hand and squeezed it, and did not release it immediately when they went into the study; she found she was in fact quite grateful for his presence at her side. She saw that Mr. Gardiner had been engaging Mr. Bennet in earnest conversation which broke off at their arrival, and she looked at her father with that expression of mingled guilt and mischief which had attended her every transgression since she had been a small child, though unfortunately there could be little comparison made between a marriage just this side of elopement and hiding Kitty's favourite doll in a tree.

She was relieved when he stood and approached her, taking her hands in his. "Well, Lizzy, I see that it still remains beyond you to manage your romantic life in a traditional manner," he said.

"I must find some way in which to distinguish myself from Jane," she said gravely.

"Yes, well, I am beginning to appreciate Jane far more than I have in the past!" said Mr. Bennet. "There is something to be said for tradition, after all. But you have my very best wishes, Lizzy, and I hope you will be very happy."

She smiled up at Darcy with an unmistakable look of affection. "Of that I have no doubt, sir, and I hope that some day you will be equally happy about it."

"Well, perhaps, but you will excuse me at the moment if I spend my time appreciating the predictable Mr. Bingley," he said dryly. "But we can discuss this further at a later date; I know you must be tired after your long journey. Tomorrow I will be meeting again with . . . your husband to discuss further steps we might undertake to discover Lydia; perhaps I shall see you at some point as well?"

She glanced at Darcy before nodding her assent.

⁂

Elizabeth's feelings on the journey to the Darcy townhouse were far more complex than she would have anticipated; it was not until the moment when she left her father and uncle behind to go to her husband's home that she felt the true extent of how her marriage had changed her life—that she had left her old life and her family behind, and that Darcy's views now must take precedence over her father's. It would not, under normal circumstances, have been an unusual discovery, but since at Pemberley her marriage had entailed only a change of bedroom, it had not felt true to her until now.

They arrived at Brook Street just as darkness was falling. Though curious to behold the place where she could expect to spend a great deal of time in the future, Elizabeth nonetheless held back slightly as the butler met them at the door.

"Mr. Darcy!" Philips said in surprise. "We had not been expecting you, sir."

"I apologize for failing to send notice, Philips; we left Pemberley rather unexpectedly," said Darcy, handing over his hat and coat.

"I will have your rooms prepared immediately, sir. Would you like some refreshment?" Philips glanced towards Elizabeth, wondering about arrangements for this unknown guest.

"Yes, if Cook could put something together, I am sure we would all appreciate it."

"Right away, sir. And, Mr. Darcy, I should mention that Colonel Fitzwilliam has been staying here; I hope that is not a problem, sir."

"Not in the least," said Darcy, wondering what would have brought his cousin to town again so shortly after his last visit, as the gentleman himself appeared in the hallway to check on the commotion.

"Darcy!" Colonel Fitzwilliam exclaimed. "What brings you here?" He kissed Georgiana's cheek warmly, and then, noticing Elizabeth, started in surprise. "Miss Bennet, this is an unexpected pleasure," he said, bowing over her hand.

"I fear that I shall have to introduce you again; you do not have her name correctly, Fitzwilliam," Darcy said significantly.

A puzzled look crossed the colonel's face as he looked back and forth between Darcy and Elizabeth, then, as light dawned, he glanced down at her hand. "Not Mrs. Darcy," he drawled, shooting a pointed look at Darcy.

Elizabeth smiled and curtsied. "It is indeed a pleasure, Colonel Fitzwilliam."

"Well!" he exclaimed with a broad smile. Turning his attention to his cousin, he said, "Darcy, you dog! And without even inviting me to the wedding! Does this mean that the pistols at dawn are off?"

Darcy looked pleased. "Yes; I have decided to wait until you challenge me instead—then I can choose rapiers and spoil your pretty looks for you, cousin. Now, may I sit down in my own house, or are you planning an inquisition before you let us past the door?"

Shaking his head in disbelief, Colonel Fitzwilliam allowed them pass. Darcy, spotting a stunned-looking Philips still hovering, took a moment to introduce him to Elizabeth properly before leading her to the large sitting room.

Once they were all settled, Darcy asked, "So, what are you doing here, Fitzwilliam?"

"Apart from drinking your port? Well, you know that I went back up to Newcastle, and no sooner had I arrived than his lordship sent me straight back here to indulge the Major General again, and then we repeated the whole cycle one more time, after which I told his Lordship that I thought it would be far more efficient for me to remain in London while he sent me instructions by post, rather than keeping the instructions in Newcastle and sending me back and forth by post. So, since you were away, and planning to shoot me at dawn as well, I imposed upon Edward—my elder brother, Mrs. Darcy—and stayed with him for two days, after which I thought it unlikely that I would survive long enough for you to shoot me, so I decamped and threw myself on the mercy of Philips, who took pity upon me and took me in. He has not allowed me to drink *too* much of your port, though, more's the pity."

"Fitzwilliam, you are welcome to every last drop of my port, and the rest of the wine cellar as well," Darcy said meaningfully, with a glance at Elizabeth.

The colonel inclined his head. "Always happy to be of service. But I suspect that you have a more interesting saga to tell, Darcy. Have you come from Hertfordshire?

Darcy laughed. "I fear it is far more complex than that. We spent some weeks in Hertfordshire, where, after a certain amount of persuasion, I managed to convince this lovely lady to accept the offer of my hand," he said, pausing to take Elizabeth's hand and kiss it lightly. She looked at him with the tender smile that always made his heart beat faster, and their eyes locked for a moment.

"You will have to become accustomed to this, Richard," interposed Georgiana. "I am afraid that they do it quite constantly."

Elizabeth coloured lightly. Darcy kissed her hand again, then held it in his own, staring at Colonel Fitzwilliam as if daring him to object. The latter merely raised an amused eyebrow. "That must have been a very short engagement, then, cousin."

"Well, I confess that we had originally intended it to be somewhat longer, but, as it happened, Elizabeth was by great coincidence about to travel with some of her family to Derbyshire, and we convinced them to stay at Pemberley. And, of course, once I had Elizabeth at Pemberley, I was not about to let her leave again, so we imposed upon your old friend the bishop to remove the remaining obstacles to immediate matrimony. Your parents attended the wedding."

Elizabeth was relieved that Colonel Fitzwilliam did not seem to find this tale in any way remarkable, and noted for future consideration what it might mean that, while the entire world saw Darcy as always behaving in a studied and careful manner, his relations all seemed to think it perfectly natural for him to be madly impulsive.

"And no one saw fit to so much as mention it to me?" Colonel Fitzwilliam said in mock indignation. "I *will* have to challenge you, Darcy. Not to mention coming up with some suitable punishment for my parents."

"It was only two days ago, Colonel Fitzwilliam," Elizabeth said amusedly.

"Two days? What in heaven's name are you doing here, then?" He sounded mildly scandalized.

"Excuse me, please," Georgiana said abruptly, and exited the room.

Colonel Fitzwilliam looked after her in concern. "Did I say something I should not have?"

Darcy looked at Elizabeth as if for permission. In response to her nod, he said, "I believe that she wished to avoid hearing the answer to your question, which touches on the unpleasant subject of George Wickham."

Colonel Fitzwilliam's face looked grim. "What has that blackguard done now? If he has so much as spoken a word to Georgiana, I swear that I will . . . pardon me, Mrs. Darcy, I am afraid that my temper has been known to get the best of me on this subject."

"I understand completely," said Elizabeth dryly.

"He has not attempted anything with Georgiana; I fear he is trying his hand at a new route to tormenting me," Darcy said, tightening his hand around Elizabeth's. "He somehow managed to convince Elizabeth's youngest sister to elope with him—he does seem to repeat the same patterns again and again—and they have been traced as far as London, but apparently have gone no further, hence our arrival today."

"I am very sorry to hear it, Mrs. Darcy," he said, his voice concerned. "Do I take it, then, that he knows of your marriage?"

"Not that we are married, but we believe that Lydia was aware of our engagement, so we must assume he knew as well," Elizabeth replied. "I cannot imagine otherwise why he would choose her; she has no dowry to speak of, and my family can offer him little."

"I have a few ideas of how to discover him," Darcy said. "Tomorrow I will meet with Mr. Bennet, who is also in London, to discuss how to resolve the situation."

"Indeed. Perhaps I should join you, Darcy. I might have a bit to add myself," said Colonel Fitzwilliam.

Darcy frowned. "Although I appreciate your willingness to help, I fail to see what you might know that I do not."

"Wickham is very skilled at playing on your emotions, Darcy. He knows that I would just as soon run him through as not," said Colonel Fitzwilliam. "That puts me at a certain advantage in dealing with him."

"It is my responsibility. Had I not felt it to be beneath my dignity to expose his behaviour to the world, this could never have happened." Darcy's voice expressed his anger at himself.

Elizabeth said gently, "I could say the same—that it is my fault for failing to reveal what I knew about him. The truth, though, is that it is the fault of only one person, and that is Mr. Wickham. I would not refuse anyone's help in this situation."

"Wise as well as beautiful; you have done well for yourself, Darcy. Listen to your wife."

"There speaks the perpetual bachelor!"

Colonel Fitzwilliam decided against pointing out that he had assisted his cousin in courting the most promising marital prospect he himself had seen in some time. "Had I your opportunities, old man, you would sing a different tune."

Darcy eyed him suspiciously, but was interrupted in whatever he might have chosen to say by the appearance of Philips, who requested a brief conference with the master. On his return a few moments later, he found Elizabeth conversing happily with Colonel Fitzwilliam. Discovering to his chagrin that he did not at all care for seeing Elizabeth smile at any other man, even his own cousin, he approached her and spoke quietly in her ear. "It seems we have a household crisis of unprecedented magnitude, my love. Apparently even my admirable staff cannot ready within a matter of an hour rooms which have been out of use for many years, and thus the rooms due to you as the lady of the house will not be ready until tomorrow. They offer you instead the finest guest room."

Her eyes sparkled up at him with amusement. "I assume that you accepted on my behalf, sir," she said mockingly, unaware of how her playfulness was affecting him.

"Indeed not, madam. I proposed an entirely different solution," he said suggestively.

Elizabeth glanced at Colonel Fitzwilliam, who was watching this interplay with interest, although he could not hear Darcy's words. "Perhaps we could discuss this later, sir," she said composedly.

"I think not, my lovely wife," he replied, helping her to her feet before scooping her up in his arms. "Good night, Fitzwilliam," he said, satisfaction evident in his voice.

"Good night, Darcy, Mrs. Darcy. I hope you sleep well." Colonel Fitzwilliam smiled broadly, raising his glass to them.

Elizabeth, in deepest embarrassment, buried her face in Darcy's shoulder. Once they were out of the room, she gazed up at him reproachfully. "And to think that I once believed that you valued propriety!"

He paused to kiss her, disregarding the servant in the hallway. "It is all a matter of priorities, my love." He pushed open the door to an upstairs room. "Right now my priority is to acquaint you with my bed." He placed her on that piece of furniture, exploring her mouth with an unhurried attentiveness to detail which roused Elizabeth into a state where she no longer felt the least interest in opposing his intentions. He stroked the soft skin of her neck, leaving trails of sensation wherever he touched, and then, sliding her gown off her shoulder, he slipped his hand under the neckline to caress her breast. She arched her back to encourage the pleasure he was giving her, and the intense shock of desire that rushed through her when he began to explore her nipple made her gasp under his lips. As he pulled away just far enough to look at her, she could see the flush of passion on his unsmiling face. "Do you still want to return downstairs, Elizabeth?" he asked, continuing to stimulate her with his skillful fingers.

Struck even through the waves of delightful sensation running through her by the oddness of his demeanour, she twined her arms around his neck. Just before she drew his face back to hers, she whispered, "I never did. I want to be with you, William."

He nibbled at her lip, then released her just long enough to throw off his cravat and coats. He lowered himself onto her as if to claim her body with his and kissed her demandingly before moving to explore her face and neck with his lips. When he reached her ear, he murmured, "Elizabeth, if you do not find a way to remove your clothing very quickly indeed, I will take matters into my own hands, and I do not guarantee that they will be wearable when I am through."

Her face lit with amusement. "It is *quite* unclear to me, sir, how you expect me to do anything of the sort when you persist in lying on top of me."

He rolled off her obligingly, but did not free her until his impatient hands had the opportunity to reacquaint themselves thoroughly with the curves of her body. Seeing his eagerness, she turned to allow him to unfasten her dress. He struggled with the tiny buttons manfully for several long moments until he gave in to his threatened impulse and pulled the sides apart by force.

"William!" she exclaimed, startled by his action. "I do not have that many dresses with me on this trip!"

He nibbled on the nape of her neck as he undid the ties of her corset. "Buy more," he instructed succinctly.

Afterwards, she lay in his arms, breathing hard, and over-whelmed once again by the pleasure he could give her. An upwelling of tenderness for him filled her, a sense of gratitude for their having discovered each other against all odds, and she gently smoothed back his hair. She was aware that something had been troubling him earlier; she did not know what it had been, but the lines of concern were erased from his forehead now. "I love you so," she whispered impulsively, and his arms tightened around her.

"My beloved Elizabeth," he replied. "You never cease to amaze me."

A smile curved her lips. "Oddly enough, I believe that I could say the same about you."

He kissed her forehead gently, thinking back on his earlier feelings. The pensive look on his face caught Elizabeth's attention, and she asked, "Is anything the matter, William, my love?"

He twisted a lock of her disheveled hair around his finger thoughtfully. With a sigh, he admitted, "There are times at which I need you so much that it worries me."

"That is a sentiment which I can certainly understand," said Elizabeth feelingly, "since it is one which I share."

"Do you?"

She raised herself on one elbow to see him better. "Yes, I do," she said slowly.

He cupped her cheek with his hand. "I did not know," he said, kissing her tenderly. "I cannot say that I am sorry to hear it."

"Misery loves company?" she asked with a smile.

"*Your* company is all I want." He paused for a moment, then added, "If only we could go back to Pemberley, just the two of us, I would be quite content. I wish that everyone would leave us alone— your father, my cousin, your sister, Wickham, even the staff here."

Elizabeth muffled a laugh in his shoulder. "Especially the staff here—what will they think of me, appearing out of nowhere and leaving a trail of torn clothing behind me?"

"They will adore you, just as I do. Well, perhaps a little differently. They will think you a great improvement over the mood that I was in during the spring—I doubt they would care if you shredded every item of clothing and drapery in the house."

"Pardon me, sir; I do not believe that *I* was the one doing the aforementioned shredding!"

"You drove me to it," he said, kissing her lingeringly. "Besides, it will provide you and Georgiana with something to do tomorrow.

There is nothing that Georgiana loves so well as shopping—she will be delighted to help you choose a new wardrobe."

"Oh, dear," said Elizabeth with amusement.

"I suggest that you choose gowns which are easy to remove," he said. "It may promote their longevity."

She stopped his mouth in his favourite manner.

***

After breakfast Darcy and Colonel Fitzwilliam departed for Gracechurch Street. Georgiana, as Darcy had predicted, was enthusiastic about a trip to the modiste, and although it hardly seemed a priority to Elizabeth, she was willing to admit that remaining in the unfamiliar townhouse all day while awaiting news was likely to be unpleasant. The stores which Georgiana patronized were of a higher quality than those Elizabeth had visited with her aunt in the past, and she became concerned over the expense as the number of items Georgiana insisted she needed continued to mount. Marrying her was already likely to cost Darcy a considerable sum to settle the affair of Lydia, and she was disinclined to spend more of his money than was needed. Georgiana did not know how to comprehend Elizabeth's reluctance, and eventually decided to leave it to her brother to explain what would be necessary to her in her role as Mrs. Darcy.

When they finally arrived back at Brook Street in the late afternoon, the gentlemen were still not returned. This delay caused Elizabeth some anxiety, and she proposed a walk in Hyde Park to distract herself, but Georgiana was tired after their day on the town and preferred to remain quietly at home. Elizabeth tried to quell her restlessness, but was relieved when Darcy and

Colonel Fitzwilliam finally appeared, both showing evidence of having had a fatiguing day indeed.

Darcy's face brightened when he saw Elizabeth, and he took a moment to take her hand in his and to whisper a private greeting. Sensing her impatience, he suggested that they confer immediately, for which he received a grateful glance.

"I am happy to be able to report that we believe that we have located Wickham, and presumably Lydia with him." Darcy seated himself beside Elizabeth. "I believe the intelligence we received today to be reliable, and had it not been so late in the day already, I would have tried to meet with them today."

"He fails to mention, Mrs. Darcy, that it was the general consensus that it would not be for the best for him to meet with Wickham personally," said Colonel Fitzwilliam, handing Darcy a glass of port. "I must compliment you for your influence on him. He took the decision relatively graciously."

"Fitzwilliam, is this really necessary?" said Darcy tiredly.

"I know that you would much prefer to do it all yourself, so yes, I believe it is necessary. In any case, the plan in fact calls for *me* to meet with Wickham, hopefully tomorrow morning, and . . . "

"I *still* do not like this part," Darcy interrupted with irritation. "I conceded to it this morning, but it is against my better judgment, and I still may not permit it, especially now that I know the area of London concerned!"

"And you say there was consensus, Colonel?" asked Elizabeth lightly. "It sounds rather more like a battlefield!" Recognizing that they were on sensitive ground, she slipped her hand into her husband's for a moment, but when she tried to draw away, he tightened his grip and would not release her.

"It had its moments," Colonel Fitzwilliam conceded. "We took the liberty of bringing you into the plans, the suggestion being that you accompany me in hopes of convincing your sister to quit her current position. Since she is not acquainted with me, I could hardly ask her to leave with me, and it was your father's opinion that she would be more likely to listen to you than to him or Mr. Gardiner."

"That is a *slight* distortion, Fitzwilliam," said Darcy. "In fact, Mr. Bennet was threatening to remove her bodily if she did not agree, and since this did not seem conducive to a successful res-olution of the situation, your involvement was proposed. I think, though, under the circumstances, it would be wiser to send Mr. Gardiner."

Elizabeth said slowly, "Obviously, I am not aware of all of the ramifications of this business, but if there were to be a way in which I could be of assistance, I would be appreciative of the opportunity." She turned to look at Darcy with anticipation.

"Elizabeth, your sentiment is much appreciated, but this is a very disreputable part of town that we are speaking of, and I am concerned for your safety," said Darcy, plainly having to force himself not to completely forbid it.

"Given that I am expected to be able to face Napoleon him-self, not to mention those mad Americans, I believe that I can manage to keep your wife safe in the middle of London, Darcy," said Colonel Fitzwilliam mildly.

"You are only one man, Fitzwilliam. It is hardly the same thing."

"What, then, if you send someone with us?"

Darcy shook his head. "I do not wish to have anyone more than necessary aware of this."

"Why not send Wilkins, then? Certainly you can trust his discretion, and he no doubt already has a good idea of the matter. He always seems to know everything that happens. I should not be surprised to discover that he could tell us what the Prince Regent ate for breakfast this morning."

Darcy looked stormy. "I will consider it. Enough of this for now."

Darcy was eventually brought to agree to abide by the original plan, although it took a great deal of persuasion on the part of his cousin. En route to Wickham's lodgings the following morning, Colonel Fitzwilliam took the opportunity to explain his strategy to Elizabeth. "You may hear me say some things that surprise you, but if you can bring yourself to make the appearance of agreement, it would be helpful. It is important that we convince Wickham that this matter is not as urgent to us as he would like to believe, and that may involve a little, ummm, bending of the truth on my part."

Elizabeth paused to digest this concept. She was certain that Darcy would not approve of this sort of negotiation, and she questioned whether it was appropriate for her to participate under the circumstances. "What, precisely, do you mean by 'bending the truth?' "

"Well, I might, for example, point out that we could buy your sister a husband who was honest and hardworking for less than Wickham is asking, despite her ruined reputation. It is true enough, after all, though perhaps not a consideration for us. It would be helpful, however, for Wickham to think we have alternatives."

She took this opportunity to ask the question which had been disturbing her. "How much do you think he will be asking?"

Colonel Fitzwilliam grimaced. "He is a fool if he takes her for less than ten thousand pounds. If your conscience is troubled by my suggestion, keep in mind that he has a long history of trying to blackmail your husband, and is perfectly willing to destroy your sister's life as a byproduct."

Elizabeth glanced at Wilkins, whose normally imperturbable mien suggested that he had no objection to lying to, cheating, and quite likely even poisoning Wickham in defense of Mr. Darcy. "I will do my best," she said finally.

"Also, I do not know how well Wickham knows you, but if he were to believe that your motives in marrying Darcy were mercenary, he might be less likely to believe that you would agree to spending large amounts of your husband's money on this matter."

She raised an eyebrow dubiously. "That may be beyond my capability, sir."

"Well, I will not encourage you to deception, but will only point out that the reason I refused to let Darcy meet with Wickham is that he is so honest that Wickham can cheat him in a minute, which only encourages him to come back with another scheme in another year or two. I am trying to convince him that it is not worth the trouble." There was a steely look in the amiable Colonel's eyes that Elizabeth had never seen before. He said nothing further on the matter, however, before they arrived at their destination.

Elizabeth was appalled to see the disreputable neighbourhood in which Wickham and Lydia had their lodgings. Upon finding the house, the Colonel rapped with his cane on the door, and announced to the woman who answered the door that they were seeking Mr. Wickham. She looked him up and down, noting the quality of his clothing, and laughed. "Well, you're welcome to see him, and if you can pay his rent, so much the better!"

A disheveled Wickham appeared a few minutes later, clearly amused to see Colonel Fitzwilliam. On noticing Elizabeth, he assumed his old pleasing manner, and bowed to her, saying, "Miss Bennet, what a delightful surprise! I had not thought to see an old friend so soon."

"It is Mrs. Darcy now, Mr. Wickham," said Elizabeth pleasantly.

"Indeed! Well, that was fast work! You *have* done well for yourself."

"Mr. Darcy did not wish to wait, and it is not my business to argue with him," she said with a deceptive appearance of calm.

"He can be overbearing, can he not?" Wickham said with an air of sympathy.

Elizabeth, trying to hide her revulsion, said with a shrug, "I think it better that he and I get along well than not, and I had no particular objection. Although it is pleasant to have the chance to share our news, Mr. Wickham, I must admit that I was hoping to see my sister."

"She is just up the stairs and to the left, though I doubt she is dressed to receive visitors." His good-humoured ease was unchanged from his days in Hertfordshire, as if he expected his former favourite to overlook the small matter of his having seduced her sister.

She inclined her head. "Thank you, sir. Colonel Fitzwilliam," she acknowledged before heading for their room.

Wilkins followed her as closely as her shadow, clearly not at all comfortable that Mr. Darcy's wife was in such quarters.

The interview with Lydia, who was indeed far from being ready to receive visitors, was even more unsatisfactory than Elizabeth had imagined. Her sister was in no wise prepared to leave her situation with Wickham. She was sure that they would marry some time or other, and it did not much signify when. She did not care for any of her friends or her family, and refused to see that her behaviour had materially affected anyone in her family, nor that it was even a cause for concern. She laughed as she spoke of what good fun it all had been, and attributed Elizabeth's dour expression to jealousy that her dear Wickham had chosen Lydia over her. When she reached the point of congratulating herself on being married before all of her elder sisters, Elizabeth's patience was at an end, but she denied herself the satisfaction of correcting Lydia's view for fear that it would reinforce such foolish thinking.

Elizabeth was apparently not the only one who found the situation difficult to bear, as Wilkins, who had been standing quietly with his eyes on the floor up until this time, cleared his throat and said pointedly, "Mrs. Darcy, I believe that it is time that we returned below."

Not trusting herself to say a word, Elizabeth swept out of the room, leaving behind her a confused Lydia, who after a moment shrugged at what obviously must have been a mistake on the part of the servant.

The tumult of Elizabeth's mind after this interview was great, and she paused for a moment on the stairs, feeling unequal to encountering Wickham while in such an agitated state. A few deep breaths were enough to restore her composure, though not without a resolution, having seen the circumstances, to support Colonel Fitzwilliam in whatever stratagem he might devise.

She entered the tiny sitting room to find Colonel Fitzwilliam.

"So, together with paying your debts, and the amount settled on Miss Bennet, that would bring the total to over twelve thousand pounds. That is preposterous, Wickham! I begin to think that this is a waste of my time. I could purchase the lady a *respectable* husband for half that amount," said Colonel Fitzwilliam with scorn.

Wickham turned his most amiable countenance on Elizabeth, clearly anticipating that she would do whatever necessary to procure her sister's marriage to him. "Mrs. Darcy, we are having some difficulty reaching an understanding here. Perhaps your gentle influence might be of assistance," he said with a charming smile.

Elizabeth felt herself growing more angry by the moment as she approached the colonel. "She is completely unrepentant," she said in a low voice. "I would rather spend a few thousand pounds to dower Mary and Kitty to counteract the effects of this scandal on their chances of marrying, and leave Lydia to her own devices."

Colonel Fitzwilliam turned to her. "You cannot seriously be proposing that we leave your sister in these straits? Wickham will abandon her, you know, and more likely sooner than later."

Elizabeth leveled on him the kind of withering stare she had seen Darcy use with great effect. "While I would *prefer* not to do so, there is a limit to how much of *my* children's inheritance I am willing to waste to rescue Lydia from her own folly!"

Looking unperturbed, Colonel Fitzwilliam suggested that she might be more comfortable waiting in the coach. Elizabeth accepted the opportunity to take her leave. No sooner was she safely ensconced in the privacy of the coach, however, than she gave in to distress over her sister's hopeless predicament. Clearly Wickham would be willing to marry her once the proper price was negotiated, but what kind of life could Lydia ever expect to have with him? She would not have thought it possible for her opinion of Wickham to fall, but she was forced to admit that she had not expected such assurance from him, and she resolved within herself to draw no limits in future to the impudence of an impudent man.

It was not long until Colonel Fitzwilliam joined her, and they lost no time in quitting the disreputable quarter in which they found themselves. No sooner had they pulled away than Colonel Fitzwilliam said with admiration in his voice, "Madam, I must recall never to be on the wrong side of a dispute with you! For someone who was concerned about misrepresenting herself, that was rather brilliant improvisation, if I may say so."

She smiled ruefully. "You give me too much credit, sir. I fear that when I am angered beyond reason I tend to make comments that I would not otherwise, and in this case I simply gave myself free rein to do so." She thought with some amusement that Darcy would have recognized her performance from the Hunsford parsonage; she had said some equally egregious and intemperate things that day. She wondered what report Wilkins would give to his master on the events of the day.

"Well, it may have turned the trick. He was much more rea-sonable in his demands at the end, and I expect that once we have let him worry over it for a day, it might improve still more," he said with satisfaction.

When they returned, it was obvious that Darcy had been waiting impatiently for them. That he had been worried about her was apparent from the fact that he took her in his arms in front of the colonel and held her tightly, his cheek resting against her hair. Although the impropriety of the situation made Elizabeth uncomfortable, she was beginning to learn that it was best to let Darcy have the reassurance he needed, however unreasonable it might seem.

"How did it go?" Darcy inquired of Colonel Fitzwilliam when he finally released Elizabeth.

"Well enough, I would say. He was surprised to see me instead of you, but was willing enough to state his price, which naturally was ridiculously high. Fortunately for us, he is apparently in severe financial straits, and not likely to refuse immediate relief. I did not have a great deal of luck in arguing him down until your lovely wife was rather forthright in her opinions of the matter. By the end, he was down to demanding payment of his debts, which he claims to amount to nearly a thousand pounds—though I will personally be surprised if it is that low—his commission purchased, and three thousand pounds for him. I counter offered to pay the debts up to a total of two thousand pounds, the commission, and to settle another thousand pounds on Miss Bennet in addition to her own, and said I would return tomorrow for his answer."

Elizabeth could not help but be shocked by the sums involved; they would have ruined the Bennets, and even for Darcy, would take up a substantial amount of his yearly income.

She cast her eyes down in humiliation over what her foolish sister was going to cost him.

"He must be fairly desperate. It could certainly have been a great deal worse," said Darcy, not seeming in the least dismayed.

"I thought so as well," replied his cousin. "I would suggest that we begin some investigation as to the true extent of the debts in Brighton—could we contact the colonel there?—and the town in Hertfordshire."

"A good plan; I will ask Mr. Bennet tonight if he will handle that. I believe that he will be happier if he has some role to play in this," Darcy said, causing Elizabeth to look up at him with a question in her eyes. "I invited him to dine with us," he said by way of response.

She knew he had made the invitation for her sake; Mr. Bennet had been anything but gracious to him since their arrival, despite all that Darcy offered to do. She smiled her thanks to him, then looked away again, thinking that her family had become even more of a liability to him than either of them could have imagined.

After Colonel Fitzwilliam had left, Darcy took both her hands in his. "What is it, my love?"

She looked up to see concern in his eyes. With a sigh, she said, "My sister is a thoughtless fool who does not care who is injured by her actions, my father is behaving badly towards you when you are doing everything in your power to save our family, I myself was once taken in by a scoundrel of boundless impudence, and this is all going to cost you a great deal of money. You are being graciousness itself about it, but I cannot help being quite ashamed of my family."

"Elizabeth, we have been through all this before, have we not? You have done nothing wrong except to have been misled by a man who is an expert at it. Your father—well, I certainly have not done anything that would make him trust me." He paused, and regarded her thoughtfully for a moment, then said in a gentler voice, "I would imagine seeing your sister this morning must have been upsetting."

As soon as he had spoken the words, she knew that he was correct about what was truly troubling her. Wrapping her arms around him, she leaned her head against his shoulder, accepting the comfort and feelings of security that she felt in his embrace. "You are right, of course," she said. "She was so unrepentant, and did not even seem to notice her surroundings, while below Wickham was freely admitting he had no intention of marrying her unless his price was met. And speaking with *him* was even worse." She shuddered as she thought back on it.

She could feel him stiffen slightly at her last words. "What did he say to you?" he asked, trying to keep his voice level.

"Oh, nothing directly offensive; it was more what he assumed, that I would understand his motivations, since he thought my reasons for marrying you to be equally mercenary— that I was no better than he—and that I would continue to be friendly with him, and support him against you."

He kissed her forehead. "He never understood you at all. My dearest love, do not give him a second thought; he is not worth it."

"You are so very good to me, William."

"That is because I enjoy being good to you, my love," he responded lightly, trying to think of what might cheer her. "Come, there is still enough time before dinner for a walk, and you have not yet seen Hyde Park. Will you allow me to show you?"

She smiled at him gratefully.

⁂

Dinner that day began as a rather tense affair. Darcy and Colonel Fitzwilliam had met with Mr. Bennet beforehand to inform him of the progress which had been made with Wickham, a discussion which had turned somewhat irate when it became clear to Mr. Bennet that Darcy did not plan to allow him to participate in any way in the financial arrangements.

Elizabeth attempted to improve matters by introducing conversation about her journey with the Gardiners which led to relating the tale of her wedding. With the blatant encouragement of Colonel Fitzwilliam, she dwelt on her interactions with Lord and Lady Derby with amusement. Darcy clearly enjoyed watching her lively rendition, and embarrassed his cousin into relating the boyhood episode which had landed him permanently on the wrong side of the bishop.

"You have yet to meet my beloved brother and his wife, though, Mrs. Darcy," said the colonel. "A true appreciation of the extent of character in the Fitzwilliam family would be seriously lacking without that reference."

"Oh, dear," said Elizabeth gaily. "This sounds somewhat dangerous."

"It is," he assured her solemnly. "There is a reason I do not stay at my family home when I am in London!"

The most surprising contribution to the discussion came from Georgiana, who evidenced a gift for mimicry that came as a surprise to Elizabeth, giving an impression of Lady Catherine de Bourgh which would not have disgraced any actress on the London stage.

It was a new view of Darcy for Mr. Bennet, who had not before seen him in comfortable company. That his new son-in-law could laugh and tease was a significant surprise, and the obvious nature of Darcy's affection for Elizabeth could not but improve his standing with Mr. Bennet. He considered for the first time the possibility that he might someday be able to enjoy Darcy's company, a cheering thought since visits to Elizabeth seemed unlikely to be pleasant if he and Darcy persisted in sparring at every meeting. There was a good deal he was willing to suffer for Lizzy's sake, and he determined to make a greater effort with Mr. Darcy.

It was the first test of his resolve when Elizabeth and Georgiana withdrew after dinner. Colonel Fitzwilliam, all too clearly attempting to disguise the discomfort between the other two men, began to tell amusing stories of his army escapades, but when he finally stopped to enjoy a little of his port, Mr. Bennet took the opportunity to offer an olive branch. "So, Mr. Darcy, have you and Lizzy considered how you plan to inform Mrs. Bennet of your marriage?"

Darcy replied courteously, "I must confess, sir, that the subject has not come up for discussion in these last few days, as we have been preoccupied with these other matters. Obviously, it is something we should attend to as soon as possible."

"If you like," Mr. Bennet offered, "I will be sending word to Longbourn tomorrow that Lydia has been found, and I can include your news as well, but if you and Lizzy prefer to inform her yourselves, I will not mention it."

Feeling somewhat suspicious of this sudden civility and cooperativeness on the part of Mr. Bennet, Darcy asked guardedly, "Do you have a recommendation, Mr. Bennet? I have not thought ahead to when we might be able to travel to Longbourn, as this agreement with Wickham will need to be finalized before I could depart."

Mr. Bennet raised his glass in Darcy's direction. "Mr. Darcy, the day that I have any useful advice on how to manage my wife, I promise to share it with you. Unfortunately, to this day I have yet to discover any."

Darcy was at a loss as to how best to respond; certainly his relationship thus far with Mr. Bennet did not allow latitude for humour about members of his family. He grasped about for what to say, wishing for Bingley's fluency of speech.

Colonel Fitzwilliam stepped in to the rescue. "Mr. Bennet, have you any plans for when you will return home?"

"There seems to be little keeping me here at the moment, since I am not to be allowed to be of any use to my daughter," he responded dryly. "All the same, I would prefer to be certain that an agreement has been reached before I return to Longbourn, so if it appears that it may happen soon, I shall wait until then."

"I would not be surprised if we reached an agreement tomorrow," said the Colonel. "We are definitely within acceptable negotiating range, if there are no surprises."

"I shall be meeting with my solicitor tomorrow," Darcy said. "I need to arrange a settlement on Elizabeth, and I can discuss the payments to Wickham at the same time."

"So, in theory, you could both be free to depart London within the next few days, if all goes well," Colonel Fitzwilliam remarked, "especially as I can hold the line here."

Darcy raised an eyebrow. "Will not the Major General expect to see your face from time to time?"

"Hang the Major General! At least dealing with Wickham makes him seem more tolerable, and I can ask no more than that."

Chapter 12

THE FOLLOWING DAY SAW a flurry of activity as the inhabitants of the Darcy townhouse scattered to their various tasks. Georgiana, having garnered her brother's support on the necessity of a new wardrobe for Mrs. Darcy, took Elizabeth back to the modiste, which while not particularly a pleasure for her, at least distracted her from the tasks at hand. It was the third day in which business had separated her from Darcy for a majority of the day, and Elizabeth had discovered that she did not care for this in the slightest.

When they returned to the house, Darcy was already there, also feeling a similar lack. Georgiana began to tell him of their day, and then, noticing how the two were gazing at one another, excused herself somewhat abruptly. She had no sooner departed the room than Elizabeth was in Darcy's arms, enjoying the exquisite sensation of completion that returning to a lover's embrace can bring.

"Oh, William," she whispered against his chest. "I missed you so much."

He caught her lips in an engaging kiss. "I think that I shall never allow you to leave my side again." He had found himself distracted all day by her absence, wondering what she was doing, and whether she was thinking of him, and to hear her acknowledgment of missing him filled him with the contentment of knowing that he was loved by the woman he adored so completely. Now that he was holding her in his arms, however, he began finding her distracting in a completely different way, and his hand began wandering down to the curve of her hips.

It was not fair, thought Elizabeth, that he could evoke a reaction from her body with such ease. She fought against the urge to press herself against him.

He pulled her closer to him as he deepened the kiss to taste the pleasures of her mouth. He could feel her response as her lips pressed against his, but her body did not melt into his in the way he so loved. When he lifted his head for a moment, he said, "Reluctant, my love?"

Elizabeth, knowing that she could be all too tempted if she allowed herself to be, said, "Georgiana is here, William. You cannot simply carry me off to bed."

He said an ungentlemanly word, which together with the irritated look on his face, produced a soft laugh from her. He nipped at her ear. "Are you laughing at me, my love?" he growled.

She could not help the mischievous look on her face. "You *are* very amusing, after all," she murmured, her words cut off by a gasp as he began to assault her neck with light kisses which seemed to send currents of energy through her.

He pressed himself against her in such a way as to leave her in no doubt as to his potent arousal. "Let us see how long you can laugh then," he replied, moving his hands seductively over her hips while his lips drifted downward to her collarbone.

"William," she protested gently, finding it very difficult not to arch her body into his enticing touch as desire began to wend its way through her. She was beginning to gain some understanding of why his family considered him impulsive, she thought. "I did miss you today," she admitted.

"I cannot say I am sorry to hear it, since you were hardly out of my thoughts all day," he replied.

"I wish that we could return to Pemberley," she said somewhat dreamily. "There were not so many people bent on taking you away from me there."

He leaned his cheek against her hair, still finding the experience of having Elizabeth express her affection for him to be a heady one. "My dearest love," he said, feeling his love for her to be greater than he could ever hope to express. "I would like nothing better than to have you completely to myself."

They remained thus, murmuring endearments, for a brief while, which came to a close when Darcy told her that he had something to show her. After a last kiss, she stood, leaving him free to fetch a paper from his desk. He handed her several closely written pages.

"What is this?" she enquired.

"It is a copy of the settlement I made on you while I was at my solicitor's office today. I thought you might like to see it."

She gave him a grateful glance, knowing that he had no responsibility to share it with her, and that in showing it to her he was respecting her desire for involvement in decisions regarding her. She read through it carefully, noting the provisions for her future should she outlive him, and for any children they might have, and paused when she reached the section regarding her annual allowance. Without looking up, she said slowly, "This is very generous, William, but I came to you without a dowry, and there is no need to settle this sort of money on me."

He tipped her chin up so that she looked at him. "Elizabeth, this is an appropriate settlement for my wife, regardless of how you came to me, and I will not treat you like a poor relation. You will have significant expenses in maintaining the standards necessary for my wife. You will," he paused, and smiled knowingly at her "for example, clearly have a substantial need for replacing clothing."

She could not help smiling at his words, but still added, "I still believe that this is far too generous."

"It is done already, my love," he said, not without pleasure. "You may as well accustom yourself to it."

She handed the papers back to him, and kissed him affectionately. "Well, I thank you, then, and I am glad you know that I did not marry you for your fortune."

"Of that I am quite clear, my dearest."

"And thank you for showing it to me; I do appreciate being involved."

He looked rather more pleased by these thanks than her earlier ones. "I have one more thing for you as well," he said.

"Am I required to guess what it is, or do I get a hint?"

"How many kisses is a hint worth?" he asked mischievously.

She put her arms around his neck and pulled his lips towards hers. "Kisses are free," she said, demonstrating her point.

When she released him, he said, "In that case, I shall not require you to guess." He reached his hands behind her neck and unhooked the chain of the small amber cross she customarily wore. From a box in his pocket he removed another necklace, this one an elegant pendant of pearls set in gold, obviously expensive yet simple enough for everyday wear, and replaced the other one by fixing it around her neck.

She lifted it to examine it more closely. "Thank you, William," she said warmly. "It is lovely. But I hope you know that you need not buy me gifts; you are all that I need."

He gathered her into his arms. "I enjoy buying you gifts, so you should accustom yourself to that as well." She laid her head upon his chest, hearing the reassuring sound of his heartbeat.

A knock came at the door, and Darcy released her to open it. Colonel Fitzwilliam entered, and Elizabeth coloured as he gave his cousin a look which made her suspect that he had no doubts as to why the door had been locked. "Excellent news, Darcy," he said exuberantly. "Wickham accepted the offer with only minor alterations, and your sister, madam," he paused to bow in Elizabeth's direction, "is at your uncle's house on Gracechurch Street."

Elizabeth pressed her hand over her heart as a look of delight came to her face. "That is wonderful news, indeed," she cried. "Thank you, thank you again and again for all you have done in this."

"It was my pleasure, Mrs. Darcy. Your husband has the more trying position of having to foot the bill," said the colonel, adroitly turning her attention back to Darcy, who did not appear pleased by his wife bestowing her bright smiles upon his cousin.

She turned a radiant look onto Darcy. "He is quite correct," she said softly. "You are the one I should be thanking, and I do thank you, again and again, in the name of all my family."

He kissed her lightly on the forehead. "It is no more than I ought to have done. Perhaps we should call at Gracechurch Street later ourselves."

The excursion to the Gardiner home went as well as could be expected. Lydia was Lydia still: untamed, unabashed, wild, noisy, and fearless, talking constantly about her upcoming wedding and all the clothes she wished to purchase for it. Elizabeth, mortified by her behaviour, tried to keep her as far as possible from Darcy, thinking he would be quite justified in thinking Lydia not worth the small fortune he was spending to rescue her. Fortunately, Lydia had no interest in someone as dull as Mr. Darcy, even now when he was known to be her brother.

Darcy spent most of the visit in the company of Mr. Bennet, a situation which placed him on the defensive even when his father-in-law was most cordial. Elizabeth, however, could tell more immediately that the brunt of her father's anger with her husband had passed, and had the satisfaction of seeing Mr. Bennet taking pains to get acquainted with him.

After a lengthy discussion, Darcy asked Elizabeth to join them, leaving Lydia to sulk over her neglect. "Elizabeth," Darcy said, "your father has informed me that he plans to depart for Longbourn tomorrow morning."

"I see nothing further that I can do in London apart from fretting, and I can do that equally well in my own library," said Mr. Bennet, with more of his old dry humour than Elizabeth had heard since their arrival in London. "Your aunt is likewise returning to London with the children tomorrow. Lydia will have to remain here until the wedding, of course. The question is as to what the two of you wish to do."

Elizabeth glanced at Darcy, whose countenance was unrevealing. He said, "We will need to be in London in two weeks for your sister's wedding, since that is when the financial arrangements are to be finalized, but in the meantime we can do as you wish—we can travel to Hertfordshire, or we can remain in town."

Having taken earlier the difficult step of acknowledging that Darcy had the right to make this decision on his wife's behalf, Mr. Bennet was pleased to see him turning the question to Elizabeth.

"We really must go to Longbourn soon in any case," Elizabeth said. "I suppose my preference would be to do so now, so that after Lydia's wedding, we would be free to return to Pemberley."

Darcy's eyes lit at the idea that Elizabeth was anxious to go home, to *their* home. They shared a glance, silently agreeing that some time alone at Pemberley was what they both needed.

Mr. Bennet grimaced slightly, less than pleased to hear that Lizzy was desirous to leave the environs of Hertfordshire. In the interest of tranquility, however, he said, "I wrote to your mother this afternoon; I am not certain whether she will receive the letter or not before I return. I elected not to mention your marriage in it, Lizzy, since I did not know whether you preferred to announce it yourself."

"We had originally planned to do so, but that was before we knew that we would be coming to London," she replied. "I have not given it any particular thought since then, given how much else has been happening. We can tell her when we arrive at Longbourn, though."

With a wry smile, Mr. Bennet said, "Now, as you know, Lizzy, your mother's nerves and I are old companions, and I have no fear of her wrath under ordinary circumstances; however, were I to neglect to inform her that one of her daughters was married, I believe that neither her nerves nor I would be likely to survive the outcome. As a result, I do plan to inform her in the calmest possible manner of your current state when I return home tomorrow, unless, of course, you choose to join me and to share the joyous news with her yourself."

Elizabeth looked up at Darcy questioningly. He said, "If you prefer to go tomorrow, Elizabeth, then we can certainly do so."

"I think that I should prefer to tell her the story my own way," Elizabeth allowed.

"Then tomorrow it shall be," said Darcy.

⁓⚶⚶⌀⁓

They arrived at Longbourn slightly after midday, and it was clear that Mr. Bennet's letter had not yet been received, as they were apparently not expected. They hurried into the vestibule, where Jane, who came running downstairs from her mother's apartment, immediately met them. As she affectionately embraced Mr. Bennet and Elizabeth, she lost not a moment in asking whether anything had been heard of the fugitives. Mr. Bennet was so well able to reassure her as to Lydia's status as to bring tears of joy to her eyes. "But we must tell my mother at once!" Jane exclaimed. "It will be such a relief to her nerves."

"She is still in her rooms, then?" asked Mr. Bennet, his reluctance to confront his wife evident.

"She has not been downstairs since this all began," Jane replied.

"Well, then, you and Lizzy should inform her at once!" said Mr. Bennet. "I shall be in the library; I need a glass of port, and I daresay that Mr. Darcy does as well, or will need it soon enough in any case."

As they walked upstairs, Jane said, "Oh, Lizzy, how I have longed for you to be home! I cannot tell you how much I have missed you!"

"Dearest Jane, you have had so much on your shoulders— how I wish I could have helped you! And I have so very much to tell you," replied Elizabeth, thinking, *including that this is my home no longer.*

Entering Mrs. Bennet's apartment, Jane said, "Look—they are arrived! My father, and Lizzy, and Mr. Darcy as well! And they bring good news!"

"Oh, what is it, what is it? Is my Lydia married?" Mrs. Bennet cried.

"Not yet," Elizabeth answered her, "though we hope she will be soon. She has been found, and is at my uncle Gardiner's house, and she and Wickham plan to marry in two weeks."

Mrs. Bennet's joy burst forth, and she was now in an irritation as violent from delight, as she had ever been fidgety from alarm and vexation. To know that her daughter would be married was enough. She was disturbed by no fear for her felicity, nor humbled by any remembrance of her misconduct.

"My dear, dear Lydia!" she cried. "This is delightful indeed! She will be married—I shall see her again!—she will be married

at sixteen!—How I long to see her! And to see dear Wickham
too! But the clothes, the wedding clothes! I will write to her
about them directly. Jane, my dear, run down to your father, and
ask him how much he will give her. I shall have a daughter married! My dear, dear Lydia! How merry we shall be together when
we meet!"

Elizabeth took a deep breath. "I do have another piece of
news, madam, and it is that you already have a daughter married."

Mrs. Bennet paused to look at her in some irritation. "Oh,
Lizzy, how you do delight in vexing me! So they *are* already married! Why did you not say so at once? You teasing, teasing girl!"

Elizabeth could not help laughing at her mother's countenance. "I fear that you misunderstand me. It is not Lydia who is
married, but I." Jane gasped in astonishment, and Elizabeth gave
her an apologetic glance as she turned back to her mother. "It is
true; once we were at Pemberley, events took on a life of their
own. Mr. Darcy's godfather is the bishop of Matlock, and it
turned out that he was absolutely determined to officiate at our
wedding, and Lord and Lady Derby to be in attendance, and Mr.
Darcy unwilling to wait until such a time as my family could
journey to Derbyshire. So we were wed last week in Matlock
Cathedral by the bishop himself, just as the most fashionable
folk do."

"Lizzy," Mrs. Bennet said weakly. "Can this be true? My sister Gardiner said nothing of it!"

Elizabeth smiled warmly. "It is true enough; we pledged Mrs.
Gardiner to secrecy when we discovered that she would be coming here before we ourselves arrived. I am sure that she was longing to tell you the entire story; it was quite the event! I wore a

lovely gown which belonged to Lady Anne, Mr. Darcy's mother, as well as a necklace of sapphires and diamonds that Mr. Darcy gave to me for the occasion, and lace in my hair. I have never been so well dressed in my life—you would not have recognized me. Lord and Lady Derby hosted the wedding breakfast for us at Derby House, and it was a very elegant affair indeed." Inwardly, she was highly amused by this presentation of the affair, so tailored to her mother's desires.

Recovering herself, Mrs. Bennet cried, "Oh, my dearest Lizzy, this is too much! Married by the bishop himself in the cathedral! And Lord and Lady Derby present! Oh, Lizzy, you must tell me all about them! This is delightful, delightful! Lydia's is nothing to it! How Mrs. Long shall envy me when I tell her! Mrs. Darcy! How well it sounds. But what shall you do about your trousseau? Oh, we must discuss this immediately, Lizzy! There is so much that I must tell you!"

"I look forward to hearing all of your excellent advice, but will you not come down to greet my husband?" asked Elizabeth with amusement.

"Oh, yes, of course! Dear Mr. Darcy! Ring the bell, Jane, for Hill. I will put on my things in a moment. And I will go to Meryton, as well, and tell the good, good news to my sister Phillips. And as I come back, I can call on Lady Lucas and Mrs. Long. Jane, run down and order the carriage. An airing would do me a great deal of good, I am sure. Oh! Here comes Hill. My dear Hill, have you heard the good news? Miss Lizzy is married, by the bishop himself and in the cathedral! And Miss Lydia is to be married as well, and you shall all have a bowl of punch, to make merry."

Mrs. Hill began instantly to express her joy. Elizabeth received her congratulations amongst the rest, and then in order to take refuge from the scene claimed that she must return to her husband. She hurried down to the library where she joined Mr. Bennet and Darcy, who seemed to be enjoying some dry humour when she arrived. She sat down by Darcy and said plaintively, "Well, I have told her. May we go back to Pemberley now?"

Catching her hand and kissing it, Darcy laughed. Surprised to see him so relaxed in the presence of her father, Elizabeth said, "Well may *you* laugh, sir! She will barely trouble you for a moment before going off to inform Mrs. Phillips, Lady Lucas, Mrs. Long, and anyone else she can find of this astonishing news!"

"I have great faith that she will find some opportunity to corner me in this next week," he reassured her cheerfully, "and I shall count on you to defend me, Elizabeth."

"And I can see that I will not dare to emerge from my library except for meals!" grumbled Mr. Bennet, as his wife's excited voice was heard from without.

Elizabeth raised her eyebrow, unconvinced by this unusual show of amity between Mr. Bennet and Darcy. They had been perfectly civil on the ride from London, which was surprising enough by itself, but to appear as if they were enjoying each other's company seemed a bit unlikely.

"I have invited your father to visit us at Pemberley this autumn, Elizabeth," Darcy said, further straining her comprehension, but Elizabeth decided that if they intended to behave as if they were civilized gentlemen, she was not going to interfere.

"That would be lovely. I hope you will be able to join us," she said with just a hint of mischief in her voice.

"I do not wish to hurry you away from your family, my love, but since Bingley does not know to expect us, I imagine that we should try to reach Netherfield as soon as we conveniently may," Darcy said, rising to his feet.

"Go on then," Mr. Bennet said dryly, waving them away. "Desert me to the tender mercies of my family—I feel certain that I will survive it somehow."

They emerged to accept the congratulations of Mrs. Bennet, which were mercifully brief as she was anxious to reach her sister as soon as possible. Once she had departed, Jane and Mary immediately requested an explanation of the happenings in London, which was provided in brief by Mr. Bennet. Elizabeth decided that he and Darcy must have reached an accommodation on the subject, since no mention was made of her husband's role in the settling of Lydia's situation.

Elizabeth could not help but notice that Jane was unusually quiet and looked rather drawn, and before they left she took the opportunity to take her aside. "Jane, you look sad," she said. "Is there anything I can do?"

Jane made a valiant effort at a smile. "No, of course, I am delighted at how well everything has worked out. You and Mr. Darcy seem very happy together, Lizzy."

"Jane," Elizabeth said with warning in her voice, "I am not so easily deceived as all that. Is everything well between you and Mr. Bingley?"

"Of course, Lizzy! I do wish that I could have been at your wedding, that is all, but I can understand why it was important to Mr. Darcy's family to have it there."

It had not occurred to Elizabeth that Jane's feelings might be hurt. She leaned close to her sister with a smile, and said very quietly in her ear, "Do you really imagine that I would marry without my dearest Jane beside me merely to please his family?"

Jane looked at her in confusion. "I do not understand you, Lizzy! Is that not what you said?"

Elizabeth smiled at her mischievously. "Should I have told her the truth instead, that we married quickly because we had to?" she said in a whisper.

Jane's eyes grew wide. "Lizzy!" she said in deep shock.

Looking amused, Elizabeth turned up her hands helplessly. "Will you not come to Netherfield soon, so we may talk more privately? I have missed you so, Jane, and you cannot imagine how much I wished you were with me in Derbyshire."

Darcy appeared at her side. "We should be leaving, my love. Poor Bingley does not know to expect us, so we must give him a little time to have preparations made for us."

She gave Jane an apologetic glance, but her sister appeared to be recovering her equilibrium. After giving her a brief embrace, she bid her adieus to the rest of her family before Darcy handed her into the carriage. As they pulled away from the house, she smiled at him ruefully. "You survived that very well, William," she said.

"To which part do you refer—the best wishes of your family, or spending the entire day without having the least opportunity to hold you in my arms?" he asked, carefully switching seats so that he could be beside her. "There are altogether too many people in Hertfordshire." He took her into his arms and kissed her hungrily.

The trip to Netherfield had never been so enjoyable. On their arrival, the butler showed them in, and announced them—incorrectly in Elizabeth's case—to Bingley. Elizabeth turned to correct him, but he had already departed. Bingley, a broad smile on his face, leaped to his feet to greet them. "Darcy! What a wonderful surprise to see you here! And Lizzy, it is a pleasure, as always! Jane will be so pleased that you have returned. Or is she with you?"

"No, we just left her at Longbourn, but I am hoping that she will visit later," Elizabeth said warmly.

"Wonderful!" Bingley announced. A look of disturbance crossed his open face as he realized that they were unaccompanied, and he said, "Errr, Darcy . . . I hardly think this is a time to be violating the proprieties. The talk here has mostly died down, but it would take very little to refuel it."

Darcy looked at him in confusion, and then comprehension suddenly came to him. He clapped Bingley on the shoulder. "Bingley, my friend, may I have the honour of presenting my wife to you?"

"Your *wife?*"

With a laugh at the stunned look on his friend's face, Darcy explained the situation. Bingley shook his head, smiling, and said, "Had I only known that it was the rapid route to matrimony, I would have insisted that Jane and I accompany you to Derbyshire. You do have all the luck, Darcy!"

Darcy looked at Elizabeth warmly. "I certainly do."

<hr />

An invitation was rapidly dispatched to Longbourn, and to Bingley's delight, Jane was able to join the Netherfield party for dinner, although when word of her acceptance arrived, Darcy could not help whispering to Elizabeth that he was surprised her father considered them adequate chaperonage under the circumstances.

"This is *Jane*," Elizabeth replied with amusement. "She does not need a chaperone; such wicked thoughts would never cross her mind!" She was a trifle worried herself as to what her sister might be thinking of her own impetuous confession earlier, though she could not imagine what else she might have told her to relieve her hurt feelings.

When Jane herself arrived, Bingley was beside himself with pleasure. It was evident that since the first news of Lydia's elopement had been received, he had not been able to spend as much time with Jane as he would have wished, owing to Mrs. Bennet's demands upon her time. Jane herself seemed slightly subdued, though Elizabeth did her best to draw her out about the events during her absence, which had clearly taken their toll on her.

Jane was equally eager to hear about the proceedings in London, and Elizabeth dwelt with some warmth on the subject of Lydia's irresponsibility, avoiding any mention of the role she had played in the negotiations with Wickham. She caught Jane stealing glances at Bingley to see how he was taking their tale, as if concerned that he might be distressed by it. Feeling that a change of subject was in order, Elizabeth began to describe her pleasure in the sights of Derbyshire. When she reached the subject of Pemberley and the delight that she had taken in it, Darcy took her hand in his with a warm smile, kissed it lightly, and then retained it in his as she went on. Somewhat inured to this behaviour on his part by this point, and feeling as if they were among close friends, if not family, she gave him an affectionate look.

By the end of dinner, however, Elizabeth was fully convinced that Jane was out of spirits. She was not happy; her normal tranquility and warmth seemed somehow lessened. However, the gentlemen were determined not to permit the ladies to withdraw after dinner, so they all adjourned to the drawing room, somewhat to the distress of Elizabeth, who had been hoping for some time alone with Jane.

She was sufficiently concerned to raise the subject when they had just a few minutes apart from the gentlemen at the pianoforte. "Jane, is aught the matter? You do not seem yourself tonight."

Jane's fair skin coloured delicately. "What could be wrong, Lizzy?" she asked a little too quickly. "Lydia is found and to be married, you are here and happy, and I have my dearest Bingley."

Elizabeth looked at her skeptically, but was reluctant to press the subject under the circumstances. However, after she had delighted the gentlemen with her musical abilities, she found the opportunity to speak quietly to Darcy. "Would you be so kind as to take Mr. Bingley off to play some billiards, or whatever it is that men do when they are by themselves? I need to speak to Jane alone."

Darcy acknowledged her request with a barely perceptible nod, but to avoid being obvious, he waited several minutes before saying, "Bingley, it has been weeks since I have had the pleasure of thrashing you at billiards. Shall we have a game?"

Bingley groaned. "Must we, Darcy? The outcome is a foregone conclusion, is it not?"

"Think of it as an opportunity to improve your skills," Darcy said with an ironic smile.

"Oh, well, if it will make you happy, I suppose we could," Bingley grumbled good-naturedly.

Darcy caught Elizabeth's hand in his for a moment as they excused themselves, giving her a warm look. Bingley laughed. "Oh, for God's sake, Darcy—we are only going as far as the billiard room!" Darcy pinned Bingley with a haughty stare that made Elizabeth burst into laughter before he himself smiled.

Elizabeth moved to sit beside Jane and took her hand between hers. "Now, dearest Jane," she said in an engaging voice, "tell me about everything."

"There is nothing really to tell; I have spent much of my time with our mother, although aunt Gardiner was more than kind in helping with that. I do hope that this can all be hushed up, though so many people know about it already."

"And you and Mr. Bingley? How goes the romance?"

Jane coloured. "There has been little time for romance, I fear. Charles has been quite attentive in visiting, though."

But could you speak to him of what you were feeling, Jane? Elizabeth wondered. "I am sorry that I could not be here with you," she said aloud. "I have worried about how you were feeling. I know how much I missed having my dearest Jane to talk to and to comfort me when I was in Derbyshire, and you were facing much worse on your own!"

Jane seemed a little relieved by her words. "I confess that I could not understand at the time why you did not return to Longbourn as I asked, and did not even send a letter or a message to me with our aunt, but now that I know of your marriage, I can see why of course you had to go with Mr. Darcy."

With a slight grimace, Elizabeth said, "I thought of writing, but felt as if I would have to tell you the whole truth if I did, and

I did not want to add to your burdens. I can see, though, that failing to write added to those burdens as well."

"I can see how happy you are with Mr. Darcy, Lizzy. I recall how unhappy you were before you left for Derbyshire, and I am so glad that you were able to work it out with him." Despite her smile, her words had an undertone of wistfulness, and Elizabeth realized Jane could be envious of her new intimacy with Darcy.

A playful look came to Elizabeth's face, and she said, "It was more a matter of accepting the inevitable! But yes, I am very happy. I confess that I had not quite understood how much closer he and I would be once we were married, and I believe that it has been good for both of us. Oh, Jane, I do want you to know him better, since you and he are the dearest people in the world to me!"

Her smile became more genuine at Elizabeth's words. "I am so glad that he and my dear Bingley are such good friends! But, Lizzy . . . will you tell me what happened at Pemberley? Were you discovered by someone? I know you had permitted him . . . some liberties before you left here."

Elizabeth coloured. "Oh, Jane, if I tell you, you will be so ashamed of me."

"Lizzy, I could never be ashamed of you!"

"Well, Jane, if you are certain you wish to know, I will tell you, but you will not like it!" Elizabeth found herself surprisingly overcome with embarrassment faced with this admission.

"If you do not wish to tell me, I shall not be offended," said Jane hesitantly.

Putting her hands to her hot cheeks, Elizabeth said, "No one found us; I fear that we found ourselves out, and it was in William's bed."

"Lizzy!" Jane's voice exhibited the deepest of shock.

"So there was only one thing to do, and . . . I told you that you would be ashamed of me!"

"Not ashamed, but, oh, Lizzy, how could you have, that is, did he . . . " Jane was clearly unable to even bring the words to her lips. "I am not upset, but . . . a bit shocked, yes. I cannot understand quite how . . . venturesome you and Mr. Darcy have been."

Elizabeth smiled with amusement. "Well, dearest Jane, if you wish an explanation, I will do my best to give one to you, but it is rather difficult since I do not know what license you have permitted Mr. Bingley, nor how you have felt about it."

It was Jane's turn to blush. "I am not so daring as you, Lizzy! We have been circumspect; he holds my hand when we are alone, and I have allowed him to kiss my cheek."

"And have you never wanted more? No, do not try to answer; that was an unfair question. If the truth is to be told, I found William's kisses very . . . pleasant, and they grew even more so with time. And the more we indulged in that pleasure, the more tempting it became to do more, and one night the temptation became too great for us. Despite everything our mother has told us about the duties of the marriage bed, it truly can bring great joy and happiness as well."

"That is reassuring, I suppose, after what she has said! But Lizzy, was it not upsetting for you, afterwards?"

Elizabeth could not prevent a smile. "Well, I was quite shocked at myself, I must admit, and disappointed at my weakness. Certainly I would not have chosen to have it happen so. I had so hoped that you and I would share a wedding! But there are ways in which it was not as surprising as it might have been.

He and I have always been out of step with the usual proce-dure—our time here was more like an engagement for us in many ways. I know that Mr. Darcy saw himself as committed to me very early on, which affected his behaviour towards me, and while I would not admit to myself what was happening, I knew some time before I accepted him that I would be marrying him."

"Yet you always denied any interest in him so vehemently!"

With a rueful smile, Elizabeth said, "My very vehemence was probably the best evidence against me! I believe as well that you saw through me on more than one occasion as far as that goes." She thought back, wondering when in fact she had gained an inkling that it was inevitable, and a memory came back to her of that first day when he had surprised her with his appearance at Longbourn, when she had asked him how long he would be stay-ing in Hertfordshire, and he had replied, "As long as necessary."

Jane squeezed her hand lightly. "Dearest Lizzy, I hope that we shall always be the best of friends, and that marriage shall not separate our hearts, no matter how far apart we may live."

Elizabeth heartily endorsed this sentiment.

Chapter 13

D<small>ARCY CAME DOWN TO</small> breakfast late the following morning with a spring in his step. If he had thought himself insatiable before, it was nothing compared to how he responded in the ambience of Netherfield and the memories it roused in him. It had been a long night of passion in which he had made love to Elizabeth again and again, intoxicated by her eagerness and her soft cries of pleasure.

When he entered the breakfast room, Bingley looked up at him from a plate of toast with a characteristic broad smile and said, "Darcy, you look to be in a fine mood this morning!"

Darcy placed his hands on the table and leaned across it towards his friend. "Bingley, I am married to the most astonishing woman in the world, and if her sister is anything like her, you will be a very happy man indeed."

Bingley's eyebrows shot up. "Oh, ho, my friend, is that how the land lies?"

Darcy gave a smug smile. "Indeed it is."

"You lucky dog!" Bingley shook his head philosophically. "You are cruel to flaunt your happiness in front of me when I must wait for weeks yet for my angel! Our wedding has yet to be rescheduled. I wish *I* had a bishop for a godfather!"

Unaccustomed to the art of deception, Darcy experienced a moment of confusion before recalling the public version of their marriage. Recovering himself, he said, "I would not, in fact, recommend our route to the altar, although I admit that the results are very satisfactory indeed."

"Darcy," said Bingley suspiciously, "what are you failing to tell me? You are without question the worst liar I know!"

Darcy gave him a quelling stare, but his spirits were too high to hold it for long. He went about helping himself to breakfast with no further attention to Bingley's comment. Bingley, realizing with glee that he had found one of those rare subjects on which his serious friend could be teased, closed in. "Come now, Darcy, confess. What happened? Did you deliberately put the idea in the bishop's head?"

"Bingley," Darcy said calmly, buttering his toast, "if I were to tell you why we married so quickly, you would feel obligated, as Elizabeth's future brother, to thrash me within an inch of my life, and that hardly seems a good omen for our future."

"Darcy! You didn't!" Bingley's voice contained elements of both shock and awe.

"And you, perhaps, could vouch for your own behaviour if you were to accidentally meet Jane alone, wearing nothing more than a rather revealing dressing gown, in the middle of the night?"

"Well, if I could, it would be because of faith in Jane, rather than myself," Bingley conceded. Could it be that Fitzwilliam

Darcy was actually admitting a failing? With a smile on his face? "Well, given the extenuating circumstances, perhaps I will refrain from thrashing you, but only if Lizzy comes downstairs with a smile on *her* face as well."

"In that case, I believe I have nothing to worry about," Darcy said with a self-satisfied air.

"Are you *enjoying* tormenting me, Darcy, or is it just happenstance?" asked Bingley.

Darcy just smiled. "Your turn will come, my friend."

❧

Bingley rode to Longbourn after breakfast, leaving Elizabeth and Darcy to make their way to the Bennet house on their own. Darcy had nostalgically ordered the curricle readied, which produced an amused laugh from Elizabeth. He took her hand in his, giving her a warmly possessive look, as they drove off, those moments from his courtship of her very much alive in both their minds.

Elizabeth brought his hand up to her cheek, then pressed a kiss on it. "By the by, I never found a chance yesterday to ask you what was so amusing to you and my father yesterday in the library."

"Why, does it strike you as odd that we should be amicable for more than ten minutes at a stretch?" he asked mockingly.

"I would say that ten minutes is quite generous for the two of you!"

"Well, he was entertaining me with stories of your childhood misadventures, and attempting to warn me that you can have moments of temper given sufficient provocation." He gave her an amused look. "I admitted to having a certain degree of experience with that already."

"What do you mean?" she said indignantly. "When have I lost my temper with you?"

He raised his eyebrows. "Hunsford."

She coloured. "Well, I try to think only of the past as its remembrance gives me pleasure, and that is one moment that I have tried hard to forget! And I do not believe that I was the only intemperate one that day."

He gave her an indulgent look. "I never suggested otherwise, my love, and you may feel perfectly free to put it completely out of your mind if it pleases you."

"I hope you did not tell my father about that!"

"Well, only selected moments," he admitted. "He seemed to find them entertaining."

"William!" she said indignantly. "I cannot believe you would do such a thing!"

"It did allow us to avoid fighting for over a quarter of an hour, which must be a record of sorts," he said defensively. "And he told far more stories than I did."

She looked at him through narrowed eyes. Her spirits were too high to allow her to be annoyed, however, and she could admit that it was precisely the kind of conversation that would have pleased Mr. Bennet immensely.

"I did tell him that you were completely justified," he added.

"Well, I shall forgive you this time."

"Pity," he said lightly.

"Why is that a pity?" she asked suspiciously.

"If you would not forgive me, I would have to take you back to Netherfield and make love to you until you did."

"You are incorrigible, William! To think I once thought you sober and restrained!"

"That was only to allow me to catch you off your guard," he teased.

"Well, however you did it, you certainly did catch me."

It was near dark when the Netherfield party returned home, Elizabeth still finding it odd to be included in that number. Once they had arrived, it was not long before she excused herself for the evening, having found it to be a rather emotional day on top of little sleep the night before. Darcy, waiting below to give her time to make her preparations before joining her, poured a glass of port for himself and one for Bingley, and settled himself to listen sympathetically to his friend's woes over his delayed wedding.

When Darcy finally felt it appropriate to retire, Bingley looked at him with a gleam in his eye. "Yes, Bingley?" he said patiently.

"Darcy," he said with an engaging grin, "Jane and I had a particularly lovely walk today. I do not know what Lizzy said to her yesterday, but if you would not mind convincing her to say a great deal more of it, I would be most appreciative."

Darcy raised an eyebrow. "Am I to understand that my wife is encouraging your fiancée in improper behaviour?"

"Apparently," said Bingley, "and with our wedding delayed, Jane's kisses may be my only hope of sanity!"

Bingley had convinced Jane to join them for dinner the next day, and had sent his carriage for her, as it seemed likely to rain. He had been pacing the floor of the sitting room ever since, waiting eagerly for her arrival, and when the sound of the carriage was finally heard, he practically dashed out to greet her. Elizabeth made to follow him, but Darcy caught her hand and held her back. "Let them have a few minutes together, my love," he said with amusement.

"You just hope to keep me to yourself, sir!" she retorted playfully.

His arm snaked out and caught her around the waist, pulling her onto his lap. "Absolutely correct, my dearest."

She wound her arms around his neck. "You, Mr. Darcy, are the most forward man of my acquaintance," she said with an impudent smile.

He stole a breathtaking kiss. "I see that you are finally beginning to understand me, Mrs. Darcy."

She nibbled playfully at his ear. "I must ask you, however, to release me, else Jane will be quite shocked by our behaviour."

"One kiss first, my love," he said. With a smile, she met his demand, and, as he had hoped, one kiss turned into rather more. She was still in his arms when Bingley escorted Jane in, causing Elizabeth to scramble off his lap ungracefully.

It was obvious that restoring her dignity was a lost cause, so she gave a guilty smile as she went to embrace Jane. She whispered an apology for embarrassing her in Jane's ear.

"No need for that, Lizzy," Jane said with a smile. "I am becoming inured to it!"

This statement, coming from Jane, was quite a surprise, and Lizzy took a closer look at her sister, only to note that her delicate lips were ever so slightly swollen. *Jane?* she wondered to herself, and a look at the brightness of Bingley's smile only added to her suspicions.

She did not have a chance to confirm her supposition, however, until after dinner when Darcy and Bingley were thoughtful enough to allow the two women to retire by themselves for a time. She turned to Jane with a look of mischief and said, "Dearest Jane, if I did not know better, I would think that you had been allowing Mr. Bingley to kiss you tonight!"

Jane blushed deeply. "Lizzy!" she exclaimed in deep embarrassment.

Elizabeth took her hand remorsefully. "I am sorry to tease, Jane. I will not raise the subject again."

"No, dearest Lizzy, I am not afraid to speak of it, only embarrassed . . . it is my own fault, you see."

She raised an eyebrow. "Mr. Bingley had nothing to do with it?"

"Oh, Lizzy, I have behaved dreadfully! It began the day after you arrived. I was telling him what a lovely talk you and I had, and how contented you seemed with marriage to Mr. Darcy. We had both been concerned, you know, after you fought on the day you became engaged—and then I just kissed him!" She looked amazed at her own temerity.

Elizabeth smiled knowingly. "Was he shocked?"

Jane coloured. "For a moment, I believe he was, but he recovered quickly. He was . . . pleased; he made that evident." She could not quite bring herself to meet Elizabeth's eyes.

"He looks very happy tonight."

"Well, to tell the truth, Lizzy, I confess I have allowed it to happen a number of times now."

Elizabeth recalled the first times Darcy had kissed her, and how ambivalent she had felt. *Of course, we were not yet engaged,* she thought, but she would have been taken aback by her own response even had they been formally committed to one another. "It can be rather surprising in its effect, can it not?" she said sympathetically.

"I had no idea, Lizzy!" she exclaimed. "It does make it a bit easier for me to understand how you and Mr. Darcy came to be caught in such compromising positions."

Elizabeth laughed. "Yes, well, a great deal of that was my fault, but Mr. Darcy was also rather more . . . demanding than your Mr. Bingley seems to have been." The look in Jane's eyes suggested that Bingley was perhaps not now quite as undemanding as he might once have been. Elizabeth took her hand and pressed it affectionately. "Do you regret kissing him, Jane?"

There was a pause as Jane considered this. "No, I do not. I cannot think that Charles and I should ever be near so daring as you and Mr. Darcy, though, Lizzy! You would think us quite dull, I am sure."

"If you are happy, then I am happy, dearest Jane."

"I confess that I am less worried about the wedding night now!" admitted Jane with a laugh.

"You will find that it comes quite naturally, I have no doubt!" They smiled at one another affectionately.

Bingley rejoined them on his own, a broad smile on his face as he spotted Jane. After a brief greeting, he turned to Elizabeth. "Lizzy, Darcy is quite the changed man these days! I have no idea how you may have accomplished it!"

"I am not certain to what you refer, Mr. Bingley," Elizabeth said cautiously.

"He just confessed to me that there was a letter he needed to finish to his steward that should have gone in yesterday's post! Unbelievable!"

"And this is so extraordinary, Mr. Bingley?" Elizabeth asked with amusement.

"Why, Darcy has always done his work promptly. He has never delayed to the last minute like this," said Bingley. "It is quite delightful to see him engaging in some of the same sins as the rest of us mere mortals."

"I have noticed that he smiles a great deal more than I ever saw in the past," added Jane.

"I will grant you that he does smile more," said Elizabeth with a laugh.

"Do you know what I find the most astonishing, though?" asked Bingley. "His tale of the events in London! Do you realize how shocking it is that Darcy let his cousin deal with Wickham? Darcy always does everything himself. I have never known him to accept help, nor share a responsibility. I believe he would have thought it a weakness to need anyone's assistance."

Elizabeth had not considered this. She thought back on all the time she had known him, and could not find a counter-example. Of course, it was a trait that they shared, and she had learned as well to rely on his support and assistance. "One of William's most redeeming characteristics is his willingness to change," she said lightly.

"For your sake, at least!" said Bingley with a broad smile.

"Of course, I cannot claim to be completely unchanged myself," Elizabeth said slowly.

Bingley and Jane exchanged a glance which suggested to Elizabeth that this topic had been raised between them before. She looked at them in mock reproach until Jane could not help laughing. "Yes, Lizzy, you are different as well. I daresay that you and Mr. Darcy are good influences on one another."

Elizabeth was not regretful when the time came to return to London. Although she had enjoyed her time with Jane and her father, the need to shield Darcy from the notice of those of her family whose vulgarity would be mortifying to him had taken its toll on her. Leaving her former home caused little distress when she would be returning there in only two months' time for Jane's wedding. Although the reason for their return to London was not a pleasant one, she was content being with Darcy.

Georgiana was delighted to see them on their arrival in Brook Street; she had missed her new sister dearly, and was anxious to tell them both of her activities in town since they had left. Colonel Fitzwilliam was unexpectedly off to Newcastle again—"the better to keep an eye on Wickham when he arrives there," said Darcy darkly. Lydia's wedding was scheduled for the following day, and a note from Mr. Gardiner awaited them with the details of the arrangements.

Elizabeth could practically see Darcy's mood deteriorating in front of her as the evening progressed, and was concerned as to the cause of it. Not wishing to raise the question in front of Georgiana, she bided her time until they retired for the night. When they finally went upstairs, Darcy stopped her before she entered her room. "Elizabeth," he said in a serious manner, "my disposition tonight is not pleasant. You might prefer your own company to mine."

She looked at him gravely, troubled by his implication that he should perhaps keep his troubles to himself. *Perhaps*, she thought, *he wishes some time to himself, and is seeking a courteous way to say that.* She suspected, however, that it was his tendency to withdraw when he was troubled, and she certainly did not wish to set a precedent in that regard. "I think that I should prefer your company, regardless of your disposition, and would hope that my company might ease your spirits. You need not pretend to a cheer that you lack."

She thought that he looked relieved, and he kissed her forehead before going to his room. "I shall join you shortly, then, my love," he said. She smiled slightly, pleased that she seemed to have made the correct decision.

After Lucy had assisted her into her nightclothes, Elizabeth sat brushing out her hair as she wondered what might be troubling Darcy. It seemed an encouraging step that he did not attempt to hide his feelings from her. She could not expect their marriage to be always without difficulties, but it was important that they face them in concert. His knock came at the adjoining door, and she bade him enter.

His expression was warm as she set down the brush and walked into his arms. He held her close to him, burying his face in her hair, letting the softness and the sweet scent of it soothe him.

As she felt him relax in her embrace, she tilted her head back to look up at him. "Can you tell me what is distressing you, my dearest?" she asked softly.

He could see her concern, and felt warmed by it; warmed, and also pleased in other ways as well. He lowered his lips to hers in a lingering kiss. "Let me lose myself in you first, my beloved, and then, if you wish, we can speak further," he said.

There are many forms of comfort, thought Elizabeth, and she was more than happy to provide relief in that form, responding as ever to the feeling of his body against hers and the pleasures of his kisses. She arched herself against him seductively, and was rewarded by an immediate response.

Their lovemaking was sweet and tender, and when Elizabeth lay in his arms afterwards, she could sense that it had lightened his humour somewhat. She stroked his cheek affectionately, and he turned his face to her. "You do not intend to forget anything for a minute, do you, my love?" he asked lightly.

"I do not wish to forget anything that relates to you. You have made it clear that when I am in distress, you wish to know about it; likewise, I would like to share in any troubles you face."

"Trapped in my own net," he said affectionately. "Very well, my love, you may do your worst, though this is not as large a matter as you seem to believe, just that the prospect of seeing George Wickham tomorrow is an unpleasant one for me."

"I can hardly fault you for that, William. It is distressing to think that anyone can care so little for the harm he does to others, and be so impudent as to suppose that he shall always escape unscathed."

Darcy sighed deeply. "It is the more distressing when he is someone you have counted as a friend."

She considered his words. Certainly, she had experienced a sense of betrayal when she realized Wickham's true character after reading Darcy's letter, and a sense of self-disgust that she had allowed herself to admire and be attracted by such a man. Her acquaintance with him, though, had been but a few short months;

Darcy had known him his entire life, and by his own report they had been companions in their youth. How much greater must be the pain of his treachery under those circumstances! Having some sense as to the depth of her husband's personal loyalties, she could only imagine what it must have cost him to dissolve a friendship that had begun so early, and with someone with such strong ties to his family. "That must be very difficult indeed," she said.

"He knows my vulnerabilities so well. If it were only money, or even dishonour, that he sought, it would be less painful. But no, he understands how much more pain he can cause me by injuring those I love. I will not be able to look at him without seeing the hurt that he has dealt first to Georgiana, now to you. It is well-nigh unbearable."

Elizabeth knew that she would have to word her next ques-tion carefully. "I have never understood why he wishes to injure you in the first place."

Darcy grimaced. "It is not as if he spends his time searching for ways to get his revenge on me; it is more that he cannot resist an opportunity when he sees one, and he can see opportunities where no one else can. As to why . . . I have always assumed that he never surmounted his jealousy about the differences in our prospects. When we were young it meant nothing, but as we grew older, he resented it more. I believe it gives him some sense of power to get the better of me in one way or another, so he continues his tricks to this day."

She nestled close to him. "I am so sorry. I do not believe that I can imagine what it would feel like to have a friend turn on you in that way. And, William . . . " she trailed off.

"Yes, my love?" He tangled his fingers in her long curls.

"Thank you for undertaking the mortification of dealing with him, for Lydia's sake."

"Sweet Elizabeth, you hardly need thank me for remedying a situation that would not have existed but for me."

"No," she said determinedly, "it exists because of Wickham's amorality, and if you play any role in it at all, it is because he knows that in a cause of compassion and honour, you will be able to get the better of yourself and work for a solution with a man you despise. I am proud of you."

He gathered her even closer to him. "My dearest love, you are very good to me, and I do not deserve such praise."

She sat up abruptly and fixed a look of mock disapproval on her face. "Are you arguing with me, Mr. Darcy?" she said, in tones which would not have been out of place for Lady Catherine de Bourgh.

She was pleased to see him laugh. "I would never dream of it, madam."

"I am glad to hear it," she replied briskly. "Otherwise I should have to punish you."

"And how, pray tell, would you accomplish that, Mrs. Darcy?" he inquired.

She took advantage of her position over him to give him a very good sense of how she intended to punish him, running her hands lightly along the lines of his body. With a wicked smile, she began to stroke and caress him in the ways she knew he found most arousing.

He reached up and drew her down on top of him. "In that case, madam," he said, between kisses, "I feel it only appropriate to warn you that I am feeling *quite* argumentative tonight."

Chapter 14

Elizabeth was pleased to discover Darcy's frame of mind substantially improved by the next morning. If not in particularly good spirits, he no longer appeared actively distressed, even when it came time to depart for St. Clements. They arrived there just before the hour to find Lydia fidgeting in her impatience for matters to proceed, and full of complaints about her stay in London. Mrs. Gardiner was clearly tempted to put in a few words of her own, but managed to restrain herself to sharing with Elizabeth some of the frustrations of the past two weeks.

Elizabeth breathed a sigh of relief when they entered the church and found that Wickham was in fact there. Her one fear had been that he would somehow fail to appear. He greeted them both in his most amiable manner, and Elizabeth was proud to see Darcy managing to be in general civil. Fortunately, the ceremony began shortly thereafter.

As Lydia came down the aisle on her uncle's arm, Elizabeth could not help thinking back to making the same journey herself in Matlock, but the similarities between the two occasions ended there. Lydia's giggling and flirtatious glances at Wickham seemed to make a mockery of what should have been a solemn occasion, and while Wickham's demeanour was more appropriate, she knew the ceremony meant nothing to him but a source of income. The curate had little interest in the occasion, since Wickham lived in the parish but was not a churchgoer, and he gabbled his way through the service as quickly as possible. At one point Elizabeth turned to Darcy and saw that his jaw had a grim set to it. With a feeling of mischief, she whispered to him, "Are you arguing with me again?" and was pleased to see the corners of his lips lift in a barely disguised smile.

The service could not end soon enough for Elizabeth, and afterwards she bore Lydia's company as well as she could manage while Darcy, Wickham, and Mr. Gardiner met with Darcy's attorney to finalize the money matters. When they returned, Lydia and Wickham set forth on the coach to Newcastle after a few more foolish comments from the bride.

"I am glad that your father did not give in to your mother and allow them to return to Longbourn," Darcy said in Elizabeth's ear.

"I was grateful that you were there when the question arose, or I fear that he might have been unable to hold his position. My mother can be very persistent."

"I am hardly surprised, though I do not believe that I am in any position to criticize anyone for being persistent," he teased. "But let us bid your aunt and uncle farewell; Georgiana will be expecting us home soon."

Their first months at Pemberley passed quickly. It was soon difficult for Elizabeth to recall a time when Mr. Darcy had not been in her thoughts constantly, and she became accustomed to the duties of the Mistress of Pemberley, with substantial assistance from Mrs. Reynolds.

One day after they had been discussing the menus, Mrs. Reynolds said, "If I may consult you on a separate matter, madam, I have been wondering whether to start preparing the nursery. It has not been used since Miss Darcy was a babe, and it is not in the best condition."

Elizabeth raised an eyebrow, wondering whether this question dealt in generalities or if Mrs. Reynolds had made some surmises. She herself had been questioning for some time the changes she was feeling in her body. She ought to have suspected that Mrs. Reynolds would miss nothing. Elizabeth had no doubts that the housekeeper was eagerly anticipating the arrival of Mr. Darcy's children, and surely she would have been watching carefully for any signs that the mistress might be increasing. "You seem to have some suspicions, Mrs. Reynolds," she said delicately.

"You have had that look about you of late, Mrs. Darcy," she acknowledged.

"I have had some suspicions of my own, but they are nothing more than that, so I would appreciate it if this went no further at this point. I have no great expertise in this matter, and I would not wish to raise any false hopes."

"You have not shared this with Mr. Darcy, I assume," Mrs. Reynolds said with the boldness of a long-time family servant. "He still seems very happy."

"Why should he not be happy?"

"Oh, madam," Mrs. Reynolds said, "I venture to guess that when informed of the situation Mr. Darcy will suffer from a case of nerves such as you will scarcely believe, and it will be all we can do to contain him. It was so when his mother was increasing, and I have no doubt that it will be all the worse for that."

It came to Elizabeth that Mrs. Reynolds had not raised this subject by accident. "Pray continue."

"The young master was quite affected by Lady Anne's illness after Miss Georgiana's birth; we thought at the time that she was unlikely to remain with us. He had always been close to his mother, though never closer than when he sat with her every day during her recovery. When he discovered that she was once again in a delicate condition a few years later, he became quite, shall I say, paralyzed with concern for her, fearing the worst. All of us tried to reassure him, but he would not speak of his worries to anyone. When his worst fears came true, he was devastated." Mrs. Reynolds paused. "To this day, I have seen that he is uncomfortable when confronted with any woman in such a condition, and I can only imagine that it will be all the worse for him when it is his wife he sees before him."

This was hardly what Elizabeth wished to hear; she had found herself feeling increasingly needy of Darcy's support and affection during this time of uncertainty. It was difficult enough for a woman as independent in spirit as she to feel so reliant on another, and the idea that he might himself be in need of support—extensive support, if Mrs. Reynolds was to be credited—was a disturbing one. It was a grave disappointment to think that his response to her condition might not be pleasure or anticipation, but rather distress; she certainly did not wish for him to suffer in any way, and she had so looked forward to surprising him with the intelligence that their family was to increase. If only she could be nearer to Jane, or to her aunt Gardiner . . . but such thoughts could bring her no satisfaction. "I see," she said slowly, beginning to realize just how alone the Mistress of Pemberley could be in some matters. She found herself wishing that she could open up her heart to Mrs. Reynolds as Georgiana and occasionally even Darcy did, but she was cognizant of the inappropriateness of such a course of action.

It occurred to her that, given the turn of the present conversation, she could, however, turn to the housekeeper for some of the information that she felt herself to be so sadly lacking. "Mrs. Reynolds, it would be helpful to me if I had more knowledge of the signs I should be watching for in myself to have more certainty as to my condition."

Mrs. Reynolds realized that the mistress, living at such a distance from her family, was left without more experienced women to turn to for assistance in these matters. Suspecting that the strong-willed Mrs. Darcy might not respond well to a motherly sympathy from her, she said briskly, "Indeed I would imagine so. One can never know for certain, of course, until the babe quickens, and I suspect you are not so far along as that, but there are certain signs which can be a good indication." She proceeded to elaborate on some of the changes which would accompany such an event, concluding that there was an excellent midwife in the district, and that Elizabeth would be in good hands should she be required.

To her attentive listener, her words served only as a confirmation of her suspicions, and she thanked Mrs. Reynolds for the advice.

The housekeeper looked at her sharply. "You might wish to consider taking Lucy into your confidence, Mrs. Darcy. She is very discreet, and would be invaluable in helping you through the more difficult times, especially if you choose not to share the news with Mr. Darcy as of yet. You can also rely on Wilkins, who has had a good deal of experience in seeing Mr. Darcy through difficult times."

Elizabeth promised to consider these thoughts. After leaving her presence, Mrs. Reynolds shook her head with a smile. Yes, she could certainly be proud of Mrs. Darcy, and grateful that she had the strength to handle some of the master's complexities. She would need help, however, and the housekeeper went off to consider how best to support her once Mr. Darcy became aware of the situation.

Meanwhile, Elizabeth laid her head on her hands. She considered how to handle the matter, finding that she was reluctant to keep a secret from her husband, yet understanding that if it was to cause him the degree of worry Mrs. Reynolds feared, it would be best to limit the time he would need to face that worry. She sighed, thinking of her husband's impressive ability to prognosticate the worst possible outcome and his propensity towards anxiety. *Why could this not be simpler?* she asked herself in some distress. *Why could he not simply be pleased and excited, as any other man would be?*

At length she resolved to wait. The Gardiners were due to arrive for their Christmas visit the following week, and would be staying for over a fortnight. After their departure, if all the signs still suggested that her suspicions were correct, she would tell him. She would certainly take advantage of her aunt's presence to discuss the matter with her, as well.

Over the next weeks, it became increasingly clear to Elizabeth that there was in fact an extensive silent conspiracy devoted to protecting Darcy from painful knowledge. Certain subtle changes began to take place within the household. Fires were built up higher in rooms when she was present, the foods served shifted further towards her preferences, with obvious attention to a potentially queasy stomach, footstools appeared near the chairs she favoured when none had been there previously, and she became aware that the footmen were taking careful note when she departed on her walks and the direction she took. The stealth with which this occurred was more convincing than anything else to Elizabeth that Mrs. Reynolds' concerns were well-founded, if her fears were shared by other servants who had been with the family for years. She found herself grateful for the quiet fuss being made over her comfort, not so much for the physical changes as for the expression of concern it represented.

She found it less difficult to keep her knowledge of her condition from Darcy than she had expected when she considered how much it might trouble him. The arrival of the Gardiners provided a helpful distraction. She was delighted to see them, and looked forward to long talks with her aunt. It was her first chance to meet the newest of the young Gardiners, now only two months old, and holding him made her dream wistfully of the time that her own child would be in her arms. She was pleased to see Darcy enjoying the company of the older Gardiner children; had his behaviour towards Georgiana not already told her that he would be a devoted father, this would have been evidence of it.

Elizabeth relied heavily on Mrs. Reynolds for the arrangements for Christmas, allowing her to dictate which servants would go home, and which would have their families join them at Pemberley. The house was decorated with holly and ivy, the midwinter greenery adding a welcome touch of informality to the stately halls of Pemberley House. Elizabeth enjoyed the quiet solemnity of the season with her family, and was pleased with the atmosphere of tranquility that attended the gathering.

It was clear that Darcy was also contented with the holiday, which was certainly livelier for the addition of the Gardiner family and Elizabeth's influence. Although he was genuinely sorry to see their guests depart, he was also grateful to have Elizabeth to himself once more. He arranged matters so that he could spend much of the day in her presence, enjoying the peace and pleasure that he experienced by her side. Snow began to fall by evening, and she convinced him to come outside to watch it with her, and in the silence of the darkness he put his arms around her, more caught by her beauty than that of nature. "Let us retire early tonight, my love," he said softly in her ear.

She looked up at him affectionately. "I thought you would never ask."

Elizabeth had felt the quickening a few days earlier, and it seemed wrong not to share her knowledge at this point, but his countenance exhibited such a happy tranquility that she had not been able to bring herself to do anything which might shatter it. After they had retired and taken their pleasure of each other, however, she knew that she could no longer delay.

"William," she began as she lay in his arms, then lapsed into silence as she realized that in her wish to avoid thinking about his reaction, she had given no thought to how to share the news with him.

"Yes, my love?" he asked affectionately, winding her hair around his hand.

"I love you very much—I hope you know that," she temporized.

"I believe that I do, but I never object to hearing it. As it happens, I adore you passionately."

She took a deep breath, but then said nothing. Her weakness in this matter was infuriating, but the truth was that she was afraid of hearing that he was upset over her state. The idea of their child was such a happy one to her that she knew it would be difficult for her if his reaction were in the least negative. She buried her head in his shoulder, trying to summon her courage.

His voice was very gentle. "Whatever it is, I will not be angry with you, my love."

There were times when she wished that he could not read her quite so well. "I do have something to tell you," she said slowly, "and I am concerned as to how you will react, but I doubt that you will be angry."

"Well, I shall attempt to brace myself," he said with a slight smile.

She despised how dependent upon his approval she felt in her present condition. Unable to bring herself to say the words, she instead took his hand and laid it on the place where the baby had begun to make himself felt. She found herself holding her breath as she awaited his understanding.

Her first indication of his comprehension came when she felt his body stiffen slightly. "What is it that you are trying to tell me, Elizabeth?" he asked, his voice level.

"That you may expect an heir to Pemberley in several months," she said, relieved to finally say the words.

Darcy felt as if a great weight had fallen in on him. He had known on some level that this moment would come sooner or later, but he had wanted so badly to deny it. Like a prisoner waiting to hear his sentence, he said, "In several months?"

"My aunt suspects it will be late in May," she said softly. The answer to her question was apparent; he evidenced no pleasure at the intelligence. *Very well,* she told herself firmly, ignoring a stab of pain, *I shall have to be pleased and excited enough for both of us.* She awaited his response, and when it became clear that none was immediately forthcoming, she anxiously added, "My dearest, have you nothing else to say?"

"Please, Elizabeth!" He caught himself, and seeing the look on her face, sighed almost imperceptibly. Yes, he needed to say something, but it would not be easy. "That is very exciting news, my love; forgive me if it takes me a little time to become accustomed to the idea." *A little time?* he asked himself mockingly. *I doubt that I shall ever become accustomed to this idea.* He gathered her to him almost convulsively. He knew that he should be expressing his delight to her, but that far he could not bring himself to go. "I love you, my sweetest, loveliest Elizabeth," he whispered, wondering how he could possibly survive it if the worst happened.

Determinedly, she said, "And now it is *your* turn to tell *me* what is troubling *you.*"

"My love, there is no need to worry about me," Darcy said in what he hoped was a reassuring voice.

Elizabeth decided to change her strategy. "William," she said teasingly, "if you do not tell me about whatever implausible conclusion you have reached, I will have to take drastic measures to make you do so."

He accepted the distraction gladly. "And how, madam, do you plan to make me speak?" he asked lightly.

She raised herself off the bed and leaned her hands on his shoulders. "By physical force, if necessary, sir!"

An unwilling smile began to tug at the corners of his mouth at the image of Elizabeth attempting to bodily subdue him. "I tremble before you, my love."

She kissed him lightly. Her voice serious again, she said, "I beg of you, William, do not exclude me. I cannot tell you how that pains me."

"Elizabeth, please believe me . . . " She could tell from his tone that he had no intention of sharing his concerns, and she had no patience for his reserve.

"I do *not* believe you, William! I am not so lacking in perception as to be unable to ascertain when something is troubling you. How would you feel if you knew that I was keeping something from you under these circumstances—would you not feel hurt and betrayed?" She knew of nothing that would be more likely to force him to speak than to indicate that he was paining her by not doing so, and she was determined not to rest until he understood her need.

She had trapped him; he recognized it immediately. With a deep sigh, he said, "Enough. Since you will not be moved, I will tell you of my reservations, although it goes against my better judgment. But please be patient with me; this will not be easy for me."

Her face softened as she relaxed back into his embrace. "Thank you, my dearest."

Darcy hardly knew how to begin to put his thoughts in order. The last thing he wanted was to bring worries to her mind that could only make matters more difficult for her, yet he knew with the instincts he had developed in his time with Elizabeth that she was correct to be concerned that secrecy on such a matter could come between them. "I cannot deny that I would like to see our children running through the halls of Pemberley," he began slowly. "At the same time, I am all too aware of the risks of child-bearing, and I find the idea of any risk to you, my dearest, well-nigh intolerable." There was no point, he thought, in saying that he would rather not have an heir than have her face that danger. There was, after all, nothing that could be done about it.

Relieved that he was sharing his concerns, she responded with logic which she hoped would ease his mind. "But there is no reason to feel that I *am* at any risk. I am young, of good health, and my mother gave birth to five children in six years with what I understand to have been remarkably little difficulty."

He sighed. "It is nothing so rational, my love. I had the mis-fortune of watching my mother go through a long illness and eventually die in childbirth, and the idea that the same could happen to you . . . " He found he could not complete his thought.

She stroked his hair tenderly, sensing the strong emotions he was working to suppress. "Will you tell me about it, love?" she asked gently.

He gave her a startled look. "About why I fear losing you?"

She smiled at him understandingly. "No, William, about your mother." She held her breath awaiting his reaction.

It did not come immediately. "Elizabeth, my dearest love, forgive me; that is a subject that I find very difficult to discuss," he finally said carefully.

Elizabeth's instinct was to reassure him that he need say nothing that he did not wish, but she knew that would not serve. She simply waited, reminding herself of the importance of this. At last he sighed. "You are not going to rest until I accommodate you, are you?"

She shook her head. "I am afraid that I will not, given that her ghost threatens to stand between us."

He acknowledged her point with a quirk of his eyebrow. "What would you like to know, then?"

She smoothed his hair from his face. "Can you tell me what happened?"

He closed his eyes, a pained look on his face. "Once, when I was young, perhaps seven or eight, I was tormenting my mother with complaints about why our family had no other children, and demanding a little brother. Her spirits were quite lively in those days, but I recall that she had tears in her eyes when she told me that the doctors had said that it would not be safe for her to have another child. I gather there was some cause for concern at my birth that led them to this conclusion. Needless to say, I felt ashamed of upsetting her, and the moment stayed with me as a result. When it became clear a few years later that she had acted against the advice of the doctors, I could tell that my father was greatly concerned, although my mother seemed not to be. I did not know who to believe, but it weighed heavily on my mind."

He sighed before continuing. "You have no doubt heard that she was very ill after Georgiana's birth. I remember that she was well and happy one day, then the next everyone was speaking in hushed whispers, and I was told that my mother might not be with us much longer. As it happened, that stage lasted for months. She was too ill even to hold Georgiana, but she seemed to find some comfort in having me sit with her, so I spent hours each day at her side, talking to her, reading aloud, or just bearing her company, and wondering if she would see the next dawn." His voice caught, and he stopped speaking.

She sought to bring him back to the present by kissing him tenderly. "Where was your father during that time?"

"I hardly saw him," Darcy said tightly, leashed anger apparent in his voice. "He knew that he was responsible for what had happened, and he could not face her. And poor Georgiana was a victim as well. None of us had time for her, and she was left to the wet-nurse and Mrs. Reynolds."

Puzzled, Elizabeth asked, "What had your father done, that he was responsible for your mother's illness?"

He turned his head to look at her, his gaze dark and penetrating. "The same that I have done, to be responsible for the risk you face."

She sat up, appalled by his words. "William, do you *blame* yourself for my condition?"

His voice was steely as he said, "You did not create the situation by yourself, and we are both aware which of us insisted on the circumstances that led to it."

"William, this is not a cause for regrets, but for rejoicing! It is a normal part of life, and you are not at fault for sharing my bed. I would have it no other way! From what little you have said, it sounds as if your mother wanted another child desperately, and was pleased by her condition. I do not know where you came upon this idea that it was something your father forced upon her, but I insist that you disabuse yourself of it immediately!"

His look was impenetrable. "She never recovered, Elizabeth. She improved, certainly, but she never regained her vitality, and was never again the lively, witty woman she once was. Yet five years later, he did it again, but that time we all knew what was to come to pass. I watched her fade away for months, and one evening I bade her goodnight, and the next morning Mrs. Reynolds told me that she was no longer with us." His voice was raw with grief.

She looked at him steadily, seeing the confusion of the boy he had been, losing his mother to death and his father to grieving, his understanding of the situation limited, but trying to take on the responsibility of an adult through it all. "William," she said gently, "would you have denied your parents the comfort of each other's love? What happened to your mother was tragic, but it was no one's fault."

He was silent for some time, moving only to stroke her hair. "Elizabeth, my family was never the same afterwards. My father grieved for years, and he and I were not the best of friends afterwards, because I reminded him too much of my mother, and I blamed him for her death. That was when George Wickham made his way into my father's confidence, and I fear made some efforts to turn him against me. It was a bitter time."

"I am so sorry, my dearest. How unfortunate that you in some ways lost both parents at the same time, and at a difficult age."

He turned onto his side to face her. "It took *you* to bring the joy back to Pemberley, my love," he said with intense feeling.

"Oh, William," she replied, her heart aching for his losses.

"I mean it, Elizabeth. There was always grief here, to one extent or another, after my mother's death, and although the loss impacted me less once I was out in society, I became trapped in another net, one of people who valued me only as a commodity. I became world-weary and cynical. There were so few people whose affection I trusted—and then I met you, with your liveliness and wit and infectious smiles, everything I had lacked for all those years." He paused for a moment to kiss her with an emotional urgency. "So you can see, my dearest, most beloved Elizabeth, why the thought of losing you torments me."

She held his face in her hands, gazing into his eyes. "I can see why my condition will raise unhappy memories for you, dearest, but you have no reason to fear for me," she said steadily. "I am not your mother, and the past is not the present. So long as you are able to tell me what you feel, we can share this burden, but I will not allow you to have the past predict the future."

He gathered her into his arms. "Darling Elizabeth," he murmured, his voice evidencing a slight quiver.

She held him tightly, speaking endearments quietly in his ear, until she felt his body releasing its tension. "All will be well, my dearest," she whispered.

"I shall require a great deal of reassurance of that," he replied in a muffled voice, turning to kiss her tenderly.

"I will be happy to reassure you whenever you like," she said lightly, "because I know that your worries are groundless." She gave him a teasing smile, then added, "I can offer this as proof of my position: as nearly as I can judge, every servant at Pemberley has known of my condition for weeks, and their only thought has been to protect *you* from the knowledge of it."

He turned a startled stare on her. "No," he said disbelievingly.

An amused smile curved her mouth. "Yes. You have a very devoted household."

He rolled onto his back, covering his face with his hands. "There is no privacy to be had as Master of Pemberley," he said with bemused regret.

"None, so far as I can see. Fortunately, you do still have a few consolations."

He raised an eyebrow at her. "What consolations do you have in mind, my love?"

She smiled slowly and ran her hand down his side slowly. "Tell me what you would like," she whispered provocatively.

"You," he said intensely. "You, now and always." He tangled his hand in her hair, pulling her head towards his, then slowly lowered his mouth to hers until they met in passionate communion.

<hr />

Elizabeth woke during the night with the feeling that something was amiss. The fire had burned down, but she could tell from his body that Darcy was wakeful as well. He was, in fact, making no effort to sleep, but was propped up on one elbow beside her, his other hand resting lightly on her side.

"William, are you well?" she asked with sleepy concern.

"Quite well," he said softly. "I am sorry to have disturbed you, my love."

"What keeps you awake so late?"

"I have been thinking."

"Now *that* is a dangerous activity. I hope it is not a serious matter."

"No." He moved his hand, caressing her body gently. "I have been thinking about our child."

She reached up to touch his cheek. His countenance seemed quite peaceful, but she was not without concern. "And have you reached any conclusions?"

He smiled and kissed her tenderly. "Only that the idea pleases me. I have never truly permitted myself to consider the possibility in the past, so it is rather new to me, but I find the thought of a child of ours to be an agreeable one." His tone shifted slightly. "Which is not to say that I am not still worried, but I have been meditating instead on the happiness this could bring."

His words brought tears to her eyes. "Oh, William," she whispered, her voice choked.

"What did I say?" he asked in dismay.

She smiled through her tears. "Nothing. I am happy to hear it. And I fear that I am quite foolishly emotional these days, so I advise you to accustom yourself to it.

He gathered her into his arms. "Elizabeth, my dearest love. You may be as emotional as you like, so long as you are mine."

"Always, my love," she said tearfully.

He slid his hand along her side, bringing it to rest cupped around her breast, somewhat more generously proportioned than usual owing to her condition. "I have been appreciating, too, some of the changes in you which I had failed to note prior to this."

With an amused look, she responded, "There are quite a number of them, I must say. And I have been feeling him move for several days now."

"You think it is a boy, then?"

"I have not the slightest idea," she said with a laugh. "I must call him something, though!"

"Well, I would prefer a girl," he said definitely. "A girl with her mother's eyes."

She raised an eyebrow. "Not an heir to Pemberley?"

"Next time." A shadow crossed his face, and she knew that his fears had not left him. "Promise me that you will take the best of care of yourself, Elizabeth."

"I promise," she said with an indulgent smile. "You need not worry about that; you have any number of servants who have been watching my every move for weeks, and I have no doubt that they would now not hesitate to report any transgression I should make to you immediately!"

"I hope that you will forgive me if I become somewhat overprotective."

"I have been anticipating it already," she said ruefully.

"Perhaps you could consider it a disability of mine." They smiled into each other's eyes. "I love you very dearly, Elizabeth." He kissed her with a gentleness that gradually changed to something very different. By the time he released her, she was feeling pleasantly breathless.

His hands began to caress her body, lingering over her abdomen. "And I have a confession to make," he continued, in a voice that made her pulses race. "I find that I enjoy the idea of my child inside you far more than I should." Had she any doubts about the manner of his enjoyment, they were quickly put to rest.

⁕

Elizabeth was pleased to discover that Darcy's warm feelings about the upcoming addition to their family persisted. Fortunately, he did not attempt to disguise his periods of anxiety, allowing himself to be reassured by his wife, as well as enduring on a few occasions lectures from Mrs. Reynolds on the subject. If pressed, Elizabeth would have admitted to feeling somewhat smothered by his attentiveness to her health and needs, but it seemed a small price to pay for his greater comfort.

Some weeks after he learned of her condition, Darcy said, "I have been wondering, my love, if it is approaching the time for us to be seeking a wet-nurse."

Elizabeth gave him a startled glance. "I had not intended to employ a wet-nurse, in fact. I see no reason why I cannot manage on my own."

"I do not wish you to have any unnecessary stress, and it seems it would be a way to ease matters for you," he said persuasively, knowing better than to insist immediately.

"William, this is a perfectly natural event, and it will be no different for me than for any other woman. The stress, as you call it, is no danger to me," she responded firmly.

Darcy frowned. "Elizabeth, I realize that you think I am being foolish, but if there is anything that can be done to allow you an easier recovery, I would feel much better if we did so."

"I shall be *recovered* in a matter of a few days! This is nothing to be concerned over!" Elizabeth looked at her husband in some frustration. She did not want his anxieties to affect their everyday family life, yet wished to be sympathetic to his needs. Finally another tack occurred to her. "William, are you aware that women who do not nurse their own babes tend to increase again much sooner than those who do?"

"That seems an unlikely story, Elizabeth," he said dubiously.

She rolled her eyes. "If you wish, I will ring for Mrs. Reynolds, and you may ask her as to the truth of it. It is hardly something I would expect a man to be aware of."

He considered this. "Are you certain of this?"

"William, it is well known among women," she said firmly.

His expression lightened. "Then by all means, let us not employ a wet-nurse, my love. I am in no hurry to repeat this process!"

Elizabeth raised an eyebrow amusedly at the alacrity with which he accepted the idea. "You do not wish this child to have younger brothers and sisters?" she teased.

"Allow me some time to recover from this experience first, I pray you!" he responded playfully, but with obvious meaning.

As her time drew nearer, the signs of stress on her husband grew somewhat greater. Elizabeth, after giving the matter some thought, requested Wilkins to attend her.

"You sent for me, madam?" asked Wilkins from the door of her sitting room.

"Yes, Wilkins; please come in and sit down." Elizabeth noted the subtle look of surprise on the valet's face.

"Yes, madam," he said, and awaited her pleasure.

"Wilkins," she said, "We have an incipient situation on our hands for which some advance planning would not be inappropriate. May I speak frankly?" He inclined his head in agreement, and she continued, "As you know, we have the expectation of adding the new heir to Pemberley to our family in the very near future, and I anticipate that the occasion of my indisposition will be a very difficult one for my husband. I wanted you to be aware of this, as it is not unlikely that you will be the one who will have to manage the situation when it occurs." She watched him for his reaction.

"Ah, yes, madam," said Wilkins carefully. "Mrs. Reynolds and I have already addressed this question."

Amused that the staff were, as usual, more aware than she anticipated, Elizabeth said, "What conclusions did you and she reach?"

He coloured slightly. "We have plans for a variety of contingencies. Should we receive notice of the situation before Mr. Darcy, we have several, umm, prepared emergencies which will require his immediate attention on other parts of the estate. If this is not possible, Mrs. Reynolds and I will remain with him, and should either of us deem it necessary, we will make liberal application of brandy, dosed with laudanum if required. Do these plans meet with your approval, madam?"

"They do. Dare I assume that you have already inducted Lucy into this conspiracy?"

He had the grace to look somewhat embarrassed. "Yes, madam."

She raised an eyebrow. "Well, I am relieved that I can leave Mr. Darcy to your capable management, then, Wilkins."

He stood and bowed to her. "I shall do my best, madam."

Chapter 15

ELIZABETH'S PAINS BEGAN JUST before dawn one fine night in May. She was grateful they were not severe initially, though it was a struggle to mimic sleep in order not to disturb her husband. She was grateful when he finally awoke and she could move more freely. She accepted his affectionate kiss, then said briskly, "I am quite hungry this morning. I think that I shall ring for Lucy to bring me breakfast immediately."

He looked at her oddly. "Too hungry to wait to be dressed?"

She surprised herself with her acting ability. "Not as hungry as that, but perhaps I was too active yesterday. I thought I might spend the morning resting."

"As you wish, my love," he said. "I am tempted to offer to bear you company, but I fear that it would not be rest that you would be getting, in that case."

She managed to smile through a strong cramp. "Another time, William, I shall be happy to take up your offer."

Fortunately, Lucy arrived shortly thereafter. Although Darcy's presence inhibited her from speaking directly, Elizabeth managed to communicate her situation in pantomime when his back was turned. Lucy's eyes widened, and she said in a nervous voice, "I will fetch your breakfast right away, madam."

It seemed to take an inordinate amount of time for her husband to ready himself for the day, but Elizabeth knew that it was only her own anxiety and increasing discomfort that made it seem so. When finally he departed with an affectionate kiss and a promise to check on her later, she breathed a sigh of relief. His departure was followed so promptly by the arrival of Mrs. Reynolds, accompanied by Lucy, that Elizabeth knew she must have been awaiting her opportunity.

"So your time is upon you, Mrs. Darcy?" Mrs. Reynolds asked briskly.

"It would appear so," replied Elizabeth with a grimace as another pain seized her. Mrs. Reynolds placed her hand over Elizabeth's abdomen, feeling the strength of the contraction.

"The midwife has been sent for, and I expect she should be here soon. Meanwhile, it does you no good to be lying so. You must walk around, Mrs. Darcy."

The idea seemed completely lacking in appeal to Elizabeth, but she obediently followed the housekeeper's instructions. "I cannot walk far in this room," she observed with a touch of amusement.

"When Mr. Darcy has left the house, you may walk in the corridor, madam."

"Where is . . . " Elizabeth paused during another pain, and Mrs. Reynolds took her arm to support her. "Where will Mr. Darcy be going?"

"Wilkins is taking care of that, madam; you need not worry about Mr. Darcy. Lucy, I think that you had best fetch Anne Fletcher," Mrs. Reynolds said.

Elizabeth raised an eyebrow as Lucy left. "Mrs. Fletcher?" she asked, wondering why on earth Mrs. Reynolds should want one of the cooks at a moment like this.

"You seem to be moving along more rapidly than I would expect, madam, judging by your pace, and Mrs. Fletcher is very experienced in these matters. She can stay with you until the midwife arrives."

A brief panic swept through Elizabeth. "You will stay, too, will you not, Mrs. Reynolds?"

Mrs. Reynolds smiled warmly and patted her hand. "Of course I will stay."

Mrs. Fletcher proved to be less concerned than the house-keeper about the imminence of the event, especially once Elizabeth admitted that the pains had been going on for some hours. She encouraged Elizabeth to partake of some soup and bread, for she would be needing her strength.

The day seemed interminable to Elizabeth as her pains con-tinued. By midafternoon she felt already exhausted, and as the pains continued to increase in their intensity and frequency, she could no longer keep a stoic silence. "Soon, Mrs. Darcy," the midwife reassured her during the interval between her pains. "Soon it will be time."

Shortly after Elizabeth cried out at one particularly agoniz-ing contraction, firm footsteps could be heard in the hallway outside, followed by the stern voice of Wilkins. "Mr. Darcy, you must come back downstairs. You cannot be with her, sir; you can do her no good. Please, sir, come down with Miss Darcy."

"I *will* see her! Out of my way, Wilkins, immediately!"

"Sir, it is not proper . . . "

"Wilkins!" Darcy's voice had become threatening.

"Oh, let him in," Elizabeth said resignedly. "He can do no worse here than anywhere else."

The midwife glanced at Mrs. Reynolds, who gave a slight nod, just as the door opened and Darcy entered, his face ashen. He knelt immediately next to Elizabeth and took her hands in his. "Elizabeth, no one told me, or I should have been here far sooner."

Elizabeth managed a slight smile. "I told them not to tell you."

"How are you, my dearest?" He pressed kisses on her hands.

"As well as can be expected." She gripped his hands tightly as a strong pain tore through her. She bit her lip to stop a cry, unwilling to behave in a manner that could increase his worries, no matter the provocation, but she could do nothing about the tears that leaked from her eyes.

"You are doing well, Mrs. Darcy," the midwife said. "A few more like that, and you will be ready to push."

"Thank God," said Elizabeth fervently as the pain eased.

Darcy looked up at the midwife. Every woman in the room was firmly ignoring his existence. "Something is wrong! It should not hurt her so much!" he exclaimed. He was not reassured by the barely disguised smiles that met his comment.

"William, it *always* hurts this much. Often much more," said Elizabeth with some exasperation.

"Are you certain?"

"Mr. Darcy, your wife is doing very well. You need have no worries," said the midwife.

The pain came again, and Mrs. Reynolds gave her a cloth to bite on. "Oh, Elizabeth," Darcy whispered, tormented by the sight of her suffering, which seemed to go on and on. Tears streamed down her face.

Mrs. Reynolds said sharply. "Mr. Darcy, I will not have you upsetting your wife. If you can do no better than that at comforting her, then begone!"

Again in a painless interval, Elizabeth could not help a weak smile at the look on Darcy's face as he received this scolding, but it seemed to serve. He took a deep breath and squared his shoulders, not taking his eyes off her for even a moment.

As the next pain took her, he said, "Look at me, Elizabeth." She looked into his eyes as if receiving strength from him, clutching forcefully at his hands. A minute later his gaze warmed as she relaxed. "You are very strong, my love!" he teased, glancing down at their entwined hands.

"William," she murmured, allowing her head to rest on his shoulder momentarily, praying this would end soon.

He whispered endearments to her as her pains came and went until the midwife announced, "Mrs. Darcy, at the next one, you must push, as hard as you may. Mr. Darcy, it is time for you to leave, sir."

"No." Darcy's voice was implacable.

"Mr. Darcy, it is most inappropriate for you to be here at all, but especially not now! I must ask you to leave!"

"No!" he snapped.

"Leave be," Mrs. Reynolds told the midwife. "He can be stubborn as a mule when he sets his mind to it."

Elizabeth gave a feeble laugh, both at the housekeeper's statement and at her husband's complete lack of reaction to it.

"Now, Mrs. Darcy. Push now!"

Afterwards, Elizabeth could remember little of the next period beyond her husband's eyes holding her and her hands clutching his fiercely. She recalled crying in excruciating pain, and Mrs. Reynolds' voice calmly detailing her progress, until she experienced a sudden release from her suffering.

"You have a son, Mrs. Darcy!" Mrs. Reynolds announced with delight. Elizabeth, unable to appreciate anything beyond the pain having come to an end, collapsed against Darcy, who by this point had all but forgotten in his intense involvement with Elizabeth that a baby was to come, and seemed taken by surprise by the news. The midwife tied off and cut the cord, and a cry filled the room. Mrs. Reynolds, a broad smile on her face, took the infant and swaddled him in the prepared cloth, then gently placed him in Elizabeth's arms.

Elizabeth stared at the tiny face surrounded by a headful of dark hair, awash with feelings she had never felt before. She tickled his small hand, feeling euphoric as he gripped her finger with his minute, perfect fingers. She turned to Darcy with a smile of ineffable happiness, only to find him gazing in complete fascination at his son.

"Mrs. Darcy, you may be more comfortable in the bed for the remainder," said the midwife gently. Mrs. Reynolds reached to take the bundle from Elizabeth's arms, but Darcy was there before her. His wife's existence clearly faded from his mind as he held his son, absorbed by the miracle before him. Mrs. Reynolds, shaking her head with amusement, helped Elizabeth up from the stool and to the bed.

"I do not believe that I shall want to sit down for a very long time!" said Elizabeth with feeling as she collapsed back against the pillows. The midwife began to massage her stomach to encourage the afterbirth.

Mrs. Reynolds approached Darcy and said briskly, "Mr. Darcy, I do not believe that you are required for this part. Give that child back to your wife, and go tell Miss Georgiana that she has a nephew, and you can return when we have finished here."

Darcy looked at her blankly for a moment, then reluctantly surrendered the infant to Mrs. Reynolds, who tucked him into Elizabeth's arms. He kissed Elizabeth's cheek lightly, then whispered in her ear, "Thank you, my love." She looked up at him, tears welling up in her eyes.

"Out, Master William!" Mrs. Reynolds demanded, and with a roll of his eyes, he obeyed. She looked over at Elizabeth, and said authoritatively, "I *told* you he would be trouble."

"You did indeed, Mrs. Reynolds!" Elizabeth agreed with a laugh before her son engaged her every thought once again.

⚜

Elizabeth was asleep by the time Darcy was permitted to return to her. The completion of the delivery, the cleansing and the first lessons from Mrs. Fletcher on putting the babe to her breast had taken the last of her energy, and she had drifted off despite a new appreciation of how uncomfortable certain portions of her would be for the next few days.

Darcy slipped into the room quietly so as not to disturb her. It was twilight, and he found the picture of his wife and son asleep together in the gathering darkness immensely appealing. He stood and watched them for several minutes before giving into temptation and gently easing the bundle out of Elizabeth's arms. The baby stirred for a moment, and Darcy froze, but then he slipped back into a deep sleep.

Darcy settled himself in an armchair beside the bed, gently cradling the baby in his arms. He traced the tiny features with his eyes and allowed himself to lightly touch the soft baby hair. He could hardly allow the reality of the moment, but the pleasure it gave him to hold his son could not be denied. He was still gazing raptly at him some time later when Elizabeth awoke.

Their eyes met and held, a silent message flowing between them. Finally Darcy said, "I had not realized that he would be quite so small."

Elizabeth smiled warmly. "He will grow faster than you think. He has the look of you about him, I think."

"Do you? I cannot see it; he looks exactly like himself. How are you, my love?"

"Well enough; I have no complaints. But we must think about a name for that young man, William."

"Richard," he said, looking down at the baby, and despite his extraordinarily gentle tone it was clear that he was making a statement rather than a suggestion.

"Am I not to be consulted on this?" Elizabeth teased. Richard had, in fact, been on the list of names she had considered, but she saw no reason to give in to him quite so quickly.

He smiled at her with mild embarrassment. "Only if you agree with me, but he really must be Richard, you see."

"And why, pray tell, *must* he be named Richard?"

"Well, mostly because if it were not for Colonel Fitzwilliam, he would never have been born."

She raised an eyebrow. "William, I have the greatest respect for your cousin, but I fail to see what he has to do with Ri—with our baby's birth."

She could see even in the growing darkness that his cheeks flushed. "It is because of something I never told you, my love. Do you recall when I returned to Hertfordshire to court you?"

"Of course."

"The truth is that it was not my idea. I had already given up on you, and decided I did not deserve you. I never expected to see you again, then Richard came along and browbeat me into trying one more time, else I should have spent the rest of my life regretting you."

She gazed at him tenderly, touched by his disclosure. "Very well, I suppose that is an acceptable reason. Richard it shall be." The subject of their discussion opened his eyes, stirred by the sound of their voices. She held out her arms for him, and Darcy somewhat reluctantly surrendered the infant. Smiling down at her baby, she tried to persuade him to nurse, with eventual success. "Mrs. Fletcher assures me that this will become easier with time," she said ruefully to William, who was watching the process with fascination.

"Will you have the nurse take him for the night?"

She considered the matter. "I think I shall. She can always bring him to me if he needs me, and I certainly need the rest. I would like to be able to enjoy our son tomorrow beyond merely falling asleep with him!"

"I assume I should stay in my own room tonight," Darcy said tentatively.

Elizabeth looked up at him. "I had hoped that you would stay with me. It would comfort me to sleep in your arms."

Darcy's happiness at this response was apparent. "It would be my pleasure, my love. You may be certain that I would prefer not to let you out of my sight! But you must first have a little supper, to keep up your strength."

"William," she said indulgently, "the baby has been born, and you do not need to watch over me so closely any longer."

"I enjoy taking care of you, Elizabeth. And remember, you need to keep your strength up for tomorrow, too."

"Well, then, I suppose that I must have my supper," she said with resigned amusement. She noted that he was watching young Richard with the intensity he usually reserved for her, and it warmed her heart to see how quickly he was becoming attached to their child.

After Elizabeth had eaten what he considered to be an adequate amount, Darcy announced that she could go to sleep whenever she wished. She felt a pang when the nurse took the baby, but was reassured in the comfort of Darcy's embrace. He kissed her chastely on the forehead before bidding her goodnight, treasuring the opportunity to hold her in his arms, and grateful beyond words that all his fears had proved unwarranted.

"By the way, William," she said drowsily as she was about to drift off to sleep, her head resting on his shoulder, "I find it hard to believe that you could be browbeaten into doing something you did not already want to do."

"Most likely not, my love. Now go to sleep; we have a great many tomorrows still ahead of us." He kissed her gently, reflecting back on those weeks in Hertfordshire when he had so desperately sought her affections, and felt a thankfulness beyond his ability to express that she had rewarded him with the gift of her love. He would be ever sensible of the warmest gratitude towards his cousin who, by convincing him to risk offering her his heart once more, had been the means of uniting them.

Acknowledgements

My first words of gratitude must be to Jane Austen for providing years of reading pleasure and creating characters who are as alive now as they were two hundred years ago. Lovers of *Pride & Prejudice* will recognize quotes and phrases from the original scattered throughout the text of this book in homage to the original writer, whose skills were far beyond mine.

This book would never have been written without the encouragement of the Austen lovers at Austen Interlude and Hyacinth Gardens, who provided inspiration and kept me on track. My writing support group—Dor, Elaine, Ellen W., Heather Lynn, and Sylvie—read the earliest drafts and offered crucial feedback. Alison provided invaluable historical information and opened my mind about Regency period manners and morals. Ellen Pickels provided technical support and proofread with a fine-toothed comb. David, Brian, Rebecca and Amanda held down the fort at home and put up with my endless hours on the computer. Thanks to all of you!

About the Author

Abigail Reynolds is a lifelong Jane Austen enthusiast and a physician. In addition to writing, she has a part-time private practice and enjoys spending time with her family. Originally from upstate New York, she studied Russian, theater, and marine biology before deciding to attend medical school. She began writing *From Lambton to Longbourn* in 2001 to spend more time with her favorite characters from *Pride & Prejudice*. Encouragement from fellow Austen fans convinced her to continue asking 'What if?', which led to four other Pemberley Variations and her modern novel, *Pemberley by the Sea*. She is currently at work on another Pemberley Variation and a sequel to *Pemberley by the Sea*. She lives in Wisconsin with her husband, two teenaged children, and a menagerie of pets.

PEMBERLEY BY THE SEA

CHAPTER 1

The sea wall marked the beginning. Cassie had first glimpsed the ocean there while her jaded college friends told stories about their past vacations on Cape Cod. They didn't know she came from a place with asphalt seas, so she pretended the ocean was just as familiar to her. But she was captivated that very first day, tasting the briny sea air blowing in off the Sound. It cleansed her of the grime of the past.

Now, ten years later, the ocean was her life's work. She'd earned the right to watch the waves lap against the pitted stones of the sea wall. Place names like Sippewisset and Chapoquoit, which once sounded so exotic, were commonplace and comfortable now. The sea still held power, though it couldn't wash away guilt as easily as the pangs of adolescent shame. Today the ocean was only itself, changeable and rich with unseen life. She was on her own to do the work of forgetting.

She felt a tug at her arm. "I'm coming," she said, her eyes straying back to the dark water. The cry of gulls echoed a horn blast as the ferry from Nantucket returned to the harbor.

Erin tapped her foot, her blonde hair streaming behind her in the salt breeze. "The music's started. You can come back here later."

That was the best thing about the ocean. It was always there when Cassie wanted it. A long summer in Woods Hole stretched ahead of her, filled with time she could devote to the research she loved. She shrugged off her wistful mood and stepped carefully down to the sidewalk. "You're in a hurry to get there."

Erin didn't meet her eyes. "I promised Scott I'd be there early to help him learn the dances."

"Scott?" Trust Erin to have already found a man, even though she'd only been there a few days. "Another summer romance? You haven't mentioned him."

"I barely know him. And maybe you'll meet somebody."

Cassie laughed. "With you there? Not likely. Besides, what would I do with a man? He'd just be in the way of work." Men were usually too dazzled by Erin's lithe beauty to pay attention to Cassie, which suited her perfectly.

They followed the rhythmic lure of fiddle music down Water Street, past the library of the Marine Biological Laboratory. Inside the brightly lit Community Hall, the swirl of dancers chased away any serious thoughts.

There were some familiar faces among the dancers—other researchers from the Marine Biological Laboratory and grad students returning for the summer. Cassie spotted one of her old lab partners across the hall and waved to her grant administrator as he danced past. Since the New England folk dances were taught on the spot, anyone could participate. The contra dances were a social center of Woods Hole, one of the few places where scientists, townspeople, and tourists crossed paths.

Cassie danced first with a gangly young grad student from

the neurophysiology lab, a newcomer to the MBL. The dance was a vigorous one, and she threw herself into it, enjoying the complex patterns and laughing at her partner's jokes about his inexperience. Erin, partnered with a good-looking man sporting a dazzled smile, moved past Cassie down the line of dancers.

Despite the crowded room, Cassie chanced upon Erin again when the music ended. The windows of the historic clapboard hall were wide open, and Cassie welcomed the cool sea breeze on her arms after the energetic dance.

"Looks like you made a conquest already," Cassie teased.

"Scott? I met him at the biotech lecture yesterday." Erin's faint blush gave her away. "But he invited me to have lunch with him tomorrow. Will you come, too? I told him I was going to bring a friend along."

Given some of Erin's bad experiences with men, Cassie could understand her caution. "I can come to make sure he meets my standards for your boyfriends, but I imagine I'll be a third wheel."

"Of course not. It'll be fine." Erin had a faraway look Cassie hadn't seen for some time. She hoped this time it was warranted. Erin deserved some good luck for once.

Then Erin's eyes widened. "Oh, God. Is that who I think it is?" She didn't sound happy about the new development.

Cassie craned her neck to see the entranceway where a broad-shouldered man with wavy brown hair was paying the entrance fee. She didn't need to see his face to recognize him, even after three years. Her stomach tied in a knot. What was Rob doing in Woods Hole? Did he know she was there? She clenched her hand until her fingernails bit into her palm. If he knew, he wouldn't care. He hadn't even bothered to say good-bye to her when she left Chapel Hill. "Yes, that's him," she said grimly.

"Do you want to leave?"

Erin's tentative voice provided the challenge Cassie needed. She wasn't going to let Rob Elliott's presence chase her away. "No. I'm going to find a partner for the next dance." Preferably one that would make Rob think she'd never given him a second thought in the last three years.

"Good for you."

Cassie looked around quickly. Most of the dancers were already partnered for the next dance, but she spotted a tall man standing alone in the shadows by the front of the hall. She set out purposefully toward him. He didn't look like a scientist, given that his clothes matched and had the air of being recently purchased. Even in chinos he gave off the air of being formally dressed. Not her type, but still, one dance with a tourist wouldn't kill her, and it was better than letting Rob see her being a wallflower.

As she came up to him, the man's classic good looks gave way to a certain ferocity of expression. Cassie hesitated for a moment, but Erin was watching, and she wasn't going to admit to losing her nerve. Although the man seemed oblivious to her presence, she asked, "Do you have a partner for the next dance?"

For a moment he said nothing, and had Cassie been more timid, she would have been cowed by the look he gave her. "I'm not planning to dance, thank you." His lips barely moved when he spoke.

She was suddenly conscious she was still wearing her lab clothes and no makeup. But she hadn't gotten where she was by giving in to her insecurities. "If you've never tried it before, it's easy to pick up. Everyone here was a beginner once."

"I don't think so." He scanned the hall as if looking for someone.

His refusal stung, leaving her with the unpleasantly familiar feeling of having been judged and found wanting, even if he was the one violating the unspoken rules of the contra dance by refusing her. She hadn't done anything wrong. She was tempted to make a response as curt and rude as his had been, but she had higher standards for her behavior. "Never mind, then."

He turned piercing dark eyes on her for a moment, and then looked away, apparently dismissing her existence.

Something about his eyes struck her, but she had no intention of exploring what it was. One rejection was enough, and she still needed a refuge from Rob. There was one place she'd be safe from any of his nasty comments. Rob wouldn't try anything in front of Jim Davidson, her old grad school advisor. He was sitting out the dance, looking a little winded. He would welcome her company.

"Hey, stranger." She slid into the folding chair next to his.

"Cassie!" Jim said warmly. "I was hoping you'd be here. I have something to show you." He rummaged around in his pockets and handed her a folded paper with a flourish. "It's the latest spawning data. We just got the numbers in."

"Finally!" Cassie unfolded the sheet and ran her finger down the columns of figures, glad to have a distraction. She whistled silently. "Are you sure of these?"

"We've double-checked everything. In case you've forgotten, the results you came up with four years ago are on the back."

"Forgotten? I still see those numbers in my sleep. But this is worse than you expected, isn't it?"

"Much. I'm not happy about it, but it's going to make a hell of a research paper. It may even show up on the mainstream news, for the five minutes most people can bring themselves to care about species we're fishing to extinction."

"It's impressive data." It had been years since she had worked on the project as one of his grad students, but the excitement of it still touched her. She did a quick calculation in her head. The ramifications would be far-reaching. But it wasn't her project anymore. Reluctantly, she handed the data sheet back.

Jim gave her a pointed look. "I'm looking for someone to write it up for publication."

The temptation was so strong she could almost taste it. "Me? Jim, that's sweet of you, but shouldn't this go to one of your students?"

"They have their own projects, and you know this study. You were there at the beginning. You want to, I know it." So Jim still knew how to play on her passion for her work.

"But you deserve the credit."

"I have plenty of publications." Jim glanced around the hall and lowered his voice. "It could help you, Cassie."

"I still have plenty of time to get my publications in. I can make it, even if I didn't get publishable results last summer."

Jim patted her arm. "I didn't mean it that way. I know you can do great research. You wrote the best dissertation I've seen in years. But anybody can run into a string of bad luck, like last year's floods, and the tenure clock doesn't stop ticking. An extra paper could give you some leeway."

It was charity, and she knew it. But so much depended on

her getting tenure, and she'd love the chance to work with Jim again. "All right. Thanks."

"Don't thank me. I'm getting a top-notch author out of it."

"You old flatterer. I'm going to tell Rose you were flirting with me." She elbowed him in the side.

Jim's devotion to his wife was well known. "You do that."

But a familiar figure was approaching them. "Jim, I finished the initial set-up, if you . . ." Rob's voice trailed off when he saw Cassie.

Cassie plastered a pleasant smile on her face. "Hi, Rob. Welcome to Woods Hole." This was her turf, and she wasn't going to cede it to Rob.

He looked as if he didn't know what to say. "Uh, hi. Want to dance?"

How typically Rob—at least typical of him since their breakup. No pleasantries, no, "Nice to see you. How have you been?" She couldn't imagine he really wanted to dance with her. She put on her best professorial look and said, "Not now, thanks. Jim's filling me in on his spawning project."

"Some things never change. See you in the morning, then, Jim." Rob ambled away toward a redheaded woman who was apparently more inclined to dance. Cassie watched as they took hands in the line of dancers.

"Sorry." Jim seemed suddenly interested in his shoes. "I was going to warn you about that."

Cassie was well practiced at looking assured when she felt nothing of the sort. "No need. I don't have any problems with Rob."

"He won't be here the whole summer, just a couple weeks, if that's any consolation. And he isn't involved with Lisa anymore."

"It doesn't matter." Cassie ignored the stab of pain. Like it or not, she would have to get used to seeing Rob, especially if she wrote the paper with Jim. It would hurt, but there wasn't anything new about that. But the spawning results were amazing. She was already thinking of how to present them.

***

Although the start of the season was a few weeks away, tourists already clogged Water Street, the sole thoroughfare through the town of Woods Hole. The low blast of a ferry horn announced the arrival of another crowd of visitors.

"Erin, this has to be quick. I have a lot of work to do." Years of friendship had taught Cassie that men came before work for Erin.

"Even you have to eat lunch, Cassie, and I want you to meet Scott." Erin placed her hand behind Cassie's elbow and urged her on.

There was nothing wrong with a sandwich at her lab bench, like every other day, but meeting Erin's latest crush was important, too. Cassie needed to check him out before Erin became too involved. "Is he from the MBL or the Oceanographic Institution?"

"Neither. He works at Cambridge Biotechnology."

An industry scientist, then, rather than a researcher. It could be worse. Cambridge Biotech was reputable, at least. "What does he do there?"

Erin scuffed her feet against the curb. "He's the president."

"He's what?" Cassie stopped dead in the middle of the sidewalk. "And you're dating him? You just applied for a job there!"

"He doesn't know about that. I don't want him to think I'm using him to get a job. And we're not really dating. Not yet, anyway."

Cassie forced herself to keep walking. Men had hurt Erin too many times, and this was asking for trouble. "What's he doing in Woods Hole if he's with Cambridge Biotech?"

"He has a summerhouse here, and he came to a lecture at the MBL. That's where I met him."

The town drawbridge, raised to allow passage of sea-faring boats to and from the inner harbor, blocked their way. Cassie was glad for the brief respite. They waited with the other pedestrians behind the safety barrier as the boats, a pleasure craft and an MBL tug, left the harbor for the dark waters of Vineyard Sound.

When the bridge finally creaked down, they made their way across to the rambling, grey-shingled restaurant on the opposite shore of the narrow channel. The Dock of the Bay Café, with its unpretentious atmosphere and view over the harbor entrance, was one of Cassie's favorites. She wondered if it would be up to the standards of the president of Cambridge Biotech.

Cassie opened the screen door and stepped onto the worn wooden floor of the restaurant. No men sitting alone. Scott must be late.

A fragment of conversation drifted past her from the nearest table. "It won't be so bad. You might even have a good time," one man said to the other.

"I doubt it," replied a deeper voice. It was the man from the dance, the one who had turned her down. "You don't know who they are or where they're from. They could be groupies. Or criminals." His tone suggested the two were equivalent.

Erin came in behind Cassie. With a bright smile, she addressed the first speaker. "Scott, it's so nice to see you again."

Cassie recognized the deeply tanned man with curly hair now. She stiffened as she realized what the subject of their conversation had been. So Scott's friend didn't like having lunch with two little nobodies from nowhere. Used to more elite society, no doubt.

"Hi, Scott." Erin drew out the chair opposite him. "This is Cassie."

He shook her hand. "Nice to meet you, Cassie. This is my friend Calder."

The tall man beside him rose to his feet. "A pleasure." He sounded like it was anything but.

Cassie watched with amusement as he shook Erin's hand without any evidence of pleasure. When he turned to her, she smiled sweetly up at him and said, "Oh, yes, we've already met."

"We have?" he asked, taken aback and clearly none too happy about the possibility.

"Oh, yes," she said mockingly. "You're the one who goes to dances even though you don't want to dance."

He continued to look puzzled for a moment, and then his brow cleared. "Oh, the dance last night, you mean. I wasn't there to dance; I was just looking for Scott. I needed to . . . ask him something," he said, his voice declaring the subject closed.

Cassie raised an eyebrow, finding no evidence of apology or regret in his tone. "Well, to each his own." Unable to resist temptation, she leaned forward and said conspiratorially, "And for the record, Erin would be the groupie, so I must be the criminal element."

For a fleeting moment, he looked uncomfortable. "What's your crime, then?"

She lowered her voice dramatically. "I murder microscopic

organisms and steal their secrets." Little did he know. She walked around the table to the empty seat by the window. Maybe if the great and powerful Calder understood she wasn't looking for a boyfriend, it wouldn't be so bad. "I hadn't realized anyone was coming with Scott."

"I just arrived last night." He seemed more interested in the menu than anything she had to say.

Scott turned to Erin as a young waitress came to take their order. "What do you recommend?"

"I'm having the Gorgonzola salad, but the best thing here is dessert. They make wonderful pies."

Calder was the last to order. "I'll take the white marlin."

He might as well have used a cattle prod on Cassie. "Did you know white marlin is a threatened species?"

"No, I didn't. In that case I'll have . . . what would you recommend?" Calder turned his dark eyes on her.

His piercing gaze made her oddly uncomfortable. It was a relief to look down at the menu. "The striped bass and the mahi-mahi are fine, though mahi-mahi won't be local. Any of the shellfish. Not the cod."

"Cod are endangered?"

"Threatened, not endangered. Overfishing is a major problem."

"I'll go with the bass, then." He handed the menu to the waitress.

Cassie felt guilty about the sharpness of her tone. Snob or not, it wasn't Calder's fault Erin had decided to arrange this ridiculous meeting. If she had thought twice before opening her mouth, she wouldn't have said anything. "Thanks. I realize it doesn't make a difference when the fish is already dead, but I hate seeing it."

"I'd rather not support that kind of thing." He checked his watch.

So much for a peace offering. If he wanted to be aloof, that was fine with her. She turned her attention to Erin, who was explaining the history of the restaurant to Scott.

There was a brief silence when the subject was exhausted. Calder seemed to have nothing to say for himself. Cassie wasn't fond of small talk herself, but she couldn't sit there silently through the whole meal. "Scott, Erin tells me you have a summerhouse here."

"Yes. I've always wanted one, and this year I finally gave in." Scott had a charming smile. For Erin's sake, Cassie hoped the charm was more than skin-deep.

"Is it here in town?"

"Just outside, on Penzance Point. Do you know where that is?"

Of course Scott's house would be in the most exclusive part of Woods Hole. No doubt the president of Cambridge Biotech could afford it easily. His summerhouse probably cost enough to fund half the research at the MBL. She wondered if she could plead a heavy workload and leave early.

"This is my tenth summer here, so I know my way around pretty well." Cassie paused as the waitress set a bowl of fisherman's stew in front of her.

"The views are stunning. Have you been out there?" Scott asked.

"No." Cassie shelled a mussel with the ease of long practice. Penzance Point was privately owned; there was a guard on the road to keep out riff-raff like her.

Calder carefully moved his French fries aside with his fork. "So you don't live here year-round?"

Cassie's smile had an edge to it. "No, I'm a college professor. I come to the MBL every summer to do my research. I've had my own lab here since I got my PhD. Before that I was working with one of the senior researchers, studying species of fish threatened by overfishing." To her satisfaction, she could see Calder taking stock of her again. What had he thought she did, waited tables for a living? It was a good thing he didn't know the rest of her background. He would probably run a mile if he knew the truth. She looked out the window to avoid his eyes, pretending interest in a sailboat coming up the channel.

"You're interested in fish populations?" Scott asked.

"That was my grad school research. Now I'm looking at the effects of fertilizer run-off on the ecology of the salt marsh."

"Salt marsh? Sounds messy." Scott sliced into his lobster tail.

Erin said, "Careful, Scott. The salt marsh is Cassie's one true love."

Cassie laughed. "That's right. It's calm, peaceful, and more reliable than a man. And it won't waste my time when I'm trying to get tenure."

Calder crossed his arms, but Cassie thought he looked more amused than anything else. At least now he wouldn't expect anything from her. Maybe she could relax a little.

"You do research too, don't you, Erin?" Scott refilled his water glass from the pitcher on the table.

"Yes, I'm helping Cassie with her study."

Calder paused, his glass halfway to his mouth. "I thought Scott said you were in biotechnology."

Erin cast a distressed look at Cassie. "I am. I'm taking the summer off from my dissertation research. Cassie and I worked here as undergraduates, and I wanted to do it one last time before I started teaching full-time."

Two lies in one sentence, but Cassie could understand why Erin didn't want Scott to know her real reason for being in Woods Hole. And a year ago the part about teaching would have been true, before Erin decided she was better suited for a job in industry than academia.

"Well, that's Woods Hole for you." Cassie gestured toward the window with her fork. "Half the population has a doctorate. There are probably enough advanced degrees in town to sink a battleship. You'd better be careful about how you talk to any odd-looking old men muttering to themselves, because they just might be Nobel laureates. It's a world unto itself, like summer camp for grown-up scientists. One little town, and it has the MBL, the Woods Hole Oceanographic Institution, the National Marine Fisheries, and a half a dozen other research groups."

Erin, no doubt grateful for the change of subject, began to tell stories of amusing Woods Hole encounters. The moment of tension passed, and Erin and Scott chatted as they ate, with occasional additions from Cassie.

Cassie noticed Calder was watching her. She wondered how far he would take his silent withdrawal. Scott and Erin were managing fine on their own. "So, are you always this talkative, or is it just the company?"

This time his dark eyes didn't move from her. "When I have something to say, I'll say it."

Cassie opened her eyes wide in a mockery of being impressed. "Well, if I have to carry the conversation all by myself, I hope you don't mind hearing about the life cycle of

Pagurus longicarpus and the impact of algal overgrowth on the population. In detail."

To her surprise, a faint smile curved his mouth. "I'm sure it will be fascinating."

So he did have a sense of humor. Unexpectedly, Cassie wanted to smile back. Just then she heard a burst of giggling from behind the counter. Several of the young women who worked in the restaurant had congregated there, looking at their table. One of them pointed at Calder, sitting with his back to them.

"You have a fan club." Cassie gestured with her head, grateful for the distraction from her awareness of him.

His smile disappeared as if it had never existed. "Damn it. Scott, I'm going back to the house before there's a scene."

"Come on, Calder, they're not doing anything. Just ignore them."

"That's easy for you to say," Calder snapped.

"If you get up and walk out of here by yourself, that will make a scene. Finish your lunch."

"I've had all I want." He tossed his napkin on the table.

Cassie, dismayed by his sudden shift of mood, noticed Erin's unhappy look. At least this could give her an excuse to leave. "I'm done, too, and I need to get back to the lab. Maybe Calder and I could go part of the way together, and you two could take your time."

Scott's face brightened. "That won't be so bad, now! Is that okay with you, Calder?"

Calder gave a grim nod and pushed back his chair. Surprised by the speed with which this was happening, Cassie fished out a ten-dollar bill from her pocket and tossed it on the table.

Scott tried to hand it back to her. "My treat."

Cassie shook her head. "Sorry. I pay my own way."

"No, please, this was my idea."

"Scott, it's been a pleasure to meet you. Let's not spoil a budding friendship with an argument." Cassie hoped her smile took any sting from her words.

This seemed to disarm him, and she followed Calder outside. He strode off down the street at a pace she had to work to keep up with. Apparently he didn't plan to offer an explanation for the scene in the restaurant. So much for wondering if she might have misjudged him. Her first impression of him had been correct. It was disappointing.

They walked most of the brief length of the town in silence before he finally said, without looking at her, "Thank you."

"Not a problem. This is where I turn off. My lab's down here."

"I'll walk you there." He didn't sound particularly pleased with the prospect.

"There's no need. It's out of your way."

He paid no attention. Rather than argue pointlessly with him, Cassie followed his lead, glad it was only a block away.

"This is it. Take care." It was hackneyed, but it was more polite than saying, "Good-bye and good riddance."

He stopped between her and the building. "I suppose you knew all along."

"Knew what?"

His lips thinned. "Who I am."

Cassie's temper began to simmer, but for Erin's sake she didn't let it show. It wouldn't do her friend any good to have Cassie argue with Calder. "Look, I have no idea what you're talking about, I have no idea what went on back there, and I suspect I'm just as happy that way."

When he didn't respond, she flashed him a quick, if somewhat less than genuine, smile. "This is it, my home away from home," she said. "Enjoy the rest of your day." She turned and walked into the building before he could make any reply.

As she ran up the stairs, she didn't see him standing and looking after her, contemplating the rarity of a woman who couldn't seem to get out of his company fast enough. Perversely, he found himself wishing she would look back, but she never did.

Check out these e-books, also by Abigail Reynolds:

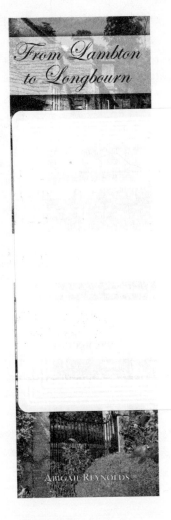

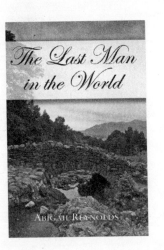